Reprinted 2017

Proudly published in 2010 by
Snowbooks Ltd.
120 Pentonville Road
London
N1 9JN
www.snowbooks.com

Paperback ISBN: 978-1-906727-208
Library Hardback ISBN: 978-1-906727-505

Illustrations Copyright © 2010 Kate Hiscock
www.slightlyeverything.com

A catalogue record for this book is available from the British Library.

www.snowbooks.com

Burton & Swinburne in

The Strange Affair of Spring Heeled Jack

When one man changes Time
Time changes everyone

Mark Hodder

About the Author

Mark Hodder is the creator and caretaker of the BLAKIANA website (www.sextonblake.co.uk), which he designed to celebrate, record and revive Sexton Blake, the most written about fictional detective in English publishing history. A former BBC writer, editor, journalist and web producer, Mark has worked in all the new and traditional medias and was based in London for most of his working life until 2008, when he relocated to Valencia in Spain to de-stress and write novels. He can most often be found at the base of a palm tree, hammering at a laptop. Mark has a degree in Cultural Studies and loves British history (1850 to 1950, in particular), good food, cutting edge gadgets, cult TV (ITC forever!), Tom Waits, and a vast assortment of oddities.

Acknowledgements

Without the faith and enthusiasm of Emma Barnes and Lou Anders, this novel might never have been published. Without the encouragement and unfailing positivity of George Mann, it might never have been written. Without the influence and genius of Mike Moorcock, it might never have been conceived. My heartfelt thanks to all.

I'd also like to express my gratitude to Saladin Ahmed, who helped with the Arabic, and Stéphane Rouvillois, who helped with the French.

A Rage to Live by Mary S. Lovell was at my side throughout this project. There are a great many biographies of Sir Richard Francis Burton but this, in my opinion, is by far the best.

To Yolanda Lerma Palomares: thank you for being so patient, so supportive, and for feeding me!

Finally, the "famous names" who feature herein are national heroes who loom large in the British consciousness. In this novel I have, with my tongue in my cheek, mercilessly trampled on their reputations and turned them into something they most definitely were not. I did so secure in the knowledge that my tampering will damage their stature not one little bit.

The First Part

In Which an Agent is Appointed and Mysteries are Investigated

A known mistake is better than an unknown truth.

—*Arabic Proverb*

Chapter 1

The Aftermath of Africa

❦

Everything Life places in your path is an opportunity.
No matter how difficult.
No matter how upsetting.
No matter how impenetrable.
No matter how you judge it.
An opportunity.
—*LIBERTINE PROPAGANDA*

❦

"By God! He's killed himself!"

Sir Richard Francis Burton staggered back and collapsed into his chair. The note Arthur Findlay had passed to him fluttered to the floor. The other men turned away, took their seats, examined their fingernails, and fiddled with their shirt collars; anything to avoid looking at their stricken colleague.

From where she stood on the threshold of the "robing room," hidden by its partially closed door, Isabel Arundell could see that her lover's normally dark and intense eyes were wide with shock; filled with a sudden vulnerability. His mouth moved spasmodically, as if he were struggling to chew and swallow something indigestible. She longed to rush to his side to comfort him and to ask what tidings had wounded him; to snatch up that note and read it; to find out who had killed himself; but such a display would be unseemly in front of the small gathering, not to mention embarrassing for Richard. He, among all men, stood on his own two feet, no matter how dire the situation. Isabel alone was aware of his sensitivity; and she would never cause it to be exposed to others.

Many people—mostly those who referred to him as "Ruffian Dick"—considered Burton's brutal good-looks to be a manifestation of his inner nature. They could never imagine that he doubted himself; though if they saw him now, so shaken, perhaps it might strike them that he wasn't quite the devil he appeared, despite the fierce moustache and forked beard.

It was difficult to see past such a powerful façade.

The Committee had only just gathered at the table, but after glancing at Burton's anguished expression, Sir Roderick Murchison, the president of the Royal Geographical Society, came to a decision.

"Let us take a moment," he muttered.

Burton stood and held up a hand in protest.

"Pray, gentlemen," he whispered hoarsely, "continue with your meeting. The scheduled debate will, of course, have to be cancelled, but if you'll allow me half an hour, perhaps I can organise my notes and make a small presentation concerning the valley of the Indus, so as to not disappoint the crowd."

"That's very good of you, Sir Richard," said one of the Committee members, Sir James Alexander. "But, really, this must have come as a terrible blow. If you would rather—"

"Just grant me thirty minutes to prepare. They have, after all, paid for their tickets."

"Very well. Thank you."

Burton turned and walked unsteadily to the door, passed through, closed it behind him, and stood facing Isabel, swaying slightly.

At five-eleven, he personally bemoaned the lost inch that would have made him a six-footer, though, to others, the breadth of his shoulders, depth of his chest, slim but muscular build, and overwhelming charisma made him seem a giant, even compared with much taller men.

He had short black hair, which he wore swept backward. His skin was swarthy and weather-beaten, giving his straight features a rather Arabic caste, which was further accentuated by his prominent cheekbones, both disfigured by scars; a smallish one on the right but a long deep and jagged one on the left, which tugged slightly at his bottom eyelid. They were the entry and exit wounds caused by a Somali spear, which had been thrust through his face during an ill-fated expedition to Berbera, on the horn of Africa.

To Isabel, those scars were the mark of an adventurous and fearless soul. Burton was in every respect her "ideal man." He was a wild, passionate and romantic figure, quite unlike the staid and emotionally cold men who moved in London's social circles. Her parents thought him unsuitable but Isabel knew there could be no other.

He stumbled forward into her arms.

"What ails you so, Dick?" she gasped, holding him by the shoulders. "What has happened?"

"John has shot himself!"

"No!" she exclaimed. "He's dead?"

Burton stepped back and wiped a sleeve across his eyes. "Not yet. But he took a bullet to the head. Isabel, I have to work up a presentation. Can I rely on you to find out where he's been taken? I must see him. I have to make my peace with him before—"

"Of course, dear. Of course! I shall make enquiries at once. Must you speak, though? No one would fault you if you were to withdraw."

"I'll speak. We'll meet later, at the hotel."

"Very well."

She kissed his cheek and left him; walked a short way along the elegant marble-floored corridor and, with a glance back, disappeared through the door to the auditorium. As it swung open and closed, Burton heard the crowd beyond grumbling with impatience. There were even some boos. They had waited long enough; they wanted blood; wanted to see him, Burton, shame and humiliate the man he'd once considered a brother: John Hanning Speke.

"I'll make an announcement," muttered a voice behind him. He turned to find that Murchison had left the Committee and was standing at his shoulder. Beads of sweat glistened on the president's bald head. His narrow face was haggard and pale.

"Is it—is it my fault, Sir Roderick?" rasped Burton.

Murchison frowned.

"Is it your fault that you possess exacting standards while, according to the calculations John Speke presented to the Society, the Nile runs uphill for ninety miles? Is it your fault that you are an erudite and confident debater while Speke can barely string two words together? Is it your fault that mischief-makers manipulated him and turned him against you? No, Richard, it is not."

Burton considered this for a moment, then said: "You speak of him so and yet you supported him. You financed his second expedition and refused me mine."

"Because he was right. Despite his slapdash measurements and his presumptions and guesswork, the Committee felt it likely that the lake he discovered was, indeed, the source of the Nile. The simple truth of the matter, Richard, is that he found it while you, I'm sorry to say, did not. I never much liked the man, may God have mercy on his soul, but fortune favoured him, and not you."

Murchison moved aside as the Committee members filed out of the robing room, heading for the presentation hall.

"I'm sorry, Richard. I have to go."

Murchison joined his fellows.

"Wait!" called Burton, pacing after him. "I should be there too."

"It's not necessary."

"It is."

"Very well. Come."

They entered the packed auditorium and stepped onto the stage amid sarcastic cheers from the crowd. Colonel William Sykes, who was hosting the debate, was already at the podium, unhappily attempting to quell the more disruptive members of the restless throng; namely, the many journalists—including the mysterious young American, Henry Morton Stanley—who seemed intent on making the occasion as newsworthy as possible. Doctor Livingstone sat behind Sykes, looking furious. Clement Markham, also seated on the stage, was chewing his nails nervously. Burton slumped into the chair beside him, drew a small notebook and a pencil from his pocket, and began to write.

Sir James Alexander, Arthur Findlay and the other geographers took their seats on the stage.

The crowd hooted and jeered.

"About time! Did you get lost?" someone shouted waggishly. A roar of approval greeted the gibe.

Murchison muttered something into the colonel's ear. Sykes nodded and retreated to join the others.

The president stepped forward, tapped his knuckles against the podium, and looked stonily at the expectant faces. The audience quietened until, aside from occasional coughs, it became silent.

Sir Roderick Murchison spoke:

"Proceedings have been delayed and for that I have to apologise—but when I explain to you the cause, you will pardon me. We have been in our Committee so profoundly affected by a dreadful calamity that has—"

He paused; cleared his throat; gathered himself.

"—that has befallen Captain Speke. A calamity by which, it pains me to report, he must surely lose his life."

Shouts of dismay and consternation erupted.

Murchison held out his hands and called, "Please! Please!"

Slowly, the noise subsided.

"We do not at present have a deal of information," he continued, "but for a letter from Lieutenant Speke's brother, which was delivered by a runner a short while ago. It tells that yesterday afternoon the lieutenant joined a hunting party on the Fuller Estate near Neston Park. At four o'clock, while he was negotiating a wall, his gun went off and severely wounded him about the head."

"Did he shoot himself, sir?" cried a voice from the back of the hall.

"Purposefully, you mean? There is nothing to suggest such a thing!"

"Captain Burton!" yelled another. "Did you pull the trigger?"

"How dare you, sir!" thundered Murchison. "That is entirely unwarranted! I will not have it!"

A barrage of questions flew from the audience, a great many of them directed at Burton.

The famous explorer tore a page from his notebook, handed it to Clement Markham, and, leaning close, muttered into his ear. Markham glanced at the paper, stood, stepped to Murchison's side and said something in a low voice.

Murchison gave a nod.

"Ladies and gentlemen," he announced. "You came to the Bath Assembly Rooms to hear a debate between Captain Sir Richard Burton and Lieutenant John Speke on the matter of the source of the Nile. I, of course, understand that you wish to hear from Sir Richard concerning this terrible accident which has befallen his colleague but, as you might suppose, he has been greatly affected and feels unable to speak at this present time. He has, however, written a short statement which will now be read by Mr Clement Markham."

Murchison moved away from the podium and Markham took his place.

In a quiet and steady tone, he read from Burton's note:

"The man I once called brother today lies gravely wounded. The differences of opinion that are known to have lain between us since his return from Africa make it more incumbent on me to publicly express my sincere feeling of admiration for his character and enterprise, and my deep sense of shock that this fate has befallen him. Whatever faith you may adhere to, I beg of you to pray for him."

Markham returned to his chair.

There was not a sound in the auditorium.

"There will be a thirty-minute recess," declared Murchison, "then Sir Richard will present a paper concerning the valley of the Indus. In the meantime, may I respectfully request your continued patience whilst we rearrange this afternoon's schedule? Thank you."

He led the small group of explorers and geographers out of the auditorium and, after brief and subdued words with Burton, they headed back to the robing room.

Sir Richard Francis Burton, his mind paralysed, his heart brimming, walked in the opposite direction until he came to one of the reading rooms. Mercifully, it was unoccupied. He entered, closed the door, and leaned against it.

He wept.

§

"I'm sorry. I can't continue."

It was the faintest of whispers.

He'd spoken for twenty-minutes, hardly knowing what he was saying, reading mechanically from his journals, his voice faint and quavering. His words had slowed then trailed off altogether.

When he looked up, he saw hundreds of pairs of eyes locked onto him; and in them there was pity.

He drew in a deep breath.

"I'm sorry," he said more loudly. "There will be no debate today."

He turned away from the crowd and, closing his ears to the shouted questions and polite applause, left the stage, pushed past Findlay and Livingstone, and practically ran to the lobby. He asked the cloakroom attendant for his overcoat, top hat and cane, and, upon receiving them, hurried out through the main doors and descended the steps to the street.

It was just past midday. Dark clouds drifted across the sky; the recent spell of fine weather was dissipating; the temperature falling.

He waved down a hansom.

"Where to, sir?" asked the driver.

"The Royal Hotel."

"Right you are. Jump aboard."

Burton clambered into the cabin and sat on the wooden seat. There were cigar butts all over the floor. He felt numb and registered nothing of his surroundings as the vehicle began to rumble over the cobbles.

He tried to summon up visions of Speke; the Speke of the past, when the young lieutenant had been a valued companion rather than a bitter enemy. His memory refused to cooperate and instead took him back to the event which lay at the root of their feud: the attack in Berbera, six years ago.

§

Berbera, the easternmost tip of Africa, on the 19th of April, 1855. Thunderstorms had been flickering on the horizon for the past few days. The air was heavy and damp.

Lieutenant Burton's party had set up camp on a rocky ridge, about three-quarters of a mile outside the town, near to the beach. Lieutenant Stroyan's tent was twelve yards off to the right of the "Rowtie" that Burton shared with Lieutenant Herne. Lieutenant Speke's was a similar distance to the left, separated from the others by the expedition's supplies and equipment, which had been secured beneath a tarpaulin.

Not far away, fifty-six camels, five horses and two mules were tethered. In addition to the four Englishmen, there were thirty-eight other men; abbans, guards, servants and camel-drivers; all armed.

With the monsoon season imminent, Berbera had been virtually abandoned during the course of the past week. An Arab caravan had lingered, but after Burton refused to offer it an escort out of the town—preferring to wait instead for a supply ship which was due any time from Aden—it had finally departed.

Now, Berbera was silent.

The expedition had retired for the night. Burton had posted three extra guards, for Somali tribes from up and down the coast had been threatening an attack for some days. They believed the British were here either to stop the lucrative slave trade or to lay claim to the small trading post.

At two-thirty in the morning, Burton was jolted of his sleep by shouts and gunfire.

He opened his eyes and stared at the roof of his tent. Orange light quivered on the canvas.

He sat up.

El Balyuz, the chief abban, burst in.

"They are attacking!" the man yelled, and a look of confusion passed over his dark face, as if he couldn't believe his own words. "Your gun, Effendi!" He handed Burton a revolver.

The explorer pushed back his bedsheets and stood; laid the pistol on the map table and pulled on his trousers; snapped his braces over his shoulders; picked up the gun.

"More bloody posturing!" he grinned across to Herne, who'd also awoken, hastily dressed, and snatched up his Colt. "It's all for show, but we shouldn't let them get too cocky. Go out the back of the tent, away from the camp fire, and ascertain their strength. Let off a few rounds over their heads, if necessary. They'll soon bugger off."

"Right you are," said Herne, and pushed through the canvas at the rear of the Rowtie.

Burton checked his gun.

"For Pete's sake, Balyuz, why have you handed me an unloaded pistol? Get me my sabre!"

He shoved the Colt into the top of his trousers and snatched his sword from the Arab.

"Speke!" he bellowed. "Stroyan!"

Almost immediately, the tent flap was pushed aside and Speke stumbled in. He was a tall, thin, pale man, with watery eyes, light brown hair, and a long bushy beard. He usually wore a mild and slightly self-conscious expression, but now his eyes were wild.

"They knocked my tent down around my ears! I almost took a beating! Is there shooting to be done?"

"I rather suppose there is" said Burton, finally realising that the situation might be more serious than he'd initially thought. "Be sharp, and arm to defend the camp!"

They waited a few moments, checking their gear and listening to the rush of men outside.

A voice came from behind them: "There's a lot of the blighters and our confounded guards have taken to their heels!" It was Herne, returning from his recce. "I took a couple of pot-shots at the mob but then got tangled in the tent ropes. A big Somali took a swipe at me with a bloody great club. I put a bullet into the bastard. Stroyan's either out cold or done for; I couldn't get near him."

Something thumped against the side of the tent. Then again. Suddenly a veritable barrage of blows pounded the canvas while war cries were raised all around. The attackers were swarming like hornets. Javelins were thrust through the opening. Daggers ripped at the material.

"Bismillah!" cursed Burton. "We're going to have to fight our way to the supplies and get ourselves more guns! Herne, there are spears tied to the tent pole at the back; get 'em!"

"Yes, sir!" responded Herne, returning to the rear of the Rowtie. Almost immediately, he ran back, crying: "They're breaking through the canvas!"

Burton swore vociferously.

"If this blasted thing comes down on us we'll be caught up good and proper. Get out! Come on! Now!"

He plunged through the tent flaps and into the night, where he found himself facing twenty or so Somali natives. Others were running around the camp, driving away the camels and pillaging the supplies. With a shout, he leaped forward and began to set about the attackers with his sabre.

Was that Lieutenant Stroyan laying over in the shadows? It was hard to tell. Burton slashed his way toward the prone figure, grimacing as clubs and spear shafts thudded against his flesh, bruising and cutting him, drawing blood.

He momentarily glanced back to see how the others were doing and saw Speke stepping backward into the tent entrance, his mouth hanging open, eyes panicked.

"Don't step back!" he roared. "They'll think that we're retiring!"

Speke looked at him with an expression of utter dismay and, right there, in the midst of battle, their friendship ended, for John Hanning Speke knew that his cowardice had been recognised.

A club struck Burton on the shoulder and, tearing his eyes away from the other Englishman, he span and swiped his blade at its owner. He was jostled back and forth. One set of hands kept pushing at his back, and he wheeled impatiently, raising his sword, only recognising El Balyuz at the very last moment.

His arm froze in mid-swing.

His head exploded with pain.

A weight pulled him sideways and he collapsed onto the stony earth.

Dazed, he reached up. A barbed javelin had transfixed his face, entering the left cheek and exiting the right, knocking out some back teeth, cutting his tongue and cracking his palette.

He fought to stay conscious.

Someone started dragging him away from the conflict.

He passed out.

In front of the Rowtie, Speke, driven to a fury by the exposure of the shameful flaw in his character, strode into the melee, raised his Dean and Adams revolver, pressed its muzzle against the chest of the man who'd downed Burton, and pulled the trigger.

The gun jammed.

"Blast it!" said Speke.

The tribesman, a massive warrior, looked down at him, smiled, and punched him over the heart.

Speke fell to his knees, gasping for air.

The Somali bent, took him by the hair, pulled him backward, and, with his other hand, groped between Speke's legs. For an instant, the Englishman had the terrifying conviction that he was going to be un-manned. The tribesman, though, was simply checking for daggers, hidden in the Arabic fashion.

Speke was thrust onto his back and his hands were quickly tied together, the cords pulled cruelly tight. Yanked upright, he was marched away from the camp, which was now being looted and destroyed.

Lieutenant Burton regained his wits and found that he was being pulled toward the beach by El Bayluz. He recovered himself sufficiently to stop his rescuer and to order the man, via sign language and writing in a patch of sand, to go and fetch the small boat which the expedition party had moored in the harbour, and to bring it to the mouth of a nearby creek.

El Bayluz nodded and ran off.

Burton lay on his back and gazed at the milky way.

'I want to live!' he thought.

A minute or so passed. He raised a hand to his face and felt the barbed point of the javelin. The only way to remove it was by sliding the complete length of the shaft through his mouth and cheeks. He took a firm grip on it, pushed, and fainted.

As the night wore on, John Speke was taunted and spat upon by his captors. With their sabres, they sliced the air inches from his face. He stood and endured it, his eyes hooded, his jaw set, expecting to die, and he wondered what Richard Burton would say about him when reporting this incident.

Don't step back! They'll think that we're retiring!

The rebuke had stung, and if Burton put it on record, Speke would be forever branded as less than a man. Damn the arrogant blackguard!

One of his captors casually thrust his spear through Speke's side. The Lieutenant cried out in pain, then fell backward as the point pierced him again, this time in the shoulder.

'This is the end,' he told himself.

He struggled back to his feet and, as the spear was stabbed at his heart, deflected it with his bound hands. The point tore the flesh behind his knuckles to the bone.

The Somali stepped back.

Speke straightened and looked at him.

"To hell with you," he said. "I won't die yellow."

The tribesman leaped in and prodded the spear into Speke's left thigh. The explorer felt the blade scrape against bone.

"Shit!" he coughed in shock, and grabbed reflexively at the shaft. He and the African fought over it; one trying to gain possession, the other struggling to retain it. The Somali let go with his left hand and used it to pull a shillelah from his belt. He swiped at Speke's right arm and the cudgel connected with a horrible crack. Speke dropped the spear shaft and crumpled to his knees, gasping with agony.

His attacker walked away, turned back, and ran at him, plunging the spear completely through the Englishman's right thigh and into the ground beyond.

Speke screamed.

Instinct took over.

With his awareness strangely separated from his body, he watched as his hands gripped the weapon, pulled it free of the ground, out through his thigh, and threw it aside. Then he stumbled into his attacker and his bound fists swept up, smashing into the man's face.

The warrior rocked back, raising a hand to his face as blood spurted from his nose.

Speke half walked, half hopped away, his disengaged mind wondering how he was staying upright with such terrible injuries.

'Where's the pain?' he mused, entirely unaware that he was afire with it.

He hobbled, barefoot, across jagged rock, down a slope and onto the shingle of the beach. Somehow, he started to run. What tatters of clothing remained on him streamed behind.

The Somali snatched up the spear and gave chase, threw the weapon, missed, and gave up.

Other tribesmen lunged for the Englishman but Speke dodged them and kept going. He outdistanced his pursuers and, when he saw that they'd given up the chase, he collapsed onto a rock and chewed through the cord that bound his wrists.

He was faint with shock and loss of blood but knew that he had to find his companions, so, as dawn broke, he pushed on until he reached Berbera. Here he was discovered by a search party led by Lieutenant Herne and was carried to the boat at the mouth of the creek. He'd run for three miles and had eleven wounds, including the two that had pierced the large muscles of his thighs.

They placed him onto a seat and he raised his head and looked at the man sitting opposite. It was Burton, his face bandaged; blood staining the linen over his cheeks.

Their eyes met.

"I'm no damned coward," whispered Speke.

§

The battle should have made them brothers. They both acted as if it had—and less than two years later they embarked together on one of the greatest expeditions in British history; a perilous trek into central Africa to search for the source of the Nile.

Side by side, they endured extreme conditions, penetrating into lands unseen by white men and skirting dangerously close to Death's realm. An infection temporarily blinded and immobilised Burton. Speke became permanently deaf in one ear after attempting to remove an insect from it with a pen-knife. They were both stricken with malaria, dysentery and crippling ulcers.

They pressed on.

Speke's resentment simmered.

He constructed his own history of the Berbera incident, excising from it the most essential element: the fact that a thrown stone had cracked against his kneecap, causing him to step back into the Rowtie's entrance. Burton had looked around at that very instant and had plainly seen the stone bounce off Speke's knee and understood the back-step for the reaction it was. He'd never for one moment doubted his companion's courage.

Speke knew the stone had been seen but chose to forget it. History, he discovered, is what you make it.

They reached the central lakes.

Burton explored a large body of water called by the local tribes "Tanganyika," which lay to the south of the Mountains of the Moon. His geographical readings suggested that it could be the Nile's source, though he was too ill to visit its northernmost shore from whence the great river should flow.

Speke, leaving his "brother" in a fevered delirium, trekked north eastward and found himself at the shore of a vast lake, which he imperiously named after the British monarch, though the tribes that lived on its shores already had a name for it: "Nyanza."

He tried to circle it; lost sight of it; found it again farther to the north—or was it the shore of a second lake?—took incomplete, incompetent measurements, and returned to Burton, the leader of the expedition, claiming to have found, on his own and without a shadow of a doubt, the true source of the great river.

They recovered a modicum of health and undertook the long march back to Zanzibar where Burton fell into a fit of despondency, blaming himself for what, by his demanding standards, was inconclusive evidence.

John Speke, less scientific, less scrupulous, less disciplined, sailed back to England ahead of Burton and en route fell under the influence of a man named Laurence Oliphant, an arch-meddler and poseur who kept a white panther as a pet. Oliphant nurtured Speke's pique, turned it into malice, and seduced him into claiming victory. No matter that it was the other man's expedition; Speke had solved the biggest geographical riddle of the age!

John Speke's last words to Burton had been: "Goodbye, old fellow; you may be quite sure I shall not go up to the Royal Geographical Society until you have come to the fore and we appear together. Make your mind quite easy about that."

The day he landed in England, Speke went straight up to the Royal Geographical Society and told Sir Roderick Murchison that the Nile question was settled.

The Society divided. Some of its members supported Burton, others supported Speke. Mischief-makers stepped in to ensure that what should have been a scientific debate rapidly degenerated into a personal feud, though Burton, now recovering his health in Aden, was barely aware of this.

Easily swayed, Speke became over-confident. He began to criticise Burton's character; a dangerous move for a man who believed that his cowardice had been witnessed by his opponent.

Word reached Burton that he was to be awarded a knighthood and should return to England at once. He did so, and stepped ashore to find himself at the centre of a maelstrom.

Even as the reclusive monarch's representative touched the sword to his shoulders and dubbed him *Sir* Richard Francis Burton, the famous explorer's thoughts were on John Speke, wondering why he was taking the offensive in such a manner.

Over the next weeks, Burton defended himself but resisted the temptation to retaliate.

Life is fickle; the fair man doesn't invariably win.

Lieutenant Speke, it gradually became apparent, had made a lucky guess; the Nyanza probably *was* the source of the Nile.

Murchison knew, as Burton had been quick to point out, that Speke's readings and calculations were badly faulted. In fact, they were downright amateurish and not at all admissible as scientific evidence. Nevertheless, there was in them the suggestion of a potential truth. This was enough; the Society funded a second expedition.

John Speke went back to Africa, this time with a young, loyal, and opinion-free soldier named James Grant. He explored the Nyanza; failed to circumnavigate it; didn't find the Nile's exit point; didn't take accurate measurements; and returned to England with another catalogue of assumptions which Burton, with icy efficiency, proceeded to pick to pieces.

A face-to-face confrontation between the two men seemed inevitable.

It was gleefully engineered by Oliphant, who had, by this time, mysteriously vanished from the public eye—into an opium den, according to rumour—to pull strings like an invisible puppeteer.

He arranged for the Bath Assembly Rooms to be the venue and September 16th, 1861, the date. To encourage Burton's participation, he made it publicly known that Speke had said: "If Burton dares to appear on the platform at Bath, I will kick him!"

Burton had fallen for it: "That settles it! By God, he *shall* kick me!"

§

The hansom drew up outside the Royal Hotel, and Burton's mind re-engaged with the present. He emerged from the cab with one idea uppermost: some day, Laurence Oliphant would pay.

He entered the hotel. The receptionist signalled to him; a message from Isabel was waiting.

He took the note and read it:

John was taken to London. On my way to Fuller's to find out exactly where.

Burton gritted his teeth. Stupid woman! Did she think she'd be welcomed by Speke's family? Did she honestly believe they'd tell her anything about his condition or whereabouts? As much as he loved her, Isabel's impatience and lack of subtlety never failed to rile him. She was the proverbial bull in a china shop; always charging at her target without considering anything that might lay in her path; always utterly confident that what she wanted to do was right, whatever anyone else might think.

He wrote a terse reply:

Left for London. Pay, pack and follow.

He looked up at the hotel receptionist.

"Please give this to Miss Arundell when she returns. Do you have a Bradshaw?"

"Traditional or atmospheric railway, sir?"

"Atmospheric."

"Yes, sir."

He was handed the train timetable. The next atmospheric train was leaving in fifty minutes. Time enough to throw a few odds and ends into a suitcase and get to the station.

§

Chapter 2

The Thing in the Alley

༜

༜

It was a fast and smooth ride to London.

Isambard Kingdom Brunel's atmospheric railway system was a triumph. It used wide-gauge tracks in the centre of which ran a fifteen-inch diameter pipe. Along the top of the pipe there was a two-inch slot, covered with a flap-valve of ox hide leather. Beneath the front carriage of each train hung a dumbbell-shaped piston, which fitted snugly into the pipe. This was connected to the carriage by a thin shaft which rose through the slot. The shaft had a small wheeled contrivance attached to it which pressed open the leather flap at the front while closing and oiling it at the back. Every three miles along the track, a station sucked air out of the pipe in front of the train and pumped it back in behind. It was this difference in air pressure which shot the carriages along the tracks at tremendous speed.

When Brunel first created the system he encountered an unexpected problem: rats ate the ox hide. He turned to his Eugenicist colleague, Francis Galton, for a solution, and the scientist had provided it in the form of specially bred oxen whose skin was both repellent and poisonous to the rodents.

The pneumatic rail system now ran the length and breadth of Great Britain and was being extended throughout the Empire, particularly in India and South Africa.

A similar method of propulsion was planned for the new London Underground railway system, though this project had been delayed since Brunel's death two years ago.

Burton arrived home at 14 Montagu Place at half past six, by which time a mist was drifting through the city streets. As he opened the wrought-iron gate and stepped to the front door, he heard a newsboy in the distance calling: "Speke shoots himself! Nile debate in uproar! Read all about it!"

He sighed and waited for the young urchin to draw closer. He recognised the soft Irish accent; it was Oscar, a refugee from the never-ending famine, whose regular round this was. The boy possessed an extraordinary facility with words, which Burton thoroughly appreciated.

The youngster approached, saw him and grinned. He was a short and rather plump lad, about eight years old, with sleepy-looking eyes and a cheeky grin marred only by crooked, yellowing teeth. He wore his hair too long and was never without a battered top hat and a flower in his buttonhole.

"Hallo Captain! I see you're after making the headlines again!"

"It's no laughing matter, Quips," replied Burton, using the nickname he'd given the newspaper boy some weeks previously. "Come into the hallway for a moment; I want to talk with you. I suppose the journalists are all blaming me?"

Oscar joined the explorer at the door and waited while he fished for his keys.

"Well now, Captain, there's much to be said in favour of modern journalism. By giving us the opinions of the uneducated, it keeps us in touch with the ignorance of the community."

"Ignorance is the word," agreed Burton. He opened the door and ushered the youngster in. "If the reaction of the crowd in Bath is anything to go by, I rather suspect that the charitable are saying Speke shot himself, the uncharitable that I shot him."

Oscar lay his bundle of newspapers on the doormat.

"You're not wrong, sir; but what do you say?"

"That no-one currently knows what happened except those who were there. That maybe it wouldn't have happened at all had I tried a little harder to bridge the divide that opened between us; been, perhaps, a little more sensitive to Speke's personal demons."

"Ah, demons, is it?" exclaimed the boy, in his high, reedy voice. "And what of your own? Are they not encouraging you to luxuriate in self reproach?"

"Luxuriate!"

"To be sure. When we blame ourselves, we feel no one else has a right to blame us. What a luxury that is!"

Burton grunted. He put his cane in an elephant foot umbrella stand, placed his topper on the hat-stand and slipped out of his overcoat.

"You are a horribly intelligent little ragamuffin, Quips."

Oscar giggled. "It's true. I'm so clever that sometimes I don't understand a single word of what I'm saying!"

Burton lifted a small bell from the hall table and rang for his housekeeper.

"But is it not the truth, Captain Burton," continued the boy, "that you only ever asked Speke to produce scientific evidence to back up his claims?"

"Absolutely. I attacked his methods but never him, though he didn't extend to me the same courtesy."

They were interrupted by the appearance of Mrs Iris Angell, who, though Burton's landlady, was also his housekeeper. She was a wide-hipped, white-haired old dame with a kindly face, square chin and gloriously blue and generous eyes.

"I hope you wiped your feet, Master Oscar!"

"Clean shoes are the measure of a gentleman, Mrs Angell," responded the boy.

"Well said. There's a freshly baked bacon and egg pie in my kitchen. Would you care for a slice?"

"Very much so!"

The old lady looked at Burton, who nodded. She went back down the stairs to her domain in the basement.

"So it's information you'll be wanting, Captain?" asked Oscar.

"I need to know where Lieutenant Speke has been taken. I know he was brought to London from Bath—but to which hospital? Can you find out?"

"Of course! I'll spread the word among the lads. I should have an answer for you within the hour."

"Very good. Miss Arundell is also making enquiries, though I fear her approach will have caused nothing but trouble."

"How so, Captain?"

"She's visiting the Speke family to offer her condolences."

Oscar winced. "By heavens! There is nothing more destructive than a woman on a charitable mission. I hope for your sake that Mr Stanley doesn't get wind of it."

Burton sighed. "Bismillah! I'd forgotten about him!"

Henry Morton Stanley, the journalist, was recently arrived in London from America. His background was somewhat mysterious; traces of a Welsh accent suggested he wasn't the authentic "Yankee" he claimed to be; and there were rumours that his name was false. Whatever the true facts about him, though, he was making a big splash as a newspaper reporter, having taken a particular interest in the various expeditions organised by the Royal Geographical Society. Befriending Doctor Livingstone, Stanley had sided with him against Burton in the Nile debate and had written some less than flattering articles in *The Empire*, including one that accused Burton of having murdered a boy who caught him urinating in the European fashion during his famous pilgrimage to Mecca. As Burton had been quick to point out, his disguise, skill with the language, and painstaking observation of customs was convincing enough to fool his fellow pilgrims into believing him an Arab over a period of many months; it was therefore quite unthinkable that he'd have been caught out making so basic mistake as to urinate standing up. Besides which, killing the boy would certainly have led to his exposure as an impostor and a summary execution.

Stanley had also attacked Isabel in the press, vilifying her for her lack of subtlety and overly headstrong character. Burton couldn't help but think that she was becoming a liability at this crucial point in his career; a situation which Stanley had spotted some time ago and was revelling in.

"Yum!" exclaimed Oscar.

Mrs Angell had reappeared with a generous slice of pie. She handed it to the youngster.

"It's nothing special but I hope it fills that bottomless hole you call a stomach!" she said.

"I have the simplest tastes, Mrs Angell" declared the news boy. "I am always satisfied with the best!"

Burton ruffled the lad's hair.

"Off you go then, Quips. There'll be a second slice waiting for when you return."

Oscar heaved a sigh of contentment, picked up his papers, and flitted out through the door which Burton held open for him.

As he closed the portal, the explorer looked at his landlady.

"You've heard the news?"

"Yes sir. May God preserve him. It must have been a terrible shock for you."

"He hated me."

"If you don't mind me saying so, sir, I think he was misguided."

"I don't disagree. Have reporters been banging on the door?"

"No, sir, they probably think you're still in Bath."

"Good. If they call, empty a bucket of slops over them. No visitors, please, Mother Angell. I don't want to see anyone until young Oscar returns." "Very well. Can I bring you something to eat?"

Burton began to climb the stairs.

"Yes, please. And a pot of coffee."

"Yes sir."

The old lady watched him as he reached the landing, turned right, and disappeared into his study. She pursed her lips. She knew Burton well enough to recognise the developing mood.

"Coffee, my eye!" she muttered as she descended to the kitchen. "He'll be through a bottle of brandy before the evening is old!"

§

Burton had, indeed, poured himself a large measure of brandy, and was now slumped in his old saddlebag armchair by the fireplace, his feet resting on the fender. He held the glass in one hand and a letter in the other. It was from 10 Downing Street and read:

Please contact the Prime Minister's office immediately upon your return to London.

He sipped the brandy and savoured the fire that sank into his belly. He was tired but not sleepy, and felt the heavy weight of depression dragging at him.

Laying his head back, and with eyes half closed, he focused his mind on his sense of hearing. It was a Sufi trick he'd learned en route to Mecca. Sight was the primary sense; when another was given precedence and the mind was allowed to wander, ideas, insights and hitherto unseen connections often bubbled up from its otherwise inaccessible depths.

He heard a bookshelf creak slightly as its wood adjusted to the changing temperature of early evening; it was the only sound from within the study, aside from his own breathing and the ticking of the clock on the mantelpiece. From beyond the two large sash windows, though, came the muffled cacophony of England's capital: voices passing on the pavement below; the clatter and chugging engines of velocipedes; the cry of a street hawker; the choppy paradiddle of a rotorchair passing overhead; a barking dog; a crying child; the rumble and hiss of steam-horses; the clip-clop of real horses; the coarse laughter of prostitutes.

He heard footsteps on the stairs.

A question came to him:

"What am I to do now?"

There was a soft knock at the door.

"Come."

Mrs Angell entered bearing a tray upon which lay a plate of sliced meats, cheese and a chunk of bread. There was also a cup and saucer, bowl of sugar and a pot of coffee. She crossed the room and lay it on the occasional table beside Burton's chair.

"It's getting unseasonably cold, sir; shall I light the fire?"

"It's alright; I'll do it. Would you take a letter for me?"

"Certainly."

The housekeeper, who often performed slight secretarial tasks for him, sat at one of the three desks, slid a sheet of blank paper onto the leather writing pad and picked up a pen. She dipped the nib into the inkwell and wrote, at Burton's dictation:

I am at home in London. Awaiting further instructions. Burton.

"Send it by runner to 10 Downing Street, please."

The old lady looked up in surprise.

"To where?"

"10 Downing Street. At once, please."

"Yes, sir."

She departed with the note. A few moments later, he heard her at the front door blowing three blasts on a whistle. Within half a minute, a dog—almost certainly a greyhound—would arrive on the doorstep and, after she'd fed the animal, the housekeeper would place the letter between its teeth and announce the destination. There'd be an acknowledging wag of the tail, and the runner would race away en route for Downing Street.

They were part of a fairly new communications system, these remarkable dogs; the first practical application of eugenics adopted by the British public. Each hound came into the world knowing every address within a fifty mile radius of its birthplace and with the ability to carry mail between those locations; barking and scratching at a recipient's door until the letter was collected. After each task was completed, the runner would wander the streets until it heard another three-whistle summons.

Messenger parakeets formed the other half of the system. These phenomenal mimics carried spoken communications. A person only had to visit a post office and give one of the birds a message, the name of the recipient and the address, and the parakeet would fly straight to the appropriate set of ears.

There was one problem; an issue that had troubled the Eugenicist scientists from the start; namely, that whatever modification to a species they made, it always seemed to bring with it an unexpected side-effect.

In the case of the parakeets, it was that they swore at, mocked and offended everyone they encountered. The person on the receiving end of the service would inevitably be given a message liberally peppered with insults not put there by the sender. Nothing, it seemed, could be done to correct this fault. Originally, it had been hoped that every household would have its own parakeet but, as it turned out, no one could bear the constant abuse in their own home. So the Post Office had stepped in and now each branch kept an aviary full of the birds.

In the runners' case, the drawback was nothing more serious than a phenomenal appetite. Though they were whiplash thin, the dogs required a square meal at every address they visited, so despite being a free system, those who used it often found themselves investing a considerable amount of money in dog food.

Burton heard the front door close. His letter was on its way.

He took a swig of brandy and reached for a cheroot; he had a taste for cheap strong tobacco.

'Explore Dahomey?' he thought, still dwelling on what he should do now that the Nile question was out of his hands; for though a new expedition was required to settle the matter once and for all, he knew that Murchison would not commission him to lead it. The Royal Geographical society was already fractured by the verbal duel he and Speke had fought; the president would doubtlessly offer the expedition to a neutral geographer.

So Dahomey? Burton had been wanting to mount an expedition into that dark and dangerous region of West Africa for some time but now it was going to be difficult to raise the money.

A private sponsor perhaps? Maybe a publishing company?

Ah, yes, then there were the books. For long he'd wanted to write a definitive translation of *The Thousand Nights and a Night*; perhaps now would be a good time to begin that ambitious project. At very least he should finish *Vikram and the Vampire*, the collected tales of Hindu devilry which were currently stacked on one of his desks, with annotations half completed.

Write books, keep a low profile, wait for his enemies to become bored.

Marry Isabel?

He looked at his empty glass; blew cigar smoke into it; held the cheroot between his teeth and reached for the decanter; poured more brandy.

For more than a year, he'd felt destined to marry Isabel Arundell; now, suddenly, he wasn't so sure. He loved her, that was certain, but he also resented her. He loved her strength and practicality but resented her overbearing personality and tendency to do things on his behalf without consulting him first; loved the fact that she tolerated his interest in all things exotic and erotic but hated her blinkered Catholicism. Charles Darwin had killed God but she and her family, like so many others, still clung to the delusion.

He sought to quell his mounting frustration with another glass. And another. And more.

At eight o'clock there came a tap at the door and Mrs Angell appeared, looking with disapproval at the drunken explorer.

"Did you even touch the coffee?" she asked.

"No, and I don't intend to," he replied. "What do you want?"

"The boy is back."

"Quips? Send him up."

"I don't think so, sir. You're in no state to receive a child."

"Send him up, blast you!"

"No."

Burton pushed himself up from his chair and stood unsteadily, his eyes blazing.

"You'll do as you're bloody well told, woman!"

"No, sir, I won't. Not when I'm told by a foul-mouthed drunkard. And I remind you that though I am your employee, you are also my tenant, and I am free to end our arrangement whenever I see fit. I shall take a message from the boy and bring it to you forthwith."

She stepped back to the landing, closing the door behind her.

Burton took a couple of steps toward the door, thought better of it, and stood swaying in the centre of the room. He looked around at the bookcases, filled with volumes about geography, religion, languages, erotica, esoterica, and ethnology; looked at the swords which rested on brackets above the fireplace; the worn boxing gloves hanging from a corner of the mantelpiece; the pistols and spears which hung in the alcoves to either side of the chimney breast; looked at the pictures on the walls, including the one of Edward, his brain-damaged younger brother, who'd been an inmate at the Surrey County Lunatic Asylum for the past three years, a result of an incident five years ago when he was beaten half to death in Ceylon after Buddhist villagers took offence at his hunting of elephants; looked at the three big desks, stacked with papers, his half-written books, maps and charts; looked at the many souvenirs of his travels, the idols and carvings, hookahs and prayer mats, knick-knacks and trinkets; looked at the door in the wall opposite the windows, which led to the small dressing room where he kept his various disguises; and looked at the dark windows and his reflection in their glass.

The question came again, and he spoke it aloud:

"What the hell am I to do?"

The door opened and Mrs Angell, her expression severe and voice cold, stepped in and said:

"Master Oscar says to tell you that Mr Speke is at the Penfold Private Sanatorium."

Burton nodded, curtly.

The old woman made to leave.

"Mrs Angell," he called.

She stopped and looked back at him.

"My language was entirely unwarranted," he mumbled, self-consciously. "My temper, too. Please accept my apologies."

She gazed at him a moment.

"Very well. But you'll take your devils out of this house, is that understood? Either that, or you remove yourself from it—permanently!"

"Agreed. Did you treat Quips to more pie?"

The old dame smiled indulgently.

"Yes, and an apple and some butter scotch."

"Thank you. Now, as you recommend, I think I shall take my devils out of the house."

"But you'll not allow them to guide you into trouble, if you please, Sir Richard."

"I'll do my best, Mother Angell."

She bobbed her head and departed.

Burton considered for a moment. It was too late in the evening to visit the hospital; that would have to wait until the morning, and if Speke didn't survive the night, then so be it. It was, however, never too late to visit the Cannibal Club. A few drinks with his Libertine friends would help to lift his spirits, and maybe Algernon Swinburne would be among them. Burton hadn't known the promising young poet for long but enjoyed his company immensely.

He made up his mind, changed his clothes, took another swig of brandy, and was just leaving the room when a tapping came at one of the windows. He crossed to it, a little clumsily, and saw a colourful parakeet sitting on the sill.

He pulled up the sash. A cloud of mist rolled in. The parakeet looked at him.

"Message from the stinking Prime Minister's office," it cackled. "You are requested to attend that prattle-brain Lord Palmerston at 10 Downing Street at nine o'clock in the morning. Please confirm, arse-face. Message ends."

Burton's brows, which usually arched low over his eyes in what appeared to be a permanent frown, shot upward. The Prime Minister wanted to meet with him personally? Why?

"Reply. Message begins. Appointment confirmed. I will be there. Message ends. Go."

"Bugger off!" squawked the parakeet, and launched itself from the sill.

Burton closed the window.

He was going to meet Lord Palmerston.

Bloody hell.

§

The Cannibal Club was located in rooms above Bartoloni's Italian restaurant in Leicester Square.

Burton found the enigmatic and rather saturnine Richard Monckton Milnes there, in company with the diminutive Algernon Swinburne and Captain Henry Murray, Doctor James Hunt, Sir Edward Brabrooke, Thomas Bendyshe and Charles Bradlaugh; hell-raisers all.

"Burton!" cried Milnes as the explorer entered. "Congratulations!"

"On what?"

"On shooting that bounder Speke! Surely it was you who pulled the trigger? Please say so!"

Burton threw himself into a chair and lit a cigar.

"It was not."

"Ah, what a shame!" exclaimed Milnes. "I was so hoping you could tell us what it feels like to murder a man. A white man, I mean!"

"Why, yes, of course!" put in Bradlaugh. "You killed that little Arab boy on the road to Mecca, didn't you?"

Burton accepted a drink from Henry Murray.

"You know damned well I didn't!" he growled. "That bastard Stanley writes nothing but scurrilous nonsense!"

"Come now, Richard!" trilled Swinburne, in his excitable, high-pitched voice, "Don't object so! Do you not agree that murder is one of the great boundaries which we must cross in order to know that we, ourselves, are truly alive?"

The famous explorer sighed and shook his head. Swinburne was young—

just twenty-four—and possessed an intuitive intelligence which appealed to the older man; but he was gullible.

"Nonsense, Algy! Don't let these Libertines mesmerise you with their misguided ideas and appallingly bad logic. They are incorrigibly perverse, especially Milnes, here."

"Hah!" yelled Bendyshe from across the room, "Swinburne's as perverse as they come! He has a taste for pain, don't you know! Likes the kiss of a whip, what!"

Swinburne giggled, twitched, and snapped his fingers. As always, his movements were fast, jerky and eccentric, as if he suffered from Saint Vitus' dance.

"It's true. I'm a follower of de Sade."

"It's a common affliction," noted Burton. "Why, I once visited a brothel in Karachi—on a research mission for Napier, you understand—"

Snorts and howls of derision came from the gathering.

"—and there witnessed a man flagellated to the point of unconsciousness. He enjoyed it!"

"Delicious!" shuddered Swinburne.

"Maybe so, if your tastes run to it," agreed Burton. "However, flagellation is one thing, murder is quite another!"

Milnes sat beside Burton, leaning close.

"But, I say, Richard," he murmured. "Don't you ever wonder at the sense of freedom one must feel when performing the act of murder? It is, after all, the greatest taboo, is it not? Break that and you are free of the shackles imposed by civilisation!"

"I'm no great enthusiast for the false pleasures and insidious suppressions of civilisation," said Burton. "And, in my opinion, Mrs Grundy requires a thorough shagging; however, as much as I might rail against the constraints of English society and culture, murder is a more fundamental matter than either."

Swinburne squealed with delight. "A thorough shagging! Oh, bravo, Richard!"

Milnes nodded. "False pleasures and insidious suppressions indeed. Pleasures which enslave, suppressions which pass judgement. Where, I ask, is freedom?"

"I don't know," answered Burton. "How can one quantify so indefinite a notion as freedom?"

"By looking to nature, dear boy! Nature red in tooth and claw! One animal kills another animal; is it found guilty? No! It remains free to do what it will, even—and, in fact, certainly—to kill again! As de Sade himself said: 'Nature has not got two voices, you know, one of them condemning all day what the other commands.'"

Burton emptied his glass in a single swallow.

"For sure, Darwin has demonstrated that Nature is a brutal and entirely pitiless process, but you seem to forget, Milnes, that the animal which kills is most often, in turn, itself killed by another animal, just as the murderer, in a supposedly civilised country, is hung for his crime!"

"Then you propose an innate natural law of justice from which we can never break free; a law which transcends culture, whatever its stage of development?"

James Hunt, passing to join a conversation between Bradlaugh and Brabrook on the other side of the room, stopped long enough to refill Burton's glass.

"Yes, I do believe some such law exists. I find the Hindu notion of karma more alluring than the Catholic absurdity of original sin."

"How is Isabel?" put in Bendyshe, who'd stepped across to join them.

Burton ignored the mischievous question and went on:

"At least karma provides a counterbalance—a penalty or reward, if you like—to acts we actually do and thoughts we actually think, rather than punishing us for the supposed sin of our actual existence or for a transgression against a wholly artificial dictate of so-called morality. It is a function of Nature rather than a judgement of an unproven God."

"By Jove! Stanley was correct when he wrote that you're a heathen!" mocked Bendyshe. "Burton joins with Darwin and says there is no God!"

"Actually, Darwin hasn't suggested any such thing. It is others who imposed that interpretation upon his *Origin of Species*."

"'There is no God, Nature sufficeth unto herself; in no wise hath she need of an author,'" quoted Swinburne. "De Sade again."

"In many respects I consider him laughable," commented Burton. "But in that instance, I wholeheartedly agree. The more I study religions, the more I'm convinced that man never worshipped anything but himself."

He quoted his own poetry:

*"Man worships self: his God is man; the struggling
of the mortal mind
to form its model as 'twould be, the perfect of itself
to find."*

Milnes took a drag from his cigar and blew a smoke ring, which rose lazily into the air. He watched it slowly disperse and said: "But this karma business, Richard; what you are proposing is that one way or another, through some sort of entirely natural process, a murderer will receive retribution. Do you then count man's judgement—the death penalty—to be natural?"

"We are natural beings, are we not?"

"Well," interrupted Bendyshe, "I sometimes wonder about Swinburne."

It was a fair point, thought Burton, for Swinburne was a very unnatural-looking man. At just five-foot-two, he had a strangely tiny body. His limbs were small and delicate, with sloping shoulders and a very long neck upon which sat a large head made even bigger by a tousled mass of carroty-red hair standing almost at right-angles to it. His mouth was weak and effeminate; his eyes huge, pale green, and dreamy.

Few poets looked so much a poet as Algernon Charles Swinburne.

"But that aside," said Bendyshe, "what if the murderer avoids the noose?"

"Guilt," proposed Burton. "A gradual but inescapable degradation of the character. A degenerative disease of the mind. Maybe a descent into madness and self-destruction."

"Or perhaps," offered Swinburne, "a tendency to mix with criminal types until the murderer is himself, inevitably, murdered."

"Well put!" agreed the famous adventurer.

"Interesting," pondered Milnes, "But, I say, we all know that murders are committed either in the heat of passion, or else with intent by an individual who's already in an advanced—if that's the appropriate word—state of mental decay. What if, though, a murder was calculated and committed by an intelligent man who performs the act only out of scientific curiosity? What if it were done only to transcend the limitations that tell us it shouldn't be done?"

"An idle motive," suggested Burton.

"Not at all, dear boy!" declared Milnes. "It's a magnificent motive! Why, the man who would undertake such an act would risk his immortal soul for science!"

"He would undoubtedly see sense and back away from the experiment," said Burton, his voice slurring slightly. "For once crossed, that barrier allows no return. However, his decision would be based on self-determined standards of behaviour rather than on any set out by civilisation or on notions of an immortal soul; for as you say, he's an intelligent man."

"It's strange," said Henry Murray, who up until now had listened in silence. "I thought that you, of all of us, would be the one most likely to approve the experiment."

"You should take my reputation with a pinch of salt."

"Must we? I rather enjoy having a devil in our midst," grinned Swinburne.

Sir Richard Francis Burton considered the susceptible young poet and wondered how to keep him out of trouble.

§

Burton was not a Libertine himself, but they considered him an honorary member of the caste and delighted in his knowledge of exotic cultures, where the stifling laws of civilisation were remarkable only by their seeming absence. He enjoyed drinking and debating with them; especially this evening; it kept his mind engaged and helped to stave off the despondency that had been creeping over him since he'd returned from Bath.

By one o'clock in the morning, though, it was dragging at him again, made worse by alcohol and exhaustion, so he bid his friends farewell and left the club.

The evening was bitterly cold—unusual for September—and the roads glistened wetly. The thickening pall wrapped each gas lamp in its own golden aureole. Burton held his overcoat tight with one hand and swung his cane with the other. London rustled and murmured around him as he walked unsteadily homewards.

A velocipede chattered past. They had started to appear on the streets two years ago, these steam-driven, one-man vehicles, and were popularly known as "penny farthings" due to their odd design, for the front wheel was nearly as tall as a man, while the back wheel was just eighteen inches in diameter.

The rider was seated high in a leather saddle, situated slightly behind the crown of the front wheel, with his feet resting in stirrups to either side, his legs held away from the piston arm and crank which pumped and span to the left of the axle. The tiny, box-like engine was attached to the frame behind and below the saddle; the small boiler, with its furnace, was under this, and the coal scuttle under that; the three elements arranged in a segmented arc over the top rear section of the main wheel. As well as providing the motive power, they were also the machine's centre of gravity and, together with the engine's internal gyroscope, made the vehicle almost impossible to knock over, despite its ungainly appearance.

By far the most remarkable feature of the penny farthing was its extraordinary efficiency. It could complete a twenty-mile journey in about an hour on just one fist-sized lump of coal. With the furnace able to hold up to four pieces and with the same number stored in the scuttle, it had a maximum range of 160 miles and could operate for about twenty hours before needing to refuel. The vehicle's main flaw, aside from the thorough shaking it meted out to the driver, was that the two slim funnels, which rose up behind the saddle, belched smoke into the already miasmal atmosphere of England's capital, adding to an already bad situation. Nevertheless, the vehicles were currently all the rage and had done much to restore the public's faith in the Engineering faction of the Technologist caste; a group that had been much maligned of late after the disastrous flooding of the undersea town of Hydroham off the Norfolk coast, and a number of fatal crashes during the attempted—and ultimately abandoned—development of gas-filled airships.

Burton watched the contraption disappear into the mist.

London had transformed while he'd been in Africa. It had filled with new machines and new breeds of animal. The Engineers and Eugenicists— the main branches of the Technologist caste—seemed unstoppable, despite protests from the Libertines, who felt that art, beauty and nobility of spirit were more essential than material progress.

The problem was that the Libertines, despite producing reams of anti-Technologist propaganda, were unclear in their message. On the one hand, there were the "True Libertines," such as the Pre-Raphaelite Brotherhood, who were basically Luddites; while on the other, there were the increasingly powerful "Rakes," whose interests ran to black magic, anarchy, sexual depravity, drug-taking, meddling and general bad-behaviour, which they justified as an attempt to "transcend the limitations of the human condition." Most Libertines, Richard Monckton Milnes being a prime example, fell somewhere between the two camps, being neither as dreamily idealistic as the one faction nor as scandalously self-indulgent as the other.

As for Sir Richard Francis Burton, he wasn't sure where he fitted. Although it was the country of his birth, England had never felt like home, probably because he'd spent most of his childhood being dragged around Europe by his restless parents. He was therefore rather surprised when he returned from the Nile expedition and found that the country's current state of social instability somewhat suited him. The rapid changes, more intensely felt in the capital than elsewhere, might be confusing to the majority of the populace but he'd always regarded his own identity as rather a transient and changeable thing, so now he felt an odd sort of empathy with the fluctuating nature of British culture.

As he walked, he slowly became aware of a tapping noise from somewhere above and realised that he'd been hearing it on and off since leaving the club. He peered up and around but saw nothing.

He continued his trek home, listening, and, yes, there it was again. Was he being followed? He looked back, but there was no suggestion of anyone on his heels until a policeman started to trail along behind him, his attention attracted by the lone, obviously rather drunk man's brutal features. After five minutes or so, the constable drew closer, saw that Burton wore the clothes of a gentleman, hesitated, then abandoned the chase.

The explorer crossed Charing Cross Road and entered a long badly lit side street. His foot hit a discarded bottle which span into the gutter with a musical tinkle. Something large flapped overhead and he looked up in time to see a huge Eugenicist-bred swan pass by, dragging a box kite behind it through the mist. A man's white face—an indistinct blur—looked down from the kite before it vanished over the rooftops. A faint voice reached Burton's ears but whatever it was the man had shouted was muffled by the water-laden air.

Last year, Speke and Grant had used the same form of transportation to make their way to the Nyanza, following the old route. It had taken a fraction of the time required by Burton's expedition. They'd set up camp in Kazeh, a small town some hundred and fifty miles south of the great lake, and here John Speke had made one of his characteristic errors of judgement by failing to properly guard his birds. They'd been eaten by lions. Without them he couldn't circumnavigate the lake; couldn't ascertain whether it was the source of the great river; and couldn't prove Burton wrong.

A few yards farther down the road, a man shuffled from the shadows of a doorway. He was a coarse-featured individual clad in canvas trousers and shirt with a rust-coloured waistcoat and a cloth cap. There were fire marks— red welts—on his face and thick forearms caused by hours spent stoking a forge.

"Can I 'elp you, mate?" he growled. "Maybe relieve you of wha'ever loose change is weighin' down yer pockits?"

Burton looked at him.

The man backed away so suddenly that his heels struck the doorstep and he sat down heavily.

"Sorry, fella!" he mumbled. "Mistook you fer somebody else, I did!"

The explorer snorted scornfully and moved on. He entered a network of narrow alleys; dark, dangerous and sordid; a dismal tentacle of poverty reaching far out of the East End into the centre of the city. Mournful windows gaped from the sides of squalid houses. Inarticulate shouts came from some of them; occasionally the sound of blows, screams and weeping; but hopeless silence came from most.

It occurred to him that the depths of London felt remarkably similar to the remotest regions of Africa.

He came to a junction, turned left, tripped and stumbled; his shin banging against a discarded crate; his trouser leg catching on a protruding nail and tearing. He spat out an oath and kicked the crate away. A rat scuttled along the side of the pavement.

Leaning against a lamp post, Burton rubbed his eyes. The taste of brandy burned uncomfortably at the back of his throat. He noticed a flier pasted to the post and read it:

Work disciplines your spirit
Work develops your character
Work strengthens your soul
Do not allow machines to do your work!

Pushing himself away, he walked along the alley and turned yet another corner—he wasn't sure where he was but knew he was proceeding in the right general direction—and found himself at the end of a long, straight lane, its worn cobbles shining beneath the haggard light of a single lamp. It was bordered by high and featureless red brick walls; the sides of warehouses. The far end opened onto what looked to be a main thoroughfare. He could vaguely see the front of a shop, possibly a butcher's, but when he tried to read the sign over the window, a velocipede clattered past it, leaving a swirling wreath of smoke which further obscured the lettering.

Burton moved on, trying to avoid pools of stinking urine, his shoes squelching in patches of mud and worse, kicking against refuse.

A litter-crab came clanking into view by the shop, its eight thick mechanical legs thudding against the road surface, the twenty-four thin arms on its belly darting this way and that, skittering back and forth over the cobbles, snatching up rubbish and throwing it through the machine's maw into the furnace within.

The crab creaked and rattled past the end of the alley and, as it did so, its siren wailed a warning. A few seconds later, it let out a deafening hiss as it ejected hot cleansing steam from the two downward-pointing funnels at its rear.

The automated cleaner vanished from sight as a tumultuous wall of white vapour boiled into the passage. Burton stopped and took a few steps backward, waiting for it to disperse. It billowed toward him, extending hot coils which slowed and became still, hanging in the air as they cooled.

Someone entered the street, their weirdly elongated shadow angling through the white cloud; a figure writ dark, skeletal and horrific by the distortion. Sudden flashes of light illuminated the roiling mist, as if it were a miniature storm. Burton waited for the shadow to shrink; to be sucked into the person to whom it belonged when he—for surely it must be a man—emerged from the vapour.

It didn't shrink.

It wasn't a shadow.

Possibly, it wasn't even a man.

The steam parted and from it sprang a bizarre apparition; a massively long-legged shape—like a carnival stilt-walker—a long dark cloak flapping from its hunched shoulders, bolts of lightning crackling around its body and head.

Burton retreated hastily until his back brought up against the wall. He blinked rapidly and licked his lips.

Was it human, this thing? Its head was large, black and shiny, with an aura of blue flame crawling around it. Red eyes peered at him maliciously. White teeth shone in a lipless grin.

The creature stalked forward, bent, its talon-like hands flexing, and Burton saw that his first impression was accurate; the thing walked on two-foot-high stilts.

Its lanky body was clad in a skin-tight white scaly suit which glittered in the dim light of the single guttering gas lamp. Something circular glowed on its chest and emitted bursts of sparks and ribbons of lightning which snaked over the thing's long limbs.

"Burton!" the apparition croaked. "Richard Francis bloody Burton!"

It suddenly pounced on him and a hand slashed sideways, slapping hard against his right ear, sending him reeling. His top hat went spinning into a puddle. He dropped his cane.

"I told you once to stay out of it!" snapped the thing. "You didn't listen!"

All of a sudden, Burton felt icily sober.

Fingers dug into his hair and yanked his head up. He felt an agonisingly powerful static charge coursing through his body. His arms and legs twitched spasmodically.

Red eyes glared into his.

"I'll not tell you again. Leave me alone!"

"W-what?" gasped Burton.

"Just stay out of it! The affair is none of your damned business!"

"What affair?"

"Don't play the innocent! I don't want to kill you, but I swear to you, if you don't keep your nose out of it, I'll break your fucking neck!"

"I have no idea what you're talking about!" protested Burton.

His head was shaken violently, causing his teeth to clack together.

"I'm talking about you organising forces against me! It's not what you're meant to be doing! Your destiny lays elsewhere. Do you understand?"

The creature rammed its forearm into Burton's face.

"I said, do you understand?"

"No!"

"Then I'll spell it out for you," growled the stilt man. He dragged Burton around and slammed him against the wall, drew back his arm and sent a fist crashing into the explorer's mouth.

"Do what—"

Again. Crack!

"—you're supposed—"

Crack!

"—to do!"

Burton sagged back against the bricks. He mumbled through split lips: "How can I possibly know what I'm supposed to do?"

The fingers in his hair jerked him up until he was looking directly into the thing's eyes, which stared down, inches from his own. They burned redly, and Burton realised that his attacker was completely insane.

Blue flame leaped from the thing's head and licked at the explorer's brow, scorching his skin.

"You are *supposed* to marry Isabel and be sent from one fucking miserable consulship to another. Your career is *supposed* to peak in three years when you debate the Nile question with Speke and the silly sod shoots himself dead. You are *supposed* to write books and die."

Burton braced his legs against the wall.

"What the hell are you babbling about?" he demanded, in a stronger voice. "The debate was cancelled. Speke shot himself yesterday—but he's not dead!"

The creature's eyes widened.

"No!" it whispered. "No!"

It gritted its teeth and snarled: "I'm a historian! I know what happened. It was 1864 not 1861. I know—"

A look of bemusement passed over its gaunt, horrible features.

"God damn it! Why does it have to be so complicated?" it whispered to itself. "Maybe if I kill you? But if the death of just one person has already done all this—?"

Burton, feeling the fingers loosening, took his chance. He jerked his head free, shoved his shoulder into his attacker's stomach, then threw himself sideways.

The apparition teetered back to the opposite wall. It clutched at it for balance and glared at Burton as he regained his footing. They stood facing each other.

"Listen to me you bastard!" snapped the creature. "For your own good, next time you see me, don't come near!"

"I don't know you!" objected Burton. "And, believe me, if I never see you again, I'll not regret it one iota!"

Lightning exploded from the apparition's chest and danced across the ground. The stilt man cried out in agony, almost falling.

Suddenly, its wild eyes dimmed and Burton saw a brief glimmer of reason in them. It looked down at itself, then at him, and in low tones said:

"The irony is that I'm running out of time. You're in my way, and you're making the situation much worse."

"What situation? Explain!" snapped the explorer.

The uncanny, spindly figure stepped forward and the irises of its eyes narrowed to pinpricks.

"Marry the bitch, Burton. Settle down. Become consul in Fernando Po, Brazil, Damascus and wherever the fuck else they send you. Write your damned books. But, above all, leave me alone! Do you understand? *Leave me the fuck alone!*"

It crouched low, glared at him, and suddenly straightened its legs, shooting vertically into the air.

Burton twisted his head to look up. His assailant soared high above the top of the warehouses, and, in mid-air, vanished.

§

Chapter 3

The Commission

"Die, my dear doctor! That's the last thing I shall do!"
—*Lord Palmerston*

∽

"Great Scott, man!" exclaimed Lord Palmerston. "What have you been up to now?"

Burton lowered himself gingerly into the chair before the Prime Minister's desk. His body was bruised; his right eye blackened; his lips cut and puffy.

"Just an accident, sir. Nothing to worry about."

"You look perfectly hideous!"

'You're a fine one to talk!' thought Burton.

For the past two years, Palmerston had been receiving Eugenicist life extension treatments. Though seventy-seven years old, he currently had a life expectancy of about a hundred and thirty. To match this, he'd received a cosmetic overhaul. The loose skin of his face had been tightened, the fatty deposits removed, and the discolourations eliminated. Paralysing toxins had been regularly injected into the wrinkles on his forehead and around his eyes and mouth, smoothing them out and giving his face the clean contours of a young man—or, thought Burton, of a waxwork, because, in his opinion, the Prime Minister appeared to have wandered out of Madam Toussaud's. There was nothing natural about him; he was a shiny mockery of himself; a freakish caricature; his face too white and mask-like, his lips too red, his sideburns too bushy, his curly hair too long and black, his midnight blue velvet suit too tight and foppish, his eau de Cologne too liberally applied, and his movements too mannered.

"I say!" declared the Prime Minister, "it's not the first time you've been knocked around, is it? I remember when you came back from Abyssinia with those dreadful wounds on your face. You seem to have a nose for trouble, Burton."

"I think it's more a case of trouble having a nose for me," muttered the adventurer.

"Hmm. Be that as it may, when I look back over your history I see one disaster after another."

Palmerston leafed through a report on his desk top. The desk was an extremely big, heavy affair of carved mahogany. Burton noticed with amusement that, just below its lip, there ran around it a horizontal band decoratively carved with scenes of a highly erotic nature.

There were not many items on the desk: a blotting pad; a silver pen in its holder; a letter holder; a carafe of water and a slender glass; and, to the Prime Minister's left, a strange device of brass and glass which sporadically emitted a slight hiss and a puff of vapour. Burton could make neither head nor tail of it, though he saw that part of the mechanism—a glass tube about as thick as his wrist—disappeared into the desk.

"You served under General Napier in the East India Army and undertook intelligence missions for him, I believe?"

"That's correct. I speak Hindustani, among other languages, and I make up well as a native. I suppose it made me a logical choice."

"How many languages do you speak?"

"Fluently? Twenty-four, so far, plus a few dialects."

"Good gracious! Remarkable!"

Palmerston pushed on through the pages. Burton found it astonishing—and ominous—that so much had been written about him.

"Napier speaks highly of you. His successor, Pringle, does not."

"Pringle is a cretinous toad."

"Is he, indeed? Is he? Bless my soul, I shall have to be a little more rigorous in my choice of appointments, then, shan't I?"

Burton coughed lightly. "My apologies," he said. "I spoke out of turn."

"According to these reports, speaking out of turn is another of your specialisms. Who was Colonel Corsellis?"

"*Is*, sir; he still lives. He was acting C. O. of the Corps when I met him."

Palmerston tried to raise his brows but they remained motionless on his taut face. He read aloud:

"*Here lies the body of Colonel Corsellis,*
The rest of the fellow, I fancy, in hell is."

The corner of Burton's mouth twitched. He'd forgotten that youthful doggerel.

"To be fair, he did *ask* me to write something about him."

"I'm sure he was delighted with the result," replied Palmerston, witheringly. His fingers tapped impatiently on the desk. He looked at Burton thoughtfully. "You were on active service with the 18th Bombay Native Infantry from '42 to '49. It appears to have been seven years of recurring insubordination and frequent sick leave."

"All the men fell ill, sir. India, at that time, was not conducive to good health. As for the insubordination; I was young. I have no other excuse."

Palmerston nodded. "We all commit errors of judgement when young. For most of us, they are forgiven and relegated to the past, where they belong. You, however, seem to have a rather stubborn albatross slung around your neck. I refer, of course, to your misjudged investigation in Karachi and the rumour that has attached to it."

"You mean my report concerning male brothels?"

"Yes."

"General Napier was concerned that a great number of British troops were visiting them. He asked me to find out exactly how corrupting the establishments and the practices therein might be. I did my job. I found out."

"You probed too far, according to Pringle."

"An interesting choice of words."

"His, Burton, not mine."

"Indeed. I have often thought that when a man selects one word over another he often reveals far more of himself than he intended."

"And what, in your opinion, does Pringle reveal?"

"The man maliciously besmirched my reputation. He accused me of indulging in the acts of depravity which I was sent to investigate. His hounding of me amounted to an irrational obsession which, I believe, suggests but one thing."

"That being?"

"His ill-repressed desire to perform those very acts himself!"

"That's quite an accusation."

"It's not an accusation, it's a supposition, and one made in a private interview. Compare that to the frenzied objections he made, in public, to my entirely imagined behaviour. His allegations have haunted my career ever since. He almost ruined me."

Palmerston nodded and turned a page.

"You were subsequently passed over for a position as Chief Interpreter?"

"In favour of a man who spoke but one language aside from his own, yes."

"That seems rather absurd."

"I'm pleased that someone finally recognises the fact."

"You sound bitter."

Burton didn't answer.

"So you left the East India Company army on medical grounds?"

"I was sick with malaria, dysentery and opthalmia."

"And syphilis," added Palmerston.

"Thank you for reminding me. The doctors didn't think I'd live. For that matter, neither did I."

"And your health now?"

"The malaria flares up now and again. A course of quinine usually quells it."

"Or a bottle of gin or two?"

"If necessary."

Another sheet of tightly written notes was turned aside.

"You returned to England in 1850 on sick leave then prepared for your now famous pilgrimage to Mecca and Medina."

"That's correct, Prime Minister. May I ask why we're reviewing my history?"

Lord Palmerston cast him a baleful look. "All in good time, Burton."

The old man surveyed the next page, then, flicking a quick glance of embarrassment at the explorer, reached into a drawer and retrieved a pair of pince-nez spectacles, which he ruefully clipped to the bridge of his nose. Their lenses were of smoked blue glass.

He cleared his throat.

"Why did you do it?"

"The pilgrimage? I was curious. Bored. Restless. I wanted to make a name for myself."

"You certainly achieved that. You completed the entire journey in disguise, as a native, speaking only Arabic?"

"Yes; as Abdullah the dervish. I wanted to be treated as one of the brethren, not as a guest. It has long been my view that an outsider, in any culture, is offered but a fragment of the truth, and that carefully dressed for his consumption, to boot. I desired authenticity."

"And you killed a boy to avoid being exposed as a non-Muslim?"

"I am, it seems, accused of that crime on a daily basis. Only last night, the question was asked of me for the umpteenth time. Did I kill a boy? No, Prime Minister; I did not. I am not guilty of murder; not of a boy nor of a woman nor of a man nor even of a dog."

"Are you capable?"

Burton sat back in his chair, surprised. This theme of murder arising again, so soon after the conversation at the Cannibal Club! It was an extraordinary coincidence and it agitated the superstitious part of his character.

"Am I capable of cold-blooded murder? I think not. Might I kill in the heat of battle or in self-defence? Of course. I may have done so in Berbera; in such circumstances it's impossible to know the outcome of your shots or the cuts of your sword."

"And what if you were in a position of authority and were required to send a man to his almost certain death?"

"I would fulfil my responsibilities."

Lord Palmerston nodded as if satisfied. He reached into his waistcoat pocket, withdrew a snuff tin, and sprinkled a small heap of the fine powder onto the side of his right hand at the base of his thumb. This he raised to his nose and snorted.

He sniffed and turned another page. Burton noticed that the Prime Minister's fingernails were carefully manicured and coated with clear varnish.

"It was in '55," continued Palmerston, "the Berbera incident. Lieutenant John Hanning Speke was one of the men who accompanied you?"

"Yes."

"Incidentally, I enquired after him last night. He's in the Penfold Private Sanatorium. He shot half his face off; they don't expect him to live."

Burton nodded, his countenance iron hard. "I know."

Palmerston regarded him.

"Another enemy?"

"Apparently so. Are you?"

If Palmerston was shocked or surprised at the brazen question, he didn't show it. Mind you, mused Burton, the man was incapable of showing anything.

"Am I your enemy? No, I am not."

"That's encouraging, anyway. Yes, Prime Minister, Lieutenant Speke did indeed accompany me into Somalia. I got a spear through the face and he was also injured. One of our companions, Lieutenant Stroyan, was killed. The following year, after brief service in the Crimea, I organised an expedition to central Africa in search of the source of the Nile. Speke accompanied me and afterwards he betrayed me. The press made the most of it and a confrontation between us was engineered. It was due to take place yesterday at the Bath Assembly Rooms. It didn't. So, that's the history done with. Perhaps now we can move on to my reason for being here?"

Palmerston's mouth opened and a mirthless cackle sounded, though his lips didn't smile.

"Oh my goodness!" he exclaimed. "You *are* an impatient man!"

"I don't deny it. And to be perfectly frank, Prime Minister, I have a hangover and I badly need a piss, so I'd appreciate it if we could bypass the niceties and get to the core of the matter."

Palmerston banged his right hand up and down on the desk, threw his head back and let loose a rapid sawing noise, which Burton—phenomenal interpreter though he was—could only guess was laughter. It rasped rhythmically for too long, passing quickly from genuine to affected, and developed a strange sibilance which, for a bizarre moment, made it seem as if the Prime Minister had developed a leak and was rapidly deflating.

Then Burton realised that the increasingly loud hiss was coming not from the man opposite but from the odd device on his desk. He turned his eyes to it in time to see the thing suddenly shake frantically. The needle of a gauge on its side swept over into a red-marked segment and, with a sound like a large bung being pulled from a container, the mechanism gave one last jerk and became silent and motionless. A wisp of steam floated from its top. The needle sank back to the left.

Palmerston closed his mouth, looked at the contraption, grunted, reached across and flipped a switch. A small door swung open and a canister popped out into the Prime Minister's hand. He twisted the lid from it and pulled a pale blue sheet of paper from within. He read the note and nodded, then looked up at Burton and announced:

"You are approved!"

"How nice," said Burton. "By whom? For what?"

"Why, by Buckingham Palace! Our monarch is offering you a job!"

For once, Burton was at a loss for words. His jaw hung loosely.

Palmerston's face stretched sideways around the mouth in what might have been an attempted grin. It was not a pretty sight.

"That's why I called you here, Burton. The palace has taken an interest in you. It has been mooted that, with your rather unusual range of skills and— shall we say *forceful?*—personality, you can do the Empire a unique service; something no other man can offer. That's why this position has been created; specifically for you."

Still Burton said nothing. His mind was racing; grappling with this entirely unexpected development—and also with the notion that someone at Buckingham Palace might somehow be listening in on this conversation.

"I must confess," continued Palmerston, "that you presented me with a quandary. I knew I had to do *something* with you but I had no idea what. Your talent for making enemies concerned me; I suspected that whatever post I gave you, you'd quickly become a liability. It was suggested, by one of my colleagues, that I should bury you in some remote consulate; Fernando Po was top of the list. Do you know it?"

A nod. The only response Burton could manage.

Marry the bitch. Settle down. Become consul in Fernando Po, Brazil, Damascus and wherever the fuck else they send you.

The words blazed through his mind.

"Who knows?" he jerked intently.

"Pardon?"

"Who knows about this interview, the job, the consulate?"

"About the job; just myself and the palace." Palmerston tapped the copper and glass apparatus. "We have communicated privately on the matter. About you being here? The palace, myself, my private secretary, the guards on the door, the butler, any of the household staff who might have seen you come in. About the consulate? The palace, myself, and Lord Russell, who suggested you for the position. Why?"

Burton knew what Lord John Russell, the Foreign Secretary, looked like. He was an elderly, bald-headed, broad-faced man who in no way resembled the apparition of last night.

"I think," said Burton slowly, "there's the distinct possibility that either the government or the royal household has a spy in its midst."

Palmerston became very still. His Adam's apple rose and fell.

"Explain," he said softly.

Rapidly, without embellishment, Burton recounted the attack of the previous evening. Palmerston listened attentively and, for all the movement he made, he might have become the waxwork he so closely resembled.

When Burton had finished, the Prime Minister asked him to describe the apparition in greater detail.

The reply came:

"He was tall and emaciated with limbs long, thin but wiry and strong. His head was encased in a large black, shiny, globular helmet around which a blue flame burned. From within the headgear red eyes, insane, glared at me. The face was skull-like: the cheeks sunken, the nose a blade, the mouth a slit. He wore a white skin-tight costume which resembled fish scales in texture. A lengthy black cloak with a white lining hung from his shoulders and a flat circular lamp-like affair was affixed to his chest, shining with a reddish light and emitting sparks. His hands were bony and talon-like. The feet and calves were encased by tight boots from which a spring-like mechanism projected, attached to two-foot high stilts."

Burton paused.

"When I was on the pilgrimage," he continued quietly, "there was much talk of evil djan—"

"Djan?" interposed Palmerston.

"Sorry. It's the plural of 'djinni,' the evil spirits that supposedly haunt the deserts. I consider myself a reasonably intelligent man, so, of course, I discounted the talk as mere superstition. However, if you were to tell me that last night I came face to face with one such, I might believe you."

"Perhaps you did," countered Palmerston. He glanced down as the instrument on his desk trembled and emitted a puff of steam. "Have you ever heard of Spring Heeled Jack?"

Burton looked surprised.

"That never occurred to me!"

Spring Heeled Jack was a bogeyman; a mythical spook used by mothers to scare naughty children into submission: 'Behave! Or Spring Heeled Jack will come for you!'

"So a spy dressed as a character from folklore?" Burton reflected. "But why? And why attack me? What interest has he in Lord Russell's suggestion that you make me a consul?"

"He may be rather more than a spy," suggested Palmerston. "Captain Burton; I want you to talk to Detective-Inspector William Trounce of Scotland Yard. In 1840, when he was a constable, he was present at The Assassination. He claimed to have seen this jumping Jack thing at the scene, and, despite opposition from his superiors, still maintains that the creature is a fact, rather than an illusion caused by panic or hysteria, as others have asserted. It nearly cost him his career. For a decade afterwards, he was the laughing stock of the Yard and only rose to his current position through dogged determination and hard work. You have your albatross; Spring Heeled Jack is his."

Burton spread his arms in a shrug.

"Talk to him to what end?"

"As a start to your second assignment. I spoke of a job. Our monarch wants to commission you as—for want of a better word—an 'agent.' It's a unique position; you will be required to investigate matters which, perhaps, lay outside of police jurisdiction, or which, due to their nature, require a rather more singular approach than Scotland Yard can offer. You will answer to Buckingham Palace and to me and you will have the authority to command the police when necessary. We live in tumultuous times, Burton. The Technologists are pushing ethical boundaries and the Libertines are pushing moral boundaries. Both castes are too powerful and both have extremist factions. The palace is concerned that science is altering our culture too much and too fast and without proper periods of reflection and consultation. For the good of the Empire, we require someone who can unveil secrets and make snap judgements; someone fearless and independent; someone like you."

"I'm honoured, sir," responded Burton, and he meant it.

"It's not an order. If you don't want the commission, you can have the consulate instead."

"I want the commission, Prime Minister."

"Good. I have an initial assignment for you, but, as I said, I want you to consider this Spring Heeled Jack affair as a second. If there is indeed a spy within the government or at the palace, unmask him! As for the original mission: find out what these are and where they are coming from—"

The Prime Minister pulled a sheet of paper from his desk drawer and slid it toward Burton. On it there was a rough sketch, in pencil, of a squat, misshapen man with a snout-like jaw, his face resembling that of a vicious dog.

"You want me to find the artist?" asked Burton.

"No. I know who the artist is; a Frenchman named Paul Gustave Doré. He's buried himself somewhere in the East End where he's been surreptitiously sketching scenes of poverty—God knows why; you know how these artists are, with their absurd notions of the nobility of the poor and whatnot. No; I want you to find the man-wolves."

Burton looked up, puzzled.

"Man-wolves? You think this is sketched from life?"

"It is. The Royal Secretary made it known to Doré that the monarch was interested in his work. In response, the artist has been posting some of his sketches to the palace. This was among them. Look on the back."

Burton turned the sketch over and saw words scrawled in an erratic hand:

'Your Majesty, there are loup-garous at large in the Cauldron and the people here are greatly afraid. There have been deaths and abductions every night, far beyond that which is the usual for this part of the city. The populace hate the police and will not consult them. I have seen one of the loup-garous with my own eyes. This sketch depicts the thing I saw. It tore out a man's heart as I watched and made away with his boy. —Doré.'

"Good lord!" exclaimed Burton.

"Personally," said Palmerston, "I think Doré has fallen in with the opium crowd and this is nothing but a drug-fuelled delusion. Maybe you can find out. With your ability to disguise yourself and adopt accents, I thought maybe you could penetrate where the police fear to tread; find this Doré chap and speak to him."

With a rattle and a whistle of steam, a second canister popped up into the contraption on the Prime Minister's desk. He took it, opened it, read the note, and offered it to Burton.

"Your salary."

Burton looked at the numbers scrawled on the paper.

For the second time that morning, his jaw went slack.

§

Last night's mist had condensed into a fog; a sickly sulphurous blanket which scratched at Burton's eyes as he waved down a hansom cab along Whitehall. It was one of the new vehicles, pulled by a steam-horse. These four-wheeled engines bore a passing resemblance to the famous Stephenson's Rocket but were a fraction of the size, being about five feet long, three feet wide and three feet tall, with a thin funnel soaring a full ten feet straight upward. From each end of the front axle two thin curved steering rods arced up and back to the driver, who sat on his "box" on the top of the cab, which was harnessed behind the engine. Levers on the hand grips controlled the speed and the brakes.

Despite the height of the funnel, smoke still had a tendency to drift into the driver's face, so he wore goggles and a leather cap for protection.

Burton climbed in and gazed out of the window as the hansom chugged away from the kerb. The ghost-like forms of London's inhabitants scuttled through the pea-souper, fading in and out of sight as if their very existence was questionable.

His hangover had vanished entirely. He felt strong and positive; he possessed a sense of purpose at last.

Palmerston's final words, though, still echoed in his ears: "This is not a job for a married man, you understand?"

Burton did understand.

Isabel would not.

Penfold Private Sanatorium, which was run by the Sisterhood of Noble Benevolence, was located in St. John's Wood, off Edgware Road.

The hansom drew up near the hospital's entrance and Burton disembarked, handing his fare up to the driver. He mounted the steps and entered the building.

The nurse at the reception desk glanced up at him.

"Oh!" she exclaimed, "Your poor face! But I'm sorry, sir, we don't treat minor wounds here! Can't you see your own doctor? You probably only need your cuts cleaned and some cream on that black eye."

Burton gave a slight smile.

"Actually, Sister, I'm here to visit Lieutenant John Speke. Which room is he in?"

She looked surprised.

"He's no longer here, sir. They took him last night."

"Took him? Who took him? Where?"

"The—um—his—" She stalled; looked confused. "His family?"

"You're asking me?"

"No! No, sir. I mean to say—yes, his family took him, I believe."

Burton frowned.

"Come now! You believe? What's going on?"

"Are you related to Lieutenant Speke, sir?"

"My name is Richard Burton. Perhaps you've heard of me?"

"Oh, I see. Yes, sir; I have. It's that—the thing is—well, the Lieutenant was removed from the sanatorium last night while Sister Raghavendra was on duty and she neglected to do the proper paperwork. We have no record of who came for him or where they took him."

"The man was on his death bed! How on earth could she allow his removal without due procedure?"

"She—she said she was taken ill and can't properly recall events, sir."

"Is that so? At what time did this occur?"

"About four in the morning. There were very few staff on duty at the time."

"And Speke was still alive?"

"Yes, sir. Though, in all honesty—and I'm sorry to say this—but it's unlikely that he survived being taken from our care."

"I'd like to see the nurse—Sister Raghavendra—if you please."

"I'm afraid she's not here. She was suspended from duty and sent home. She was very upset."

"Where does she live?"

"Oh, I can't tell you that, Mr Burton. It's against policy."

"To *hell* with your policies, Sister! They obviously count for nothing!"

The nurse's eyes widened in shock. "Sir!"

Burton pulled his wallet from his pocket and took out a folded document. He showed it to the nurse.

"Look at this signature, young lady. Do you recognise it?"

"No. Yes. It's—my goodness!—it's the same as the one on pound notes!"

"Now read this paragraph here," he instructed, indicating a short block of text with his finger.

She did so, pursed her lips, and nodded.

"Very well, sir. It seems I have no choice. Sister Raghavendra lives here—"

She scribbled an address onto a sheet of paper and handed it to him.

"Thank you," he said, and turned to leave, satisfied with the effectiveness of the document which Palmerston had issued to him that morning.

"Sir Burton!" she called after him.

He looked back.

She smiled. "Rub castor oil around your eye. It will reduce the bruising."

He winked at her.

§

Outside, Burton found the hansom still standing at the kerb. He hailed the driver: "Hi, cabbie, still here?"

"Oh aye, sir. Thought it best to wait for the fares to come to me, 'stead o' drivin' through this stinker lookin' for 'em!"

"Can you take me to 3 Bayham Street, near Mornington Crescent?"

"Wiv me eyes closed, sir—which in this 'ere mess o' fog is just as well. 'Op in!"

Burton settled on the seat and closed the door. He rubbed his itchy eyes as the steam-horse growled and the cabin lurched into motion. His skin felt grimy; thinly coated with soot and other pollutants. He wondered whether Limehouse had been evacuated. During the previous fog—two weeks ago— toxic gasses had settled into the Thames basin and a great mob of sailors, criminals, drug addicts and illegal immigrants—mainly Lascars, Dacoits, Chinamen, Africans and Irish refugees—had swept into Whitechapel, where they'd rioted for three days. When the fog cleared, and they returned to their hovels and opium dens, it was found that they'd piled hundreds of corpses—asphyxiation victims— along Commercial Road. With the risk of a cholera epidemic and a boom in the already unmanageable rat population, the government had called in the Army to clear and burn the bodies. Ever since, the newspapers had been calling for an all-out assault on Limehouse, demanding that it be cleared and razed to the ground. This, thought Burton, was unlikely to happen. The opium trade needed Limehouse and, he suspected, there were powerful forces in the Empire which needed the opium trade.

It took far longer to reach Mornington Crescent than it should have; the cabbie took two wrong turns and, when he finally delivered his passenger to Bayham Street, he seemed beside himself with embarrassment.

"Never done that 'afore, I swears to you, guv'nor!" he moaned. "As sure as me name's Montague Penniforth, I knows every nook and cranny of this 'ere city! But this 'particuliar' has befuddled me senses! I can 'ardly think straight, let alone guide this smokin' horse in the right direction!"

Burton knew what the man meant; some ingredient in the fog was causing him to feel slightly dizzy too; which, after a hard night's drinking was the last thing he needed.

"Don't worry yourself about it, Mr Penniforth," he said. "Here's a couple of bob extra. Why don't you pack up for the morning? Go spend some time with your missus!"

"Cor blimey!" coughed Penniforth. "You must be jokin'! Daisy would have me guts for garters if I turned up on the doorstep 'afore midnight. She can't stand the sight o' me!"

Burton laughed.

"Wait here, then, if you don't mind. I shan't be long and I'll promise you another shilling!"

"Me lucky day!" grinned the cabbie. "I'll have a draw on me pipe while I wait; get some *decent* fumes into me lungs!"

Burton left Montague Penniforth cleaning out the bowl of a filthy old cherrywood and crossed the pavement to peer at the house numbers. Number 3 was a four-storey terrace. A dim glow emanated from the fanlight window above the front door. He yanked at the bell-pull and heard a distant jangle.

After a minute, the portal was opened by an elderly woman in mourning dress, her face concealed behind a weeping veil of black crepe.

"Yes?" she whispered. There was an edge of suspicion to her voice, for though her visitor was obviously a gentleman, his face was cut, bruised, and barbarous in aspect.

"My apologies, ma'am," said Burton, courteously. "Do you have a Sister Raghavendra here?"

"Yes, sir. On the third floor. Are you from the sanatorium?"

"I've just come from there, yes," he replied. It wasn't quite an answer to the question she'd asked but she didn't seem to notice and appeared to be mollified by his deep, polite and melodious voice.

"If you wish to see her, sir, I should act as chaperone," she noted, in her frail tones.

"That will be acceptable, thank you."

"Pray, come in out of the fog, then. You can wait in the hallway."

Burton ran the soles of his shoes over the iron boot-scraper on the doorstep then stepped into the dingy hall, the walls of which were crowded with framed paintings and photographs, display plates and crucifixes. The landlady closed the door behind him and took a small silver finger-bell from her sleeve. In response to its tinkling ring, a sturdy young girl hurried out from the parlour. Flour powdered her hands, forearms and nose. She gave a clumsy curtsey.

"Mum?"

"Run up to Sister Raghavendra, Polly, and tell her she has a visitor; a Mr—?"

"Captain Burton." He always preferred to use his military rank; "Sir Burton" sounded a mite pretentious.

"A Captain Burton. You may advise Sister Raghavendra that I will escort the gentleman up to her sitting room if she wishes to receive him."

"Yes, Mum!"

The maid thumped up the stairs and out of sight.

"An ungainly girl but she serves me well. My name is Mrs Emily Wheeltapper, Captain. My late husband was Captain Anthony Wheeltapper of the 17th Lancers. He fell at Balaclava. I have been in mourning these seven years since. He was a fine man."

"My sympathy, ma'am."

"Will you take a cup of tea, Captain?"

"Please don't trouble yourself. My business will be brief."

"Is the poor girl in difficulty? She came home in tears this morning. Has something happened at the sanatorium?"

"That's what I'm here to find out, Mrs Wheeltapper."

Polly's heavy tread thundered down the stairs.

"She says to come on up, mum," she reported.

"Thank you, Polly. Now back to the kitchen with you. Those scones won't cook themselves. Follow me, please, Captain Burton."

The old widow slowly ascended, followed patiently by her visitor.

On the third landing, they were met by Sister Raghavendra. She was, Burton guessed, in her mid-twenties. She was also extremely beautiful, with dark almond-shaped eyes and dusky skin. Her nose was small and straight; her lips full and sensual, with a squarish shape more often found in South Americans; and her black hair, though pinned up, was obviously very long and lustrous.

His nostrils detected the scent of jasmine.

She reminded Burton of a Persian girl he'd once bedded, and a thrill of desire rippled through him as her eyes met his.

"You are Captain Burton?" she asked, in a soft, slightly accented voice. "You have come about Lieutenant Speke, I suppose? Come into my sitting room, please."

He followed her into a small and sparsely ornamented chamber and sat in the armchair to which she gestured. She and Mrs Wheeltapper settled onto the sofa.

He noticed a statuette of Ganesha on the mantelpiece; a nurse's headdress, which had been thrown carelessly onto a table; a small bottle of laudanum on a dresser.

Sister Raghavendra sat with her back held very straight and her hands folded gracefully on her lap. She was still in her work clothes; a floor-length, high-collared and long-sleeved pale grey dress over which she wore a short white jacket.

"With Mrs Wheeltapper's permission," said Burton gently, "I would like to ask you about the events of last night, when John Speke was removed from the sanatorium."

The old widow patted her lodger's hand. "Is that alright with you, my dear?"

"Perfectly," answered the nurse, with a trace of imperiousness in her voice. "I will answer any question as best I can, Captain Burton."

"I'm happy to hear that. Perhaps you could tell me what occurred?"

"I'll tell you as much as I know. I came on duty at midnight. My shift is from twelve until six. I was assigned to Lieutenant Speke; my duty being simply to sit with him and monitor his condition. Forgive me for being blunt, Captain, but he wasn't expected to live for long; the left side of his face and head were extremely badly damaged. The presence of a nurse was not entirely necessary in a medical sense, for there was nothing that could be done to save him, but it is our practice to never leave a dying man alone in case he recovers himself in his final moments to make a statement or request or confession."

"I understand."

"I passed four hours reading to him and was then interrupted by a man who entered the room."

She paused and put a hand up to her throat; took a breath and continued:

"I cannot describe him. I cannot see him in my mind's eye. I remember—I remember only his soft tread as he came in, then—I—I—"

Droplets of sweat appeared on Sister Raghavendra's forehead. She bit her lip and pulled at her collar.

"Did I faint?" she asked. "But why should I have done so?"

"What is your next clear memory?" asked Burton.

"I was—was, um—I was inside the entrance by the reception desk, wheeling a trolley past it and, somehow, I felt satisfied that Lieutenant Speke was in good hands."

"Whose?"

"Well, I thought his family's but—I—I don't know!"

She lowered her face into her hands.

Mrs Wheeltapper stroked her tenant's arm and crooned wordlessly.

Sir Richard Francis Burton had not only listened to the girl's words; he'd also been absorbing her accent, and with the phenomenal skill that was his, had identified her—or at least her family—as native to the Mysore region of Southern India; specifically, to the Bangalore district.

He now spoke to her in her own dialect:

"You have fallen under a spell, young lady. I recognise the signs, as you, a nurse, would recognise the symptoms of an illness. The presence of a newly opened bottle of laudanum on your dresser suggests to me that you are suffering from a headache. This further leads me to believe that you've experienced a traumatic shock and the memory of it has been sealed within the depths of your mind. Believe me when I say that it will do you no good if it remains there, hidden away like a festering cancer. It must be sought out, exposed and acknowledged; confronted, subdued, and defeated. Sister Raghavendra, I possess the power of magnetic influence. If you permit it—if you place yourself under my protection and send this worthy old woman away—I may be able to break through the spell to discover that which is concealed. My intentions concern only your well-being; you should neither fear me nor my skill as a mesmerist."

The nurse looked up and her exquisite eyes were wide with wonder and delight.

"You speak my tongue!" she exclaimed, in her own language.

"Yes, and I know Bangalore. Will you trust me, Sister?"

She reached out her hands to him; he leaned forward and took them.

"My name is Sadhvi," she breathed. "Please help me to remember. I don't want to lose my job without even knowing the reason why."

"Here," interrupted Mrs Wheeltapper, wheezily. "What's all this? I'll brook no hanky panky in my premises! And what was all that gobbledygook? Not sweet nothings, I hope; not bold as brass in front of a poor old widow woman!"

Burton smiled at her and released the nurse's hands.

"No, Mrs Wheeltapper; nothing like that. It just so happens that I know the sister's town of birth and speak her native language. She was moved to hear it again."

"It's true," put in the nurse. "You cannot imagine, Mrs Wheeltapper, how it gladdens my heart to be so reminded of my childhood home!"

The old lady threw up her hands.

"Ooooh!" she cried, with more life in her voice than Burton had heard yet. "Ooooh! How lovely! How wonderful for you, my dear!"

"It is! It is!" nodded Sister Raghavendra. "Ma'am, I feel positive that you can trust the good Captain to behave with the utmost decorum. I would speak with him awhile, if you don't mind, in my own tongue; of his travels in my homeland. It would be dreadfully boring for you. Why not continue with whatever you were doing? I smell cooking—were you performing miracles in the kitchen again?"

The landlady raised a gnarled hand to her veil and tittered behind it.

"Silly girl!" she chortled. "You know very well that Polly cooks to my directions and inevitably adds her own special ingredient: utter incompetence!"

The three of them laughed.

"Mrs Wheeltapper," said Burton. "A few months ago the monarch honoured me with a knighthood. I can give you my word that I would never tarnish that title with any act of impropriety."

Even as he spoke, Burton wondered whether he could trust himself to keep such a promise.

"Good gracious!" the old widow cooed. "A knight! A 'Sir' in my own home! Well I never did! I never did indeed!"

She reached up and lifted her veil. The baggy, liver-spotted face beneath, as ancient as it was, had obviously been attractive in its day, and was made so again by the unrestrained smile which it directed at the famous explorer. Two teeth were missing, the rest were yellowed, but the pale blue eyes twinkled with good humour, and Burton couldn't help but grin back.

"Forgive me!" pleaded the widow. "I treated you like a common visitor when you are obviously a man of culture, as was my dear Tony, may he rest in peace. I shall give you both your privacy!"

She stood.

Burton got to his feet and escorted her to the door.

"A gallant gentleman!" she sighed. "How lovely!"

"It has been a delight to meet you, Mrs Wheeltapper. I shall talk with Sister Raghavendra awhile, then depart—but may I call again some time? I know of the 17th Lancers and would be very much interested in hearing of your late husband's service with them."

A tear trickled from the old woman's cheek.

"Captain Sir Burton," she said "You are welcome to call on me whenever the inclination takes you!"

"Thank you, ma'am."

He closed the door after her and returned to Sadhvi Raghavendra, who, in truth, was the real reason he might consider a repeat visit to 3 Bayham Street.

"What do you know of mesmerism?" he asked as he sat down.

"I saw it practised many times when I was a child," she replied.

"Are you scared of it?"

"No. I want to know what it is that I can't remember. If that means placing me in a trance, so be it."

"Good girl. Wait a moment; let me pull this chair a little closer."

Burton shifted the armchair until he was sitting face to face with the nurse.

He looked her in the eye and spoke in her language.

"Allow yourself to relax. Keep your eyes on mine."

Two pairs of dark fathomless eyes locked together.

"You have long lashes," said the girl.

"As do you. Don't speak now. Relax. Copy my breathing. Imagine your first breath goes into your right lung. Inhale slowly; exhale slowly. The next breath goes to the left lung. Slowly in. Slowly out. And the next into the middle of your chest. In. Out."

As her respiration adopted the Sufi rhythm that he was teaching her, Sister

Raghavendra became entirely motionless but for an almost undetectable rocking, which Burton could see was timed to her heartbeat.

He murmured further instructions, guiding her into a cycle of four breaths, each directed to a different part of her body.

Her mind, subdued by the complexity of the exercise, gradually gave itself over to him. He could see it in her luminous eyes, as her pupils expanded wider and wider.

Suddenly, the black circles closed inward from the sides, forming perpendicular lines, and the deep brown irises blazed a bright pink. Something malevolent regarded him.

Burton blinked in surprise but the illusion—if that's what it was—was gone in an instant.

Her eyes were brown. Her pupils were wide black circles. She was entranced.

Recovering himself, he spoke to her: "I want you to return to last night; place yourself in Penfold Private Sanatorium; in Lieutenant Speke's room. You've been reading to him but now you are interrupted. A man enters the room."

"Yes," she replied softly. "I hear a slight creak as the door swings open. I look up from my book. There is a footstep and he is there."

"Describe him. In detail."

A shudder ran through her body.

"Such a man! I've never seen the like! His frock coat is of crushed black velvet; his shirt, trousers, shoes and hat are all black, too; and his pointed fingernails are painted black; but his skin and hair—straight hair, so long that it falls past his collar—they are whiter than snow! He's an albino! There is no trace of colour on him except in the eyes, which are of a dreadful pink with vertical pupils like a cat's."

Burton started. Those same eyes had looked out of the girls head just moments ago!

"There is something wrong with his face," she continued. "His upper and lower jaws are pushed a little too far forward, almost forming a muzzle; and his teeth—when he smiles—are all canines!

"He enters the room, looks at the Lieutenant; looks at me; then tells me to fetch a trolley. I must obey. It's as if I have no will of my own."

"So you leave the room?"

"For a moment, and when I return there are three—three—"

She stopped and whimpered.

"Don't worry," soothed Burton, "I am here with you. You are perfectly safe. Tell me what you can see in the room."

"There are three men. I—I think they are men. Maybe something else. They are short and wear red cloaks with hoods and they are each sort of—sort of *twisted*; their bodies are too long and too narrow in the hip; their chests too deep and wide; legs too short. Their faces, though—their faces are—"

"Yes?"

"Oh, save me! They are the faces of dogs!"

Burton sat back in surprise.

He reached into his jacket and drew the sketch by Doré from his pocket. He unfolded it and showed it to the girl.

"Like this?"

She recoiled away from him and began to tremble violently.

"Yes! Please—please tell me—what are they?" Her voice rose in volume and pitch. "What are they?"

He took her hands in his and stroked their backs with his thumbs. Her skin felt smooth, soft and warm. The heady scent of jasmine filled his nostrils.

"Shhh. Don't be afraid. It's over, Sadhvi. It is in the past."

"But they aren't human!"

"Perhaps not. Tell me what happens next."

"I walk back into Lieutenant Speke's room with the trolley, see the—the three things—then the albino jumps from behind me and restrains me, with a hand over my mouth. He is so strong! I can't move! The dog—dog-men—they lift Lieutenant Speke from his bed, place him on the trolley and wheel him out of the room."

"There are no other nurses? No one else sees them?"

"No, I don't think so—but you have made me realise something; the sanatorium, or at least this wing of it, seems very quiet; more so than it should be, even at such an early hour."

"So the dog creatures leave the room—and then?"

"Then the man turns me, looks into my eyes and tells me to forget; to remember only that Speke's family took the lieutenant. He leaves the room and I follow him along the corridor toward reception. I feel strange. There are nurses standing motionless and, as he passes them, he says something to each in a low voice. We reach reception, and I see the trolley standing empty by the desk. The albino orders me to move over to it and I obey. He speaks to the nurse at the desk and she starts to blink and look around. Then he walks toward the main door and, as he passes me, he says 'awake!'"

She sighed and visibly relaxed.

"He's gone."

"And now you find yourself pushing the trolley and remembering nothing of what just happened?" put in Burton.

"Yes."

"Very well. Close your eyes now. Concentrate on the rhythm of your breathing."

Sister Raghavendra's hands fell from his and she leaned back on the sofa. Her head drooped.

"Sadhvi," he murmured, "I'm going to count down from ten. With each number, you will feel yourself awakening. When I reach zero, you will be fully conscious, alert, refreshed, and you will remember everything. You will not be afraid. Ten. Nine. Eight. Seven—"

As he counted, her eyelids fluttered and opened; her pupils shrank into focus; she looked at him; her hand flew to her mouth and she cried: "Dear God! Did that really happen?"

"Yes, Sadhvi, it happened. A combination of shock and mesmeric suggestion caused you to bury the memories—but we have managed to uncover them."

"Those dog-things were abominations!"

"I suspect the Eugenicists have been at work."

"They can't! They can't do that to humans!"

"Maybe they didn't, Sadhvi. Maybe they did it to dogs. Or to wolves."

Her eyes widened.

"Yes," she whispered. "Wolves!"

"What's the motive for abducting Speke, though? That's what puzzles me," continued Burton, thoughtfully.

He stood up.

"Anyway; thank you Sister Raghavendra. You've been very helpful."

She rose from the sofa, stepped forward and placed her hands on his chest.

"Captain, that albino fellow—he's—he's *evil*. I felt it. You will be careful, won't you?"

Burton couldn't help himself; his hands slipped around her slim waist and he pulled her close, looking down into her deep, soulful eyes.

"Oh!" she gasped—but it wasn't a protest.

"I'll be careful," he whispered throatily. "And when the mystery is solved, shall I return to tell you about it?"

"Yes. Come back, please, Captain Burton."

§

It was midday, but London, buried in the heart of the congealing fog, was deprived of light. It tried to generate its own—gas lamps and windows blazed into the murk—but their fierce illumination was immediately crushed and reduced to vague patches of yellow, orange, and red. Between them, the vast and sickening gloom writhed like a living entity, consuming all.

"That you, guv'nor?" came a gruff voice from above.

"Yes, Mr Penniforth. You're still breathing?"

"Aye. Been 'avin' a smoke o' me pipe. There ain't nuffink like a whiff o' Latakia for fumigatin' the bellows! Get yourself comfy while I light the bullseyes. An' call me Monty."

Burton climbed into the hansom. "Bellows?" he grunted. "I should think your lungs are more like a couple of turbines if they can deal with fog and Latakia! Take me to Scotland Yard, would you?"

"Right ho. Half a mo', sir!"

While his passenger settled, Penniforth climbed down from the box, struck a lucifer, and put the match to the lamps hanging from the front of the engine, and the front and rear of the cabin. He then hoisted himself back up, wrapped his scarf around the lower half of his face, straightened his goggles, gave the peak of his cap a tug, and took hold of the steering bars.

The machine coughed and spluttered and belched smoke into the already laden atmosphere. It lurched away from the kerb, pulling the cab behind it.

"Hoff we go, into the great unknown!" muttered Penniforth.

As he carefully steered the machine out of Mornington Crescent and into Hampstead Road, there came a mighty crash and tinkling of broken glass from somewhere far to the left.

"Watch out!" he exclaimed softly. "You don't want to be drivin' into a shop window, do you! Irresponsible, I calls it, bein' in charge of a vehicle in these 'ere weather conditions!"

By the time the hansom cab reached Tottenham Court Road, the "blacks" were falling: coal dust coalescing with particles of ice in the upper layers of fog before drifting to the ground like black snowflakes. It was an ugly sight.

Penniforth pushed on, guided more by instinct and his incredible knowledge of the city's geography than by his eyes. Even so, he steered down the wrong road on more than one occasion.

The steam-horse gurgled and popped.

"Don't you start complainin'!" the cabbie advised it. "You're the one wiv a nice hot boiler! It's cold enough up here to freeze the whatsits off a thingummybob!"

The engine emitted a whistling sigh.

"Oh, it's like that, is it? Feelin' discontentified, are you?"

It hissed and grumbled.

"Why don't you just watch where you're a-going and stop botherin' me wiv the benny-fits of your wisdom?"

It rattled and clanged over a bump in the road.

"Yup, that's it, ol' girl! Giddy up! Over the hurdles!"

The hansom panted through Leicester Square and on down Charing Cross Road, passing the antiquarian bookshops—whose volumes were now both obscure and obscured—and continuing on to Trafalgar Square, where Monty had to carefully steer around an overturned fruit wagon and the dead horse that had collapsed in its harness. Apples squished under the hansom's wheels and were ground into the cobbles; and the resultant mush was quickly blackening by falling soot.

Along Whitehall the engine chugged, then left into Great Scotland Yard, until, outside the grim old edifice of the police headquarters—a looming shadow in the darkness—Penniforth brought it to a standstill.

"There you go, guv'nor!" he called, knocking on the roof.

Sir Richard Francis Burton disembarked and tossed a couple of coins up to the driver.

"Toddle off for a pie and some ale, Monty. You deserve it. If you get back here in an hour, I'll have another fare for you."

"That's right gen'rous of you, guv'nor. You can rely on me; I'll be here waitin' when you're ready."

"Good man!"

Burton entered Scotland Yard.

A valet stepped forward and took his coat, hat and cane, shaking the soot from them onto the already grimy floor.

Burton crossed to the front desk. A small plaque on it read: *J. D. Pepperwick – Clerk*. He addressed the man to which it referred.

"Is Detective-Inspector Trounce available? I'd like to speak with him, if possible."

"Your name, sir?"

"Sir Richard Francis Burton."

The clerk, a gaunt fellow with thick spectacles, a red nose and a straggly moustache, looked surprised.

"Not the explorer chappie, surely?"

"The very same."

"Good gracious! Do you want to talk to the inspector about yesterday's shooting?"

"Perhaps. Would you take a look at this?"

Burton held out his authorisation. The clerk took it, unfolded it, saw the signature, and read the text above it with meticulous care, dwelling on each separate word.

"I say!" he finally exclaimed. "You're an important fellow!"

"So—?" said Burton slowly, suggestively inclining his head and raising his eyebrows.

The clerk got the message.

"So," he responded, "I'll call Detective-Inspector Trounce—on the double!"

He saluted smartly and turned to a contrivance affixed to the wall behind him. It was a large, flat brass panel which somewhat resembled a honeycomb, divided as it was into rows of small hexagonal compartments. Into these, snug in circular fittings, there were clipped round domed lids with looped handles. A name was engraved onto each one.

The clerk reached for the lid marked 'D. I. Trounce' and pulled it from the frame. It came away pulling a long segmented tube behind it. He twisted open the lid and blew into the tube. Burton knew that at the other end a little valve was popping out of an identical lid and emitting a whistle. A moment later a tinny voice came from the tube: "Yes? What is it?"

Holding its end to his mouth, the clerk spoke into it. Though his voice was muffled, Burton heard him say: "Sir Richard Burton, the Africa chap, is here to see you, sir. He has, um, *special* authorisation. Says he wants to talk to you about the shooting of John Speke at Bath yesterday."

He transferred the tube to his ear and listened, then put it back to his mouth and said "Yes, sir."

He replaced the lid, lifting it back to its compartment, and the tube automatically snaked back in before it.

He smiled at Burton.

"The inspector will see you straight away. Second floor, office number nineteen. The stairs are through that door there, sir," he advised, pointing to the left.

Burton nodded and made for the doors, pushed through them and climbed the stairs. They were wooden and needed brushing. He came to the second floor and moved along a panelled corridor looking at the many closed doors. The sound of a woman weeping came from behind one.

About halfway down the passage he found number nineteen and knocked upon it.

"Come!" barked a voice from within.

Burton entered and found himself in a medium-sized, high-ceilinged, square and shadowy room. Its dark corners lay behind a thin veil of blue cigar smoke. There was a very tall narrow window in the opposite wall; a fireplace with quietly crackling logs in its hearth to his right; and a row of large filing cabinets lining the wall to his left. A red and threadbare rug covered the centre of the floor; a hat stand supported a battered bowler and dusty overcoat by the door; and a big portrait of Sir Robert Peel hung over the fireplace. Gas lamps flickered dimly in the alcoves to either side of the chimney breast. A lit candle wavered on the heavy desk beneath the window. It cast an orange light over the left side of Detective-Inspector Trounce's face.

He was sitting behind the desk, facing the door, but stood as Burton entered.

Trounce was short, big-boned and heavily muscled. He possessed wide shoulders, an enormous chest and the merest hint of a paunch. He was a man, decided Burton, to whom the word "blunt" could be most aptly be applied. He had thick, blunt-ended fingers, a short blunt nose, and, under a large outward-sweeping brown moustache, an aggressive chin that suggested a bluntness of character, too.

The police officer extended a hand and shook Burton's.

"I'm pleased to meet you, Sir Burton," he said, indicating a chair as he sat in his own.

"Please," his visitor replied, "Captain, will do." He pulled the chair over to the desk and sat down.

"You served in the military?" Trounce's voice was deep with a slightly guttural rasp.

"Yes, in the 18th Bombay Native Infantry."

"Ah. I didn't know. The newspapers only ever mention the expeditions. Anyway, how can I help you, Captain? Something to do with Lieutenant Speke's accident, I suppose?"

"Actually, no. Something to do with Spring Heeled Jack."

Trounce jumped back to his feet. In an instant, his face hardened and his eyes turned cold.

"Then you can leave this office at once, sir! Who put you up to this? Was it that little prig, Honesty? I'll take the mockery no more!"

Burton remained seated, crossed his legs, and pulled a couple of cigars from his jacket pocket.

"Would you care to smoke, Inspector?" he asked.

Trounce glared at him and said: "I don't know what it has to do with you, but let me make something very clear: I will *never* deny what I saw!"

"I don't doubt it. Sit and calm down, man! Have a cigar."

Trounce remained standing.

Burton sighed.

"Inspector, as you can see, I have a black eye, a cut lip, a burnt brow and a number of very painful bruises. Do you want to know how I got them?"

"How?"

"Last night, I was set upon by a creature who fits the description of Spring Heeled Jack."

Trounce dropped into his chair.

He distractedly took the proffered cigar, cut it, held it to the candle, placed it to his lips and inhaled the sweet smoke. His eyes never left Burton's face.

"Tell me what happened. Describe him," he muttered, the blue smoke puffing from his mouth.

Burton cut and lit his own cigar and recounted the events of the previous evening.

When he'd finished, Trounce leaned forward and the candle flame reflected in his eager blue eyes.

"That's him, Captain Burton! That's him! So he's back!"

"Buckingham Palace and the Prime Minister have asked me to look into the matter, and I was told that you are the expert. So, you see, you overreacted. I'm not here to mock; rather, I thought perhaps we could work together."

The Detective-Inspector got up and crossed to the filing cabinets; slid open one of the bottom drawers and, without having to search for it, selected a well-thumbed file and took it back to the desk.

"My apologies. Mention of that devil never fails to get my goat. I've had to put up with a great deal of derision over the years. Well now, tell me: what do you know of him?"

"Virtually nothing. Until last night, I thought he was a fairy story; and I didn't even make *that* connection until Palmerston brought his name up in relation to my attacker."

"In that case, I shall give you a brief history."

Without consulting the report, Trounce—who obviously knew the facts by heart—gave an account of its contents:

"The first sighting was twenty-four years ago, in 1837, when a gentleman reported seeing a grotesque figure leaping over the gate of a cemetery near the Bedlam mental hospital. A few days later, it was October, a fifteen-year-old servant girl named Mary Stevens, who'd just visited her parents in Battersea, was returning to her employer's home on Lavender Hill via Cut Throat Lane when she was grabbed by someone—or some*thing*—fitting the same description as your attacker. It was a sexual assault, Captain Burton— her clothes were ripped from her body and her flesh was squeezed and caressed in an aggressive manner. Not surprisingly, the girl screamed, which attracted the attention of several local residents, who came to investigate the commotion. Upon hearing them approach, the assailant bounded away, making tremendous jumps, and is said to have vanished in mid-air.

"The following day, in the same neighbourhood, the creature sprang out of an alleyway onto the side of a passing brougham and demanded to know the whereabouts of 'Lizzie,' whoever she may be. The terrified coachman lost control of his horses and crashed the carriage into the side of a shop, suffering serious injuries. There were a great many witnesses, all of whom reported that the 'ghost'—as it was referred to at the time—escaped by vaulting over a nine-foot high wall. According to one witness, the creature was laughing insanely and babbling in a fairly incoherent manner something about history and ancestors."

"And its appearance?" interrupted Burton.

"Again, apart from minor variations which can be attributed to the usual unreliability of witnesses, the various descriptions are remarkably consistent and tally with what you saw. Can I offer you a drink? There's a decanter of red wine in the top left filing drawer."

Burton shook his head.

"No thank you. I must confess, I rather overdid it last night."

"It happens to the best of us," replied Trounce, with a wry smile. He reached across to a brass lid on the desktop, identical to the ones Burton had seen on the wall downstairs, and lifted it. A tube snaked out from the desk. Trounce opened the lid and blew into the tube. A moment later, a voice answered.

"Pepperwick," the Detective-Inspector said into the mouthpiece. "Would you have a pot of coffee and a couple of cups sent up? And give my appointments to Detective-Inspector Spearing until further notice. I don't want to be disturbed."

He put the tube to his ear; back to his mouth; said "Thank you," then replaced the lid and put it back on the desk.

"So, to continue: throughout late 1837 and early '38 there were a great many sightings of this so-called ghost or devil, which seemed to be haunting an area within the triangle formed by Camberwell, Battersea and Lambeth, and, incidentally, it was during this period that it acquired the nickname by which we still know it. Several young girls were attacked but all escaped physically unharmed, though molested. However, the shock caused a couple of them to lose their minds. In addition, two witnesses to Jack's 'manifestations'—if I may refer to his appearances that way—died of heart failure. I point this out because some newspapers reported the incidents as 'wicked pranks.' Personally, Captain, I cannot classify as a prank any action that results in the loss of life or sanity.

"We now come to one of the most well-documented and widely reported cases; that of Jane Alsop. On the 19th of February, 1838, at a quarter to nine in the evening, the bell was rung at the gate of a secluded cottage on Bearbinder Lane in the village of Old Ford, near Hertford, north of London.

"Jane Alsop, an eighteen-year-old, was inside the cottage with her parents and two sisters. She went to the front door and opened it, walked down the path, and approached a shadowy figure standing at the gate. In her statement to the local police, she said that it appeared to be an extremely tall angular man who was wrapped in a cloak and wearing some sort of helmet.

"She asked what he wanted and he replied that he was a policeman and that he needed a light. He told her that someone had been seen loitering in the neighbourhood.

"The girl fetched a candle from the cottage and handed it to the waiting figure. As she did so, it threw back its cloak to reveal itself as Spring Heeled Jack. Grabbing her, it tore her dress down to her waist before she managed to break free and run back along the path. Jack followed and caught her at the threshold of the front door. He was pulling her hair and yanking at her slip when her younger sister entered the hallway, witnessed the scene, and let out a loud scream of terror. At this, the older sister came running and managed to drag Jane from the thing's grasp. She pushed him back and slammed the front door in his face. The apparition then bounded away and vanished into the night."

There came a knock at the door.

"Come!" cried Trounce.

A short white-haired woman shuffled in bearing a tray.

"Coffee, sir,"

"Thank you, Gladys."

The woman padded over to the desk and lay down the tray. She poured two cups and silently withdrew, closing the door behind her.

Burton flicked his cigar stub into the hearth.

"Milk?" asked Trounce.

"No. Just sugar."

The famous explorer shovelled four teaspoonfuls into the steaming liquid.

"By Jove!" blurted Trounce. "You have a sweet tooth!"

"A taste I picked up in Arabia. So what happened next?"

"Jane subsequently gave the most complete description of Spring Heeled Jack we have on record and, I can confirm, it matches yours in every respect, even down to the blue flame flickering around its head.

"Eight days later, another eighteen-year-old girl, Lucy Scales, and her younger sister, Lisa, were passing through Green Dragon Alley on the outskirts of Limehouse when they spotted a figure slumped in an angle of the passage and draped over by a cloak. The person appeared to be in distress; the sisters heard groans of pain. Lucy approached it and asked whether she could help, at which the figure raised its head, which was clad in a black helmet around which blue fire raged. The creature screamed and a tongue of flame leapt from its head to Lucy's face, blinding her and sending her staggering backward. She dropped to the ground and was stricken with violent fits which continued for many hours after the encounter. Lisa held Lucy, called for help and—*my God!*"

Trounce's eyes widened and he stared at Burton, his mouth working.

"What is it?" asked the explorer, puzzled.

"I—I'd forgotten!"

"Forgotten what?"

"My God!" repeated Trounce, in a whisper.

"Spit it out, man!" snapped Burton.

The detective cleared his throat and continued, speaking slowly and with apparent amazement:

"As Lucy lay in her sister's arms, Spring Heeled Jack walked quickly away. Lisa reported that he was talking to himself in a high-pitched, crazy-sounding voice. Most of his words, she said, were unintelligible. There was, however, one phrase that came to her clearly."

Trounce paused. He looked at the man opposite, who asked: "What was it?"

"Apparently," replied Trounce, "he shouted, 'This is your fault, Burton!'"

Sir Richard Francis Burton felt icy fingers tickling his spine.

The two men looked at one another.

Shadows shifted across the walls and the sound of a mournful foghorn pushed at the window pane.

"Coincidence, of course," whispered Trounce.

"Obviously," replied Burton, in an equally hushed tone. "In 1838, I was seventeen years old and living with my parents and brother in Italy. I'd spent very little of my life in England and had certainly never encountered or even heard of Spring Heeled Jack."

Another pause.

Trounce shook himself, opened the report and looked down at it.

"Anyway, now we come to my own encounter," he said, brusquely, "which occurred on the 10th of June, 1840; perhaps the most infamous date in English history."

Burton nodded: "The day of The Assassination."

§

Chapter 4

The Assassination

✌

ASSASSINATION HAS NEVER CHANGED THE HISTORY OF THE WORLD.
—BENJAMIN DISRAELI

✌

Dennis the Dip slowed down Police Constable William Trounce by five minutes; five minutes in which the eighteen-year-old policeman could have become a national hero rather than the laughing stock of Scotland Yard.

Constable Trounce's beat incorporated Constitution Hill, and he always timed it so that he got there at six o'clock, just as Queen Victoria and her husband emerged from the "Garden Gate" of Buckingham Palace in their open-topped carriage for their afternoon spin around Green Park. For the twenty-year-old queen, the daily ritual was a breath of fresh air—so far as the word "fresh" could be applied London's malodorous atmosphere—an hour's escape from the stifling formality of Buckingham Palace, with its dusty footmen and haughty butlers, servile advisers and fussing maids; while for the citizens who gathered along the route, it was a chance to cheer or boo her, depending on their opinion of her four-month reign.

Trounce was usually quick to warn those who jeered to "move along."

Today, though, as he proceeded along the Mall, Trounce spotted Dennis the Dip and decided to follow him. The notorious pickpocket was, as usual, dressed as a gentleman and looked entirely at ease among the well-heeled crowd which sauntered back and forth along the ceremonial avenue. It was a disguise. Had he opened his mouth to speak, the chopped and diced version of the English language that emerged would have immediately marked Dennis as a native of London's East End, otherwise known as "the Cauldron."

He scrubbed-up well, did Dennis, thought Trounce, as he slowed his pace and kept his eyes on the meandering crook.

The pickpocket was obviously looking for a mark and, when he found it, Trounce would swoop. It would be a nice feather in his cap if his very first arrest ended the career of this particular villain.

However, it soon became apparent that Dennis was rather indecisive today. He wondered from one side of the avenue to the other; trailed first one man then the next; stopped by a doorway and eyed passers-by; and all the time his skilful fingers remained in plain view. They didn't plunge into a single pocket; not even his own.

After a while, Trounce grew bored, so he walked over to the petty crook and stood facing him.

"What ho, old son! What do you think you're up to then?"

"Oh bleedin' 'eck, I ain't up to nuffink, am I!" whined Dennis. "Jest givin' me Sunday best an airing, that's all."

"It's Wednesday, Dennis."

"No law agin' wearin' a Sunday suit on a Wednesday, is there?"

The crook's rodent-like eyes swivelled right and left as if seeking an escape route.

Trounce unhooked his truncheon from his belt and pushed its end into Dennis' chest.

"I'm watching you, laddie. Those fingers of yours will be slipping into where they're not welcome before too long, and, when they do, *my* fingers will be closing over your shoulder, mark my words. We'll soon have you out of that suit and wearing the broad arrow. There are no pockets in prison uniforms, did you know that?"

"Yus. But you ain't got no cause to threaten me!"

"Haven't I, now? Haven't I? Well, see it stays that way, Dennis my lad. Now hop it! I don't want to see you in this neck of the woods again!"

With a vicious look at the young constable, the pickpocket spat onto the pavement and scurried away.

Constable Trounce grinned and resumed his beat.

At the end of the Mall he passed Buckingham Palace, where the queen had recently taken up residence, and turned right onto Green Park. Rather than walk along Constitution Hill itself, he preferred to pace along on the grass, thus positioning himself behind any crowd that might gather along the queen's route. In his experience, the troublemakers usually hid at the back, where they could more easily take to their heels should anyone object to their catcalls.

Her Majesty's carriage, drawn by four horses—the front left ridden by a postilion—was already on the path a little way ahead. There were four outriders with her; two in front of the vehicle and two some yards behind it.

Trounce increased his pace to catch up, walking down a gentle slope which gave him an excellent view of the scene.

Despite the mild weather, the crowd was sparse today. There were no protests and few hurrahs.

He jumped at the sound of a gunshot.

What the hell?

Breaking into a run, he scanned the scene ahead and saw a man wearing a top hat, blue frock-coat and white breeches walking beside, and to the right of, the slow-moving carriage. He was throwing down a smoking flintlock and drawing, with his left hand, a second gun from his coat.

In an instant, horror sucked the heat from Trounce's body and time slowed to a crawl.

His legs pumped; his boots thudded into the grass; he heard himself shout "No!"

He saw heads turning toward the man.

His breath thundered in his ears.

The man's left arm came up.

The queen stood, raising her hands to the white lace around her throat.

Her husband reached for her.

A second man leaped forward and grabbed the gunman.

"No, Edward!" came a faint yell.

The scene seemed to freeze; the two men entwined; their faces, even from this distance, so similar, like brothers; each person in the crowd poised in mid-motion, some stepping forward, some stepping back. The queen standing, wearing a cream-coloured dress and bonnet. Her consort leaning forward, in a top hat and red jacket. The outriders turning their horses.

"Christ!" thought Trounce. "Christ, no! Please, no!"

Suddenly a freakish creature flew past him.

What the hell? A—a stilt-walker?

Tall, loose-limbed, bouncing on what seemed to be spring-loaded stilts, it stopped just ahead of the constable, who stumbled and fell to his knees.

"Stop, Edward!" the weird apparition bellowed.

A bolt of lightning shot from its side into the ground and the lean figure staggered, groaning and clutching at itself.

Below, the two struggling men turned and looked up.

A puff of smoke from the pistol.

Blood spraying from Queen Victoria's head.

"Merciful heaven!" gasped Trounce.

A detonation echoing away over the park; rippling into the distance, taking with it the consequences of the heinous act; history, quite literally, in the making; expanding outwards to envelop the Empire.

"No," groaned the stilt-walker. "No!"

It turned and Trounce saw the face: crazy eyes, a thin blade of a nose, a mouth stretched into a rictus grin, drawn and lined features, pale beneath a sheen of sweat, twisted in agony.

The thing was wearing a big round black helmet and a black cloak beneath which there was a white, tight-fitting body suit. Some sort of flat lantern hung on the chest, spitting fire. There were scorch marks on the material around it.

The odd figure bobbed on the short stilts then bounded forward and leaped right over the police constable's head.

Trounce toppled onto the grass, rolled over and looked behind him. The costumed figure was nowhere to be seen. It had vanished.

Christ almighty. Christ almighty.

Screams.

Trounce looked down the slope.

Victoria had flopped backward out of the carriage onto the ground. Her husband was scrambling after her.

The assassin was still struggling with the other man but, as Trounce watched, the gunman was suddenly thrown off his feet by his assailant. His head hit the low wrought-iron fence which bordered the path. He went limp and lay still.

The crowd surged around the royal carriage. The outriders plunged through the throng and attempted to hold the panicked people back, away from the stricken monarch. A police whistle blew frantically.

'That's me,' thought Trounce. 'That's me blowing the whistle.'

A figure detached itself from the mob and started running across the park, north-westward, heading for Piccadilly.

It was the man who'd grappled with the assassin.

Trounce took off in pursuit. It seemed the right thing to do.

The thought occurred to him that police-issue boots were ill-designed for running.

"For goodness' sake!" he gasped to himself. "Concentrate!"

He raced past the outriders.

A dazed young man, squinting through a monocle, wandered into his path and Trounce barrelled into him, shoving him aside with a curse.

His quarry angled up a slope and disappeared into the heavily wooded upper corner of the park. Trounce grunted with satisfaction; he knew there was a high wall behind those trees.

He was breathing heavily and had a stitch in his side by the time he got to the edge of the woods. He stopped there, gulping air, eyeing the gloomy spaces beneath the boughs; listening for movement.

Distant screams and shouts were sounding from behind him. Police whistles were blasting from different points around the park as constables converged on the scene.

A rustle came from the trees. A movement.

Trounce took hold of his truncheon.

"Step out into the open, sir!" he commanded. "I saw what happened; there's nothing to worry about. Come on; let's be having you!"

No reply.

"Sir! I saw you trying to protect the queen. I just need you to—"

There was a flurry of leaves, and suddenly Trounce found himself confronted by the stilt-walking man again, leaping out of the thicket.

Taken by surprise, Trounce stepped back, lost his footing, and fell onto his bottom.

"How—how—?" he stuttered.

The thing—phantom, devil, illusion; whatever it was—crouched as if to spring.

Reflexively, Trounce whipped his arm back and hurled his truncheon. The club struck the creature in the chest, hitting the lamp-like object affixed there. Fiery sparks erupted and rained onto the grass. The apparition stumbled.

"Damn!" it cursed in a clear human voice, then turned and sprang to the constable's right, leaping away in huge bounds.

Trounce got to his feet and watched the thing heading eastward. It took a massive leap into the air and, twenty feet above the ground, winked out of existence. The air seemed to fold around it.

Trounce stood, his arms dangling at his sides, his mouth open and his eyes wide.

A minute passed before, as if waking from a dream, he roused himself and looked down the sloping grass to the royal carriage. Then he looked back at the thicket. His quarry—the man who tackled the assassin—must still be in there somewhere.

He entered the trees and began to search, calling: "There's no point hiding, sir. Please show yourself!"

Ten minutes later he admitted defeat. He'd found a top hat laying on the ground, but that's all. The man had escaped.

He trudged down the slope toward the chaotic scene below, his mind blank.

Other constables had arrived and were pushing the growing crowd back, helped by the queen's outriders.

Trounce pushed past the onlookers—some silent, some sobbing, some talking in hushed tones, some shouting or screaming—and crossed to where the assassin lay. The man's head was pinned to the top of the low railings, held at an awkward angle, the spike of an upright projecting from his left eye, blood pooling beneath. It was a grisly sight.

Two flintlocks lay on the ground nearby.

Odd, thought Trounce, the way the assassin and the man who tried to stop him looked so alike.

He found himself standing helpless, unable to do anything, his mind numbed.

Off to his left, a moustachioed man was calmly watching the scene with a smile on his face. A smile!

A memory stirred. A case he'd read about from two or three years ago; something concerning a girl being attacked by—by a ghost which escaped by taking prodigious leaps—by a thing that breathed fire—by a creature known as—Spring Heeled Jack!

§

Chapter 5

The Birth of the Libertines

৶

WE WILL NOT DEFINE OURSELVES BY THE IDEALS YOU ENFORCE.

WE SCORN THE SOCIAL ATTITUDES THAT YOU PERPETUATE.

WE NEITHER RESPECT NOR CONFORM WITH THE VIEWS OF OUR ELDERS.

WE THINK AND ACT AGAINST THE TIDES OF POPULAR OPINION.

WE SNEER AT YOUR DOGMA. WE LAUGH AT YOUR RULES.

WE ARE ANARCHY. WE ARE CHAOS. WE ARE INDIVIDUALS.

WE ARE THE RAKES.

—*FROM THE RAKE MANIFESTO*

৶

The candle guttered and died, sending a coil of smoke toward the high ceiling.

The two men allowed a silence to stretch between them.

Detective-Inspector Trounce broke it:

"They said I panicked and ran away from the scene," he murmured. "Said that my claim to have seen Spring Heeled Jack was just an attempt to justify my 'moment of cowardice.' Had it not been for the fact that I was wet behind the ears—I'd only been on active duty for a fortnight—they would've drummed me out of the force. As it was, I was laughed at, taunted and passed over for promotion for more than a decade. I had to prove myself over and over; earn respect the hard way. They have long memories here in the Yard, Captain Burton. They still call me 'Pouncer Trounce,' and there are whisperings from certain quarters even all these years later."

"You mentioned someone named Honesty?" asked Burton.

"Detective-Inspector Honesty. Not a bad man by any stretch; but unimaginative; a bit of a stick-in-the-mud. He has the ear of the Chief Commissioner and neither of them have time for what they regard as my hysterical fantasy."

"No one understands your situation better than I," said Burton, sympathetically. "I am 'Blackguard Burton' or 'Ruffian Dick'—or far worse—to many, all because of a report I wrote in Karachi, just five years after the death of Victoria. A report written, I should add, in response to a direct order."

Trounce grunted. "When a man gets a stain on his character—justified or not—it doesn't wash off."

He drained his coffee cup and took a couple of cigars from a box on his desk, offering one to Burton, who took it. When they were lit, Trounce threw the lucifer into the fireplace without bothering to relight the candle. He sat back and considered the man sitting opposite.

There was something, he reckoned, untamed about Burton. The man looked like a prize-fighter, with those dark, direct, and smouldering eyes, the heavy jaw and the prominent, hard chin.

'By Jove!' he thought, "If this man were the desperado he appears, what great crimes might he commit!'

Yet, for all Burton's tremendous animalism and air of repressed ferocity, there was something about him which appealed to Trounce. Instinctively, he knew that he'd always get the unvarnished truth from the famous explorer.

"Anyway," he continued, "after the events of that day, I was suspended from duty for a month and played no part in the subsequent investigation. As you of course know, the man—"

"Just a moment, Detective-Inspector," interrupted Burton, holding up his hand. "The Assassination was some twenty years ago and, like you, I was nineteen years old at the time; just enrolling into Oxford University, as a matter of fact. Unlike you, I wasn't at the scene or even in the country and received the news of Victoria's death 'over the grapevine,' as it were. The facts of the investigation, as they emerged and were reported in the newspapers, were spread out over a period of weeks. I cannot claim to have read them all and, besides, my memory needs refreshing. So please make no assumptions about my knowledge, unless it is to assume that I know nothing at all."

Trounce gave a curt and appreciative nod of his head.

"Understood, Captain. The man who wrestled with the assassin after he fired the first shot, which missed the queen, was never found. The newspapers christened him the 'Mystery Hero.' I have always been convinced that he was somehow related to the shootist—their physical resemblance was remarkable—but, unfortunately, my superiors didn't place much stock in my impressions from that day; few other witnesses noted the likeness; and, besides, all the gunman's relatives were traced and questioned and the man was not among them.

"As for the assassin himself: Edward Oxford was born in Birmingham in 1822; one of seven children. His father was a brutal alcoholic who beat his wife and children on an almost daily basis. He was eventually certified insane and committed to an asylum where he died after choking on his own tongue during a fit of some sort. The grandfather, incidentally, had also been a lunatic.

"His mother, Hannah, separated from her husband when Edward was seven years old. She moved with the boy and one of his sisters to Lambeth where, after the lad completed his schooling, he began working as a barman in various public houses, including The Hat and Feathers, which is on the corner of Green Dragon Alley."

"Ah ha! So you have a connection between Oxford and Spring Heeled Jack, aside from The Assassination, I mean!" exclaimed Burton, his eyes gleaming.

"Yes. At the time of the Lucy Scales incident, Oxford was working in the pub; he was actually behind the bar when the encounter was taking place around the corner. Apparently, when he heard about the attack he began to laugh hysterically and had to be restrained and sedated by a doctor."

"Interesting. Pray continue, Inspector."

"Oxford continued to live with his mother and sister in lodgings at West Place, West Square, Lambeth. By 1840, he was the pot boy in The Hog in the Pound on Oxford Street but in May of that year he quit the job. On the 4th, he bought a pair of pistols from an old school friend for the sum of two pounds, and for the next four weeks he practised with them at various shooting galleries around London. These were the weapons with which, the following month, he killed Queen Victoria."

"His motive?" asked Burton.

"In his room there were found papers which he'd written in order to suggest that he was a member of a secret society entitled 'Young England' but these were proven to be nothing but the rantings of a sick mind. No such group existed. Edward Oxford was insane, there's no doubt of it. He was known to occasionally cry for no apparent reason and to talk incoherent nonsense. The Lucy Scales incident definitely triggered a deterioration in his mental state.

"He often stated, according to his associates, that he wanted to be remembered throughout history. It was his pet obsession. The Yard detectives concluded that his motive was simply to achieve that fame—or, rather, infamy.

"The police investigation ended there. My colleagues were satisfied that a madman shot the queen and was then himself killed by an unknown person. With the subsequent onset of the constitutional crisis and widespread social unrest, the police had more to worry about than tracing the Mystery Hero, who, as far as most were concerned, had done the country a favour by saving it the cost of a hanging."

"But you weren't satisfied," suggested Burton, shrewdly.

"Not a bit. I kept digging. The coincidence of Edward Oxford being around the corner when Lucy Scales was attacked was too much for me to swallow. So I started searching for more connections between him and Spring Heeled Jack."

"And found them?"

"Yes. After the death of Victoria, The Hog in the Pound gained a measure of notoriety thanks to Oxford having worked there. It immediately became the regular drinking hole for a group of young aristocrats who reckoned themselves philosophers; their philosophy being that mankind is shackled in chains of its own making."

"The Libertine philosophy."

"Exactly. The Hog in the Pound is where the Libertine movement began."

"So the Mad Marquess was among the young aristocrats?"

"Yes. What do you know about him?"

"Just the reputation. And that he was the man who founded the Libertine movement."

"The *bad* reputation!"

"Even worse than mine, apparently," smiled Burton.

Trounce chuckled.

"Henry de La Poer Beresford, the 3rd Marquess of Waterford. His history is colourful, to say the least. He succeeded to the marquessate after his father died—in the mid-twenties—and inherited the Curraghmore Estate in County Waterford, in the Republic of Ireland. He immediately set about disposing of the family fortune as quickly as possible, mainly by betting on horses and gambling in clubs.

"He first achieved notoriety in 1837 when, after a successful fox-hunt near Melton Mowbray, he and his party got stupendously drunk, entered the town, found half a dozen cans of red paint, and proceeded to daub it all over the buildings on the high street. Thus the saying 'painting the town red!'"

"The folly of youth," commented Burton.

"That same year," continued Trounce, "he escaped the famine and moved to an estate just north of Hertford, near the village of Waterford, though the name is a coincidence—there's no connection with County Waterford."

"It seems a big coincidence!"

"I suppose so, though I don't read anything significant into it. My suspicion is that the man's vanity—which, incidentally, knew no limits—made him choose that location. Perhaps he fancied himself as the Marquess of an English estate, in addition to the Irish one. He lived in a rambling old half-derelict mansion, appropriately named 'Darkening Towers,' on considerable acreage to the west of the village."

"Wait a minute. If Waterford is just outside Hertford, it must be fairly close to Old Ford."

"Well spotted. Darkening Towers is about three miles from the Alsop cottage."

"Does Jane Alsop still live there?"

"Yes. She's Jane Pipkiss now. She lives in the cottage with her husband, Benton—they married in 1843—and their children; a daughter and a son.

"Anyway, between '37 and '40, Beresford continually clashed with the local constabulary for drunken brawling, vandalism, and a number of brutal pranks which he played on local women. The man seemed to have no respect for the law, did absolutely anything for a bet, and displayed a strong streak of sadism."

"The Marquis de Sade holds an allure for certain types," said Burton. "You should meet my friend Swinburne."

"Really?" replied Trounce flatly, with an eyebrow raised.

"Well, maybe not."

"Anyway, after the death of Victoria, Beresford and his cronies started drinking in The Hog in the Pound, obviously attracted by its notoriety as 'the assassin's pub.' As their numbers grew and their anarchistic philosophy took form, they became the Libertines."

Burton frowned.

"But what's their connection with Jack?"

Trounce gazed at the burning log in the fireplace, as if the past could be glimpsed in the flames.

"By '43, the creature had become like the bogeyman of folklore. Whenever a sexual molestation occurred, the public was quick to cry 'Spring Heeled Jack!' whether there was any evidence of his involvement or not, and there were a great number of pranks committed in his name by young bloods dressed in costume. As time passed, it became more difficult to separate the genuine incidents from those performed by copycats. Then, during '43, there was a new outbreak of sightings in the Battersea, Lambeth and Camberwell triangle. They appear to have been genuine. I shan't go through them now, Captain, but you can borrow this report and read the details yourself.

"Henry Beresford seemed to be galvanised by the reappearance of the creature. He held Spring Heeled Jack up as some sort of Libertine god—called it a 'trans-natural entity'—a being entirely free of restraint, with no conscience or self-doubt; a thing that did whatever it wanted, whenever it wanted.

"As the Mad Marquess's ranting increased, the Libertine group split into two; into what are now known as the 'True Libertines,' who offer the more reasonable proposition that art, culture and beauty are essential to the human spirit and who, nowadays, concern themselves mostly with railing against the detrimental influence of the Technologists' machinery; and into the far more extremist 'Rakes,' led by Beresford, who seek to overthrow society's legal, moral, ethical and behavioural boundaries. Confounded scoundrels, the lot of them!"

"It would seem," pondered Burton, "that if Spring Heeled Jack is a man, then the Mad Marquess is your obvious suspect."

"He most certainly was," agreed Trounce, "but for certain difficulties. For one, physically and facially he in no way resembled the creature I saw. For another, he possessed rock-solid alibis for the times when Mary Stevens and Lucy Scales were attacked. And for a third, though the folklore of Spring Heeled Jack has grown these twenty-years past, the creature itself has been absent until the attack on you last night, which, from your description, I have no doubt was committed by the apparition I saw back in June 1840."

"Which presents a difficulty because?"

"Because Henry de La Poer Beresford, the 3rd Marquess of Waterford, died two years ago. He fell from his horse and broke his neck."

Burton's eyes lost focus as he reviewed all that Trounce had told him. The connections between Oxford, Beresford and Spring Heeled Jack were circumstantial at best, coincidental at worst, yet possessed an undeniable allure; he sensed that an undiscovered truth lay concealed somewhere in the tangled web.

"There's something else," said Trounce, quietly.

Burton looked at him.

"When Spring Heeled Jack leaped past me toward the queen's carriage," said the Detective-Inspector, "there was an aura of blue fire around his head and sparks and electrical charges shooting from his body. His costume was burned in places, and, when he turned, his face was stricken with pain.

"After he vanished, I pursued the Mystery Hero across the park and was again confronted by the apparition, this time by the woods in the park's north-western corner.

"The creature moves exceedingly fast but I cannot for the life of me see how it got there without passing me. Also, the Spring Heeled Jack that jumped out of the trees was not aflame, had no burn marks upon its suit, and displayed no signs of pain. In other words, Captain, I am convinced that there are at least two Spring Heeled Jacks!"

"Phew!" breathed Burton, "As if matters weren't complicated enough!"

He stood.

"You've been of immense help, Detective-Inspector. I'm indebted to you."

Trounce got to his feet and held the report out to Burton, who took it.

"You can pay that debt by keeping me informed, Captain. My superiors will not allow me to actively investigate this case, which they regard as so much nonsense, so I'm counting on you to solve the mystery. Please remember, too, that when I'm off duty, I'm entirely at your disposal."

They shook hands.

"Thank you, Inspector Trounce—"

"William."

"William. I shall be sure to alert you to whatever progress I might make; I give you my word."

As Burton turned to leave, Trounce said:

"One last thing, Captain."

"Yes?"

"In the past, Spring Heeled Jack has always committed a number of assaults during a period of days before then vanishing for weeks, months or years at a time."

"So you think another attack is due?"

"Imminently."

§

It was mid-afternoon by the time Burton stepped out of Scotland Yard to be engulfed by the silence of the "London particular."

The soot was still falling.

Like a blind man, he tapped along the pavement with his cane until he found the kerb.

His eyes started to water and a stinging sensation burned his nostrils.

"Monty!" he bellowed.

A towering shadow loomed to his right and he stepped back with his heart hammering in his chest, expecting the uncanny stilt-walker to emerge from the cloud; but no, the shape was too bulky.

"That you, guv'nor?"

"Yes! By heaven!"

"Aye. It's a thick 'un, ain't it? I can hardly see the end o' me nose!"

Montague Penniforth materialised at Burton's side.

"Bismillah!" uttered the King's agent. "I didn't realise you were a giant!"

It was true; Penniforth was enormous, standing at least six-foot-five, and heavily-muscled, too.

"Me muvver's to blame," the cabbie confessed. "She fed me too much porridge an' molasses!"

Burton noticed with astonishment that the man was still smoking his cherrywood.

"I'm glad you're here, Monty, but you should've gone home; you can't possibly drive in this!"

"Oh don'tcha worry yourself about that; we'll just have to inch along a bit slow, like—but I'll get you to wherever you want to go, guv'nor, you can be sure o' that. Come on, the hansom's over here."

Burton followed Penniforth along the kerb until the cab hove into view. As he clambered into it, he said: "Do you think you can find Montagu Place?"

"O' course! It's named after me, ain't it?"

Miraculously—because it seemed impossible—Montague Penniforth did find Montagu Place, though it took the rest of the afternoon. Burton gave him a very generous tip and, nurturing an idea that had occurred to him during the excruciatingly slow ride, he asked the cabbie to call on him the next day, or, if the fog precluded that, as soon as possible after it had cleared.

With a sigh of relief, the famous explorer stepped into his home.

Sir Richard Francis Burton had lived at 14 Montagu Place for just over a year. It was a four-storey structure, with a basement flat. Most of its floors divided into two large rooms. The basement was Mrs Iris Angell's domain; her sitting room—cluttered with all manner of framed pictures, decorative ceramics, ornaments, mementoes and knick-knacks—her bedroom, a bathroom, a larder and the kitchen, which was the worthy old soul's pride and joy. It was fitted with every convenience a cook could possibly desire, and a great deal more besides, for the late Mr Thomas Franklin Angell had been an ardent Technologist and a brilliant amateur inventor. A great many of her kitchen and household utensils and tools were entirely unique, having been designed and constructed by her late husband but never patented. The widow had told Burton that the attic was also filled with "Tom's fancies," though the explorer had never been up there to find out exactly what she meant.

At the end of the basement hallway, opposite the bottom of the staircase, a door opened onto steps leading up to an empty high-walled yard at the back of which lay what used to be a stable but was now an empty garage.

On the ground floor, there was a reception room and a seldom-used dining chamber.

The first floor was dominated by Burton's study, the costume and disguise room, a small water closet, and an empty chamber which the explorer was thinking of converting into a laboratory or photographic darkroom.

Up the stairs, the second floor held his bedroom, a dressing room and a spare bedchamber for guests; while on the topmost floor, there was the library—which contained his huge collection of books and manuscripts—and a storage room.

When Burton entered his study he found five suitcases lined up beside the door and the maid, Elsie Carpenter, dusting the mantelpiece.

"Run along, Miss Elsie; there's a good girl."

"Yes, sir," she said, bobbing her head, and left the room. She was fifteen years old and visited the house each day, from eight in the morning to four in the afternoon, to do Mrs Angell's bidding.

Burton found a note on his main desk and read it:

Tuesday 17th September 1861

Dearest Dick

I had a horrible time at the Fuller's. They were most unwelcoming and entirely unforthcoming concerning John's whereabouts, telling me only that he had been transported to London. I feel they went out of their way to conceal the truth from me. Perhaps if I apply to Sir Roderick Murchison he will intercede on our behalf? I understand that he is leaving Bath for London this afternoon (17th).

I have returned your luggage and am now setting out for home. I sent a parakeet to mother asking whether, in view of the circumstances, she and father would be prepared to receive you. She replied that they are not. Do not worry, my love, their disapproval will subside once we are married.

I shall call on you on Thursday afternoon.

I cannot bear these times apart.

Your loving,

Isabel

Burton dropped the note back onto the desk, sat down, and wrote a letter to Lord Palmerston. He felt sure that on his recommendation the Prime Minister would summon Sir Richard Mayne, the Chief Commissioner, and order him to put Detective-Inspector Trounce in charge of the Spring Heeled Jack case. He sealed the letter in an envelope and wrote upon it "Urgent. Attn. Lord Palmerston" and signed it with his new codename—Abdullah— to ensure that it would be delivered straight to the Prime Minister's hand.

He went downstairs, took a whistle from the hall table, opened the front door and gave it three quick blasts. Moments later, a runner leaped over the gate and landed on the doorstep, its tail wagging. Burton pulled a biscuit tin from under the hall table, opened its lid, and withdrew a chunk of ham. Mrs Angell always ensured that something tasty was in that tin. He placed the meat on the doorstep and the greyhound eagerly wolfed it down. After it had finished, it licked its lips, looked at the letter Burton held out, and took it between its teeth.

He bent over the dog's ear and said: "10 Downing Street, Whitehall."

The runner turned and bounded back over the gate, vanishing into the fog.

Burton returned to his study and paced over to the fireplace. The maid had evidently lit the fire earlier, for it was burning, though in a desultory manner. He poked the life back into it, used it to light a cigar, and sank into his armchair.

As Palmerston had detailed that morning, Burton's life had so far been remarkable, but he felt that this day, perhaps, had been the most astonishing of them all.

He shook his head in wonder. Only yesterday he'd been agonising over what to do next!

Resting his head on the embroidered antimacassar, he closed his eyes and allowed his thoughts to roam. They took him to 1841, the year he'd begun to study the Arabic language, the year the British Empire almost collapsed.

The government of the time, led by Lord Melbourne, had flown into a panic in the wake of Queen Victoria's death. There was only one clear successor to the throne: her uncle Ernest Augustus I, the Duke of Cumberland and King of Hanover, the fifth son of King George III. However, the thought of him becoming the king of England filled almost everyone with horror, for sixty-nine-year-old Ernest had, without a doubt, inherited his father's madness. There were persistent rumours that he'd brutally murdered his valet in 1810, fathered a son by Princess Sophia—who happened to be his own sister—and had indecently assaulted Lady Lyndhurst. He was also an extreme conservative, and thus out of step with the more liberal politics which were sweeping Britain at the time. Besides, it would mean reuniting the royal houses of Hanover and the United Kingdom, which had only been separated three years before, after Victoria came to power.

In the immediate aftermath of The Assassination, the populace took to the streets to protest at the possibility of Ernest becoming their king. Riots broke out in several cities. A bomb exploded near the Houses of Parliament.

The government declared a constitutional crisis, the Duke of Cumberland's accession was blocked, and regal powers were passed to a council of high officials, among them, the then Foreign Secretary, Lord Palmerston. These men turned their attention to an item of legislation which had been due for presentation in August of 1840. It was the Regency Act, prepared when Victoria declared her first pregnancy and designed to allow her husband, Prince Albert of Saxe-Coburg and Gotha, to be designated Regent in the event of his wife's death before their child reached the age of majority.

Palmerston, who'd been intensely disliked by Victoria due to his propensity for acting without going through a proper consultation processes, knew a good thing when he saw it. With a political sleight of hand, he and his fellow council members back-dated the Regency Act to make it effective from the time the royal couple's child had been conceived, rather than from the time of its birth. The Act was then rushed through Parliament and approved unanimously.

It was, of course, sheer hocus-pocus.

The unborn child had died with Victoria, so Act or no Act, the Prince Regent had no right to the throne. To achieve that, further manipulations were needed. The constitution required a rewrite.

Ernest Augustus I was, of course, furious. Had Hanover been any larger than a small English county, he may well have declared war. As it was, he looked on helplessly while the British politicians made the necessary adjustments and signed away his rights of accession.

In April 1842, the throne of the British Empire was passed to the House of Saxe-Coburg and Gotha.

Albert became King.

§

Chapter 6

The Hog in the Pound

cs

"THE GOVERNMENT IS THE EMPIRE'S BRAIN.
THE TECHNOLOGISTS ARE THE EMPIRE'S MUSCLE.
THE LIBERTINES ARE THE EMPIRE'S IMAGINATION.
AND I, GOD HELP ME, MUST BE THE EMPIRE'S CONSCIENCE."
—HIS MAJESTY, KING ALBERT

cs

Wednesday tried and failed to dawn. It wasn't until late morning that the fog allowed a smudge of daylight to filter through.

Sir Richard Francis Burton had spent the previous evening pondering the report Detective-Inspector Trounce had loaned him. There was one aspect of it that he and the Yard man hadn't discussed: in every description given by witnesses—even those where the apparition was said to be a ghost or a devil—its age was estimated as "early-forties." Yet twenty-four years had passed since the first manifestation. If Jack had been in his early-forties when he pounced on Mary Stevens then he should be nigh on sixty-five by now. The face Burton had seen beneath the globular helmet had been lined with madness and pain but certainly not with age.

He was beginning to agree with Trounce that the Spring Heeled Jack phenomenon might involve more than one person—and perhaps more than one generation.

As was his habit, he slept lightly and restlessly, awoke early and wrote for three hours before taking breakfast.

Throughout the rest of the morning, the gas lamps glowed in both his study and the library upstairs, as he brought down stacks of books and searched through them for references to any mythical being that might resemble his assailant.

While he was at it, he kept his eyes open for information concerning wolf-men, too.

In the latter case, there was a plethora of references to *loup-garous*—or *werewolves*. Tales had been told of half-man, half-wolf creatures all over the world and throughout history.

The same could not be said for Spring Heeled Jack; Burton found but one mention of a stilt-walking spirit. He was smoking a hookah while studying the reference when Algernon Swinburne called at one o'clock.

The poet stood on tiptoe and peered over a wall of books at Burton, who'd absently-mindedly muttered "send him in" when Mrs Angell announced his friend's arrival. It was plain that the great explorer was in one of his "scholarly funks"—as Swinburne called them—and was blind to all but the book in his hand.

"Boo!" said the poet.

"Moko Jumbi," announced Burton.

"Eh?"

The explorer looked up.

"Oh, hello Algy. There's nothing. No reference I can find that at all resembles Spring Heeled Jack with the exception of the Caribbean's 'Moko Jumbi,' which is represented in carnivals by stilt-walking dancers. The origin is definitely African. Moko is a god of the Congo region; the word means 'diviner.' As for 'jumbi,' I believe it roughly equates with the Arabian 'djinni' and probably has its origin in the Congolese word 'zumbi.' So: 'Diviner Spirit.' Interesting."

"Is it?" said Swinburne. "Why are you researching Spring Heeled Jack? Are you joining the Rakes? And why do you have a black eye?"

"The one gave me the other."

"What? What? Are you telling me that Spring Heeled Jack whacked you in the eye?" exclaimed Swinburne, moving around the books to sit in the armchair facing Burton's. His elbow caught a stack and sent volumes cascading to the floor.

Burton sighed.

"Do you consider 'whacked' to be a suitable word for an up-and-coming poet?"

"Shut up and answer the question!"

"If I shut up I can hardly—"

"Richard!" screeched Swinburne, bouncing in his seat.

Burton laughed. Isabel had once commented that, when he did this, it looked like it hurt him, and Swinburne saw the truth of her observation now. His friend's upper lip curled, revealing over-long canines, and the eyes seemed to wince, as if seldom-used muscles had come into play. Three deep-chested barks, then the face fell back to its normal savage aspect and the penetrating eyes levelled at Swinburne's own pale green orbs.

"It's true, Algy. I was attacked by Spring Heeled Jack after leaving you at the Cannibal Club," he said, putting his book aside. He proceeded to describe the incident.

"Great heavens, but that's wonderful!" enthused Swinburne when he'd finished. "Fancy being punched in the head by a myth! I don't believe you, of course. Have you eaten?"

"I can assure you that I'm telling the truth and it felt far from wonderful. No, I haven't."

"Come on then; let's go for tiffin at The Black Toad."

Burton put the hookah aside and stood. "Very well, but go easy on the ale. Last time we lunched there, I had to carry you out over my shoulder."

"Funny," chuckled the little poet. "I don't remember that at all!"

As he leaped up, his foot clipped another pile of books and sent it crashing down.

A couple of minutes later, the two men, with overcoats buttoned up to their necks, top hats at a jaunty angle on their heads, and canes swinging in their hands, strolled out of 14 Montagu Place and headed east toward Baker Street.

The fog had turned from a deep hellish red to a pustulant pale yellow. People, animals and vehicles moved cautiously through it. Sound was muted. Even the sudden report of a nearby velocipede's boiler exploding, and the rider's yells as his calves were scalded, sounded strangely muffled.

"Algy," said Burton, "you've knocked around with a Rake or two. Why their enthusiasm for Spring Heeled Jack? What exactly is their philosophy?"

"They're extremists," declared the poet. "Anarchists. Nihilists. Very naughty boys. They claim that all moral codes and social conventions are entirely artificial and that by following them a man is willingly allowing his authentic identity to be suppressed."

They crossed Gloucester Place and entered Dorset Street, Swinburne hurrying along with his characteristically springy step and nervous movements. As they passed the corner, the sweet odour of roasting chestnuts caressed their nostrils; one of the rare pleasurable scents the streets of London could offer. Burton tipped his hat at the vendor.

"Afternoon, Mr Grub. How's business?"

"Rotten! No one can see me in this blinkin' pea-souper. Can I do you a bag?"

"Sorry, old son. I'm on my way for a nosh-up at the pub!"

"Ah well. Enjoy, Cap'n!"

It was one of Burton's great talents, this ability to communicate with anyone, whatever their social standing. Some of his acquaintances sneered at it; they considered it indecorous to converse with the hoi polloi, but their opinions did little to influence him.

"The difference between a True Libertine and a Rake," said Swinburne as they moved on, "is that the one is concerned with how and what an individual should contribute to society, while the other is concerned only with how society shapes the individual."

"You make the Libertines sound rather virtuous. That's not their reputation."

"No, no! Don't misunderstand me! Both branches of the movement are thoroughly disreputable by Mrs Grundy's puritanical standards. Our mother of propriety stamps her little foot at the merest whiff of scandal; and the Libertines stink of it, not least because sexuality is a focal point for their cause. They identify it as the area where the Empire's hypocrisy is most apparent; and they are wickedly unrestrained in their support of eroticism, pornography, pederasty, de Sade, and all manner of vices."

A gentleman, walking past at this moment, muttered "I say!" as he caught some of the poet's words. Swinburne chuckled and raised his voice so that other passers-by might hear:

"The True Libertine points to the thousands of prostitutes on London's streets and says: 'Look! Sex for sale! This is what these woman—and men!— have resorted to in order to survive in this so-called civilisation! Where are your much-vaunted morals now, Society? Where is your restraint; your puritan ethic? And these prostitutes have customers! Men whose sexual tastes cannot be satisfied within your rules of so-called decency! You, Society, generate the very thing you denigrate!'"

Burton glanced around as heads turned and disapproving glares were cast at his companion. Swinburne continued regardless; sermonising with more than a little relish:

"The Rake, meanwhile, celebrates the sexual act as the one place where men and women are literally and metaphorically stripped naked and reduced to their purest nature—I mean 'pure' in the sense of unaffected; the one occasion when we are most liable to shed the artificial skin of Society and gain a sense of our own fundamental identity."

The two men turned right into Baker Street.

"The Rakes say of shame: what is it? Of virtue: we can miss it. Of sin: we can kiss it. And it's no longer sin!"

Burton gave a derisive snort. However, after a moment of thought, he conceded: "I can sympathise with the general sentiment. Any intelligent man can see that the hypocritical politeness and studied mannerisms of our civilisation suppress and oppress in equal measure. They certainly serve to obliterate difference, enforcing a regime that discourages intellectual, emotional and sexual freedoms. Far better for Society that its citizens are built according to its dictates, rather than in their own image. It makes them better slaves."

"Here! Here!" agreed Swinburne. "Those who allow their identity to be formed by the Empire are nothing but the willing fuel for it! This is why the Libertines, and the Rakes in particular, offend, disconcert—even frighten—people. The movement pushes at boundaries which the masses aren't even aware of *until* they are pushed; and it is those boundaries that define most people's identities and which tell them that they're a valued member of a stable society. People like to feel wanted, to know they have their part to play, even if it's only as fuel for the Empire's furnace! My goodness, look at that!"

Swinburne pointed to where an elephantine shape was emerging from the miasma. It was one of the new dray horses—a mega-dray—which the Eugenicists had recently developed. These gigantic beasts stood fifteen feet high at the shoulder (measuring them in "hands" had been deemed ridiculous) and were immensely strong. The cargo wagons they towed were often the size of small houses.

Burton and Swinburne pressed against the wall of the building beside them as the towering animal plodded closer, trying to move as far from it as possible; and with good reason, for mega-drays had no control over their bladders or bowels and were over-productive in both departments. This had proven a serious problem in London's already filthy streets until an enterprising member of the Technologist caste had invented the automated cleaners, popularly known as "litter-crabs," which now roamed the city every night scooping up the mess.

Sure enough, as the horse came abreast of their position, towing an omnibus behind it, large boulders of manure thudded onto the road, splattering across the pavement, narrowly missing the two men.

The mega-dray faded into the lazily swirling pall.

Burton and Swinburne walked on.

"Where does Spring Heeled Jack enter into it, Algy?" asked the King's agent.

"According to the Mad Marquess," answered Swinburne, "if we transcend the borders that define us, we will gain what he termed 'trans-natural' powers. Spring Heeled Jack jumping over a house, he maintained, is an illustration of this, for Jack is the ultimate example of a being who dances to nobody's fiddle but his own; law or no law; morals or no morals. This freedom is, apparently, the next step in our evolution."

Burton shook his head.

"Being liberated is one thing; sexually assaulting young girls is quite another," he objected. "By God! Poor old Darwin's theory seems to have proven dangerous for everyone. It's all but destroyed the Church; Darwin himself has been forced into hiding; and now it's being used to justify sexual aggression against innocents! Surely, Algy, such acts are indicative of regression rather than evolution? If we must remove suppressions in order to evolve—and in that much, I agree with the Rakes—should there not also come a self-generated code of conduct that disallows such acts of depravity? Evolution should move us away from animalistic behaviour, not toward it!"

Swinburne shrugged and said: "The Rakes specialise in being bestial. They glory in perversion, black magic, drugs and crime. They want to break taboos, laws and doctrines, all of which they view as artificial and oppressive."

The Black Toad came into sight.

"Praise the Lord!" enthused Swinburne. "I'm parched!"

"Can you last a little longer?" asked Burton. "I have it in mind to bypass this place and walk on to The Hog in the Pound on Oxford Street."

"Ah, you want to see the birthplace of the Libertines, hey? Certainly, let's leg it over there. But why the sudden interest, Richard?"

Burton told Swinburne the story of Spring Heeled Jack's tenuous connection with Edward Oxford.

Half an hour later, they arrived outside The Hog in the Pound. It was a dark, overweight building; ancient, timbered, crooked and begrimed. A litter-crab had broken down in the road outside the premises and curious onlookers had gathered around. It was collapsed with its four right legs curled underneath. Half of the thin litter-collector arms on its stomach had been crushed or bent out of shape, and steam wafted sluggishly from a split in its raised side. One of the left legs twitched repetitively.

Swinburne giggled.

"You see," he announced at the top of his voice. "The spirit of the Libertines still haunts The Hog in the Pound! All machines that pass here must surely die! Hoorah for art and poetry! Down with the Technologists!"

They entered the public house and pushed through the dimly lit, low-ceilinged taproom—where a thirsty mob of manual labourers, clerks, shopkeepers, businessmen and city gents were swilling away the soot that lined their throats—to the parlour, which was considerably lighter and less well-attended. Hanging their coats and hats on the stand beside the door, they crossed to a table and made themselves comfortable. A barmaid took their order: a glass of port for Burton and a pint of bitter for Swinburne. They both chose steak and ale pie for their meal.

"So this is where it all happened," observed Swinburne, looking around at the smoke-stained, wood-panelled chamber. "The very room where the Mad Marquess preached to his followers."

"A sermon of lawlessness, madness and self-indulgence, by the sound of it."

"Not to begin with. At first it was fairly mild Luddite stuff. Machines are ugly. Machines steal our jobs. Machines dehumanise us. The usual sort of thing. Personally, I think the Marquess was pandering to the crowd; I don't think he much believed in his own preaching."

"What makes you say that?"

"The fact that he was known to have struck up a close friendship with Isambard Kingdom Brunel back in '37. They were often seen together at the Athenaeum Club. If Beresford was truly a Luddite, why the blazes was he so often seen in deep conversation with the leader of the emerging Technologist movement?

"By '43, if I remember rightly, he stopped railing against the Technologists altogether and, instead, introduced the idea of the trans-natural man. That became his obsession, and he became much more the extremist. Ah! The drinks! Thank you, my dear. Cheers, Richard!"

Swinburne took a gulp from his pint, which seemed enormous in his tiny hand. He wiped froth from his upper lip then continued:

"Delicious! The problem for the Marquess was that most of his followers were more interested in opposing the Technologists than they were in all the evolving man bunkum, so in 1848, a more palatable version of his preachings was developed by a small breakaway group, comprised of painters, poets and critics, and led by William Holman Hunt, John Everett Millais and my friend Dante Gabriel Rossetti."

"The Pre-Raphaelite Brotherhood."

"That's what the core group call themselves, though they and their many followers have more generally become known as the True Libertines.

"Over the past twenty years or so, their brand of Libertarianism has transformed into a celebration of the so-called nobility of the human spirit. They look at the humble labourer and declare that he is a thing of beauty, this hard done by man, whose very existence is threatened by the ugly, job-stealing machines."

He grinned.

"I must admit, though, that the True Libertines are mostly the listless elite, foppish painters, languorous authors, lazy philosophers, or half-mad poets like me. They—perhaps I should say 'we,' for I do count myself among their number—*we* would rather wax lyrical about the labourer than actually pick up a shovel ourselves."

"You don't fool me, little 'un," said Burton. "You're a half-arsed Libertine at best!"

"I confess; I'm merely a dabbler!" laughed the poet. "Anyway, to get back to the subject of my little discourse, Henry Beresford and his remaining supporters renamed themselves the Rakes and the rest you know; they're a bunch of lawless rascals who delight in mischief! And, of course, they received a huge boost when Darwin published *The Origin of Species*. Who needs morality when God is dead?"

"I wonder what would Darwin himself say about it?" pondered the King's agent.

"Perhaps he'd agree with your theory of a natural system of justice; the idea that we all have an individual built-in moral sense which brings rewards for our good deeds and punishments for our bad. I suspect that he'd see it as a function that assists in the survival of the species."

"Maybe so, if he's still alive. With every religion declaring jihad against him, he might have discovered that scientific realism can't protect against the vengeance of a dead god."

"Do you believe the rumours that the Technologists are sheltering him?"

"It wouldn't surprise me. Francis Galton, the head of the Eugenicist faction, is his cousin. But back to the Rakes, Algy; do they still idolise Spring Heeled Jack?"

"If anything, more so. Their new leader, Beresford's protégé, is more extreme even than *he* was."

"And who is this new leader?"

"You know of him. His name is—Ah ha! Here's the food!"

The barmaid placed a steaming plate before each man, lay cutlery on the table, and asked: "Another round, gents?"

"Yes," said Swinburne. "No. Wait. Bring us a bottle of red wine, instead. Does that suit you, Richard?"

Burton nodded and the barmaid smiled toothily and departed.

"Oliphant," declared Swinburne.

"Pardon?"

"The leader of the Rake faction for the past two years: Laurence Oliphant."

§

By the afternoon, the fog had turned a rusty brown and flakes of soot were once again drifting lazily through it.

Swinburne got drunk and staggered off into the smothering murk with no clear destination in mind. He would undoubtedly end up unconscious in a gentlemen's club or brothel; his behaviour had been deteriorating these past weeks.

'What that lad needs,' thought Burton, 'is a purpose.'

The King's agent had managed to talk with the manager of The Hog in the Pound before departing. He'd learned that the original owner of the pub—the man who'd employed Edward Oxford and witnessed the birth of the True Libertines and Rakes—was named Joseph Robinson.

"He's an elderly gent, now, sir" the manager had advised. "A few years back, 1856 it was, he tired of the daily journey to and fro—he's always lived in Battersea, you see—so he sold up and bought himself a public house closer to home; a nice little place called The Tremors."

"Strange name for a pub!" Burton had commented.

"Aye, 'tis. If you ever go there, ask him about it; there's a story!"

Burton got home at six and hadn't been there for more then ten minutes when a loud detonation sounded outside the house. It was followed by the clang of the doorbell. A minute later Mrs Angell knocked on the study door and announced the arrival of Mr Montague Penniforth, "who's leaving   a trail of soot on the carpet."

The doorway darkened behind her as the giant cabbie ducked and stepped through. He was wrapped in a calf-length red greatcoat, wore white britches, knee-high boots and a tricorn hat; all peppered with black flakes.

"I'm sorry, good lady," he said. "My mistake. Forgot to wipe me feet. You see, I'm preoccupied, like, on account of the fact that me crankshaft just broke and flew a good forty feet in the air afore it came back down to earth in three pieces."

He shrugged at Burton, who was seated at the main desk. "I'm sorry, guv'nor, but I don't think I'll be takin' you anywhere 'til I get the bleedin' thing replaced; beggin' your pardin for the bad langwidge, ma'am!"

Mrs Angell sniffed, muttered "I wouldn't mind so much if they were normal-sized feet!" and glided out of the room with a haughty air.

Burton stood and shook his visitor's hand.

"Hang up your hat and coat, Monty. A brandy?"

"Don't mind if I do, sir."

Burton poured a couple of generous measures and, after Penniforth had divested himself of his outer layers, handed him a glass and gestured to one of the armchairs by the fireplace.

The men sat opposite each other and the cabbie gave a satisfied sigh.

"Blimey," he said, "Takin' a brandy in the house of a toff; who'd have thought?"

"A toff, Monty?"

"'Scuse me, guv'nor!"

Burton gave a wry smile. "I've not properly introduced myself, have I?"

"No need, sir. I reads the papers. You're Sir Richard Burton, the Africa gentleman. A reg'lar Livingstone, you are!"

"Ouch!" winced Burton.

Penniforth looked bemused.

"It's not a comparison I'm keen on," explained the explorer.

"Ah. Competition?"

"Different ideas. I say, you enjoyed that brandy! Another?"

The cabbie looked in surprise at his empty glass.

"I wouldn't say no, if it ain't an imposition, sir; I didn't notice that one go down the pipe!"

Burton handed over the decanter.

"Here help yourself. Tell me, Monty, how well do you know the East End?"

The big man looked up in surprise—and forget to stop pouring the brandy until his glass was filled almost to the brim.

"Oof!" he gasped. "The Cauldron! I can look after meself but I wouldn't recommend it it to no one but them what's tired o' life. I lives in Cheapside, what's in spittin' distance o' Whitechapel. So I knows the East End. I knows all o' London. It's me job."

"Have you heard anything about wolves in the area?"

Penniforth's face—a solid, clean-shaven, weather-beaten and square affair, framed by curly brown hair—paled slightly.

"Aye, somethin' of the sort. It's said they're more men than wolves; monsters what have been comin' out after dark these weeks past. You ain't gonna ask me to go a-huntin' wiv you, I hope?"

"Just that."

Montague Penniforth swallowed his over-filled glass of brandy in a single gulp.

"Bloody 'ell," he gasped.

"You can refuse, of course," said Burton. "I know the Cauldron is dangerous enough even without monsters running around it, but one way or another I intend to go there tonight. I was hoping that you'd come with me, as you know your way around. I'll pay you generously."

Penniforth reached up and scratched his head through his thick curls.

"The thing is, sir, that you bein' a toff 'n' all—a-beggin' your pardin—it'll make you a target for every scallywag what sets eyes on you. An' in the East End, every bugger what sets eyes on you will be a scallywag!"

Burton stood up.

"Wait here. Finish the brandy if you like. I'll be about fifteen minutes."

He strode across his study and disappeared through a door.

Penniforth refilled his glass and looked around. He'd never seen a room like this. It was crammed with books and weapons and pictures and charts and things he didn't even know the name of. He got to his feet and wandered around, examining the old flintlocks, the modern pistols, the curved knives and the great variety of swords; it was the weapons that appealed to him most.

The cabbie had often exclaimed to his wife "'Ow the other 'alf live!" but this man Burton, he didn't seem to belong to the other half; he was one of a kind. He acted like a gentleman but he'd the face of a brute. He was of the 'upper crust' but he spoke to the cabbie like they were equals. He was famous but he had no airs and graces. Strange!

The door leading to the stairs opened and a rough-looking oldster with a long white beard stepped in; an ex-seaman if his rolling gait was any indication.

"Hallo, pa!" greeted Penniforth. "You lookin' for the master of the 'ouse?"

"Yus," croaked the new arrival, blinking beneath his beetling white eyebrows. "The beggar owes me three 'n' six an' I can't wait no longer!"

"Ho, he does, does he?"

"Yus. Where is 'e, the rat?"

Penniforth lay down his glass and pushed out his chest.

"'Here now, you'd better watch your tongue, mister!"

"My tongue, is it?" wheezed the old man. "What yer gonna do abaht it, ay?"

"For a start, me ol' mucker," growled Penniforth, "I'll pick you up by the collar of that two 'undred year old coat o' yours, an' by the seat of them scabby-lookin' pants, an' I'll throw you out o' this 'ouse right into the gutter, make no mistake!"

"Oh yer will, will yer!"

"Yes I blinkin' well will!"

The oldster let loose a bark of laughter and suddenly grew much taller and a lot wider.

"There'll be no need for that, my good fellow!" came Sir Richard Francis Burton's voice.

Montague Penniforth staggered backward.

"My sainted aunt!" he cried. "It's that African ju-ju!"

"No, Monty, it's a white wig, powder in my beard, a little stage make-up to cover the scars, some old clothes, and a spot of play acting!" said the old man, who suddenly didn't seem so old.

"Lord almighty! You had me proper fooled! You're a blinkin' artist, guv'nor!"

"So you'll think I'll pass muster in the Cauldron?"

"Cor blimey, yes; no one will look at you twice!"

"Jolly good! Then it just remains for us to arm ourselves and we'll be off, if you're agreeable?"

"Right ho, sir; right ho!"

Burton crossed to the bureau which stood against the wall between the two windows and, opening a drawer, pulled from it a brace of modern pistols.

He handed one of the six-shooters to the giant cabbie.

"It's loaded, so be careful. And Monty, this is only to be used in the very last resort, is that understood?"

"Yes, sir."

"If you have to draw it, be careful where you point it and only pull the trigger if there's no other option."

"Right you are, guv'nor."

"Good. Let's be off, then. I'm afraid we'll have to pay one of your competitors to take us there."

"Don't worry about that," said Penniforth. "We cabbies have an understandin' between ourselves. An' whatever chap takes us, I'll 'ave him arrange for me steam-horse to be towed away from outside your 'ouse, too."

They pushed their pistols into their belts, buttoned up their coats, and left the house.

Chapter 7

The Cauldron

For nigh on five hours, Sir Richard Burton and Montague Penniforth had been trudging around the crowded streets, courts, alleys and cul de sacs of Whitechapel with the fog churning around them and the unspeakable filth sticking to their boots.

The honeycomb of narrow, uneven passages, bordered by the most decrepit and crowded tenements in the city, was flowing with raw sewerage and rubbish of every description, including occasional corpses. The stench was overpowering and both men had vomited more than once.

They passed tall houses—"rookeries"—mostly of wood, which slumped upon their own foundations as if tired of standing; houses whose gaping windows were devoid of glass; patched, instead, with paper or cloth or broken pieces of wood; windows from which slops and cracked chamberpots were emptied; from which defeated eyes gazed blankly.

Lines of rope stretched across the alleys, decorated with flea-ridden rags; clothes put out to be washed by the polluted rain; later to dry in the rancid air; but currently marinating in the toxic vapour.

Time and again the two men were approached by girls barely out of childhood, who materialised out of the fog with matted hair and bare feet, smeared with excrement up to their knees, covered only by a rough coat or a thin, torn dress or a man's shirt which hung loosely over their bones; who offered themselves for a few coppers; who lowered the price when refused; who begged and wheedled and finally cursed viciously when the men pushed past.

Time and again they were approached by boys and men in every variety of torn and filthy apparel, who demanded and bullied and threatened and finally, when the pistols appeared, spat and swore and sidled away.

Time and again they passed skeletal women sitting hunched in dark corners clutching tiny bundles to their breast; poverty and starvation gnawing at them; too weak and hopeless to even raise their heads as the two men walked quietly by.

Burton, the author, the man who'd described in minute detail the character and practices of cultures far removed from his own, felt that he could never find the words to depict the utter squalor of the Cauldron. The dirt and decay, the putrescence and rot and garbage, the viciousness and violence, the despair and emptiness; it was far beyond anything he'd witnessed in the darkest depths of Africa, amid the so-called "primitives."

Thus far tonight, the two men had drunk sour-tasting beer in four malodorous public houses. It was the fifth that delivered what they were looking for.

They were approached Stepney, when Burton mumbled, "There's another public house ahead. I have to get this foul taste out of my mouth. We'll take a gin or rum or something; anything, so long as it's not that piss-water they call ale."

The cabbie nodded wordlessly and stumbled on, his big feet squelching through the slime.

The pub—The White Lion—halfway down a short and crooked lane, bulged out over the mud as if about to collapse into it. The orange light from its windows oozed into the fog and was smeared across the uneven road surface and opposite wall. Shouts, screams, snatches of song, and the wheeze of an accordion came from within the premises.

Burton pushed open the door and they entered; Penniforth bending to avoid knocking his head on the low ceiling.

"Buy us a drink, dad?" asked a man of Burton before he'd taken two paces toward the bar.

"Buy yer own fuckin' drink," he replied, in character.

"Watch yer mouth, you old git!" came the reply.

"Watch yours!" warned Penniforth, his massive fist pushing up under the man's chin.

"Steady mate, no 'arm done," whined the individual, turning away.

They shouldered through the crowd to the counter and ordered gins.

The barman asked to see their money first.

Leaning on the scarred wood, they gulped down the spirit and immediately ordered another round.

"Thirsty, aint'cha?" commented the man beside Penniforth.

"Yus," grunted the cabbie.

"Me too. I always gets a thirst on after fightin' with the missus."

"Been givin' you earache, 'as she?"

"Not 'alf, the bleedin' cow. I ain't seen you in 'ere before."

"I ain't been 'ere afore."

"That your old fella?" the man nodded toward Burton.

"Yus," answered Penniforth, gruffly. "Nosey, ain'tcha?"

"Just bein' neighbourly, that's all. If yer don't wanna talk, it ain't no skin off my nose!"

"Yer, well, fair enough. I thought I'd get 'im out o' Mile End for an 'oliday!"

The other man laughed.

"An 'oliday in Stepney! That's rich!"

"At least you don't 'ave bleedin' monsters runnin' around at night!" exclaimed the cabbie.

Burton smiled appreciatively into his glass. Good chap, Monty! Quick work!

He ordered more drinks and included a beer for their new acquaintance.

"'Ere yer go, mate; get that down yer neck," he rasped, sliding the pint over.

"Ta dad, much appreciated. The name's Fred, by the way. Fred Spooner."

"I'm Frank Baker," offered Burton. "This is me son, Monty."

They drank each others' health.

Over in the corner, the man with the accordion began to squeeze out another tune and the crowd roared out its bawdy lyrics, which, as far as Burton could make out, told of the various places visited by a pair of bloomers belonging to Old Ma Tucker.

He waited patiently, the odour of old sweat and bad breath and acidic beer and stale piss clogging his nostrils. He didn't have to wait for long.

"So they're in Mile End now, are they?" shouted Spooner above the noise.

"Yus," said Penniforth.

"It'll be 'ere next, then," said the East Ender, with an air of resignation. "My mate over in Wapping lost 'is tenant to 'em last week."

"Wotcher mean 'lost'?"

"They snatched one of the kids what roomed at 'is place. That's what they do; they steal the nippers, though most of the kids what were taken 'ave come back since. They took 'em from Whitechapel first, then Shadwell, Wapping these weeks past, and now I guess it's Mile End's turn."

"Bloody 'ell. What are they?"

"Dunno, mate. Dogs. Wolves. Men. Summick inbetween. You know they explode?"

"Explode?" uttered Burton. "What do yer mean?"

"I've 'eard of three occasions when it's 'appened: they burst into flames for no reason and burn like dry straw 'til there ain't nuffink of 'em left! I wish the 'ole lot o' them would go up like that. It's Hell draggin' them back, if yer arsk me!"

"It's a rum do, that's fer sure!" said Burton.

"Come on, pa; we'd better be off," urged Penniforth.

"I'll finish me drink first," objected Burton.

"'Urry it up then!"

"You seen an artist around?" Burton asked Spooner.

"Aye. Slick Sid Sedgewick is the best in the business. Why, you got a scam?"

"No, mate. Not a con artist. I mean an artist what draws and paints."

Spooner spluttered into his glass.

"You gotta be jokin'! A paintin' artist around 'ere!"

"I just 'eard there was one, that's all."

"What is it, dad? You wanna get yer portrait done 'n' hanged in the National bleedin' Gallery?"

"Alright, alright!" protested Burton.

He and Penniforth swigged back the last of their gin and bid Spooner farewell.

"Good luck to yer!" he said, as they pushed away from the bar and heaved their way through the throng to the door.

They burst out into the alleyway hoping for a breath of fresh air and getting quite the opposite.

It was well past midnight. The atmosphere was thick, loathsome and catarrhic.

"Wapping's about a mile away as the crow flies," said Burton in a low voice. "Probably considerably farther through this maze."

"Don't worry, guv'nor, I knows the way."

"Are you up for it?"

"In for a penny, in for a pound."

"Good man! And well done; the way you got information out of that Spooner fellow was admirable! Thanks to you, we now know where the loup-garous are hunting."

"The what?"

"Men-wolves."

They resumed their trek through the hellish back streets and, once again, were accosted every few minutes with varying degrees of pleading and promised violence. Only their pistols and Montague Penniforth's great size kept the knife-men, club wielders and garrotters at bay.

Even those deterrents failed as they crossed Cable Street and entered the outskirts of Wapping.

They'd just passed along Juniper Street and turned left into an unnamed alley when, from dark doorways to either side, a gang of men hurled themselves out and threw a large blanket over Penniforth, tripping him and, as he crashed to the ground, piling on top of him. He struggled and yelled but with five heavy-set thugs applying their full weight, he was helpless.

Meanwhile, Burton found himself surrounded by three hard-eyed men;

two in front of him and one behind; each sneering; each waving a dagger threateningly.

He stood still, maintaining his guise as an elderly seaman, his back a little crooked, his eyes peering short-sightedly at the gang.

"W-what do yer want?" he stuttered, weakly.

"What 'ave you got?" replied one of the men; the apparent leader. He was tall, rat-faced, with a tangled black beard and lank hair.

"Nuffink."

"Is that so? Funny, 'cos I see a nice pair o' strong boots on yer feet, an' word 'as reached me that there's a pistol under that there warm-lookin' coat o' yours. Don't go for it if yer wanna live."

Burton heard the man behind taking a step forward.

'Just one more, my friend,' he thought.

"An' that bowler you're a-wearing on your 'ead will look just fine an' dandy on mine, I reckons."

"Ummph!" came Penniforth's voice from inside the blanket.

The step was taken.

Burton whirled and straightened, his right arm shot up, and his fist connected with the man's chin with such force that the jawbone broke with an audible snap and the crook's feet left the ground.

Before the man had landed on his back, Burton was facing front and springing at the leader. Taken aback, Rat-face stabbed at him reflexively, the dagger aimed at his throat, but Burton swivelled, brought his own arm up under his opponent's, hooked his elbow and wrist around it, and jerked upward. With a nauseating crunch, Rat-face's arm splintered. His scream was cut short by a ferocious uppercut. He flopped backward, out cold.

As the third man closed in, others left the blanket to come to his assistance. It was a stupid mistake. Penniforth erupted out of it with a bellow of rage, ripping the material asunder.

While the cabbie lay into the gang, Burton took off his bowler and tossed it at the remaining knife-man's face. Momentarily distracted, the crook ducked and his beady eyes wavered, missing Burton's next lightning fast movement. Before he realised what had happened, the East Ender felt his wrist clutched in a grip of such strength that his fingers opened involuntarily and the dagger fell from them. He was yanked forward and his erstwhile victim's forehead smashed into the bridge of his nose. The thief collapsed to his knees, blood spurting from his face, his wrist still held, as if in a vice. He looked up, half-dazed, and the eyes that met his blazed with sullen rage.

"N-no," he stammered.

"Yes," said Burton.

He twisted the man's arm out of its socket and put an end to the high-pitched shriek with a chop to the neck.

The limp crook crumpled into a yellowish puddle.

Burton turned to see how Penniforth was getting on and laughed.

The giant cabbie was grinning, with three unconscious men at his feet. He was holding the other two upside down, a hand around an ankle of each.

"What shall I do with the rubbish, guv'nor?" he asked.

Burton recovered his slime-stained bowler.

"Just drop it in the street like everyone else does around here."

He turned and caught sight of four squat figures passing the far end of the alley. They were gone in an instant, leaving him with a vague impression of floor length scarlet cloaks with big hoods, totally enveloping the wearers. A new order of nuns perhaps, come to aid the poor? Yet there had been something disturbing about those four shapes; something—what was it?— Yes, something about their gait.

"Monty!" he snapped, and started running.

The cabbie dropped the crooks and followed. They reached the end of the passage and Burton looked to the right just in time to see a glimpse of red cloth sliding past the edge of a wall.

"Come on!"

He raced to the corner and peered down a dank alleyway no wider than the span of his arms. Far ahead, the four red cloaks were consumed by billowing fog.

Burton sped on, occasionally slipping in the slime, almost falling, with Monty on his heels.

An arched entrance opened onto yet another backstreet; almost pitch black, with just a glimmer of candlelight bleeding into the cloud from the gaps in a bordered-up window.

A flash of red passed through the light.

Through one dark passageway after another, they pursued the short, cowled figures, only ever catching fleeting glimpses, never seeming to close with their quarry.

"By heck!" panted Penniforth. "They're fast! Who are they? Why are we chasin' them?"

"I don't know! There's just something odd about them! There!" Burton pointed ahead to where the four flowing shapes passed through an aura of light cast by a solitary gas lamp.

They pounded along until they reached the patch of brightness and there Burton skidded to a halt.

He bent and quickly examined the mud. There were four sets of footprints in it.

"They're running bare-foot on the balls of their feet and—look at this!—triangular pads and four toes, and, if I'm not mistaken, these indentations indicate claws! They're the loup-garous, Monty!"

A terrified shout suddenly echoed from somewhere close.

Without another word, Burton plunged ahead. Monty followed, pulling the pistol from inside his greatcoat.

They emerged into a cobbled square with the vague mist-shrouded mouths of alleyways opening into each of its sides.

A man and a boy stood in its centre. The four robed figures were circling them with a predatory lope. Liquid snarling reached Burton's ears.

"For God's sake 'elp us!" pleaded the man. "They're going to—"

One of the things swooped forward and leaped onto his chest, momentarily obscuring him with its red robe. Then it dropped back and stalked away, leaving him standing there, his throat missing.

A fountain of blood arced out and splashed onto the cobbles.

The boy let loose a wailing cry.

The man dropped to his knees then keeled over onto his face, blood pooling out around him.

Penniforth raised his pistol and fired.

The detonation sounded terrific as it echoed from the walls.

The shot missed its target—Burton clearly saw the edge of a red brick explode as the bullet hit it—but, unexpectedly, as if set off by the noise, one of the creatures suddenly burst into flames which raged with such intensity that, within seconds, the figure was reduced to ashes before their eyes.

The remaining three creatures, in unison, sprang upon the boy. He screeched and struggled.

Penniforth fired again, hitting one of the creatures in the arm.

It howled and released its grip on the youngster, whirled, and bounded toward the big cabbie. As it did so, its hood fell back.

Burton jumped forward to intercept it and saw a diabolical face with a furrowed brow, deeply set bloodshot eyes gleaming above a wrinkled snout; a huge drooling mouth filled with long sharp canines; and a shaggy head of tangled hair out of which pointed ears projected.

The pistol banged again, its flash reflected in the thing's eyes as it ducked down, jumped up, and swiped at Burton. He felt an impact on the side of his head. The square somersaulted. Bells rang in his ears. He thudded into the ground and, through a shrinking tunnel of darkness, saw the writhing, screaming boy carried out of sight; saw a pistol fall and clatter onto the cobbles; saw a shower of red; saw—nothing.

§

"Hold onto this," whispered a heavily-accented voice in his ear. A scrap of paper was pushed into his hand. His fingers closed around it automatically. For a moment he thought it had been handed to him by Arthur Findlay, and he knew the words written upon it.

John Speke had shot himself in the head.

Footsteps milling around.

Voices.

"Where you going, Gus?"

"Anywhere that I don't have to look at that mess!"

Hands lifting him, holding him upright; fingers wandering from pocket to pocket.

"Steady, old timer," said a hoarse voice.

Something moving in his belt.

"Bugger me, lookit this; anuvver pistol!" Deep voice.

"Let's see that!" Hoarse voice.

"Check if it's loaded." Whiny voice.

The sound of running footsteps as someone departed in a hurry.

"Oy! Come back wiv that, you thievin' git!" Whiny voice.

"Ah, let the silly sod scarper; we'll catch up wiv 'im later." Deep voice.

"Hey, dad, you wiv us?" Whiny voice.

Burton opened his eyes.

A fat, greasy individual was supporting him by the left arm; a small pockmarked man, with legs distorted by rickets, held his right. People were standing around, holding candles or oil lamps, some looking at him, others staring at the mess on the cobbles where a butcher's cart had dropped its load of offal.

Except—

Burton doubled over and vomited for the fourth time that night.

The two men, Hoarse voice and Whiny voice, backed away, cursing.

The King's agent, remembering his disguise, straightened but kept his back hunched. He wiped his mouth with his sleeve and looked again at the ripped and shredded intestines and organs that were spread messily across the cobbles. His eyes followed their long bloody trail, past the outspread legs, across the torn thigh with its bone glinting wetly in the lamplight, and into the hollowed out ribcage.

Above tattered scraps of coat and shirt and skin, the glazed eyes of Montague Penniforth stared up through the fog at whatever lay beyond.

"It were the dog things," hissed Whiny voice.

A gaunt, elderly man limped forward. He had a peg-leg and three fingers missing from his right hand.

"Where are you from, Mister?" he said, in a surprisingly gentle voice.

"Mile End," mumbled Burton.

"You've been lucky; the dogs didn't kill you."

"They weren't dogs. And they took a little kid," said the King's agent, noticing the corpse of the child's companion.

"They always do. Why don't you get off 'ome? We'll sort this lot out."

"Sort it out? What do yer mean?"

"I mean we'll get rid o' the stiffs; beggin yer pardin if that fella was yer boy."

"What'll yer do with them?"

"The usual."

Burton knew what that meant: what was left of Monty would be thrown into the Thames.

He put a hand to his forehead.

How many deaths must he have on his conscience? First Lieutenant Stroyan in Berbera; then Speke, who must surely have died by now; and, tonight, Montague Penniforth.

He felt sick; he hadn't bargained for this; but what could he do? He couldn't call the police—or even an undertaker to come and collect Monty's remains. No matter how much he wanted the big cabbie to receive a decent burial—and Lord knows he'd willingly pay for it himself—there was no way to get the cadaver out of the East End without arousing suspicion; and if his disguise failed him, he himself would probably end up in the river.

His head throbbed. He felt wet blood in his hair.

He dropped his hand and clenched it; fingernails digging into his palm. In the other hand, something got in their way. The note from Findlay!

No, wait, not from Findlay—so, from whom?

He waited until Throaty voice, Whiny voice and Peg-leg were distracted, then surreptitiously unscrewed the paper and glanced at the words on it:

Mes yeux discernent mieux les choses que la puplart ici. Je vois à travers votre masque. Rencontrez moi vers la Thames, au bout de Mews Street dans moins d'une heure.

'My eyes are more discerning than most here. I see through your mask. Meet me at the Thames end of Mews Street within the hour.'

He put the note in his pocket and moved over to Peg-leg's side.

"'Ere, mate, I gotta get to Mews Street" he grumbled in a low voice. "Which way is it?"

"What's yer business there?" asked Peg-leg, his rheumy eyes looking Burton up and down.

"*My* business, that's what!" responded Burton.

"Alright fella, no need to get shirty. That alley over there; take it down to the river then turn right 'n' follow the bank-side road 'til you come to a pawn shop what's closed an' boarded up. That's the corner of Mews Street. You gonna be alright on your own? You know your shooter got pinched?"

"Yus, the thievin' bastards. I'll manage, matey. Me bruvver is expectin' me an' I'm already a good five hours late!"

"Stopped off at a boozer, hey?"

"Yus."

"Sorry abaht yer boy, dad. Fucking bad way to go."

Burton forced himself to give a heartless East End shrug and moved away, shuffling into the clouded mouth of the alley that the one-legged man had indicated. The increasing distance between himself and Penniforth strained behind him; stretched to snapping point—but didn't snap. It, like Stroyan's death and like Speke's suicide, would pull at his heart for the rest of his life; he knew that; and he realised the commission he'd received from Palmerston— to be "King's agent"—carried with it a terribly heavy price.

The alley was cramped, almost entirely devoid of light, and ran crookedly down a slight slope toward the river. Burton kept his fingers on the right-hand wall and allowed it to guide him. He repeatedly stumbled over prone bodies. Some cursed when his foot struck them; others moaned; most remained silent.

His mouth felt sour with vomit and alcohol. The toxic fog burned his eyes and nostrils. He wanted to go home and forget this disastrous expedition. He wanted to forget *all* his disastrous expeditions.

Dammit Burton! Settle down! Become consul in Fernando Po, Brazil, Damascus and wherever the fuck else they send you! Write your damned books!

He walked on, and when a man stepped into his path and said "'Oo do we 'ave 'ere then?" Burton didn't reply or miss a step but simply rammed a fist as hard as he could into the man's stomach.

He kept going, leaving the wretch laying in the foetal position behind him.

Every few yards, his hand fell away from the wall as he encountered junctions with other passages. Each time, he walked ahead keeping his arm outstretched until he came to the opposite corner. Eventually, instead of a corner, he found railings spanning his path, and by the intensity of the stench realised that he'd crossed the Thames-side road and was beside the river. He returned to the other side of the street, found the wall, and staggered on in a westward direction.

As he pushed on through the bilious fog, the fumes seeped into his bloodstream, starving his brain of oxygen. He began to feel a familiar sensation; a feeling which had haunted his malarial deliriums in Africa. It was the notion that he was a divided identity; that two persons existed within him, ever fighting to thwart and oppose each other.

The death of Penniforth became their battlefield. Pervading guilt struggled with a savage desire for revenge; the impulse to flee from this King's agent role wrestled with the determination to find out where the loup-garous came from and why they were, apparently, abducting children.

"Monsieur!"

The word was hissed from a doorway.

Burton stopped and fought a sudden wave of dizziness. He could just about make out a figure crouched in a rectangle of denser shadow.

"Monsieur!" came the whisper again.

"Doré?" he said, softly.

"Oui, Monsieur."

Burton moved into the doorway and said, in French:

"How did you recognise me, Doré?"

"Pah! You think you can fool an artist's eye with a dab of stage make-up and a toupee? I have seen your picture in the newspaper, Monsieur Burton. I could not mistake you; those sullen eyes; the cheekbones; the fierce mouth. You have the brow of a god and the jaw of a devil!"

Burton grunted.

"What are you doing here, Doré? The East End is no place for a Frenchman."

"I am not merely a Frenchman; I am an artist."

"And you possess a cast iron stomach if you can put up with the stink of this place."

"I have grown used to it."

In the absence of anything but the dimmest of lights—from three red blemishes floating over the nearby river bank; perhaps the lights of a merchant vessel or barge—Burton could barely see the Frenchman. He had a vague impression of rags, a long beard and wild hair.

"You look like an old vagrant."

"Mais oui! I owe my survival to that fact! They think I possess nothing, so they leave me alone, and quietly and secretly I draw them. But you, Monsieur; why are you in the Cauldron? It is because of the loup-garous, no?"

"Yes. I've been commissioned to find out where they come from and what they are doing."

"Where they come from I do not know—but what they are doing?—they are stealing the chimney sweeps."

"They're doing *what*?"

"Mais je te jure que c'est vrai! These loup-garous, they are most particular. They take children but not *any* children; just the boys who work as sweeps."

"Why the devil would werewolves kidnap chimney sweeps?"

"This question I cannot answer. You should see The Beetle."

"Who—or what—is The Beetle?"

"He is the president of the League of Chimney Sweeps."

"They have a league?"

"Oui, Monsieur. I regret, though, that I know not where you should look for the boy."

"My young friend Quips might know."

"He is a sweep?"

"No, a newsboy."

"Ah, oui oui, he will know. These children, they—what is the expression?—'stick together,' no? I have heard that a word given to one is passed to the next and the next and spreads across your Empire faster than a fire through a dry forest."

"It's true. Anything else, Monsieur Doré? You know nothing of where the loup-garous come from?"

"Mais no. I can tell you that they have been hunting here for two months and that their raids now come every night, but I can tell you no more. I must go. It is late and I am tired."

"Very well. Thank you for your time, Monsieur. Please be careful. I understand that art is your life, but I would not like to hear that you had died for it."

"You will not. I am nearly finished here. The sketches I have taken, Monsieur Burton; they will make me *famous*!"

"I'll keep an eye open for your work," replied Burton. "Tell me, how can I get out of the Cauldron?"

"Keep going along this road; that way—" He pointed, a vague motion in the darkness. "It is not far. You will come to the bridge."

"Thank you. Goodbye, Monsieur Doré. Be safe."

"Au revoir, Monsieur Burton."

§

It was past five in the morning by the time Sir Richard Francis Burton collapsed onto his bed and into a deep sleep.

After his meeting with the French artist, he'd made his way past the Tower of London, following the fog-dulled cacophony of the ever-awake London Docks, until he reached London Bridge. He'd then walked northward away from the Thames. As the river receded behind him, the murk thinned somewhat and a greater number of working gas lamps enabled him to better get his bearings. He trudged all the way to Liverpool Street and there waved down a hansom of the old horse-pulled variety.

At home, under the conviction that his malaria was about to flare up again, he'd dosed himself with quinine before divesting himself of the disguise and washing the soot from his face. Then, gratefully, he slid between crisp, clean sheets and fell into a deep sleep.

He dreamed of Isabel.

It was a strange dream. He was standing on a low rocky hill overlooking Damascus and a black horse was pounding up the slope toward him, its hooves drumming noisily on the ground. As it came closer, he saw that it was ridden by Isabel, who was wrapped in Arabian clothing and rode not as a woman, side-saddle, but as a man. She radiated strength and happiness.

The animal skidded to a halt and reared before coming to rest in front of him, its sweat-flecked sides heaving.

Isabel reached up and pulled aside her veil.

"Hurry, Dick; you'll be late!" she urged, in her deep contralto voice.

From behind him he heard a distant noise, a clacking. He wanted to turn to see what it was but she stopped him.

"No! There's no time! You have to come with me!"

The sound was drawing closer.

"Dick! Come on!"

Now he noticed that there was a second horse, tethered to Isabel's. She gestured at it, urging him to mount.

Clack! Clack! Clack! Clack!

What *was* that? He started to turn.

"No Dick! No!"

Clack! Clack! Clack! Clack!

He twisted and looked up at the hill behind him. A freakish figure was bounding down it, approaching fast, taking huge leaps.

Clack! Clack! Clack! Clack!

The sound of its stilts hitting the rock.

Isabel screamed.

The thing gave an insane and triumphant yell, its red eyes blazing.

Burton awoke with a start and sat up.

Clack! Clack! Clack! Clack!

A moment's disorientation, then he recognised the sound; someone was hammering at the front door. He glanced at the pocket watch on his bedside table as he dragged himself out of the warm sheets. It was seven o'clock. He'd been asleep for less than two hours.

He threw his *jubbah* around himself; the long and loose outer garment he'd worn while on his pilgrimage to Mecca, which he now used as a night robe, and headed down the stairs.

Mrs Angell reached the front door before him and he could hear her indignant tones as he descended.

"Have you come to arrest him? No? Then your business can wait until a more civilised hour!" she was saying.

"I'm most dreadfully sorry, ma'am," came a male voice, "but it's a police emergency. Captain Burton's presence is required."

"Where?" demanded Burton, as he reached the last flight of stairs and started down them.

"Ah, Captain!" exclaimed the visitor, a young constable, stepping into the hall.

"Sir!" objected Mrs Angell.

"It's alright, Mother," said Burton. "Come in Constable—?"

"Kapoor, sir."

"Come up to my study. Mrs Angell, back to bed with you."

The old woman looked from one man to the other.

"Should I make a pot of tea first?"

Burton glanced enquiringly at Kapoor but the constable shook his head and said, "There's no time, sir; but thank you, ma'am."

The landlady bobbed and returned to her basement domain while the two men climbed the stairs and entered the study.

Burton made to light the fire but the policeman stopped him with a gesture.

"Would you dress as fast as possible, please, Captain Burton? Spring Heeled Jack has attacked again!"

§

Chapter 8

Marvel's Wood

"Detective-Inspector Trounce would like you at the scene as quickly as possible, Captain," said Constable Kapoor. "I have a rotorchair waiting for you outside."

"Where did the attack occur?" asked Burton.

"Near Chislehurst. I'll wait here, sir."

Without further ado, Burton raced up to his bedroom, poured water from a jug into a basin and splashed it onto his face, scrubbing away the last vestiges of soot, before hurriedly dressing. His body was aching after having maintained an old man's posture for so many hours, and his mind felt sluggish from lack of sleep, though he knew from past experience that it would clear soon enough. He had the ability to defer sleep when necessary, often going for days at a time without any before then taking to his bed for a prolonged bout of unconsciousness.

He joined Constable Kapoor on the first landing and they descended to the hall, where Burton put on his overcoat and top hat and picked up his cane. At the policeman's recommendation, he wrapped a scarf around his throat. They left the house.

The sun had risen and was sending lazy shafts of light into the pale yellow fog. Black flakes were suspended in the pall; neither falling nor swirling about.

Two rotorchairs waited at the side of the road. Burton was surprised he hadn't heard them land but then remembered his dream and the sound of hooves thudding up the hill.

"One was flown by me; the other by another constable who's gone back to the Yard," explained Kapoor. "Have you been in one before?"

"No."

"It's quite simple to operate, Captain," said the policeman, and, as they came to the nearest rotorchair, he quickly ran through the controls.

Burton inspected the contraption. It looked like a big studded leather armchair such as could be found in gentlemen's clubs and private libraries. It was affixed to a sled-like frame of polished wood and brass, the runners of which curled up gracefully at either end. In the forward part of this frame, from a control box situated just in front of a foot-board, three levers, similar to those found in railway signal boxes, but curved, angled back to the driver's position. The middle lever controlled altitude, while those to either side of it steered the vehicle to the left or right. The foot-board, when pressed forward with the toes, increased the rotorchair's velocity and forward motion; when pressed backward with the heels, slowed the vehicle; and when pushed all the way back, caused it to hover.

Affixed to the the back of the chair, a vaguely umbrella-like canopy protected the driver from the down-draft caused by the four short, flat and wide wings which rotated at the top of a shaft rising from the engine; this situated behind the chair. This engine was a larger version of the ones used for velocipedes and operated with the same remarkable efficiency.

Kapoor handed Burton a pair of round leather-lined goggles.

"You'll need to wear these, Captain, and you'll have to fly hatless unless you want to lose your topper. There's a storage compartment under the seat. Put it there with your cane, then we'll get going."

Burton did as advised, then climbed into the chair and secured himself with the belt attached to it.

"I'll ascend first. I'll wait for you above the fog," said the constable. He moved to the back of the vehicle and the explorer heard him fiddling with the engine, which coughed into life and started to quietly chug, making the seat vibrate.

Moments later, a second engine spluttered and roared, its pitch and volume increasing rapidly, to be joined seconds later by a rattling thrum, like the noise of a snare drum.

The fog rolled away, revealing a wide expanse of Montagu Place. A gentleman, suddenly exposed on the opposite pavement, clutched at the brim of his hat.

The racket faded upward and tendrils of vapour came snaking back toward Burton.

He allowed a minute to pass then took hold of the middle lever and gently pulled it while simultaneously pressing his toes down softly on the footboard.

The wings above his head jerked, turned, began to rotate, then suddenly transformed into a circular blur.

The fog whipped away again.

The rotorchair scraped over the cobbles then slid into the air. The ground dropped away and vanished as the mist closed up beneath the vehicle.

Strangely, there was very little sense of movement.

Entombed in the cloud, Burton felt as if he'd been transported to Limbo, until suddenly his rotorchair burst out of it and he was dazzled by the low morning sun. Grabbing at the left lever, he yanked it to turn the vehicle away from the blazing orb. The rotorchair gyrated crazily. He clutched at the right lever; struggled to stabilise the car; and eventually got it under control.

The blanket of fog stretched from horizon to horizon. Though dirty, it was made eye-wateringly bright by the sun.

Burton experimented with the controls until he felt comfortable with them then turned the rotorchair slowly until it faced Constable Kapoor's machine. A column of steam, like an umbilical cord, streamed from the policeman's vehicle to the cloud below.

For a moment they hovered, facing each other, then the policeman banked his machine and flew off in a south easterly direction. Burton followed the leading vehicle's white plume. He took deep breaths of the wonderfully fresh air, feeling his tiredness dissipate as the oxygen cleaned out the night's contaminations.

The rotorchairs picked up speed and flew across the enshrouded city; over Soho, the Thames and Waterloo Bridge, Elephant and Castle, Peckham, and on to Lewisham, where the thick pall below started to break up, revealing glimpses of houses, streets and gardens.

Burton had never flown before and he was thoroughly enjoying the sensation. He thought of John Speke sitting in a box kite being towed by a giant swan over East Africa and felt a pang of jealousy—then intense regret. Bismillah! It was only three days ago that he'd learned John had shot himself!

Soon, woods and tracks of cultivated land started to separate the clumps of houses and the fog retreated, reduced to a white mist, which lay in heavier ribbons along the courses of rivers, canals and streams.

The rotorchair ahead of Burton started to lose altitude. He gently pushed the middle lever and felt his own machine sink.

They flew on for a mile, past the outskirts of Chislehurst, then Kapoor angled his machine slightly more eastward and descended, with Burton following. They landed in a field near cottages on the edge of a village, which Burton would later learn was named Mickleham. There were six rotorchairs already parked on the grass beside a mud-caked traction engine to which a plough was attached.

Even before the wings of Kapoor's rotorchair had stopped spinning, the young constable was out of it and sprinting across the grass to where a couple of policemen stood by a garden gate outside a ramshackle old dwelling. He spoke to them briefly then came running back, reaching Burton just as he stepped out of his machine.

"No!" he shouted above the noise of the engines. "We have to go up again!"

"Why; what's happening?"

"Spring Heeled Jack is still in the area! They've chased him northward. We'll have to circle; see if we can spot anything. We'll spread out and fly low, Captain; cover as much ground as we can. Look out for a group of villagers and policemen—but keep me in sight and head my way if you see me land!"

Burton jumped back into the rotorchair, buckled himself in and powered up the wings.

He took off and followed Kapoor. The vapour trails they'd made on their way to the field were still hanging in the air.

Burton bore to the west until the other machine was a mere speck in the sky off to his right, with an irregular white line extending out behind it. They flew back past Chislehurst, the King's agent peering at the landscape to the right, left, and ahead.

Five minutes later he saw figures gathered on a golf course. He steered his rotorchair toward it and, as he approached and descended, saw that it was a crowd of constables and townspeople. The latter were milling about, brandishing shovels and broom handles.

People scattered as he landed the machine, thudding into the grass rather too heavily.

A burly man came running over; it was Detective-Inspector Trounce.

"Captain Burton!" he yelled. "It's gone into Marvel's Wood, there!"—he waved his cane at a wide expanse of forest on the eastern edge of the course— "Fly over, see if you can drive it out!"

The King's agent nodded and took to the air again.

As his machine slid over the trees, he flew it as low as he dared, sending loose leaves flying in every direction as branches whipped about beneath the rotorchair's downdraught.

Leaning over the side, Burton scanned the woods below, seeing flashes of the ground through the foliage. He passed at a slow speed around the outer part of the wood then began to spiral inward.

Despite his heavy overcoat, he was feeling cold. The past few days had pushed his body too far; he'd been drunk, attacked and beaten; had spent an entire night in the noxious atmosphere of the East End; and had slept a mere two hours. The quinine he'd taken last night might stave off a malarial attack but he was nevertheless concerned; he needed proper rest.

Something moved below but he'd flown past before he could see what it was. He dug his heels into the footboard, bringing the rotorchair to a stop, then turned it around to face the way he'd come. To avoid flying back into his machine's trail of steam, he reduced his altitude until the runners were brushing the top of the trees, then inched it forward while looking down through the agitated branches.

Burton was leaning over the right side when the rotorchair suddenly lurched heavily to the left, shaking horribly as the wings sliced into twigs and leaves. His toes instinctively pressed hard on the footboard and he yanked back the middle lever, sending the rotorchair soaring upward, spinning wildly on its axis. As he fought with the levers, he became aware, through the edge of his goggles, of a large shape clinging to the side of the machine, unbalancing it.

He turned his head and looked into the eyes of Spring Heeled Jack.

The creature's mouth was moving as if shouting something but, though its face was very close to Burton's, the words were obliterated by the roar of the engines and drumming of the wings. It reached out and grabbed his wrist.

The rotorchair spiralled downward.

Burton struggled to free himself but everything was happening too fast. He'd barely registered the presence of Spring Heeled Jack before the rotorchair plunged into the woods, keeling over sideways, its wings snapping and shooting away, one arcing high into the air, the others clattering through the branches.

The vehicle twisted and tumbled, knocking its driver this way and that as it fell through the foliage, hit the ground back-end first, then toppled onto its side and came to rest.

Steam screamed through a rent in its boiler and Burton, shaken but conscious enough to fear an explosion, fumbled with the buckle straps, finally released them, and crawled out of and away from the machine.

He lay panting, face down in the loam.

Rustling footsteps approached and, as Burton rolled over onto his back, a foot—or, rather, a stilt—was placed to either side of him.

Spring Heeled Jack, light dappling his face, stood astride the King's agent and gazed down at him. He squatted.

"Who are you?" the creature asked.

Blue flame formed a corona around its head; sparks spat from its chest. The eyes blazed with madness.

"You know damned well who I am," said Burton.

"I don't. I've never seen you before, though I must admit, I feel I should know you."

"Never seen me! You gave me this damned black eye!"

Even as he said it, though, Burton thought about Trounce's suggestion that there might be more than one of the stilted creatures. "Or maybe that was your brother?" he added.

The creature grinned.

"I don't have a brother. I don't even have parents!"

It threw back its head and let loose a peal of insane laughter, then looked down and ran its eyes over Burton's face.

"Where have I seen you before?" it muttered. "Famous, are you?"

"Comparatively," answered Burton. He started using his feet and elbows to shift himself out from between Spring Heeled Jack's stilts but the thing reached down and grasped the front of his coat.

"Stay still," it commanded. "Yes, I know you now. Sir Richard Francis Burton! One of the great Victorians!"

"What the hell is a Victorian?"

Shouts sounded in the distance—the police and townspeople approaching—and, beyond them, the thrum of Constable Kapoor's rotorchair.

"Listen Burton," hissed Jack. "I have no idea why you're here but you have to leave me alone to do what I have to do. I know it's not a good thing but I don't mean the girls any harm. If you or anyone else stops me, I can't get back and I won't be able to repair the damage. Everything will stay this way—and it's wrong! It's all wrong! This is not the way things are meant to be! Do you understand?"

Burton shook his head.

"Not in the slightest. Let me up, damn it!"

Jack hesitated then released his grip.

Burton slid from between the stilts and scrambled to his feet, looking up at the strange apparition.

Spring Heeled Jack was a man, he could see that now, but his costume was bizarre and there was an unearthly air about him.

"So what exactly is it you need to do?" he asked the stilt-walker.

"Restore, Burton! Restore!"

"Restore what?"

"Myself. You. Everything! Do you honestly think the world should have talking orang-utans in it? Isn't it obvious to you that something is desperately wrong?"

"Talking orang—?" began Burton.

"Captain Burton!" interrupted a distant shout. Detective-Inspector Trounce.

The chopping of Kapoor's rotorchair was close now.

Jack looked up through the canopy of leaves overhead.

"The mist has cleared and the sun is high enough. I should be able to recharge."

"Charge at what? You're speaking in riddles, man!" barked the King's agent.

"Time to go," muttered Jack, then suddenly burst into laughter. "Time to go!"

Burton leaped at him but Jack sidestepped swiftly and the explorer crashed past, landing in a tangle of roots. He rolled to his feet just as Jack flashed by and made off into the trees.

"Bloody hell!" cursed Burton, and set off in pursuit.

Despite having to duck under low branches, his quarry moved fast, taking long loping strides, while Burton was hampered by projecting roots, tangled vines and his own exhaustion. He managed to keep up until Jack burst out of the trees onto the golf course some way north of where the police and townsfolk were milling about; there Jack started to bound ahead on his spring-loaded stilts.

A police whistle blew and a roar went up from the crowd, which, waving makeshift weapons, surged after the strangely-costumed man.

Burton stopped and watched, puzzled.

Rather than running away, Spring Heeled Jack seemed to be circling the golf course, almost as if he were toying with his pursuers. Only Constable Kapoor, in his rotorchair, could keep pace with him, but there was little he could do but follow.

"What the devil are you playing at?" muttered Burton, as Jack, who'd receded into the distance, turned southward and hopped along the edge of the course before then changing direction to race north eastward, back toward Burton, who stood on the border of the wood.

The King's agent ran out to intercept him only to have Jack spring a clear fifteen feet over his head.

"Stay out of it, Burton!" shouted the stilt man

He took six long bounds, then suddenly launched himself high into the air until, twenty feet up, and just in front of Kapoor's rotorchair, he vanished.

Burton had the impression of some sort of bubble momentarily forming around Jack, its edge touching the front of the flying machine. When it, and the stilt man, disappeared, so did part of the vehicle.

The rotorchair flew apart and, leaving a spiralling ribbon of steam behind it, plunged to the ground, which it hit with an appalling crash. The boiler exploded and pieces of metal went spinning into the air.

From different directions, Burton, Trounce, and a number of constables ran over to the wreckage.

Constable Kapoor's broken body dangled from the upside-down seat, his expression frozen in shock, blood streaming from his torn body down his neck, across his face, over his motionless eyes, and into his hair from whence it dribbled onto the ripped turf.

"God damn it," breathed Detective-Inspector Trounce, leaning with both hands upon his cane. "He was going to be promoted next week."

He stood deep in thought for a moment then shook himself and spoke to a nearby constable.

"Bennett, fetch Sergeant Piper, would you?"

The constable nodded and moved away.

"What the blazes is that thing, Captain Burton?" asked Trounce.

"A man, of that I'm certain," responded the famous explorer. "And a madman, at that."

"The same as I saw at assassination?"

"It can't be; it didn't appear old enough."

"Great heavens, this is too bizarre! What happened in the woods?"

"He spoke nonsense; said I was a Victorian."

"What's that?"

"I haven't the vaguest idea, though it's fair to assume it has something to do with the late queen. He said that if we stop him doing what he needs to do, everything will stay this way; and what he needs to do is 'restore.'"

"Restore what?"

"'Myself. You. Everything,' whatever that means. Then he mentioned talking orang-utans and said he had to charge at something again."

Trounce shrugged.

"None of it makes any sense! It's the ravings of a lunatic!"

"I don't disagree," said Burton.

Trounce turned to an approaching police sergeant who saluted smartly.

"Ah, Piper, the men seem to have the crowd under control."

"Yes, sir. I think they'll be off to their homes soon, now that the jumping man has gone."

"Good. Good. I want you to post a couple of men here and organise for poor Kapoor to be transported to the morgue."

"Right you are, sir. He was a fine man. I'll see to it that he's not left here any longer than needs be."

"Thank you. Captain Burton, would you come with me please? There are a couple of police velocipedes over by the club house; we'll ride them back to Mickleham. I want you to meet the girl who was attacked. Oh, and by the way, Sir Richard Mayne assigned me to the Spring Heeled Jack case, and I suspect I'm indebted to you for that. My gratitude."

"Best man for the job," said Burton, succinctly. "Wait a moment while I retrieve my hat and cane."

He returned to his stricken rotorchair for the items, then rejoined Trounce, who sent four constables into the woods to drag the vehicle out.

The two men started toward the club house.

"Who's the girl?" asked Burton.

"Her name is Angela Tew. Fifteen years old. That's about as much as I know at the moment. Before dawn this morning a parakeet arrived at Scotland Yard. It'd been sent by Mickleham's bobby and stated that the girl had been attacked by the fabled Spring Heeled Jack. I was roused from my bed at about a quarter past six and dashed down here with a few men by rotorchair, having first sent Kapoor to fetch you. When we got here the villagers were on the rampage. They'd spotted Jack loitering at the edge of a field and chased him around the outskirts of Chislehurst and as far as Marvel's Wood. We ran along with them. Idiot that I am, I left the rotorchairs parked in Mickleham and by the time I realised how useful they'd be, it was too late to go back for them. I'm still not accustomed to the damned things, Captain. If I'd had horses, I'd have employed them without a second thought, but, frankly, this new technology is difficult for a traditional old bobby like me to cope with. Anyway, you arrived just as we reached the golf course. So now let's see the girl and find out what happened."

"It's strange," mused Burton, as they came to the club house and approached a line of police velocipedes which, guarded by a constable, were parked outside it. "He has this supernatural ability to vanish into thin air, which I've witnessed twice now, so why didn't he do so straight away?"

"I have no idea," answered Trounce, then said to the policeman: "Constable, I have to commandeer a couple of penny farthings."

"That's quite all right, sir; help yourself," replied his subordinate.

Burton stepped to one of the boneshakers and unclipped a small bellows from the side of its furnace. He inserted the nozzle into a valve and started pumping until steam began to vent from another valve set in the small boiler just below the engine. Then he placed the bellows back in its holder, twisted a toggle switch on the engine and gave the small wheel beside it a couple of turns. The piston rod jerked and smoke puffed from the two tall, thin funnels.

He heard the whine of the gyroscope and kicked the parking stand up; the velocipede didn't need it any more.

Holding onto the frame, Burton placed his left foot on the lower mounting bar, heaved himself up, swung himself between the front wheel and the funnels, slipped his right foot into the right stirrup, then boosted himself up into the saddle and put his left foot into the left stirrup. It was done in one smooth motion and, though the penny farthing rocked, the gyroscope kept it stable.

He looked to his right and saw that Trounce had also mounted and was in the act of slipping his cane into the holder that was affixed to the vehicle's frame.

Both men released the brakes. The piston arms moved slowly at first but rapidly picked up speed, the crank pins whirled, steam hissed, the men engaged the gears, and the velocipedes went panting into the road.

"Spring Heeled Jack made mention of the fact that the mist had cleared and the sun was up," called Burton, as they clattered toward Mickleham, "It seemed significant to him."

"Are you suggesting that he can't vanish at night?" returned Trounce.

"No. Remember, the first time I saw him he *did* vanish at night!"

"Then what?"

"I don't know!"

"This business presents one confounded puzzle after another!" exclaimed Trounce.

They came to the outskirts of Chislehurst, rode through the town, now a-bustle with the morning market, out the other side, and down a country lane toward the village.

The mist had dispersed entirely and the sky was a jumbled mass of clouds with patches of blue sky occasionally peeking through.

From the brow of a low hill, Burton recognised Mickleham ahead, and a few minutes later he and Detective-Inspector Trounce parked their velocipedes at the side of the same field the King's agent had landed in earlier that morning.

The two constables were still on duty by the gate of the ramshackle cottage. It was to this that Trounce led Burton.

The Yard man knocked on the front door and it was opened by a man in corduroy trousers, shirt and braces, with tousled hair, long sideburns, and wire-framed spectacles.

"Police?" he asked, in a lowered voice.

"Yes, sir. I'm Detective-Inspector Trounce of Scotland Yard. This is my associate, Captain Burton. You are Mr Tew?"

"Yes. Edward. Come in."

They stepped across the threshold and found that the door opened directly into a fairly cramped and low-roofed sitting room. On a threadbare sofa, a pretty young girl lay within her mother's protective embrace. The woman was large, matronly, tearful and shaking uncontrollably. The girl was wide-eyed and, thought Burton, rather too thin.

"Angela, these are policemen from London," said Edward Tew, gently.

"She can't speak. She's too upset," interrupted the mother. "I know what she feels! I know!"

"Quiet now, Tilly," said Tew. "The girl is calm enough now. Go make a pot of tea; give the gentlemen room to sit down."

"No! Leave her alone. I—she—she can't talk!"

"Yes I can, mother," whispered the girl.

The woman turned and kissed her daughter's cheek; held her hands.

"Are you sure? You don't have to. It'll just be questions, questions, questions!"

"Tilly, please!" snapped Edward Tew.

"It's alright, mother," whispered the girl.

With a sniff and lowered eyes, the mother nodded, stood and left the room.

"Sit with your daughter, Mr Tew," said Trounce, gesturing to the sofa as he lowered himself onto a wooden chair next to a small table on which a vase of flowers stood.

Tew did so, while Burton sat in the one armchair.

"Now then; it's Angela, isn't it?" the detective asked, in a kindly voice.

"Yes, sir," answered the girl, quietly.

"Would you tell me what happened? Try not to miss anything out. Every detail is important."

Angela Tew nodded, and her throat worked compulsively for a moment.

"I work as maid for the Longthorns, sir; them what lives in the grand old house on St. Paul's Wood Hill. I was a-going there this morning and left here at—at—"

"At about ten to five," put in her father. "She works from five in the morning until two in the afternoon. Go on, Angey."

"So I took me the short cut through Hoblingwell Wood."

"Isn't it rather dark at that time of morning?" asked Trounce. "Dark, I mean, to be wandering through the woods?"

"It's very dark, sir, aye, but the path is straight and I takes an oil lamp with me to light the way. I goes that way all the time, I does."

"And what happened?"

"I was a good way along the path when a man stepped out from the trees. I couldn't see him properly, so I lifted the lamp and I says: 'Who's that there?' Then I saw he was very tall and had big long legs like one of them circus folks what walks on sticks. I tells you, sir, round here we all know the stories about the ghost what's called Spring Heeled Jack and I ain't stupid. I saw what he was and recognised him straight off from the tales. So I turned and started a-running as fast as I could but I hardly got two steps afore he grabbed me up from behind and clapped his hand over me mouth. Then he—he—"

She put her arm across her face, hiding her eyes in her elbow. "I can't say it, father!"

Edward Tew patted his daughter's back and looked pleadingly at Detective-Inspector Trounce. The Yard man nodded and Tew took up the story.

"Jumping Jack took the neck of her dress at the front and ripped it down to her waist, taking her underclothes with it. He turned her and bent her backward, putting his face—" A muffled sob came from the girl and Tew blinked rapidly, his mouth opening and closing. He looked at his two visitors and touched the middle of his chest.

"Here," he whispered.

Burton clenched his jaw. The girl was only fifteen!

She looked up suddenly, and angrily smeared the tears from her cheeks with the heels of her hands.

"He bent me backward until I thought I might break in half. Then he let me up a little, looked into me face with them terrible eyes of his, and he said: 'Not you.'"

The King's agent leaned forward eagerly.

"Miss Tew, this is very important: are you absolutely sure that's what he said?"

She nodded.

"Clear as a bell it was. 'Not you!' he said. Then he let go of me and hopped away like a horrible big cricket."

"Before you screamed?"

"Yes. I didn't give voice, sir, until I was at the garden gate. I was a-running too hard."

Burton and Trounce looked at one another.

"Did he say anything else?" asked Burton, turning back to the girl.

"Nothing, sir."

"Can you describe him for me?"

The girl gave a description that exactly matched the man Burton had just encountered in Marvel's Wood.

A few minutes later, the two men left the cottage. As he stepped out, Burton cast a glance back and saw the mother, Tilly Tew, standing in the opposite doorway. She was looking at him with a strangely furtive expression on her face.

They opened the gate and walked back into the field.

"Odd," said Trounce. "In past attacks, he's always done a bunk after being interrupted. You'll remember the case of Mary Stevens, for example. She screamed, people came running, and Jack skedaddled."

"Probably not the same Jack, Inspector."

"Well, be that as it may, this time he put his hand over her mouth, the assault was conducted in relative silence and no one came to her assistance. Yet he didn't—for want of a better expression—go all the way. Instead, he tore her dress and got a good eyeful—but then let her go. Why?"

"He said 'Not you'—which suggests he was looking for a specific girl and got the wrong one. I have to get back to London. Can I take one of the rotorchairs?"

"Help yourself. Park it outside your house and I'll send a constable along for it later. What's your next move?"

"Sleep. I'm exhausted and my malaria is threatening to take hold. And you?"

"I'm going to talk some more with the Tew family. I'm looking for a link between his victims."

"Good man. We'll talk again soon, Trounce."

"I'm certain of it; our spring-heeled friend will be back, you can be sure of that. Where will he appear, though? That's the question. Where?"

"One more thing, Inspector," said Burton. "Pay close attention to the mother, Tilly. There was something about her expression when we left that leads me to suspect she knows more than she's letting on!"

§

Chapter 9

The Battersea Brigade

∽

CONQUER THYSELF, TILL THOU HAS DONE THIS, THOU ART BUT A SLAVE;
FOR IT IS ALMOST AS WELL TO BE SUBJECTED TO ANOTHER'S APPETITE AS TO THINE
OWN.
—SIR RICHARD FRANCIS BURTON

∽

By two o'clock that afternoon, Burton was back at work. He'd slept for a couple of hours, washed, dressed and eaten lunch, and had then sent two messages; one by runner to the Prime Minister requesting an audience; the other by parakeet to Swinburne asking him to call early this evening.

An hour later, a reply from 10 Downing Street landed on his windowsill.

"Message from that degenerate idle-headed lout Lord Palmerston. Come at once. Message ends."

"No reply," said Burton.

"Up your spout!" screeched the parakeet as it flew off.

Forty minutes later, Burton, having walked briskly through the thinning fog, which was still clinging to central London, was once again sitting opposite Lord Palmerston, who, while hurriedly scribbling notes in the margins of a document, spoke without looking up:

"What is it, Burton? I'm busy and I don't require progress reports. Just write up the case when it's done and send it to me."

"A man died."

"Who? How?"

"A cab driver named Montague Penniforth. He accompanied me to the East End and was there killed by a werewolf."

Palmerston looked up for the first time.

"A werewolf? You saw it?"

"I saw four. Penniforth was torn apart. I had no way to take care of his body without placing myself in jeopardy. He was a good man and didn't deserve an East End funeral."

"The Thames, you mean?"

"Yes." Burton clenched his fists. "I was a damned fool. I shouldn't have got him involved."

The Prime Minister lay his pen to one side and rested his hands in front of him with fingers entwined. He spoke in a slow and level tone:

"The commission you have received from His Majesty the King is a unique one. You must regard yourself as a commander in the field of battle and, on occasion, His Majesty's servants will be required to serve. It's highly likely, given the nature of your missions, that some of those servants will be killed or injured. They fall for the Empire."

"Penniforth was a cabbie not a soldier!" objected Burton.

"He was the King's servant, as are we all."

"And are all who fall while in his service to be dumped unceremoniously into the river like discarded slops?"

Palmerston pulled a sheet of paper from his desk drawer and wrote upon it. He slid it across to Burton.

"Wherever possible in such circumstances, get a message to this address. My team will come and clean up the mess. The fallen will be treated with respect. Funerals will be arranged and paid for. Widows will be granted a state pension."

The King's agent looked at the names written above the address.

"Burke and Hare!" he exclaimed. "Code names?"

"Actually, no; coincidence! The resurrectionist Burke was hanged in '29 and his partner, Hare, died a blind beggar ten years ago. My two agents, Damien Burke and Gregory Hare, are cut from an entirely different cloth. Good men, if a little gloomy in outlook."

"Montague Penniforth had a wife named Daisy and lived in Cheapside. That's all I know about him."

"I'll put Burke and Hare onto it. They'll soon find the woman and I'll see to it that she's provided for. I have a lot to do, Captain Burton. Are we finished?"

Burton stood. "Yes, sir."

"Then let us both get back to work."

Palmerston returned to his scribbling and Burton turned to leave. As he reached the door, the Prime Minister spoke again:

"You might consider taking an assistant."

Burton looked back but Lord Palmerston was bent over his document, writing furiously.

§

Propriety demands that young women do not visit the homes of bachelors without a chaperone but Isabel Arundell didn't give two hoots for propriety. She was well aware that Society was already looking down its ever-so-haughty nose at her because she'd accompanied her fiancé to Bath and stayed in the same hotel as him, though, heaven forbid, not in the same room. Now she was wilfully breaking another taboo by visiting him at his home independently— and not for the first time.

Her wilful destruction of her own reputation bothered her not a bit, for she knew that when she and Richard were married they'd leave the country to live abroad. He would work as a government consul and she would gather around herself a new group of friends, preferably non-English, among whom she'd be considered an exotic bloom; a delicate rose among the darker and, she imagined, rather less sophisticated blossoms of Damascus or, perhaps, South America.

She had it all worked out, and, generally, what Isabel Arundell wanted, Isabel Arundell got.

When she arrived at 14 Montagu Place that afternoon, she was reluctantly allowed into the house by Mrs Angell, who had the brazen effrontery, in Isabel's opinion, to ask whether the "young miss" was sure this visit was entirely wise. The kindly old dame then suggested that if Isabel was determined to go through with it, then perhaps she—Mrs Angell—should remain at her side throughout, to satisfy social mores.

Isabel impatiently dismissed the well-meant offer and, without further ado, she marched up the stairs and entered the study.

Burton was slumped in his saddlebag armchair by the fire, wrapped in his *jubbah*, smoking one of his disreputable cheroots and staring into the room's thick blue haze of tobacco smoke. He'd been there since his return from Downing Street an hour ago and had barely moved a muscle. His mind was far away and he was completely unaware that Isabel had entered.

"For goodness' sake, Dick," she chided, "I've stepped out of one fog and into another! If you must be—"

She stopped, gasped, and raised her gloved hands to her mouth, for she'd noticed that a yellowing bruise curved around one of his eyes, a livid and much darker one marked his left temple, there were scratches and grazes all over his face, and he looked somewhat as if the charge of the Light Brigade had galloped over him.

"What—what—what—?" she stuttered.

His eyes turned slowly toward her and she saw his pupils shrink into focus.

"Ah," he said, and stood. "Isabel, my apologies; I forgot you were coming."

"Your face, Dick!" she exclaimed, and she suddenly flung herself into his arms. "Your face! What on earth has happened!"

He kissed her forehead and stepped back, holding her at arm's length.

"Everything, Isabel. Everything has happened. My life seems to have changed in an instant! I have been commissioned by the King himself!"

"The King? Commissioned? Dick, I don't understand. And why are you bruised and cut so?"

"Sit down. I'll endeavour to explain. But, Isabel, you must prepare yourself. Remember the Arabic proverb I taught you: *in lam yakhun ma tureed, fa'ariid ma yakhoon.*"

She translated: "'When what you want doesn't happen, learn to want what does.'"

She sat and frowned and waited while he went to the bureau and poured her a tonic.

He returned and handed her the glass but remained standing. His expression was unreadable.

"The Foreign Office was going to offer me a consulship in Fernando Po," he began.

She interrupted: "Yes, I have sent many a letter to Lord Russell recommending you for just such a post. Though I requested Damascus."

"You did what?" he muttered in surprise. "You thought it acceptable to write to Lord Russell on my behalf without first consulting with me?"

"Don't be bullish, Dick. We've spoken about a consulship often. But, pray, tell me what happened to you!"

"In due course. And I should say there is a great difference between a conversation shared between us and a begging letter sent to a government minister."

"It was hardly that!" she cried.

"Be that as it may, you should neither speak nor write on my behalf unless expressly asked by me to do so."

"I was trying to help you!"

"And in doing so made it appear that I lacked the wherewithal to forward my own career. By myself perhaps I could have secured Damascus. As it is, your intervention earned me an invitation to Fernando Po. They offered me a governmental crumb when I wanted a governmental loaf. Do you know where Fernando Po is?"

"No," she whispered, a tear rolling down her cheek. This visit wasn't going at all as she had planned.

"It's a Spanish island off the west coast of Africa; an insignificant, disease-ridden flea-pit, widely regarded as 'the white man's graveyard.' A man who is made consul of Fernando Po is a man the Foreign Office wants out of the way. The fact that Lord Russell suggested it for me means only one thing: I have irritated him. Except, of course, I haven't. In fact, I've had no contact with him at all."

"It was me! It's my fault! Oh, I'm so sorry, Dick; I wanted only the best for you!"

"And achieved the worst," he noted, ruthlessly.

Isabel hid her face in her hands and wept.

"Isabel," said Burton softly. "When the king honoured me with a knighthood, I thought my future was secured—*our* future. Then came John's betrayal. Why he did it, I know not. He'd been a younger brother to me but he was weak and allowed himself to be manipulated by a malignant force. I'd striven like no man to make a name for myself: in India, I had to overcome disappointments and the jealous opposition of officers; in Arabia, I risked execution by taking the pilgrimage to Mecca; in Berbera, I was nearly killed by natives; and in central Africa, I almost died from illness and exhaustion. It all became worthless when he turned against me and tarnished my reputation. The things he suggested! By God! I should have horsewhipped him! But sentiment caused me to stay my hand and in that pause, the harm was done. When he shot himself, it might have been my head he levelled the gun at for all the damage it did me; for now, on top of all the malicious lies he'd told, I am blamed for his attempted suicide. On Monday, when I learned what he'd done, the Richard Burton you met in Boulogne ten years ago—the Burton you fell in love with—that man ceased to exist."

"No, Richard! Don't say that!" she wailed.

"It's true. You would have married a broken man—but for one thing."

"What?" she whimpered.

"That evening, I was physically assaulted."

Isabel blinked rapidly.

"You were attacked? By whom?"

"By a thing out of myth and folklore; by a seemingly supernatural being; by Spring Heeled Jack."

She stared at him wordlessly.

"It's true, Isabel. Then, on Tuesday morning, I was summoned by Palmerston and he offered me a post on behalf of the king. I have become a—well, there's no real name for it; Palmerston calls me the 'King's agent,' though 'investigator' or 'researcher' or even 'detective' might do just as well. One of my first commissions is to discover more about the very creature that assaulted me."

Isabel Arundell suddenly rose to her feet and crossed the room to one of the windows. She looked out of it as she spoke.

"This is poppycock, Dick," she snapped, decisively. "Has your malaria returned?"

He moved back to the bureau, beside her, and poured himself a glass of port.

"Do you mean to suggest that I might be delusional?"

There was a deep sadness in his voice. She swung around at the sound of it.

"Spring Heeled Jack is a children's story!"

"And if I were also to tell you that I've seen werewolves in London?"

"Werewolves! Richard! Listen to what you are saying!"

"I know how it sounds, Isabel, but I also know what I saw. Furthermore, a man died and it was my fault. It taught me a painful lesson: that this post I now hold brings with it immense danger, not just for me, but for those close to me, too."

"I can't—I can't—" she stammered. "Dear God! You mean to give me up?"

She clutched at her chest as if her heart were failing.

"You know what manner of man am I," he replied. "Discovery is my mania. Africa is closed to me now and, anyway, I have little desire for the ill-health that expeditions bring with them. The last almost killed me, and I would rather die on my feet than on my back. Besides, geographical exploration is but one form of discovery; there are others; and the king has given me the opportunity to use my mania in a fashion I had hitherto never imagined. I can—"

"Stop!" commanded Isabel. Her chin went up and her eyes flashed dangerously. "And what of me, Richard? Answer me that! What of me?"

Ignoring the great ache that suddenly gripped his heart, Sir Richard Francis Burton answered.

§

Despite her flaws, Burton loved Isabel, and despite his, she returned that love. She was meant to be his wife, that he could not dispute, yet he had defied Destiny and wilfully forced his life down a different path.

He was left empty and emotionless; yet he suddenly acquired a heightened self-awareness, too, and experienced an intensification of the feverish sensation that his personality was split.

As the afternoon gave way to early evening, he fell once again into a deep contemplation—almost a self-induced trance—under the spell of which he explored the presence of the invisible *doppelgänger* which seemed to occupy the same armchair as himself. Oddly, he found that he now associated this second Richard Burton not with the delirium of malaria but with Spring Heeled Jack.

He and his double, he intuitively recognised, existed at a point of divergence. To one of them, a path was open which led to Fernando Po, Brazil, Damascus and *"wherever the fuck else they send you."* For the other, the path was that of the King's agent, its destination shrouded.

The stilt-walker, Burton was certain, had somehow foreseen this choice. Jack, whatever he was, was not a spy, as he and Palmerston had initially suspected. Oh no, nothing so pedestrian as that! It wasn't just *what* the strangely-costumed man had said but also the *way* he'd said it that forced upon Burton the conception that Jack possessed an uncanny knowledge of his—Burton's—future; knowledge which could never be gained from spying, no matter how efficient.

In India, he'd seen much that defied rational thought. Human beings, he was convinced, possessed a "force of will" which could extend their senses beyond the limits of sight, hearing, taste or touch. Could it, he wondered, even transcend the restrictions of time? Was Spring Heeled Jack a true clairvoyant? If he was, then he obviously spent far too much time dwelling upon the future, for his grasp of the present seemed tenuous at best; he had expressed astonishment when Burton revealed that the Nile debate—and Speke's accident—had already occurred.

'I'm a historian!' he'd claimed. 'I know what happened. It was 1864 not 1861.'

Happened. Past tense, though he spoke of 1864, which was three years in the future.

Curious.

There was an obvious—though hard to accept—explanation for the discrepancies in Jack's perception of time: he simply wasn't of this world. The creature had, after all, twice vanished before Burton's very eyes and, back in 1840, had done the same in full view of Detective-Inspector Trounce. Plainly, this was a feat no mere mortal could achieve.

What's more, everything could be explained—Jack's inconsistent character and appearance; his confusion about time; his seeming to be in two places at once; his apparent agelessness—if it were accepted that he was a supernatural being whose habitat lay beyond the realms of normal time and space. Perhaps Burton's first impression had been correct: could he be an uncorked djinni? A demon? A malevolent spirit? Moko, the Congo's god of divination?

The King's agent emerged from his contemplation having come to two conclusions. The first was that, for the time being, the bizarre apparition should be treated as one being rather than as two or more. The second was that Time was a key element in understanding Spring Heeled Jack.

He stood and rubbed a crick out of his neck. As always, focusing his mind on one thing had helped him to forget another, and, though his meeting with Isabel had been painful, he wasn't immobilised by depression, as he'd sometimes been in the past. In fact, he was feeling surprisingly positive.

It was eight o'clock.

Burton crossed to the window and looked down at Montagu Place. The fog had reduced to a watery mist, liberally punctuated with coronas of light from gas lamps and windows. The usual hustle and bustle had returned to the streets of London; the rattling velocipedes, gasping steam-horses, old-fashioned horse-drawn vehicles, pantechnicons, and, above all, the seething mass of humanity.

Usually, when he looked upon such a scene, Burton, ever the outsider, felt a fierce longing for the wide open spaces of Arabia. This evening, though, there was an unfamiliar cosiness about London, almost a familiarity. He'd never felt this before. England had always seemed strange to him; stifling and repressive.

'I am changing,' he thought. 'I hardly know myself.'

A flash of red caught his attention: Swinburne stepping out of a hansom. The poet's arrival was signalled by shrill screams and cries as he squabbled with the driver over the fare. Swinburne had the fixed idea that the fare from one place in London to any other was a shilling, and would argue hysterically with any cabbie who said otherwise—which they all did. On this occasion, as so often happened, the driver, embarrassed by the histrionics, gave up and accepted the coin.

Swinburne came bobbing across the street with that peculiar dancing gait of his.

He jangled the front doorbell.

'Everyone uses the bell,' thought Burton, 'except policemen. They knock.'

Moments later, Burton heard Mrs Angell's voice and the piping tones of Algernon, footsteps on the stairs, and the staccato rap of a cane of his study door.

He turned from the window and called "Come in, Algy!"

Swinburne bounced in and enthusiastically announced: "Glory to Man in the highest! For Man is the master of things."

"And what's prompted that declaration?" enquired Burton.

"I just saw one of the new rotorships! It was huge! How godlike we have become that we can send tonnes of metal gliding through the air! My hat! You've acquired new bruises! Was it Jack again? I saw in the evening edition that he pounced on a girl in the early hours."

"A rotorship? What did it look like? I haven't seen one yet."

Swinburne threw himself into an armchair, hooking a leg over its arm.

He placed his top hat onto the end of his cane, held up the stick and made the hat spin.

"A vast platform, Richard; flat and oval shaped; with a great many pylons extending horizontally from its edge, and, at their ends, vertical shafts at the tip of which great wings were spinning so fast that only a circular blur was visible. It was leaving an enormous trail of steam. Did he beat you up again?"

"On its way to India, perhaps," mused Burton.

"Yes, I should think so. But listen to this: it had propaganda painted on its keel. Enormous words!"

"Saying what?"

"Saying: 'Citizen! The Society of Friends of the Air Force summons you to its ranks! Help to build more ships like this!'"

Burton raised an eyebrow.

"The Technologists are certainly on the up as far as public opinion is concerned. It seems they intend to make the most of it!"

"What a sight it was," enthused Swinburne. "I expect it could circle the globe without landing once! So tell me about the pummelling."

"I'm surprised at your enthusiasm," commented Burton, ignoring the question. "I thought you Libertines were dead set against such machines. You know they'll be used to conquer the so-called uncivilised."

"Well, yes, of course," responded Swinburne, airily. "But one can't help but be impressed by such impossibilities as flying ships of metal! Not with dreams, but with blood and with iron, shall a nation be moulded to last! Anyway, old chap, answer my confounded question! How come the new bruises?"

"Oh," said Burton. "Just a tumble or two. I was clobbered by a werewolf, then, a few hours later, Spring Heeled Jack dragged my rotorchair out of the sky and sent me crashing through some tree tops."

Swinburne grinned. "Yes, but really, what happened?"

"Exactly that."

The young poet threw his topper at the explorer in exasperation. Burton caught it and tossed it back.

Swinburne sighed, and said: "If you don't want to explain, jolly good; but at least tell me what's on the menu for tonight? Alcoholic excesses? Or maybe something different for a change? I've been thinking it might be fun to try opium."

Blake slipped out of his *jubbah* and reached for his jacket, which he'd thrown carelessly over the back of a chair.

"You'll stay well away from that stuff, Algernon. Your self-destructive streak is dangerous enough as it is. Alcohol is going to kill you slowly, I have no doubt. Opium will do the job with far greater efficiency!"

He buttoned up his jacket. "Why you want to do away with yourself, I cannot fathom," he continued.

"Pshaw!" objected Swinburne, jumping up and pressing his topper down over his wild carroty hair. "I have no intention of killing myself. I'm just bored, Richard. Terribly, terribly bored. The ennui of this pointless existence gnaws at my bones."

He began to dance crazily around the room.

"I'm a poet! I need stimulation! I need danger! I need to tread that thin line 'twixt life and death, else I have no experience worth writing about!"

Burton gazed at the capering little slope-shouldered man. "You are serious?"

"Of course! You yourself write poetry. You know that the form is but a container. What have I, a twenty-four year old, to pour into that container but the pathetic dribblings of an immature dilettante? Do you know what they wrote about me in the *Spectator*? They said: 'He has some literary talent but it is decidedly not of a poetical kind. We do not believe any criticism will help to improve Mr Swinburne.'

"I want to improve! I want to be a *great* poet or I am nothing, Richard! To do that I must truly live. And a man can only truly live when Death is his permanent companion. Did I ever tell you about the time I climbed Culver Cliff on the Isle of Wight?"

Burton shook his head. Swinburne stopped his bizarre hopping and they crossed to the door, went out and started down the stairs.

"It was Christmas, 1854," said his friend. "I was seventeen and my father had refused to buy me a commission as a cavalry officer. Denied a role in the war, how could I tell whether I possessed courage or not? It was all very well to dream of forlorn hopes and cavalry charges but for all I knew, when faced with the reality of war, I might be a coward! I had to test myself, Richard; so that Christmas I walked to the eastern headland of the island."

They exited the house and turned up their collars. It was getting colder.

"Where are we going?" asked Swinburne.

"Battersea."

"Battersea? Why, what's there."

"The Tremors."

"Is that an affliction?"

"It's a public house. This way. I want to find my local paper boy first."

"Why all the way to Battersea just for a drink?"

"I'll tell you when we get there! Continue your story."

"You know Culver Cliff? It's a great face of chalk cut through with bands of flint. Very sheer. So I decided to climb it as a test of my mettle. On the first attempt, I came to an impassable overhang and had to make my way down again to choose a different route. I started back up, setting my teeth and swearing to myself that I would not come down alive again—if I did return to the foot of that blessed cliff, it would be in a fragmentary condition! So I edged my way up and the wind blew into the crevasses and hollows and made a sound like an anthem from the Eton Chapel organ. Then, as I edged ever higher, a cloud of seagulls burst from a cave and wheeled around me and for a moment I feared they would peck my eyes out. But still I ascended, though every muscle complained. I had almost reached the top when the chalk beneath my footholds crumbled away and I was left dangling by my hands from a ledge which just gave my fingers room enough to cling and hold on while I swung my feet sideways until I found purchase. I was able to pull myself up and over the lip of the cliff and there I lay so exhausted that I began to lose consciousness. It was only the thought that I might roll back over the edge that roused me."

"And thus you proved your courage to your satisfaction," asked Burton.

"Yes, but I learned more than that. I learned that I can only truly live when Death threatens; and I can only write great poems when I feel Life coursing through my veins. My enemy is ennui, Richard. It will kill me more surely and more foully than either alcohol or opium, of that I am certain."

Burton pondered this until, a few minutes later, they caught up with young Oscar in Portman Square.

"I say, Quips!"

"What ho, Captain! You'll be taking an evening edition?" smiled the youngster.

"No lad; I need information that I won't find in the newspaper. It's worth a bob or two."

"A couple of years ago, Captain, I thought that money was the most important thing in life; now that I'm older, I know that it is! You have yourself a deal. What is it that you're after knowing?"

"I need to meet with The Beetle, the president of the League of Chimney Sweeps."

Algernon Swinburne looked up at Burton in astonishment.

"Oof!" exclaimed Oscar. "That's a tall order! He's a secretive sort!"

Burton's reply was lost as a diligence thundered past, pulled by four horses. He waited until it had disappeared into Wigmore Street then repeated: "But you can find him? Is it possible?"

"I'll knock on your door tomorrow morning, sir. One thing: if you want to talk with The Beetle, you'll have to take him some books. He's mad for reading, so he is."

"Reading what?"

"Anything at all, Captain, though he prefers poetry and factual to fiction."

"Very well. Thank you, Quips. Here's a shilling to be going on with."

Oscar touched his cap, winked, moved away, and yelled: "Evenin' paper! Confederate forces enter state of Kentucky! Read all about it!"

"What an extraordinary child!" exclaimed Swinburne.

"Yes, indeed. He's destined for great things, is young Oscar Wilde," answered Burton.

"But see here, my friend," shrilled the poet, "I'll be left in the dark no longer! Spring Heeled Jack, a werewolf, and The Beetle. What extraordinary affair have you got yourself involved in? It's time to tell all, Richard. I'll not move another step until you do."

Burton considered his friend for a moment. Then:

"I'll tell you, but can I trust you to keep it under your hat?"

"Yes."

"Your word?"

"My word."

"In that case, once we're in a hansom and on our way to Battersea, I'll explain."

He swung around and strode out of the square, with Swinburne bouncing at his side.

"Wait!" demanded the poet. "We aren't catching a hansom now?"

"Not yet. There's a place I want to visit."

"What place?"

"You'll see."

"Why must you be so insufferably mysterious?"

They made their way through the early evening crowd of perambulators, hawkers, labourers, buskers, beggars, vagabonds, dollymops and thieves until they reached Vere Street. There Burton stopped outside a narrow premises which stood hunched between a hardware shop and the Museum of Anatomy. Beside its bright yellow door, a tall blue-curtained window had stuck upon its inside a sheet of paper upon which was written in a swirling hand, the legend:

The astonishing COUNTESS SABINA, seventh daughter, CHEIROMANTIST, PROGNOSTICATOR, tells your past, present and future, gives full names, tells exact thought or question on your mind without one word spoken; reunites the separated; removes evil influences; truthful predictions and satisfaction guaranteed. Consultations from 11am until 2pm and from 6pm to 9pm. Please enter and wait until called.

"You're joking!" said Swinburne.

"Not at all."

Burton had heard about this place from Richard Monckton Milnes. He and the older man had long shared an interest in the occult and Monckton Milnes had once told Burton there was no better palmist in all London than this one.

They entered.

Beyond the front door the adventurer and his companion found a short and non-too-clean passageway of naked floorboards and cracked plaster walls lit by an oil lamp which hung from the stained ceiling. They walked its length and pushed through a thick purple velvet curtain, entering a small rectangular room which smelled of stale sandalwood incense. Wooden chairs lined the undecorated walls. Only one was occupied; sat upon by a tall skinny and prematurely balding young man with watery eyes and bad teeth, which he bared at them in what passed for a smile.

"The wife's in there!" he said, in a reedy voice, nodding toward a door beside the curtained entrance. "If you wait with me until she finishes, you can then go in."

Burton and Swinburne sat. The room's two gas lamps sent shadows snaking across their faces. Swinburne's hair took on the appearance of fire.

The man stared at Burton.

"My goodness, you've been in the wars! Did you fall?"

"Yes he did. Down the stairs in a brothel," interposed Swinburne, crossing his legs.

"Great heavens!"

"They were throwing him out. Said his tastes were too exotic."

"Er-erotic?" spluttered the man.

"No. Exotic. You know what I mean, I'm sure." He made the sound of a swishing cane.

"Why, y-yes, of-of course."

Burton grinned savagely, looking like the very devil himself. "You fool, Algy!" he whispered.

The man cleared his throat once, twice, three times, before managing: "Eroti—I mean exotic, hey? What? I say! And—er—well—tally ho!"

"Are you familiar with the Kama Sutra of Vatsyayana?" asked Swinburne.

"The, um, the—the K-Kama—?"

"It offers guidance in the art of lovemaking. This gentleman has just begun translating it from the original Sanscrit."

"The—the—ar-ar-art of—?" The man swallowed with an audible gulp.

The door opened and a woman swept into the room. She was tall, enormously fat, and wore the most voluminous dress Burton had ever seen. She reminded him of Isambard Kingdom Brunel's megalithic transatlantic liner, the *S. S. Titan*.

"Thank God!" exclaimed the thin man. "I mean, I say, you've finished, my little lamb!"

"Yes," she said, in a booming voice, her double chins wobbling. "We must go home at once, Reginald. There are things we must discuss!"

He stood, and Burton was sure he could see the man's knees knocking together.

"Th-things, Lammykins?"

"*Things*, Reginald!"

She pushed aside the curtain and squeezed her bulk into the corridor. Her husband followed, casting a last glance at Swinburne, who winked and said in a stage whisper: "The Kama Sutra!"

He chuckled as the man dived after his wife.

Another woman stepped from the doorway. She was of indeterminate age; either elderly but very well preserved or young and terribly worn, Burton couldn't decide which. Her hair was chestnut brown, shot through with grey, and hung freely to the small of her back, defying the conservative styles of the day; her face was angular and may once have been beautiful; certainly, her large, dark, slightly slanted eyes still were. The lips, though, were thin and framed by deep lines. She wore a black dress with a cream-coloured shawl. Her hands were bare; the nails bitten and unpainted.

"You wish an insight into the future?" she asked, in a musical, slightly accented voice, looking from one man to the other.

Burton stood.

"I do. My friend will wait."

She nodded and stepped aside so that he might pass through to the room beyond. It was small, sparsely furnished, and dominated by a tall blue curtain; the same he'd seen from the outside. A dim lamp hung low over a round table. Shelves lined the walls and were packed with trinkets and baubles of an esoteric nature.

The Countess Sabina closed the door and moved to a chair. She and Burton sat, facing each other across the table.

She considered him.

In the ill-lit chamber, with the flickering light shining from directly above, Burton's eyes were shadowy sockets and the deep scar on his left cheek stood out vividly.

"Your face will be known for long," the countess blurted.

"I beg your pardon?"

"I'm sorry. Sometimes I don't know why I say what I say. It is an aspect of my gift—of my powers. It is for you to decide the meaning. Give me your hand. The right."

He held out his hand, palm upward. She took hold of it and bent close, tracing its lines with a finger.

"Small hands," she muttered, almost inaudibly. "This—hmm—such restlessness. No roots. You have seen much. Truly *seen*."

She looked up at him. "You are of the People, sir. I am certain of that."

"You mean the gypsy race? It's true that I bear the name Burton."

"Ah! One of the great families. Your other hand please, Mr Burton."

He held out his left hand. She took it, without releasing the right, and examined it closely.

"What! So strange!" she whispered, almost as if addressing herself. "This cannot be. Separate roads to tread; separate destinations at which to settle; one of small glories that will become great long after he has passed; another of great victories won in secrecy and never revealed. This cannot be; for both paths are trodden! Both paths! How is this possible?"

Burton felt his flesh crawling.

The woman's hands gripped his own tightly. She started swaying back and forth slightly and a low moan escaped her.

He'd seen this sort of thing before, in India and Arabia, and watched fascinated as she slipped into a trance.

"I will speak, Captain," she muttered.

He started. How did she know his rank?

"I will speak. I will speak. I will speak of—of—of a time that is not a time. Of a time that could be. No! Wait. I do not understand. Of a time that *should* be? Should? Should? What is this I see? What?"

She fell silent and rocked backward, forward, backward, forward.

"For you, the wrong path is the right path!" she suddenly announced loudly. "Captain Burton: the wrong path is the right path! The way ahead offers choices that should never be offered and challenges that should never be faced. It is false, this path; yet you walk it and it is best that you do so. But what of the other? What of the other? What of that which was spoken but doesn't manifest? The truth is broken and the lie is lived! Kill him, Captain!" She suddenly threw her head back and screamed: "*Kill him!*"

The room fell silent and she slumped forward. He withdrew his hands. The door clicked behind him.

"I say, is everything all right?" came Swinburne's voice.

"Leave us a moment, Algy. I'll be out shortly."

The poet grunted and closed the door.

Burton moved around the table and, taking the countess by the shoulders, pulled her upright. Her head fell back, revealing eyes that showed only the whites; the pupils had rolled up into the sockets.

The King's agent crooned a low chant in an ancient language and made a couple of strange passes across her face with his left hand. His words throbbed rhythmically and, gradually, she began to rock again, in time with the chant. Then he stopped and said: "Awake!"

Her pupils snapped down and into focus.

She gasped and clutched at his forearm, holding it tightly.

"I cannot help you!" she mumbled, and a tear fell from her long eyelashes. "Your very existence is not as it should be and yet, at the same time, it is *exactly* as it should be! Listen to the echoes, Captain; the points of time's rhythm, for each is a crossroads. Time is like music. The same refrain emerges again and again, though different in form. What does this mean? What am I saying?"

"Countess," said Burton. "You have told me what I myself have half suspected. Something, somehow, is not as it should be. I know who holds the secret to this mystery and I mean to get it from him."

"The stilt-walker," she hissed.

"Yes. You see much!"

"Beware the stilt-walker. And the panther and the ape, too."

"What are they?"

"I can tell you no more. Please, leave me now. I must retire. I am exhausted."

Burton straightened. He pulled two guineas from his pocket and lay them on the table.

"Thank you, Countess Sabina."

"That is too much, Captain Burton."

"It is what your reading has been worth to me. There is no greater cheiromantist in all London, of that I am certain."

"Thank you, sir."

Burton left and, with Swinburne, departed the premises.

"It sounded like you were strangling her," noted the poet.

"I can assure you that I wasn't," replied the King's agent. "Keep your eyes peeled for a hansom. Let's get to Battersea and The Tremors. I need a drink."

They picked up a cab a few minutes later and, as it chugged southward, skirted around Hyde Park, and headed down Sloane Street toward Chelsea Bridge, Burton told Swinburne about his new post, about Spring Heeled Jack, and about his theory that the stilt-walker was a supernatural being—possibly Moko of Africa's Congo region. He also told the poet about the East End werewolves.

Swinburne spent the entire journey with his wide eyes fixed on his friend.

Finally, as they crossed the Thames and rattled past the prodigious and brightly lit power station, with its four massive copper rods towering against the night sky, the poet said quietly: "You have always been an inveterate story-teller, Richard; this, though, beats any of your Arabian nights tales!"

"It's certainly as strange as anything recounted by Scheherazade," agreed Burton.

"So we're going to The Tremors to speak to its landlord?"

"Yes. Joseph Robinson, the man who employed Queen Victoria's assassin."

"I'll tell you what I like about your new job, shall I?" said Swinburne.

"What's that?"

"It seems to involve a lot of public houses!"

"Too many. Listen, Algy; I want us both to cut back on the drinking. We've been going at it hammer and tongs these weeks past; letting our frustrations get the better of us. It's time we took ourselves in hand."

"That's easy for you to say, old thing," responded Swinburne. "You have this new job to keep you occupied. Me, though; all I have is my writing, and it's not been well-received!"

The hansom steamed past Battersea Fields, and stopped on Dock Leaf Lane, where its two passengers disembarked. They paid the driver, crossed the road, and entered The Tremors; a small half-timbered pub with smoke-blackened oak beams pitted with the fissures and cracks of age, tilting floors, and crazily askew walls.

There were two rooms, both cosily lit and warmed by log fires, and both containing a few tables and a smattering of customers. Burton and Swinburne passed through them and sat on stools at the counter. An ancient, bald and stooped, grey-bearded man with a merry gnome-like face, rounded the corner of the bar, wiping his hands on a cloth. A high collar encased his thick neck and he wore an unfashionably long jacket.

"Evening gents," he said, in a creaky but jovial voice. "Deerstalker? Finest ale south of the river!"

Burton nodded, and asked: "Are you Joseph Robinson?"

"Aye, sir, that's me," responded the landlord. He held a tankard to a barrel and twisted the tap. "Has someone been talking, then?"

"I was at The Hog in the Pound yesterday. The manager mentioned you."

"Oh ho! That old boozer! My my, what times I had there, I can tell you!" He placed the frothing tankard in front of Burton and looked at Swinburne. "Same for you, lad?"

The poet nodded.

"I was told to ask you about the name of this place," said Burton. "The Tremors. Apparently there's a story behind it?"

Start with a straightforward question, he thought; get him talking first then move onto the subject of Edward Oxford.

"Oh aye, yes sir, that there is!" exclaimed Robinson. "Let me serve them what's waiting then I'll come tell you all about it."

He placed Swinburne's beer in front of the poet, glanced curiously at the little red-headed man, and left them, walking to the other end of the bar where a corpulent customer stood rattling coins in his hand.

"Will you be embarking on any more expeditions, Richard, or has this new role taken over?" asked Swinburne.

"It's very much taken over, Algy. It feels *right*, somehow. It's given me a purpose. Although I must admit, I'm none too keen on the confinements and hustle and bustle of London."

"Perhaps if it offers you action enough, you'll feel less like a caged tiger. What's Isabel's opinion?"

The answer came in a flat, cold tone: "There is no longer an Isabel."

The little poet lowered his glass, leaving white froth on his upper lip, and looked at his friend in astonishment.

"No Isabel? You mean you've parted ways?"

"This role I've taken on is not compatible with marriage."

"Good lord! I would never have believed it! How did she take it?"

"Not well. I don't want to discuss it, Algernon. It's a mite painful. A fresh wound, so to speak."

"I'm sorry, Richard. Truly, I am."

"You're a good chap, Algy. Here comes old Robinson; let's listen to his tale."

The landlord came lumbering back and treated them to a gap-toothed smile through his bushy beard.

"It was the power station, you see," he announced, leaning his elbows upon the counter. "When Isambard Kingdom Brunel proposed it back in '37, the local community wasn't too happy. Oh no no no, we weren't happy at all. Who'd want that blooming eyesore on their doorstep? And, on top of that, we was afraid. When they started drilling the four holes, no one knew what would happen. Right down into the crust of the Earth they was pushing them blooming great copper rods, so's they could—um—confound the German fleet—no—um—what is it?"

"Conduct the geothermal heat," put in Burton, helpfully.

"That's the one! I remember them saying they'd be able to light the whole blooming city with electricity! What a load of cobblers that turned out to be! The only thing they've ever managed to light is the blooming power station itself! Anyways, back in the day, folks around here was mighty afraid that the crust of the Earth would split wide open and swallow up the whole area, so me, being the young firebrand I was back then, I went and organised the Battersea Brigade."

"A protest group?" asked Swinburne.

"Yes, laddie. I wasn't much older than you but I was doing alright for myself. I'd taken over my old pa's public house—The Hog in the Pound, where you were yesterday, sir—and, being placed slap bang in Oxford Street, it was doing fine business."

"But you lived in Battersea?" asked Burton.

"Aye. My folks, bless 'em, had lived here all their blooming lives. Old dad used to walk—walk, mind you!—to The Hog and back every day. Three miles there; three miles back! So when he got tired of that, he made me manager, and I did the blooming foot-slog instead!

"Anyways, like I was a-telling you, I recruited a bunch of locals and formed the Brigade—and I don't mind admitting that it turned into a nice little earner for me!"

"How so?" asked Burton, pushing his empty tankard forward.

The old man started refilling it.

"It struck me that if we were to stand against those Technologist devils then we'd need a spot of 'Dutch courage,' so to speak. So every Saturday, I used to ship the Brigade up to The Hog in three or four broughams, and give 'em all a drink for free. Heh! Once they got that down their necks they soon wanted more; only, of course, that weren't for free. Ha ha! Those Battersea Brigade meetings always turned into right old knees-ups, I can tell you! I made a tidy profit, thank you very much; and even more a few years later when I had the Brigade in the taproom and those Libertine rapscallions in the parlour!"

"The Libertines?" asked Burton, innocently.

"Why yes, sir, the—" He took Swinburne's empty tankard and started to refill it.

"I'll have a large brandy, too, if you please," said the poet. "And have something for yourself on me."

"Much obliged, sir. Most decent of you. I'll take a whisky. The Libertines; why, the whole thing started at The Hog in the Pound, ain't that right, Ted?"

This last was addressed to an ancient old fellow who'd just arrived at the bar. He stood beside Swinburne, who marvelled at his weather-beaten skin and bald pate, huge beak-like nose and long pointed chin. He looked like Punchinello, and, when he spoke, he sounded like him, too; his tone sharp, snappy and aggressive, seemingly the voice of a much younger man.

"What's that, Bob? The Libertines? Bah! Bounders and cads! 'Specially that blackguard Beresford!"

"May I buy you a drink, Mr—?" asked Burton.

"Toppletree. Ted Toppletree. Very good of you, sir. Very good indeed. Most generous. Deerstalker. Best ale south of the river. Never mind the dog, sir."

This last was directed at Swinburne, whose trouser leg was being pulled at by a small Basset hound.

The poet jerked his ankle away only to have the dog lunge forward and bite his shoe.

"I say!" he shrilled.

"He's only playing with you, sir. Do you want to buy 'im? He's the best tracker you'll ever find; can sniff out anything. Fidget's his name."

"No!" squealed Swinburne. "Confound the beast! Why won't he leave me alone?"

"He's taken a right shine to you! Here, Fidget! Sit! Sit!"

The old man pulled the hound away from the poet. It sat, gazing longingly at Swinburne's ankles.

"You sure you wouldn't like to buy 'im, sir?"

"I've never been surer of anything!"

Swinburne took a long gulp of ale. "I do believe you may be right about this beer! Very tasty!" he enthused, keeping a suspicious eye directed toward the dog. His upper lip was now entirely concealed behind a frothy white moustache. "Perhaps little Fidget will calm down if we offer him a bowl?"

Joseph Robinson placed a pint before Toppletree who took a swig, then announced: "Scum!"

Burton and Swinburne looked confused.

"Edward Oxford, I mean," explained the old man. "It was him. That's why Beresford and his mob came to The Hog."

Swinburne swallowed his brandy in a single gulp and pushed the glass toward Robinson. He glanced ruefully at Burton and shrugged.

The King's agent, who was sipping his drink with more restraint, said: "Edward Oxford? The assassin?"

"Of course!" barked Toppletree. "Bob, here, employed the bugger!"

Robinson handed the old man his beer and poured more brandy into Swinburne's glass. "It's true," he said. "Oxford used to work for me at The Hog before he went potty and shot the queen dead, may she rest in peace and he rot in hell."

"My Aunt Bessie's sacred hat!" exclaimed Swinburne. "You knew him? You actually *knew* the man who killed Queen Victoria?"

"Knew him!" exploded Toppletree. "This silly arse *paid* him!"

"I didn't pay him to blooming well assassinate the queen!" objected Robinson.

"Might as well have done. 'Twas your money he used to buy the pistols."

Robinson bridled, sticking his chest out over his not inconsiderable paunch and raising his clenched fists. "Watch your mouth, Ted. The bastard earned his money fair and square. What he did with it weren't my responsibility."

Toppletree, or Punchinello, as Swinburne couldn't help but think of him, grinned and his eyes twinkled mischievously.

"Ruffled feathers!" he exclaimed. "Guilty conscience, Bob?"

"Shut your trap!"

"Heh heh!"

Robinson suddenly relaxed.

"You old git!" he chuckled.

"Easy target!"

"Stow it, old man!"

"So what was Oxford like?" interposed Swinburne, eyeing the Basset hound, which gazed back with a forlorn expression.

'Well done, Algy!' thought Burton, pleased that his friend was steering the conversation back in the right direction. He remembered Monty doing the same, under very similar circumstances, not much less than twenty-four hours ago. Repetitive themes, just as Countess Sabina had suggested; as if time were music, presenting the same refrain.

Listen to the echoes, Captain; the points of time's rhythm, for each is a crossroads.

"Blooming heck, you can knock 'em back!" observed Robinson, noting that Swinburne's brandy glass and tankard were both empty again.

"Another round, if you please!" requested the little poet. "Include your good self."

"Ta very much. Edward Oxford? He was barmy. Talked to himself all the time. The customers treated him like the village idiot. Laughed at him. Teased him. Mighty popular with the Brigade, though, he was; always asking after their families, befriending their kids; and he was a blooming good barman, too. Fast on his feet with a good head for figures. Never once gave the wrong change. Kept the taps clean and the ale flowing. I ask you, gents; how was I to know he was a killer?"

Burton said solemnly: "You can never tell what's at the back of a man's mind."

"True!" snapped Punchinello. "If I'd known, I'd have killed the sod."

They all grunted in agreement.

Burton surreptitiously checked his pocket watch. It was twenty minutes past midnight.

"So the Libertines frequented the Hog in the Pound just because Oxford had worked there?" he asked.

"Exactly so," said Robinson, serving the fresh drinks. "And I can tell you, at first it was only the fact that they dressed like gentlemen that stopped me booting them out!"

"That and the money they spent," snorted Punchinello.

Swinburne looked at the oldster at his side.

"So you were one of the Battersea Brigade?"

"I was. And I nearly came to blows with that Beresford bastard."

"How come?"

"You've read the evening paper? About the attack? This morning? The girl? Spring Heeled Jack?"

Sir Richard Francis Burton tensed and placed his tankard back on the bar in case they noticed his shaking hand.

"Yes," said Swinburne. "It was fairly vague. The girl hallucinated, surely. Spring Heeled Jack is just a bogeyman."

"Nope. That devil's real, right enough. Ain't that so, Bob?"

The old barman nodded. "Aye. Attacked a couple of our girls, he did."

"Your girls?" asked Burton.

"The Brigade's. Bartholomew Stevens' lass and Dave Alsop's."

Burton's eyebrows rose. Stevens! Alsop!

"The attacks happened around the time Dave moved up to a little place north of the city, on account of getting work as a blacksmith," explained Robinson. "'But though he was well away from the power station, he still used to ride down to the Hog occasionally for a drink with the old mob."

"Nice chap, he was," muttered Punchinello.

"Aye, it's true. Then that devil had a go at his daughter right on the doorstep of his blooming house. That was in '38, just a few months after Jumping Jack had attacked Bart Stevens' girl."

"What happened there?" asked Burton.

"Mary, her name was; she was set upon not far from here but screamed loudly enough to attract help and the devil hopped it. Well, a few years passed, then we had The Assassination and old Beresford, the Mad Marquess, started bringing his chaps to The Hog. After a while, a rumour went round that he was Spring Heeled Jack. Dave and Bart got wind of it and they, and Ted here, were all set to beat the living daylights out of him, ain't that right, Ted?"

"Yup. We was going to pulverise the bastard."

"But I stopped the blooming hot-heads!" said Robinson. "I was all for giving Spring Heeled Jack a good hammering but I didn't want no trouble in my pub unless it was for good reason; so I told old Bart to bring along young Mary to have a look at Beresford; see if she recognised him."

"And she didn't?"

"Nope," confirmed Robinson. "She'd never seen him before. Said he was nothing like the devil who attacked her. Jack had a thin face; Beresford was a moon-faced git."

"So no duffing up of the Mad Marquess," said Punchinello, regretfully.

"What happened to the Battersea Brigade?" asked the King's agent.

"Hah!" snorted Punchinello. "Turned into a drinking club. Never did a single thing. No opposition to the power station!"

"By the mid 'forties, most had drifted away," put in Robinson.

"To where?" asked Swinburne.

"Well now, let me see. Alsop, Fraser, Ed Chorley, Carl Goodkind, Sid Skinner and Mark Waite have all kicked the bucket; Bart Stevens moved out to Essex; Old Shepherd took his family to South Africa; Fred Adams moved out of London, Chislehurst way—"

"Chislehurst?" asked Burton.

"Or thereabouts, yes. Edmund Cottle is one of my regulars, like Ted, here; Arnie Lovitt is still in the neighbourhood; his girl and her husband drink here every Friday night, though I doubt I'll see them for a while, the poor sods—their daughter, Lucy, went loopy a couple of weeks back; I hear they're putting her in Bedlam—and Eric Saydso is hanging on but probably won't be around for much longer; he's a consumptive. That's the lot; there was fourteen of us in all, plus the various wives and kids."

"So the Brigade disbanded," noted Burton, "and then you gave up The Hog in the Pound?"

"That's right. I got tired of the blooming place and all those Libertine idiots, so I sold up and bought this little boozer and—to answer your original question, sir—I named it The Tremors on account of the fact that people around here was so certain that the Technologists' power station would cause earthquakes and the like."

"You've certainly had a high old time of it!" observed Burton. "What with the Technologists, the Libertines, Edward Oxford and Spring Heeled Jack!"

Punchinello blew out a breath and said: "He attracts crackpots!"

Robinson laughed. "You've been my customer for nigh on thirty years, Edward Toppletree, so you may well be right! Anyway, gents, I have customers to serve. Give me a shout when you're ready for a top up."

He gave them a nod and shuffled away.

"Nice talking to you," said Punchinello. "I'm going to to sit by the fire and smoke me pipe. You positive you don't want to buy Fidget, here? His nose might be the eighth blinkin' wonder of the world!"

"Positive!" replied Swinburne.

They bid him farewell and watched as he shuffled away with the dog at his heels.

"What do you think, Richard?" asked Swinburne quietly.

"I think," responded Burton, "that we just picked up some very useful information and I'd better speak to Detective-Inspector Trounce first thing tomorrow!"

§

Chapter 10

Beetle and Panther

Wearing loose fitting white cotton kurta pyjamas, a saffron-coloured turban upon his head, and with his already swarthy skin darkened with walnut oil, Sir Richard Francis Burton strode purposefully along the bank of the Limehouse Cut canal. He'd made his way there through the disreputable streets of Limehouse unmolested by the rogues who inhabited London's great melting pot. The people of this district kept themselves to themselves, only mingling when there was a shady deal to be made or a dirty deed to be done.

Without a disguise, Burton appeared barbarous enough to have probably avoided trouble. He was cautious though, and felt it best to take on the character of a foreigner. The guise of a Sikh was an obvious choice, for Sikhs possessed a reputation—undeserved, as it happened—for ferocity. This, together with his forked beard and terrible, magnetic eyes, gave him such a fearsome aspect that people quickly stepped out of his path as he swung along, and he'd arrived at the bank of the canal without having been even once approached.

Late last night, after he and Swinburne made their way home from Battersea, Burton had slept much more deeply than usual, not waking until nine in the morning. After bolting down a grilled kipper and a round of toast, he'd gone to Scotland Yard to present Detective-Inspector Trounce with the list of Battersea Brigade members.

"By Jove!" the policeman had exclaimed. "I can't believe they missed this; though I suppose it's understandable under the circumstances. The Yard didn't have a detective branch until the early 'forties, and I guess the fact that the Alsop attack happened near Epping tripped them up. There was no reason to look for a connection between the girls' fathers. I'll look into this, Captain Burton. In fact, I'll go down to Battersea myself today."

An hour later, back at 14 Montagu Place, Burton found a message waiting for him from Oscar Wilde. Through the "boys' network," the youngster had arranged a meeting for him with The Beetle. The appointment was for three o'clock, and the venue was strange, to say the least.

Burton was almost there.

Along the sides of Limehouse Cut—a commercial waterway which linked the lower reaches of the River Lea with the Thames—some of the city's most active factories belched black smoke into the air and gave a meagre wage to the thousands of workers who toiled within. Many of these men, women and children had yellow, red, green or blue skin, permanently coloured by the industrial dyes they worked with; others were disfigured by scorch marks and blisters from hours spent next to furnaces or kilns; and all had callused hands, hard bony bodies, and the haunted look of starvation in their eyes.

Burton walked past the huge, towering premises until he came to one particular building which, unlike its neighbours, had been abandoned. Standing seven storeys high, and with nearly every window either missing, broken or cracked, it silently loomed over the busy canal; a shell; its chimneys impotent, its entrances bricked up.

He circled it by passing through an arched passageway which gave access to Broomfield Street, crossing its barren frontage with the blocked loading bays and empty stables, then returning back along a second covered alley to the narrow docks at the side of the canal.

People saw and ignored him. That was the way of things in Limehouse.

Beside the dock, on the factory's wall, in a niche down which rusting gutter pipes ran, he found what he was looking for: iron rungs set into the brickwork.

He shifted the bag that was slung across his shoulders, moving it so that it hung against the small of his back, then began to climb, testing each hold before putting his weight on it.

There had been a second message waiting for him at home that morning when he returned from Scotland Yard. It was from Isabel; and read:

You will change your mind. We are destined for one another; I knew that the moment I saw you ten years ago. I will wait. For as long as it takes, I will wait.

He'd sat considering it for some time, absently running a forefinger along the scar on his cheek. Then he'd composed and sent a terse reply:

Do not wait. Live your life.

It was brutal, he knew, but as with an amputation, a fast and clean cut is the quickest to heal.

He continued upward until he eventually reached the top of the ladder, then heaved himself over the parapet and sat for a moment to catch his breath, looking across the flat roof at the two long skylights, the cracked panes of which had been made opaque by soot. In the centre of the roof, between the two rows of glass, eight chimneys soared high into the air. It was the third from the eastern side that interested him.

He gingerly picked his way across the debris-covered roof, avoiding the areas that sagged, until he reached the nearest skylight. He skirted around its edge then moved over to the chimney.

It had rungs affixed to it, running from the base all the way to the top. Once again, he climbed, marvelling at the view of London which unfurled beneath him.

A cold breeze was blowing, making his loose attire flap, though he was kept warm by a thermal vest.

He stopped, hooked an arm through a rung, and rested. He was halfway up and could see, far away, through the dirty haze and angled columns of smoke which rose like a forest from the city, the magnificent dome of St Paul's. A few specks flew between him and the cathedral; rotorchairs and swans, the divergent forms of air transport developed by those two powerful factions within the Technologist caste, the Engineers and the Eugenicists.

He sighed. It had come just too late for him, this new technology. If he'd had the advantage of the swans, as John Speke had during his second expedition, recent history would have been very different indeed.

He continued his ascent, giving silent thanks that he didn't suffer from a fear of heights.

Minutes later he reached the top and swung himself over to sit with one leg to either side of the chimney's lip. The breeze tugged at him but with a foot hooked through one of the rungs and his knees clamped tightly against the brickwork, he felt reasonably secure.

He noticed that another set of metal rungs descended into the darkness of the flue.

Burton pulled his shoulder bag around, opened it, took out a bound notebook, and started to read.

For ten minutes he sat there, outlined against broken clouds and patches of blue sky, perched a precarious three-hundred and fifty feet above the ground, the book in his hand, his noble brow furrowed with concentration, his savage jaw clenched, his clothes fluttering wildly.

Eventually, there came a furtive rustle and scrape from within the chimney.

Burton listened but didn't react.

The hiss of falling soot.

The scuffing of a boot against metal.

Moments of silence.

Then a quiet, sibilant voice:

"What are you reading?"

Without shifting his eyes from his notebook, Burton replied:

"It's my own translation of the *Behdristan*, which is an imitation of the *Gulistan* of Sa'df, the celebrated Persian poet. It is written in prose and verse, and treats of ethics and education, though it abounds in moral anecdotes, aphorisms, and amusing stories, too."

"And the original author?" hissed the voice.

"Niir-ed-Di'n Abd-er-Rahman; the Light of Religion, Servant of the Merciful. He was born, it's believed, in 1414 in a small town called Ja'm, near Herat, the capital of Khurasin, and adopted Jami as his takhallus, or poetical name. He is considered the last of the great Persian writers."

"I want it," whispered the voice from the darkness.

"It is yours," responded the King's agent. "And I have other volumes here." He patted his shoulder bag.

"What are they?"

"My own works: *Goa and the Blue Mountains*, *Scinde or the Unhappy Valley*, and *A Personal Narrative of a Pilgrimage to El-Medinah and Meccah*."

"You are an author?"

"Among other things, yes."

"Indian?"

"No, this is a disguise I adopted in order to travel unmolested."

"Limehouse is dangerous."

"Yes."

There was a pause, then the sepulchral tones came again:

"What do you ask in return for the books?"

"I ask to be permitted to help."

"To help? To help with what?"

"Some hours ago, in Wapping, I saw wolf-like creatures snatch a boy from the street. I know he isn't the first to have been taken, and I know that all the missing boys are chimney sweeps."

A long silence followed.

Burton closed his notebook, placed it in his bag, then removed the bag from his shoulders and lowered it by the strap into the darkness.

A small mottled hand, so pale it was almost blue, reached out of the shadow within the flue and took the bag. A satisfied sigh echoed up from below.

Burton said: "The books are yours, whether you give me any information or not."

"Thank you," came the response. "It is true; the League of Chimney Sweeps is under attack and we do not know why."

"How many boys have been taken?"

"Twenty-eight."

Burton whistled.

"As many as that!"

"They all returned but nine. Nine are still missing. Ten if you include the latest, Aubrey Baxter, the boy you saw abducted."

"They are the ones most recently taken?"

"No, not at all. Most come back; some don't."

"And what of those who returned? What did they have to say?"

"They remember nothing."

"Really? Nothing at all?"

"They don't even remember the wolves. There is one thing, though."

"What?" asked Burton.

"All the boys who were taken; when they reappeared, they each bore a mark upon the forehead, between the eyes, about an inch above the bridge of the nose."

"A mark?"

"A small bruise surrounding a pin-prick."

"Like that made by a syringe?"

"I have never seen the mark made by a syringe, but I imagine so, yes."

"Can you arrange for me to meet one of these boys?"

"Are you the police?"

"No."

"Wait."

Burton waited. He watched a swan flying past in the near distance, a box kite trailing behind it, a man sitting in the kite, gripping the long reins.

"Here," hissed The Beetle.

The King's agent looked down and saw the worm-coloured arm reaching up out of the darkness. A piece of paper was held in the small fingers. He bent, stretched down, and took it.

Upon the paper two addresses had been written.

"Most of the boys live in the Cauldron," murmured the hidden sweep, "but that is too dangerous a place for such as you."

'Don't I know it!' thought Burton.

"There are some lodging houses which I rent in safer areas, such as these two. If you wait until tomorrow, I will see to it that you are expected; just say you have been sent by The Beetle. The first is where you'll find Billy Tupper, one of the fellows who returned. The second is a boarding house where three of the boys who are still missing lodged."

"Their names?"

"Jacob Spratt, Rajish Thakarta, and Benny Whymper. All these boys were taken whilst visiting fellow sweeps in the East End."

"Thank you. This is very useful. Is there anything else you can tell me?"

"On the other side of the paper I've listed all the boys who were taken and the dates of their abductions. I know nothing more."

"Then I'll take my leave of you, with thanks. If I learn anything about these kidnappings, I'll return."

"Drop three stones into the chimney. I'll respond. Bring more books."

"On what subject?"

"Philosophy, travel, art, poetry, anything."

"You fascinate me," said Burton. "Won't you come out of the shadow?"

There was no reply.

"Are you still there?"

Silence.

§

Both his cases were at a temporary standstill, so Burton spent the rest of the day catching up with his correspondence and various writing projects. He was surprised to find, in *The Empire,* an article by Henry Morton Stanley which, in reviewing the status of the Nile debate, gave well-balanced consideration to both positions. Burton's theory that the great river flowed out of the as yet unexplored northern shore of Lake Tanganyika was presented as a possibility in need of further investigation. John Speke's proposal that the Nyanza was the source was deemed more probably correct but, again, further expeditions were required. As for the explorers themselves, Burton, Stanley claimed, had been a victim of severe misfortune when fever prevented him from circumnavigating Tanganyika, while Speke had lacked the skills and experience necessary for geographical surveys and had made serious mistakes. Stanley was also highly critical of Speke's "renaming" of Nyanza. There was no need, he wrote, for a "Lake Albert" in central Africa.

It was a surprising turnaround, thought Burton, for he'd considered Stanley an implacable enemy; one of the men who'd stoked the fires of Speke's misplaced resentment against him.

What was the damned Yankee up to?

The answer came a few minutes later when he opened a letter from Sir Roderick Murchison. It was many pages long and covered a range of topics, though was mainly concerned with the financial mess Burton had left behind upon his departure from Zanzibar two years ago. The explorer had denied full payment to most of the porters who'd accompanied him and Speke for seven hundred miles into unexplored territory then seven hundred miles back again. The porters had not, Burton asserted, remained true to their contract, having mutinied and deserted in droves, and therefore did not deserve full payment.

Unfortunately, the British Consul at Zanzibar, Christopher Rigby, was yet another of Burton's foes. They had known each other back in India, and Rigby had never forgiven the explorer for repeatedly beating him out of his usual first place position in language examinations. Rigby was now getting his revenge by using his official position to stir up trouble, causing the payment affair to drag on for two tedious years.

This, however, was old news. What really caught Burton's attention was a paragraph in which Sir Roderick revealed that Henry Morton Stanley had received approval from his editor to mount an expedition of his own to settle the Nile question once and for all.

I have thus, wrote Murchison, *made available to him the fruits of your labours, which I am certain will be of invaluable assistance in this fresh endeavour. Please rest assured, my dear Burton, that your place in history is secure, and it will ever be stated that the results of Stanley's expedition, whatever they may be, would not have been possible were it not for your outstanding achievements, which, as it were, have 'blazed a trail' for all who follow.*

Again, Sir Richard Francis Burton was suddenly aware of that peculiar sense of being divided, for he knew that this news would have once infuriated him, yet now he felt nothing. Geographical exploration now belonged, he sensed, to another version of himself; to the doppelgänger.

He spent the next few hours writing up his case notes, creating a copy of the Spring Heeled Jack reports that Detective-Inspector Trounce had loaned him, and designing a filing system in which to keep records of his cases.

At ten o'clock that evening, Trounce called at the house.

"You've cracked it, old chap!" he announced, dropping into an armchair and accepting a proffered glass of whisky. "I've had a right old foot slog around the Battersea district today but every twinge of my bunions is worth it! Listen to this!"

Burton sat down and sipped his port while the policeman spoke.

"Of those Brigade members on your list, seven have daughters and the rest can be ignored for now. I shall deal with the seven one by one. The first is Martin Shepherd, still living, sixty-one years old, married to Louisa Buckle. They had two sons and a daughter, Jennifer. She was born in 1822. In 1838, aged sixteen, she was molested by what she described as 'a hopping demon' while crossing Battersea Fields. She was shocked but unharmed and the family never reported the incident. In 1842, she married a man named Thomas Shoemaker and they had a daughter, Sarah, who, coincidentally, is now sixteen. The whole family emigrated to South Africa soon after the girl's birth. Do you mind if I smoke my pipe?"

"Not at all," replied Burton. "You think the 'hopping demon' was Spring Heeled Jack?"

"It sounds like it, doesn't it? Shame I can't interview Jennifer Shoemaker. I don't think it's necessary, though; and you'll probably agree when you hear the rest of it. Let's move on to Brigade member number two: Mr Bartholomew Stevens."

"Mary Stevens' father."

"Yes."

Trounce started pushing tobacco into the bowl of a stained meerschaum.

"Bartholomew married Elisabeth Pringle in 1821 and the following year Mary was born. As you know, she was attacked by Jack in '37, when she was fifteen years old. Five years later she married a man named Albert Fairweather and the whole family moved to Essex where they now live. The Fairweathers have four children; three boys and a girl. The daughter, Connie, is now seventeen.

"Our third chap is Carl Goodkind, who passed away five years ago. He left a widow, Emily, who still lives. They had one child, a daughter, Deborah, who, in 1838, was committed to Bedlam, having suddenly gone insane for no clear reason; at least, none that I could get Mrs Goodkind to talk about. Deborah died in the asylum twelve years ago."

"Spring Heeled Jack again?" pondered Burton.

"You've seen the files, Captain. You know there are recorded cases of his victims losing their minds. So yes, I rather suspect that Deborah Goodkind was another such. And we shouldn't be surprised that the assault was never spoken of—even to other members of the Brigade—for you know the shame and embarrassment that attaches to mental aberrations."

The King's agent nodded thoughtfully.

"The fourth man is Edwin Fraser, born 1780, died earlier this year at the grand old age of eighty-one. He married May Wells and had a daughter, Lizzie Fraser, in 1823. Apparently she was a happy and intelligent child until the age of fourteen when, after a mental breakdown, she became morose and reclusive. Nevertheless, she found a husband in Desmond Steephill and gave birth to a daughter, Marian, in 1847. She would have turned fourteen in a couple of months."

"Would have?"

Trounce took a long draw on his pipe and blew a column of blue smoke into the air.

"Last month," he said, quietly, "Lizzie poisoned herself, her husband, and her daughter."

"By gad!"

"According to the coroner's report, there were bruises on the young girl's arms, as if she'd been gripped tightly, and scratches on her chest. They were not made the same day as the poisoning."

Trounce looked directly at Burton, and through the tobacco smoke his blue eyes seemed to shine as if lit from within.

"I think," he said, "that Lizzie Fraser was the Lizzie that Spring Heeled Jack asked after when he caused the brougham to crash back in '37. Furthermore, I think he found and assaulted her, causing her subsequent mental breakdown. I also believe that, last month, he attacked her daughter, Marian, and that Lizzie, in an insane attempt to escape his attentions, poisoned herself and her family."

"Great heavens, man!" exclaimed Burton. "Are you suggesting that the fiend is specifically targeting the womenfolk of Battersea Brigade members?"

"Yes, Captain, I am. Listen to the rest, then tell me if I'm wrong!

"The fifth of our seven is fifty-nine-year-old Mr Frederick Adams, who married Virginia Jones in 1821. You've met their daughter."

"I have?"

"Tilly Adams, born 1822, married Edward Tew in 1845, gave birth to Angela Tew in 1846."

"I'll be damned!"

"Exactly."

"I did some poking about in Mrs Tew's past," said Trounce. "She was bedridden for reasons unknown for the greater part of 1839."

"So I was right about that strange look she gave me when we were leaving her cottage," revealed Burton. "Sort of secretive and resentful."

"Yes. As you suggested, she was hiding something. I have no doubt that she knew her daughter's attacker," said Trounce. "Because she herself had been one of his victims more than two decades ago. Can a trouble you for a refill?"

"Certainly," responded Burton, reaching for the bottle. He topped up the Yard man's glass.

"And number six?"

"Mr David Alsop, now deceased. Married Jemma Bucklestone. Daughter: Jane Alsop. Attacked aged eighteen in 1838. Married Benton Pipkiss in 1843. Their daughter, Alicia Pipkiss, was born three years later. Like Connie Fairweather, she's in the age group that Spring Heeled Jack attacks but has not been assaulted."

"Yet," observed Burton.

"Yet," agreed Trounce. "Those are our two next possible targets. The seventh member of the Brigade we can count out. Mr Arnold Lovitt married June Dibble and they had a daughter, Sarah. It wasn't reported at the time but Sarah admitted to me that she was sexually molested in 1839 and in describing her assailant, she gave a pretty good portrayal of our stilt walker. A couple of years later, she married Donald Harkness and they had three children, including a girl, Lucy Harkness. Three weeks ago, Lucy fell into a coma from which she hasn't emerged. The family's doctor has labelled it an 'hysterical fit caused by severe mental trauma.' A trauma which, I'll wager, was caused by you-know-who."

Burton grunted and said: "So in every case where a member of the Battersea Brigade had a daughter, that daughter was attacked by Spring Heeled Jack. And of the granddaughters, all have been attacked recently, it seems, accept Connie Fairweather and Alicia Pipkiss."

"Yes. Which beggars the question: what the hell is he playing at?"

Burton stood and paced up and down.

"You've posted constables at the girls' homes?"

"They are being watched every minute of the day," confirmed Trounce. "The Fairweather family won't be around for much longer, though; they're preparing to emigrate to Australia. That, at least, might put the girl out of harm's way."

"There seem to be two main elements to this mystery," Burton declared. "The man who assassinated Queen Victoria, and the female descendants of one particular group of regulars who drank at the pub where he worked. Perhaps we should count the late Marquess of Waterford as a third."

"There's another," said Trounce.

"There is? What?"

"You."

§

That night, he dreamed again of Isabel.

She was bent low over a blazing fire, and its orange light made her face diabolical.

In her hand, she held a bound notebook; one of his journals; a detailed chapter of his extraordinary life.

With her features contorted by a hellish fury, she threw the volume into the flames, and Burton felt a chunk of his existence melting away.

She picked up another volume, fed it to the fire, and hissed in satisfaction as another part of him was turned to ashes.

One by one, she burned his journals.

Sir Richard Francis Burton was consumed, reduced to an empty shell of deeds done; the man himself removed.

He cried out desperately: "Stop!"

Isabel raised her eyes, glared at him, and lifted a thick and heavy tome.

"No!" he shouted, "Please!" for this, he knew, was his magnum opus.

"Everything you are," she said, with an air of finality, "must be rewritten."

She dropped the book into the flames.

Burton jerked awake, a sheen of sweat upon his brow.

"The deuce take it!" he cursed, pushing back the blankets and wrapping himself in his *jubbah*. He stood, parted the curtains—it was still dark outside—then leaned over his water basin and splashed his face.

He left his bedroom and walked down the stairs to the study, opened the door and entered.

The coal in the hearth was glowing softly. Above, on the mantelpiece, a candle glimmered.

It was six o'clock in the morning; too early for Mrs Angell to have lit candles, besides which, she wouldn't have done it; she'd have stoked the fire, opened the curtains, and returned to the basement to await his awakening and request for coffee.

He closed the door behind him and stood listening. Then he calmly crossed to the fireplace and took a rapier down from a bracket on the chimney breast.

He shrugged off the *jubbah*, threw it on a chair, and faced the room, standing in his pyjamas, holding the sword point downward.

"Show yourself," he said, softly.

A figure stepped out from the shadows to the left, from between a bookcase and the curtained windows.

The man was an albino, his skin and shoulder-length hair startlingly white, his eyes pink, with vertical pupils; the eyes of a cat. Of average height and build, he was dressed entirely in black, and held a top hat in his left hand and a silver-topped cane in his right. His pointed fingernails were also black.

By far the most remarkable thing about him, though, was his face, the jaws of which seemed to protrude unnaturally, giving the impression of a carnivorous muzzle.

Undoubtedly, this was the man who'd abducted John Speke and mesmerised Sister Raghavendra.

"I've been waiting, Sir Richard."

The voice was a seductive purr; oily and repellent.

"For how long?"

"An hour or so. Don't worry; I kept myself occupied. I've been reading your notes."

"Is privacy a notion you find difficult to comprehend?"

"What possible advantage would I gain from respecting your privacy?"

"Perhaps the reputation of a gentleman?" said Burton, cuttingly.

The albino made a noise that may have been a laugh, though it sounded like a growl.

Burton raised the point of his rapier.

"Is Lieutenant Speke alive?" he asked.

"Yes."

"Why did you take him?"

"Things might go a lot better for you if you abandon such questions. You've been asking too many of late, though your investigation has amounted to little more than an extended crawl from one public house to another."

"People gather in public houses. They're a natural source of information. You've been watching me?"

"Of course. From the moment you broke my mesmeric hold over the nurse."

"I saw your eyes in hers."

"And I saw you through them."

"I've heard such things are possible, though I've never seen it done before; not even in India. And, incidentally, you can stop staring at me like that. I'm no mean mesmerist myself and I won't succumb to your magnetic influence."

The intruder shrugged and stepped into the middle of the room. His eyes burned redly in the candlelight. He placed his top hat onto a desk.

"You don't recognise me," he said. "I'm not surprised. I am somewhat altered."

"So tell me who you are and what you want before you get the hell out of my house," answered the King's agent.

In one lightning swift movement, the albino drew a sword from his cane, touched its tip to Burton's rapier, lay the sheath on a desk, and said:

"Laurence Oliphant, most definitely not at your service."

Burton stepped back in surprise and his shoulder blades bumped the mantelpiece.

"Good lord! What have you done to yourself?" he exclaimed.

Oliphant, who'd stepped forward to keep his blade against Burton's, applied a slight pressure to it.

"The True Libertines may rail against Technology," he said, "but the Rakes view the work of the Eugenicists as an opportunity. What better way to transcend human limitations than by quite literally becoming something a little more than human?"

"You've been hanging around with the wrong people," observed Burton.

Oliphant ignored the gibe and tapped his sword against the rapier, once, twice, before purring:

"And to answer your earlier question, what I want is for you to stop poking your nose into matters that don't concern you. I am quite serious, Sir Richard. I will force the issue if I must. Do you care to test me?"

Burton held his blade firmly and responded:

"I'm counted one of the finest swordsmen in Europe, Oliphant."

There was a blur of motion; an instant which passed so quickly that it might never have happened.

Burton felt a sudden warmth on his cheek. He reached up and touched it. His fingers came away wet with blood.

"And I," breathed Oliphant, "am the fastest. Don't worry; for your vanity's sake, I have merely reopened that old scar of yours rather than adding a new."

"Most thoughtful," muttered Burton, icily. He stepped forward and thrust at the albino's shoulder. His rapier was nonchalantly parried and ripped from his hand by his opponent's whirling blade. It hit a desk, bounced, and landed point-first in one of the bookcases.

Oliphant, whose sword-tip was now touching Burton just below the left eye, gave a momentary glance backward.

"My dear fellow!" he oozed. "How unfortunate. You seem to have impaled James Tuckey's *Narrative of an Expedition to Explore the River Zaire.*"

He lowered his weapon and stepped back.

"Take down another blade."

Burton, who'd never before been disarmed in combat, reached up and slid his hand along the chimney breast until his fingers found a weapon. Without taking his eyes from the intruder, he lowered it, gripped the hilt, and raised the blade until it touched Oliphant's.

The albino smiled, revealing even, pointed teeth.

"Are you sure you want to continue? There's no need. Agree to abandon your investigation, and I'll take my leave of you."

"I don't think so," countered Burton.

"Come now! Throw it over, Sir Richard! Why not settle down instead? Marry that girl of yours. Maybe apply for a governmental post and write your books."

'Bismillah!' thought Burton. 'He's practically quoting Spring Heeled Jack!'

"Yes, that's one option," he replied. "The other is that you tell me exactly what's going on. Shall we start with why you abducted John Speke, or should we go back a little further and talk about why you turned him against me after the Nile expedition? Or maybe we can discuss the werewolf creatures you had with you at the hospital?"

He took a chance:

"Or would you prefer a little chat about Spring Heeled Jack?"

A muscle twitched at the corner of a pink eye and Burton knew that he'd hit home. He wasn't working on two cases; he was working on one!

Oliphant's sword scraped down the rapier and made a lazy thrust at Burton's heart. The King's agent turned it aside and stepped to the left, flicking his point toward Oliphant's throat; a feint; he brought it down and stabbed at an area just below the albino's collar bone. His blade was met, turned, twisted and almost torn from his hand again. This time, though, his riposte was fast and effective and Oliphant, not meeting resistance from the expected direction, found his point rising higher than intended. The end of Burton's rapier danced forward beneath it, pierced the sleeve of the albino's velvet frock coat, and penetrated his wrist. It was a move—the *manchette*—that the adventurer had developed himself in Boulogne while under the tutelage of the famed Monsieur Constantine.

Laurence Oliphant sprang back and stood clutching his wrist, his lips curled.

With feline eyes following his every move, Burton circled his opponent; walked past the bureau and windows, behind his primary desk, crossed in front of a bookcase, then stopped, blocking the door.

He used the back of his hand to wipe the blood from his cheek.

"En guard!" he snapped, and adopted the position.

Oliphant hissed poisonously and followed suit. Their weapons met.

In a flurry of motion, the duel commenced. The two blades clashed, scraped, lunged, parried and whirled in attack and riposte, filling the room with the tink tink tink of metal against metal. Even with his wounded wrist, Burton's opponent possessed greater speed than any he'd faced before; but Oliphant had a fault: his eyes signalled every move, and the King's agent was thus able to defend against the blindingly fast onslaught. However, finding an opening in the albino's defence proved far more difficult, and, as the two men battled back and forth across the candle-lit study, the competition quickly became, at least for Burton, one of endurance.

"Give it up!" gasped Oliphant.

"Where is Speke?" ground out Burton. "I demand an answer!"

"The only one you'll get," growled his foe, "is *this*!"

The albino's blade accelerated to such a speed that it became almost invisible. Burton's instincts took over; his many years of study and practice in the art of swordsmanship saved him over and over as he desperately blocked and turned aside the darting point. Again and again he was forced to step back, until he was brought up against a bookcase and found himself unable to manoeuvre. Worse, he was tiring, and he saw in the pink eyes that Oliphant recognised the fact.

He feinted, avoided the counter-attack, and plunged his blade forward.

A red line appeared on Oliphant's cheek and blood sprayed out behind Burton's flashing blade.

"One for one!" he barked and, seeing his opponent momentarily disconcerted, attempted another of his own moves, the *une-deux*, which against any normal opponent would have sent their weapon flying out of their grip while almost breaking their wrist.

Laurence Oliphant was not a normal opponent.

With a howl of fury he slipped his blade through Burton's attack and renewed his assault.

The deadly tip of his sword flew in from every direction and Burton, with the bookcase at his back and his arm muscles burning, found his defences breached. Scratches began to materialise on his forearms; slashes appeared as if by magic in the material of his pyjamas; a puncture wound marked his neck.

He was breathing heavily and starting to feel light-headed. His left hand, held outward and downward for balance, kept knocking against something; a distraction which grew increasingly irritating as his defence continued to falter and Oliphant's weapon found its target again and again.

At the exact instant he saw in his opponent's eyes that the killing thrust was coming, his hand closed over the obstruction and yanked it. A second rapier whipped upward and James Tuckey's *Narrative of an Expedition to Explore the River Zaire* flew from the end of it, hitting Oliphant square on the nose.

The albino stumbled backward.

As Burton's newly acquired blade came down, his other came up, and this time his *une-deux* succeeded. Oliphant's sword went spinning away to land near one of the windows. The King's agent immediately dropped both rapiers, sprang in close, and sent a terrific right cross cracking into his enemy's ear.

The intruder's head snapped sideways and he toppled to the floor, knocking over a table and crashing into a chair, which splintered into pieces under him.

Rolling to his knees, Oliphant ducked under a second punch, and swiped upward, his fingernails clawing through pyjamas and lacerating the skin beneath.

Burton grabbed for his opponent's arm, intending to pull him into a *jambuvanthee* Indian wrestling hold, but his bare foot landed on a sharp fragment of wood and twisted under him. He lost his balanced and staggered.

The albino kicked out, his heels thumping into Burton's hip. The King's agent fell back against the bookcase with a loud bang and volumes tumbled down around him. He slid to the floor, snatched up a chair leg, and scrambled back to his feet just in time to see his opponent leaping away.

Laurence Oliphant grabbed his cane, scooped up his blade and sheathed it, and propelled himself through the glass of the window. The loud smash was immediately followed by the tinkle of glass as the shattered pane rained onto the pavement below.

Burton raced over and looked out. No normal human could have survived that drop, yet there was Oliphant, hatless and bloodied, sprinting toward the western end of Montagu Place. He ran past roadworks, which had appeared on the street the previous evening, and vanished around the corner.

Sir Richard Francis Burton, dripping blood, his pyjamas hanging in shreds, opened his bureau and poured himself a large brandy, which he swallowed in a single gulp.

He crossed to the fireplace and fell into his armchair, let loose a deep sigh, then immediately stood again, wondering how the hell Oliphant had got into the house.

A few minutes later, he found the answer: the tradesman's entrance below the front door was open and beside it, in the hallway, dressed in her nightgown, stood Mrs Iris Angell.

Her eyes were wide, staring blankly at the wall.

"Come on, Mother Angell," said Burton gently, and guided her into her parlour. He sat her down and began crooning in that same ancient tongue he'd used to bring Countess Sabina out of her trance.

He knew he had to be thorough now. It wasn't merely a case of disengaging the woman from her hypnotic stupor; he had to probe the depths of her mind to remove any lingering suggestions planted by the arch mesmerist, for it wouldn't do to have her spying for Oliphant, or, even worse, slipping poison into Burton's food.

"Hellfire!" he thought. "What have I got myself into?"

§

Chapter 11

The Sweeps

PAM IS ANTI-SLAVERY
PAM IS PRO-CHILD-LABOUR
CHILD LABOUR IS SLAVERY
VOTE OUT THE HYPOCRITE!
VOTE IN DISRAELI!

—*GRAFFITI*

Later that morning, after he'd arranged for a glazier to replace his broken window, Burton called at Algernon Swinburne's lodgings on Grafton Way, Fitzroy Square.

"By James!" exclaimed the poet, screeching with laughter. "You're more battered each time I see you! What happened this time? An escaped tiger?"

"More like a white panther," muttered Burton, noticing the dark circles under his friend's eyes. Swinburne had obviously continued drinking after their visit to The Tremors and was suffering the consequences.

The poet examined the explorer's face and hands, his eyes lingering on the cuts and puncture wounds.

"They must sting deliciously," he commented.

"That's not the word I'd choose," replied Burton, wryly. "It was Oliphant. When was the last time you saw him?"

"Laurence Oliphant! Humm, maybe eighteen months ago?"

"Describe him."

"Average build; he has a bald pate with a fringe of curly brown hair around the ears; a bushy beard; rather feline features; magnetic eyes."

"Complexion?"

"Pale; I can't remember his eye colour. Why?"

"Because the man I encountered last night—who claimed to be him— was a pink-eyed albino; clean-shaven with a full head of hair. Get your coat and hat on, Algy; we have work to do."

"So it wasn't Oliphant, then. Where are we going?"

"I think it was. He said he'd had work done by the Eugenicists, and you know how much they can change a man. Look at Palmerston! You told me Oliphant owned a white panther. I suspect that he's now closer than ever to his pet!"

Swinburne tied his bootlaces, slipped into his coat and pushed a bowler hat down over his hair.

They left the flat and hailed a cab.

While they steamed south-eastward, Burton told his friend about the latest developments: of his meeting with The Beetle and of Detective-Inspector Trounce's discoveries; then he explained: "We're going to Elephant and Castle to question one of the boys who returned after being abducted by the loup-garous. He remembers nothing, apparently; due, I believe, to a mesmeric spell cast by the albino. Maybe I can break through it, as I did with Sister Raghavendra. After that, we'll take a look at the rooms which were occupied by boys who're still missing."

"Ah ha! You intend a spot of clue-hunting, like Edgar Allan Poe's detective, Auguste Dupin?"

"Yes, something like that."

While crossing Waterloo Bridge, their conveyance broke down and they had to hail a second vehicle. This—a horse-drawn "growler"—took them the rest of the way across the river, past the railway station, onward down London Road and New Kent Road, and into the tangled streets of Elephant and Castle.

They stopped and disembarked on the corner of William De Montmorency Close. Burton paid the fare and shut Swinburne up when the poet started to complain.

"Never mind whether it's a shilling or not," he said. "Look over there! Something's up!"

Swinburne followed his friend's gaze and saw, farther along the road, a crowd of people gathered around a red-brick terraced house.

"Is that our place?"

"I fear so."

They approached the throng and glimpsed police helmets among the hats, bonnets and caps. Burton pushed through and tapped one of the uniformed men on the shoulder.

"What's the story, Constable?" he asked.

The man turned and gave him a doubtful look. Burton was dressed and spoke like a gentleman but had the appearance of a battered pugilist.

"And who might you be, sir?" he asked, haughtily.

"Sir Richard Burton; here's my authorisation."

A voice in the crowd exclaimed: "Blimey! They've sent a 'Sir.' Now we're gettin' somewhere! You'll collar the bugger what done away with the nipper, won't you, yer lordship? We want to see the devil crapped, we does!"

The crowd cheered.

"Crapped?" whispered Swinburne.

"Hanged," translated Burton.

"I'm not sure about this, sir," said the constable, hesitantly.

"Who's your superior?" demanded Burton. "Take it and show it to him."

The policeman looked again at the paper Burton had handed to him. He nodded. "Just a tick, sir." He left them and entered the house.

"Murdered!" said the man in the crowd. "And not even ten years old."

"A little angel, 'e was," came a woman's voice.

"Aye, wouldn't say boo to a goose," agreed another.

"Fancy killin' a nipper!"

"It ain't English!"

"It's one o' them bleedin' foreigners what done it, I'll lay money on it!"

The constable appeared in the doorway and indicated that Burton should enter the premises. The King's agent, with Swinburne in his wake, pushed through the onlookers and stepped into the house.

"Upstairs, sir," said the policeman.

They ascended. There were three bedrooms. A dead child lay in one.

A man stepped forward with outstretched hand. He was small and slightly built but with a wiry strength about him. His brown moustache was flamboyantly wide, waxed, and curled upward at the ends. His lacquered hair was parted in the middle. He possessed grey eyes, with a monocle clenched in the right.

"Thomas Manfred Honesty," he said. "Detective-Inspector."

"A reassuring surname for a policeman," observed Swinburne.

Burton shook the man's hand. So this was Trounce's erstwhile tormentor!

"I'm Captain Burton, acting on behalf of His Majesty. This is Algernon Swinburne. He's assisting me."

Honesty looked askance at Swinburne, who fluttered his eyelashes.

"Ahem! Yes, well, the boy," the detective spluttered, waving his hand toward the prone figure. "William Tupper. Orphan. Age uncertain. Ten years? Chimney sweep. Damn shame. Pitiful really."

Burton stepped over to the corpse and crouched beside it. The boy was tiny, even for his age. His thin neck was covered in blood; its source, a small hole at the base of the chin.

"Stiletto," offered Honesty. "In. Up. Pierced the brain."

"No," countered Burton. "A swordstick, such as gentlemen carry. A stiletto blade typically has a triangular, round, square or diamond cross section without sharpened edges, whereas the rapier style of blade, which is most often used in swordsticks, is either diamond in cross-section, with or without fluting, or a flattened hexagonal; in either case, with sharpened edges. Look closely at this wound, Inspector; you can see it was made by a hexagonal blade which cut as well as pierced as it entered."

Honesty dropped to his knees and leaned close to the boy, adjusting his monocle and peering at the grisly hole above the larynx, his nose just inches from the wound. He whistled.

"Agreed. Rapier. But swordstick? Why?"

"In this day and age, can a man walk down the street in possession of a sword without being accosted by the police? No. It had to be disguised."

"Point taken. Sorry. Pun unintended. And this?"

He indicated the boy's forehead. There was a small bruise between the eyes, with a pinprick in its centre.

"I don't know," answered Burton. "But it looks like the mark left by a syringe."

"Syringe? An injection?"

"Or an extraction."

The Yard man stood and scratched his chin.

"Syringe first? Swordstick second?"

"No, Detective-Inspector; the syringe mark is a few days old. Look at the yellowing of the bruise."

"Hmm. Unconnected then. Though odd. Very odd. And the motive?"

"I was on my way here to question the boy. I think he was killed to stop him talking. Right now, I'm afraid I can't tell you any more than that, but I'm working in harness with your colleague, Detective-Inspector Trounce, and will report to him. The two of you can then confer over this dastardly affair."

Honesty sniffed.

"Pouncer Trounce. Good man. Has imagination. Too much. You can't tell me more?"

"I have more facts to gather before I can piece together the full story and present a report."

"I want to be involved. Don't like this. Children murdered. It's wrong!"

"When the occasion arises, I'll be sure to let you get a shot at those responsible, Detective-Inspector Honesty."

"Good. Better come downstairs. Another fact for you."

"Downstairs?"

"The kitchen," said Honesty. "Mr and Mrs Payne. Householders. Let the room. How could the boy afford it?"

"The League of Chimney Sweeps paid his rent," explained Burton. "It's an admirable organisation."

He and Swinburne followed the Yard man down the stairs. The poet looked around eagerly, soaking in the atmosphere of the murder scene, the raw emotion of it.

They trooped through the hall and into the small, narrow kitchen, which smelled of boiled cabbage and animal fat.

"A moment, Constable Krishnamurthy," said Honesty to a policeman.

"Yes, sir," came the response, and the uniformed man stepped out of the room, revealing, behind him, the figures of Mr and Mrs Payne.

They were frozen in mid-movement; the old woman standing, pouring tea, which had overflowed the cup and saucer, pooled across the kitchen table and dribbled to the floor; the man in mid-step, his right hand holding a sandwich raised to his mouth. They were both looking toward a door which opened onto a small back yard.

Burton examined them for a moment, staring into their motionless eyes.

"Transfixed by psychic magnetism," he said.

"I see," responded Detective-Inspector Honesty. "Mental domination."

"Yes. I'll bring them out of it."

For the next few minutes, the Yard man looked on in bafflement as Burton chanted and waved his hands about in front of the immobilised couple. Slowly, blinking in confusion, they regained their wits and were led into the parlour, where they sank into chairs. They remembered a knock at their back door, a man with white skin, white hair, and pink eyes—and nothing else.

When Honesty revealed to them the fate of their young lodger, the woman became hysterical, the man spat expletives into the room, and Burton and Swinburne left.

They passed through the crowd outside, ignoring the questions shouted at them, and swiftly walked away.

"You should have foreseen this, Richard," advised the poet, his voice uncharacteristically grim. "Oliphant read your notes."

"I know. Confounded fool that I am!" cursed Burton. "I never considered that the bastard would come here first and do away with the poor little soul. How the hell could I have overlooked the possibility? I'll never forgive myself!"

"Don't be an idiot. You overlooked it because infanticide is unimaginable," offered Swinburne. "No one normal would consider such an option. But Richard, when I say you should have foreseen it, I don't mean to censure you because you didn't; I mean to suggest that this new role of yours requires a different way of thinking. You have to attune that phenomenal intellect of yours to deviant possibilities like this."

"You're right, Algy, but I must confess: I'm doubting myself. First Monty Penniforth, now Billy Tupper; how many innocent lives are to be lost due to my negligence?" Swinburne suddenly hopped up and down and screeched: "For crying out loud, Richard, you didn't gut the cabbie or stab the child!

Others did—and you have to stop them before they commit further atrocities!"

"Alright! Alright! Come on, let's check the missing boys' rooms; maybe we can get some idea of why they weren't returned like Tupper and the others."

The second address supplied to Burton by The Beetle was less than half a mile away, on Tainted Row, which, despite its name, was a fairly respectable street of once handsome Georgian houses, now mostly divided into flats and individual chambers. Their destination was a three-storey residence which stood on the corner. Its various rooms were rented out by the landlord, Ebenezer Smike, to the League of Chimney Sweeps.

Smike was a careworn-looking individual, with a sallow complexion and uneven eyes, gaunt cheeks and a long asymmetrical jaw, all of which gave his face a peculiarly bent quality. The fact that he regarded his visitors from the corner of his eyes, with his face slightly turned away, accentuated this impression. He wore a long threadbare dressing gown of a bilious green hue; and beneath it a pale yellow shirt, black and white chequered trousers, and a pair of worn tartan slippers.

"The League is still paying rent on the rooms," he explained, as he led them up the stairs, "though they stand empty. I ain't touched 'em. Here you are."

He opened a door, revealing a small chamber containing a bed, a table and chair, a wardrobe and a water basin.

Burton stepped in and surveyed the room; looked at the clothes in the wardrobe—a shirt, a waistcoat, a pair of trousers and a pair of soft shoes—and at the comb, tin soldier and bag of bull's-eyes on the table. A soot-stained flannel hung over the edge of the basin. A well-thumbed penny dreadful—*Robin Hood's Peril*—lay on the bed.

"This was Benny Whymper's room," said Smike.

Two small boys had appeared and were standing behind the landlord, watching the proceedings. Swinburne smiled at them and asked: "Are you lads sweeps, too?"

"Yes, mister," said one.

The next room, Jacob Spratt's, was almost identical to the first. A pair of slippers poked out from beneath the bed; a mirror leaned against the wall over the wash basin; a tattered notepad containing childish drawings, mainly of locomotives, lay on the table.

Swinburne examined himself in the mirror and groaned.

"I've modelled for the Pre-Raphaelites," he muttered, "but I don't think they'd want to paint me today. I look awful!"

The final room, which had belonged to Rajish Thakarta, contained a great many toy soldiers which the boy had cleverly carved from pieces of wood. His pen-knife was on the table, alongside a tattered book embossed with Sanskrit lettering. Burton recognised it as the *Bhagavad-Gita*.

The wardrobe contained rather more clothes than those in the other rooms, including a small sherwani, the long coat-like garment common to South Asia. The boy obviously clung to his roots, though an orphan and far from his homeland.

As they moved back into the hallway, Burton stopped and looked thoughtful. He glanced at Swinburne, then at the two little chimney sweeps who were sheltering shyly behind Ebenezer Smike, then went into each of the three rooms once again and looked at the footwear in each.

He came out and suddenly squatted on his haunches and smiled at the two boys. Swinburne grinned, amazed at the way his friend's habitually ferocious expression seemed to melt away.

"I have two shillings, lads," said Burton. "Would you like to earn them; a bob apiece?"

"Not half!" they both hollered enthusiastically. They pushed past their landlord to stand before him.

"What do we have to do, mister?" asked one.

"What's your name, son?"

"Charlie, sir; this is Ned."

"Well, Charlie and Ned, all you have to do is answer a question."

"Yes, sir?"

"Were the three boys who occupied these rooms tall?"

"Oh yes sir!" they chorused.

"Regular giants, they were!" cried the youngster named Ned.

Burton nodded.

"So older, eh?"

"No, not a bit of it! Just big 'uns, is all, sir!"

"Good lads," encouraged Burton. "Now, I have another question. If you think carefully about it and answer it truthfully, I'll add a sixpence each."

"Crumbs!" breathed Charlie.

"First of all," said Burton, "do you know the other boys who've disappeared recently?"

"Yes, mister."

"I'm aware that most of them have come back. It's the ones who haven't that I want to ask you about."

"That'll be Jacob, Raj and Benny, and Paul Kelly, Ed Trip, Mickey Smith, Lofty Sanderson, Thicko Chris Williams, and Ben Prentiss," said Charlie, counting the names off on his fingers.

"And Aubrey Baxter," added Ned. "He was snatched the other night."

"And those boys," said Burton. "Were they tall, too?"

"I say! They certainly were!" cried Charlie excitedly. "They're some o' the tallest sweeps in the League, ain't that right, Ned?"

"Excepting Aubrey, what's a nipper like us, yes; bean poles the lot of 'em!" responded Ned.

"Thank you boys; here are your wages."

He placed the coins in their eager little hands and rose to his feet, turning to Ebenezer Smike as the children scampered away as if afraid he might change his mind and demand the money back.

"Thank you, Mr Smike. We won't take up any more of your time."

"You've seen all you need?"

"Yes, I believe so. We'll leave you in peace."

Smike accompanied them to the front door and, as they stood on the step and shook his hand, asked: "The young 'uns, sir; will they be back?"

"That I can't answer, I'm afraid," replied Burton.

He and Swinburne took their leave and strolled toward New Kent Road, intending to pick up a cab there.

"Interesting," muttered Burton. "It's the tall boys who aren't returning. What does that mean, I wonder?"

"But I say!" cried Swinburne. "What the dickens put you on that particular track?"

"You did! When you were looking into the mirror in Jacob Spratt's room I realised that it was leaning against the wall at an angle exactly suited to someone of your height; considerably taller than little Ned and Charlie. I then checked the shoes and slippers in the rooms and saw that they were all of a comparatively large size."

"Auguste Dupin!" screeched the poet excitedly, jumping around the older man like a whirling dervish.

"Calm down, you silly ass!" chuckled the King's agent.

Swinburne, though he became uncharacteristically silent, did not calm down. As they walked along, his gait became increasingly eccentric, until he was practically skipping, and he wrung his hands together excitedly, twitching and jerking as if on the verge of a fit.

By the time they'd waved down a hansom and were chugging homeward, the poet could contain himself no longer, and exploded: "It's obvious, Richard! It's obvious!"

"What is?"

"That I have to masquerade as a chimney sweep!"

"What the devil do you mean?"

"You must see The Beetle again and arrange for me to join the League. I'll work in the Cauldron and will put myself in harm's way until I get abducted!"

"Don't be bloody ridiculous!" snapped Burton. "I have enough deaths on my conscience; I'll not add yours."

"You don't have any choice. If you don't help me, I'll do it despite you!"

Burton's eyes blazed.

"Blast you, you little squirt! It's suicide!"

"No, Richard. It's the only way to find out where the werewolves come from and where the boys are being taken. Look at me: I'm the same height as Jacob and Rajish and Benny and the other missing lads! I'll wander the streets after dark until I get myself kidnapped, and, somehow, by hook or by crook, I'll get a message to you!"

"I forbid it, Algernon! I absolutely forbid it! For all you know, the boys have been killed. And how the hell will you send a message?"

"I'll carry a parakeet with me!"

"It won't work! You'll not find one that'll be content to sit in your pocket without swearing at the top of its voice. It'll attract attention and you'll end up with your throat cut, if not by the loup-garous then by an East Ender."

"I don't know how then, Richard, but I'll find a way. It's our only hope of solving this case!"

"Our only hope? What do you mean our? Since when did you become my assistant?"

"Since just now—and I'll not be dissuaded; this plan will work and you know it!"

"I know no such thing."

Their argument raged on until they reached Swinburne's lodgings, by which point Burton had concluded that nothing he could do or say would convince the little poet of the madness of the scheme. He was even tempted to mesmerise his friend but Swinburne's personality was so eccentric that his behaviour under magnetic influence was impossible to predict and might prove just as dangerous as his crazy plan. So, reluctantly, he agreed to talk to The Beetle later in the day.

At the back of his mind, an idea was emerging, and he realised that a return visit to Battersea would also be required.

§

When he arrived home, Sir Richard Francis Burton found that the roadworks were now right outside his house. The two workmen were obviously toiling with far greater efficiency that the average labourer; digging a deep narrow trench and filling it in behind them as they progressed.

"Fast blighters, ain't they, Cap'n?" came a voice.

It was Mr Grub, the chestnut vendor.

"They are indeed, Mr Grub," agreed Burton. "You're taking the day off?"

"Not by choice. Some idiot lost control of his penny farthing and knocked my Dutch oven over. Put a whacking great dent in it. I had to send it off to my brother-in-law, the metalsmith, to hammer it back into shape. A darned hazard, all these new contraptions, don't you think?"

"I do, Mr Grub; I do. I wonder what they're up to?"

"The diggers? They're laying a pipe. Probably a new gas main."

Burton looked at the two workmen; funny looking chaps, he thought. More like gravediggers than labourers.

He bid Mr Grub farewell and entered his home.

Mrs Angell confronted him in the hallway.

"Now then, sir," she said, with hands on hips and a tapping foot. "They finished the new window a half hour ago and I've made your room ship-shape again—but I would very much like to know what all that nonsense was about. I've put up with your ungodly carousing on countless occasions but you've never caused such mayhem before. Who was that white-skinned scoundrel?"

"Make us a pot of tea, Mother Angell, and I'll join you in the dining room. I think it's time I told you about my new job!"

§

Chapter 12

The Resurrectionists

&

WHEN MY MOTHER DIED I WAS VERY YOUNG,
AND MY FATHER SOLD ME WHILE YET MY TONGUE
COULD SCARCELY CRY "'WEEP! 'WEEP! 'WEEP! 'WEEP!'"
SO YOUR CHIMNEYS I SWEEP, AND IN SOOT I SLEEP.
—WILLIAM BLAKE, SONGS OF INNOCENCE

&

Thwack!

"Please—no—yes—aah!"

Thwack!

"Oh my—my—eeh-yow!"

Thwack!

"Oh! Ah!—Oh! Ha! Ha!—It burns!"

Again and again, the leather belt struck Algernon Swinburne's buttocks with terrific force, sending wave after wave of pleasure coursing through his diminutive body. He shrieked and howled and gibbered rapturously until, finally, Master Sweep Vincent Sneed grew tired, threw the belt aside, took his hand from the back of the poet's neck, stepped away from the wooden crate over which Swinburne was bent, and wiped his sweaty brow.

"Let that be a lesson to yer," he snarled. "I'll 'ave none o' your back-chat, you little toe-rag. Stand up straight!"

Swinburne stood, rubbing his backside through his trousers. He was wearing a flat cap, a stained white collarless calico shirt, a threadbare waistcoat, fingerless woollen gloves, and trousers that were too short—they stopped some inches above his ankles. On his feet were ill-fitting boots with loose soles. His face, hands and clothes were smeared with soot and his teeth had been made to look yellow and rotten.

"Sorry, Mr Sneed," he whined.

"Shut yer cake-hole. I don't want another peep outa yer. Pack the tools. We've got a job on an' it's gettin' late."

Swinburne left the crate—which the Master Sweep used as a table—and limped over to the workbench where the brushes and poles, which he'd been cleaning all morning, were laid out. He started packing them into a long canvas holdall.

Sneed plonked himself onto a stool and sat with legs akimbo, elbows on knees, and a bottle of moonshine in his right hand. He watched Swinburne and sneered. The League had supplied him with this new boy three days ago and the little git was too mouthy by half.

"I'll beat some respeck inter yer, that I will," he mumbled. "Yer blinkin' whipper-snapper."

In aspect, Sneed resembled a stoat. His thin black hair was long and greasy, combed backward over his narrow skull, with his gleaming scalp shining through it. His low forehead slid down into a pockmarked and sly-looking face, the whole of which seemed to have been pulled forward by his gargantuan nose; so much so that his beady black eyes, rather then being to either side of it, seemed to be *on* the sides of the astonishing protuberance. That nose had earned him his nickname, which he despised with a passion. Woe betide anyone who uttered the words "The Conk" within range of his little cauliflower ears!

His small lipless mouth and receding chin were partially hidden by a ragged, nicotine-stained moustache and beard. Through the tangled hair, two big uneven front teeth could be glimpsed.

Over his short, thin but powerful frame, The Conk was wearing baggy canvas trousers held up by a pair of braces, a filthy shirt with a red cravat, and a bizarre blue surtout with epaulettes, which may well have been a relic from Admiral Nelson's day.

"29 Hanbury Street, Spitalfields," he grunted. "One flue, narrow. We'll take a goose, just in case."

Swinburne stifled a yawn. He'd experienced three days of exhausting work. His hands were cut and blistered. His pores were clogged with soot.

"Ain't you finished yet?"

"Yes," answered the poet. "All packed."

"So shove it in the wagon and 'itch up the 'orse. Do I 'ave to tell yer everything?"

Swinburne went out into the yard and did as directed. His buttocks were burning from the beating he'd taken. He would have whistled happily were he not so tired.

A little later, he and The Conk, wrapped in overcoats and with their caps pulled down tightly, were seated at the front of the wagon and heading north westward across Whitchapel. As the vehicle rumbled over the cobbles, its bumps and jolts sent pain lancing up through the poet's sensitised backside.

"Heavenly!" he muttered gleefully.

"What's that?" grunted The Conk.

"Nothing, sir," Swinburne replied. "I was just thinking about the job."

"Think about steering this old nag. There'll be time to think about the bleedin' job when we get there."

It was half past four. Spots of rain began to fall. The weather, unpredictable as ever, was taking a turn for the worse but it could never rain hard enough to wash away the stench of the East End. After three days, Swinburne's nose was becoming attuned to it, blocking out the mephitic stink. There were always surprises, though; areas where the putrid gases threatened to overpower him and bring up what little he had in his stomach.

The sights, too, were sickening. The streets were crowded with the worst dregs of humanity; most of them shuffling, slumping or sprawling aimlessly, their eyes desolate, their poverty having pushed them into an animal—almost vegetative—state. Others moved about, seeking a pocket to pick, a mug to rob, or a mark to swindle. There were beggars, prostitutes, pimps, drug addicts and drunkards in profusion; children, too, playing desultory games in puddles of filth; and, occasionally, the white bonnets of the Sisterhood of Noble Benevolence could be seen bobbing through the mob; the women travelling in threes, trying to do good—distributing gruel and roughly woven blankets—managing to move through this destitute hell without being harmed; how, no one knew, though some claimed they possessed a supernatural grace which protected them.

There were labourers, too: hawkers, costermongers, carpenters and coopers, tanners, slaughterhouse workers and builders. There were publicans, of course, and pawnbrokers, betting touts and undertakers; but the majority of the employed were invisible; locked away in the workhouses and factories, where they slaved back-breaking hour after back-breaking hour in return for a short sleep on a hard bed and a daily bowl of slop.

Through this milling throng, the wagon passed. Swinburne steered it along tight lanes bordered by rookeries whose gables leaned precariously inward, threatening to topple into each other, burying anyone on the cobbles beneath.

Grimy water dripped onto him from strings of hanging garments.

The sweep and his apprentice stopped and picked up a goose from a poulterer's, pushing it into a sack which The Conk kept squeezed between his legs as they continued their journey.

"It's a struggler," he noted, approvingly.

Ten minutes or so later they reached the Truman Brewery and turned into Hanbury Street, drawing up outside number 29. The premises was a large building with many rooms and an ironmonger's shop at the front. A notice in the window announced: "*Rooms to Let. Apply Within only if Respectable. Strictly No Foreigners.*"

"'obble the 'orse and unload the 'quipment," ordered Sneed, jumping down to the pavement. With the sack in his hand, he went into the shop while Swinburne chained the horse's ankles together.

The poet dragged the heavy holdall from the back of the wagon and waited. A moment later Sneed emerged and gestured to a second door.

"This way," he grunted, pushing it open.

Swinburne followed his master down a passageway and through a second door which opened onto a back yard; a patchwork of stone, grass and dirt. It was surrounded by a high wooden fence and contained a small shed and a privy. Three steps rose to a back door, which The Conk knocked on. It was opened by an elderly crinoline-clad woman, her hair in curl-papers, who gestured for them to enter.

They moved through a scullery and kitchen into a short hallway then passed through a door to the right and found themselves in a small parlour.

"Alright, ma'am; you can leave us to it," said Sneed.

"Mind you don't chip me china," advised the old lady as she departed.

Swinburne looked around but couldn't see any china.

The room smelled musty and damp.

"Jump to it!" snapped The Conk. "Lay out the sacking."

He sat on a shabby armchair and pulled the bottle of moonshine from his pocket, taking swigs, watching Swinburne work, and giving the sack between his knees an occasional slap.

Swinburne soon had the floor and furniture, what there was of it, covered.

The Master Sweep slipped the bottle back into his jacket, slid off the chair and poked his head into the fireplace, looking up.

"Nope," he grunted. "You'll not get up there. Why The Beetle 'ad to send me a hulking great helephant like you I don't know."

Swinburne grinned. He'd been called many things in his time but "hulking great helephant" was a first.

The Conk twisted, shot out a hand and slapped the poet's face. Swinburne gasped.

"You can wipe that smile off yer ugly mug!" snarled The Conk. "You've got too much hattitude, you 'ave."

They returned to the wagon outside and Swinburne untied the ropes which secured the ladder. Sneed slid it off—it was too heavy for Swinburne—and heaved it up until its top rested against the side of the roof, its topmost rung just below the eaves.

"Get up there and drop down the rope, an' be quick about it!"

"Yes, sir," said the poet, whose face was stinging pleasantly.

While The Conk returned to the room behind the shop, Swinburne wound a long length of rope around his little shoulders then scrambled up the ladder. He now faced his most dangerous task; he had to cross the sloping roof to the chimney pot; a sloping roof whose tiles were slick from the spitting rain.

Lifting himself off the top rung and over the eaves, he lay on his right hip and pressed the sides of his boots against the wet surface. With his palms flat against the tiles, he began to push himself up. Bit by bit, he advanced over the shingles toward the ridge.

It took nearly ten painstaking minutes but he made it without slipping and, with a sigh of relief, stood and braced himself against the chimney. He unravelled the rope and lowered it into the flue.

"About bleedin' time, you lazy bugger," came a hollow voice from below.

The rope jumped and jerked as The Conk tied its end around the goose's legs. Swinburne could hear the bird honking in distress.

"Alright, up with her," came Sneed's command.

Swinburne started to haul the unfortunate—and very heavy—goose up the shaft. Its panicked flapping and cries echoed up the flue.

This was the method they used to loosen the caked soot from the inside of the chimney when the space was too narrow for Swinburne to climb up and do it himself. Though he felt sympathy for the traumatised bird, the poet preferred it this way, for climbing a flue was an intensely difficult and dangerous affair, as the bruises and grazes on his knees, elbows, shoulders and hands testified.

All the way to the top, he pulled the fowl, until its flapping wings came into view amid a cloud of soot; then he lowered the blackened bird down again; his shoulders afire with the effort; the rope slipping through his hands and ripping his blisters.

"Done!" echoed Sneed's voice. "Get down 'ere!"

Dropping the rope into the chimney, Swinburne sat, twisted himself around, lay flat, and gingerly made his way down over the tiles.

The spits and spots of rain gave way to a more serious shower and the increasing gloom made it difficult to locate the top of the ladder, which projected just a couple of inches over the eaves. Swinburne—tiny, excitable and over-sensitive—was not, however, a man who felt fear, and despite the precariousness of his position, he remained calm as he carefully shifted himself over the slick shingles at the edge of the roof until the toe of his left boot bumped the ladder. He manoeuvred onto the topmost rung and climbed down until, with a sigh of relief, he felt his boots touch the pavement.

By now, his whole body was aching and he longed for a brandy. It had been three days since his last drink and he was finding sobriety thoroughly disagreeable.

He returned to The Conk, who snarled: "Too slow, boy! This ain't a bleedin' 'oliday!"

"Sorry, sir; the roof was wet."

"I'll 'ave none o' yer excuses! Finish the job!"

The sweep sat back and took a swig of moonshine while Swinburne knelt on the sacking, which was now covered with the soot the goose had loosened from the flue, and started removing the rods from the long holdall. He affixed the large round flat and stiff-bristled brush to the end of one and pushed it up the chimney. Soot showered down and billowed around him. Screwing a second rod into the end of the first, he pushed again, with the same result. This routine continued until he stopped feeling any resistance from the brush, which meant that it was now poking out of the top of the chimney. He then reversed the process, unscrewing the rods one by one and pulling them down until the brush reappeared.

Sneed, who was by now quite drunk, mumbled: "Job done. Pack up."

'Of course I will,' thought Swinburne. 'You must be exhausted with all you've done!'

He placed the rods and brush back into the holdall then rolled up each piece of sacking, carefully catching all the soot in the material. Nevertheless, once done, there remained a layer of black powder over every surface in the room, and this he had to clean up with a dustpan and brush and a damp rag.

As he was finishing, a broomcat poked its head around the door, surveyed the room, and licked its lips.

"Just in time. Grub up!" exclaimed Swinburne, as the feline sidled in and started to walk up and down the length of the room. Its long, statically-charged hair would attract the last remnants of soot, then, once every inch of floor had been covered, the broomcat would lick itself clean and digest the particles.

It was past seven o'clock by the time they steered the wagon out of Hanbury Street. Coins jingled in Sneed's pocket; in short measure they'd be exchanged for ale, though he'd have to keep a few back in order to pay the League of Chimney Sweeps, thus avoiding a visit from the organisation's infamous "punishers."

Had Swinburne been a real member of the League, he'd have received payment from them at the end of each week; a fixed amount, no matter how many jobs he had or hadn't done. It was a good system for the young boys, who were assured of a regular income while being protected from the worst brutalities inflicted by the Master Sweeps, who'd themselves been League members until they turned fourteen years of age.

Once ejected and no longer under the auspices of The Beetle, the ex-League members soon fell prey to the degradations of the East End, for scarcely any of them could afford to live elsewhere. They had their own union—The Brotherhood of Master Sweeps—but without the iron hand of The Beetle to run it, the corrupting influence of poverty, crime, and alcohol quickly caused little boys like Charlie and Ned to degenerate into sadistic louts like Vincent Sneed. In the Cauldron, that was the natural order; and even Charles Darwin would have been hard pressed to find any signs of evolution here.

Algernon Swinburne drew the wagon to a halt outside the poulterer's and handed the reins over to The Conk. He jumped down and took a sack from the back; it contained the dead goose, its neck having been broken by Sneed after its horrible ordeal in the chimney.

"You can clean the 'quipment in the morning," announced Sneed in an uncharacteristic fit of generosity. He clicked his tongue and shook the reins and the horse moved off. Swinburne would have to make his own way back later. For now, he had another job to do.

He entered the poulterer's shop.

"Evening, Mr Jambory," he said cheerfully to the tall, fat, treble-chinned proprietor.

"Hullo, sonny. I told you she was a flapper! You're as black as pitch!"

"She certainly was, sir. Very efficient! Very efficient indeed!"

"Jolly good show. Take her out back and get her plucked then."

Swinburne nodded and carried the sack through to the small yard behind the shop. He sat on a small stool, pulled out the bird, and started yanking out the blackened feathers.

The rain dribbled down the back of his neck. It turned the feathers and soot into a grey mush around his feet.

Half his mind seemed to disengage, dozing, while the remaining half guided his fingers over the goose. He shivered with exhaustion and cold.

Slightly under an hour later, Swinburne presented the pink carcass to Mr Jambory.

"Good lad!" exclaimed the fat man. "Are you hungry?"

"Starving!" admitted Swinburne.

"How about a glass of milk and some bread and dripping?"

To the poet, who'd eaten in London's best restaurants, this sounded like food of the gods.

"Wow! Yes please!" he gasped.

Some time later, feeling much recovered and with his stomach comfortably full, Swinburne was walking through the thinning crowd on Commercial Road when he was hailed from the other side. He looked across and saw a small ragamuffin with sandy blonde hair, wearing a too-big cap, a too-big greatcoat, and too-big boots. It was Willy Cornish; a fellow member of the League of Chimney Sweeps.

"Hallo Carrots!" cried Willy, crossing the road. "Been on a job?"

"Yes, up Whitechapel way. What are you up to?"

Willy lowered his voice and leaned close, his blue eyes very wide.

"Have you heard about the Squirrel Hill cemetery?"

"No, what about it?"

"Resurrectionists!"

"What?"

"Resurrectionists! They've been digging up the dead 'uns on Squirrel Hill! Wanna come and have a look? Maybe we can catch 'em at it!"

Swinburne hesitated. He was dog-tired. On the other hand, Squirrel Hill wasn't far away and he'd embarked on this adventure not just to help Richard Burton but also to experience life in its raw and bloody nakedness; seeking inspiration for his poetry; a quest for creative authenticity. Men digging up cadavers to sell to crooked medical practitioners—could life be any less embellished than that?

He nodded. "Alright Willy, let's go and spy on the grave robbers!"

"Really?" said Willy. He hadn't expected that answer. Most boys, if they were able, were rushing home now that it was dark, afraid of the werewolves. "You're not scared?"

"No. Are you?"

Willy stuck out his chest. "Course not!"

Swinburne's normally springy step was decidedly heavy as he trudged through the rain with his young companion. Willy, by contrast, jumped about excitedly and created extravagant plans for capturing the resurrectionists; plans which included booby-trapped pits, dropping nets, manacles and blindfolds; and which inevitably climaxed with gibbets and bodies kicking at the end of swinging ropes.

"You're a bloodthirsty little beggar, Willy Cornish," observed the poet, "and your plans are admirable if a mite impractical. Perhaps we should settle for reconnaissance for the time being."

"Re-conny-who?" responded the boy.

"Reconnaissance. It means we go and find out what the ghouls are up to and, if we see them, we run like blazes to get help!"

"'Spose so, Carrots," said Willy disappointedly. "I'd much rather capture the fellows myself though!"

They turned off Commercial Road and followed an unlit alley down toward Hardinge Street. A girl, perhaps twelve years old, stepped out of a doorway and gave them a price. Even in the gloom, Swinburne could see Willy's face burning red. He shook his head at the girl and pushed his companion on.

They emerged onto Hardinge, which was quiet, though the perennial hubbub of the city could, of course, be heard in the background, and followed it down to the corner of Squirrel Hill, then began to climb the steep incline. There were no houses nearby, no people, and just one gas lamp, right at the top beside the cemetery gates.

"Keep quiet now, Carrots," advised Willy. "We don't want to scare the rogues away!"

Swinburne followed his little friend up to the corner of the tree-lined burial ground and squatted with him in the shadows next to a wall.

They listened but could hear nothing but the rain pattering on the pavement and rustling through the leaves of the trees.

"Give me a leg up," said Willy.

Swinburne sighed, thinking of the sacking mattress and thin blanket waiting for him back at Sneed's place. He bent, hooked his hands around Willy's knee, and lifted. The boy grabbed the top of the wall and pulled himself up, lay flat, and extended a hand down to the poet, who took it and scrambled after him.

They dropped into the cemetery.

"I'm soaking wet," complained Swinburne.

"Shhh!"

Willy crept forward through the undergrowth and Swinburne followed.

A snapping noise came from somewhere ahead.

"What was that?" hissed Swinburne.

"Shhh!" repeated Willy. Then, in the faintest of whispers:

"Resurrectionists!"

They came to a headstone, all tangled about with weeds and creepers, and moved from it to the next and the next, slowly approaching an area of darkness from which slight sounds of movement could be heard.

Swinburne forgot his tiredness and discomfort. He was now eager to witness whatever sepulchral events were occurring ahead. He began to shake and twitch with excitement.

Willy crawled on and poked his head over the top of a granite slab. He quickly ducked back, turned, and gestured for Swinburne to join him.

On his hands and knees, the poet quietly moved to his friend's side and peeked over the stone.

Through the falling rain, he could see vague shapes moving.

He lowered his head and put his mouth next to Willy's ear.

"We have to get closer!"

The boy nodded and pointed to a mausoleum which loomed out of the darkness to their right.

"We can go around that," he breathed.

Staying as low as possible, they sneaked across the uneven ground, through dripping bushes and patches of mud, past tilted crosses and stone angels whose shadowy eyes seemed to weep, until they reached the base of the bulky monument. Sheltered from view, but also from the glimmering light of the distant gas lamp, they fumbled their way through blackness. At the far corner, they stopped.

"We'll count them," whispered Swinburne, "then go back the way we've come. We'll hot foot it to the tavern on the corner of Commercial Road and rouse some men. If we're lucky, we can get a mob to come back with us and catch the scoundrels in the act!"

He and Willy looked around the edge of the mausoleum.

There were seven figures, some bending, some crouching, in the rain. They were all cloaked and hooded. Strange noises reached Swinburne's ears; snuffles and crunches, cracking and ripping.

One of the men stood, and it seemed to Swinburne that he was quite short in stature. He held a stick in his hand, which he raised to his hood.

A chill wave of revulsion sudden numbed the poet.

It wasn't a stick. It was an arm, with a hand flapping at its end.

The figure pulled it away from its hood, tearing off a strip of polluted, wormy flesh.

Swinburne collapsed back into the shadow of the tomb, dragging the boy with him.

"Jesus Christ!" he moaned. "They aren't robbing the graves; they're eating the corpses!"

He could feel Willy Cornish trembling uncontrollably at his side.

"I want to go home," sobbed the youngster.

Swinburne hugged him close.

"Go!" he whispered. "Get out of here as fast as you can, Willy. Go quietly, stay in the shadows, get over the wall and run. Hurry to the tavern and tell what you've seen. Go now!"

The youngster wiped his nose on his wet sleeve, sniffed, and wriggled away.

Swinburne peered around the corner again. Two of the figures were dragging a coffin out of the water-logged earth, its rotten wood splitting, the sides falling away, the lid collapsing. The other five men, their hooded cloaks wrapped tightly around them, shambled closer, gathered around the coffin, and bent over its putrid contents. They pushed the pieces of lid aside and reached in. Swinburne heard bones breaking. He tasted bile in the back of his throat.

What happened next occurred so suddenly that Swinburne found himself acting without knowing what he was doing.

Something—maybe the snap of a twig or a careless movement—attracted the cannibalistic grave robbers. As one, their heads turned, and Swinburne knew straight away that Willy Cornish had been spotted.

The poet rose to his feet and stepped away from the mausoleum.

"Hey!" he shouted.

Seven hoods swung in his direction and seven sets of seething red eyes fixed on him. One of the figures took two steps forward and the dim lamp light angled across its face, revealing a wrinkled snout and white canines.

Loup-garous!

For the first time in his life, Swinburne experienced fear. He turned and started to run but went pelting into a gravestone, stumbled, lost his balance and fell. His legs kicked franticly as he tried to crawl into the shadows but when claws dug into his ankle he knew that the creatures were upon him. He was dragged back over the wet soil, his fingers digging into it but finding no purchase.

Hands gripped and lifted him, and a dread of being torn apart and eaten alive overpowered him, pushing him to the brink of unconsciousness.

The wolf-men snarled and gripped his limbs tightly, pushed their snouts into his clothing and sniffed at it. They grunted and began to move, the ground rushing past Swinburne's eyes as they raced across it.

In the last seconds of awareness, before he fainted, Swinburne realised that he was being borne away.

§

Chapter 13

Dog, Cat and Mouse

꿍

"THE UNIVERSE WE OBSERVE HAS PRECISELY THE PROPERTIES WE
SHOULD EXPECT IF THERE IS, AT BOTTOM, NO DESIGN, NO PURPOSE,
NO EVIL, NO GOOD, NOTHING BUT BLIND, PITILESS INDIFFERENCE"
—*CHARLES DARWIN*

꿍

The morning after he and Algernon Swinburne had visited Elephant and
Castle, Sir Richard Francis Burton once again donned his Sikh disguise,
made his way to the abandoned factory beside the Limehouse Cut, and
climbed the chimney. He dropped three pebbles down the flue, one after the
other, and, moments later, had his second interview with The Beetle. He and
the president of the League of Chimney Sweeps, who once again remained in
the darkness, arranged for Swinburne's apprenticeship with Vincent Sneed,
then Burton handed over a gift of books and departed.

He made his way to the poet's lodgings and outlined the plan. Swinburne
was beside himself with delight and immediately started making his
preparations.

Burton then had a meeting with Detective-Inspector Trounce at Scotland
Yard. He told him about the latest developments, including his suspicion

that Oliphant knew something about Spring Heeled Jack, and learned in turn that the two girls, Connie Fairweather and Alicia Pipkiss, had so far been going about their business as normal; there had been no sign of Spring Heeled Jack.

The King's agent arrived back at 14 Montagu Place at two-thirty. As he paid the cab driver, he noticed that the road works had stopped outside his home, the trench had been filled in, and new cobbles covered it. A thick pipe which hadn't been there before was running up the side of the house. It disappeared into the brickwork just below one of his study windows.

"What's the new pipe?" he asked Mrs Angell, as he wiped his feet on the doormat.

"Something to do with the gas supply," she answered. "I must say, they worked tremendously fast."

He mounted the stairs and went up to his study, passed through it to his dressing room, and removed the Sikh costume and make up. Half an hour later, he was dressed comfortably, seated at a desk, and picking at his lunch while reading the latest edition of *The Empire*.

There was a knock at the door and Mrs Angell entered at his bidding.

"The two workmen wish to see you, sir."

"Workmen?"

"The ones who put the new gas main in."

"What do they want?"

"I don't know but they are very insistent."

"Very well; send them up."

"Yes, sir."

She withdrew and moments later two men entered. The were both dressed identically in long black surtouts, with black waistcoats underneath. Their white shirts had high cheek-scraping "Gladstone" collars, the starched points of which threatened to pierce their eyeballs at every turn of the head. Pale yellow cravats encased their necks. Their high-waisted breeches ended just below their knees, giving way to pale yellow tights. They wore buckled shoes.

All in all, their style was at least fifty years out of date.

"Good afternoon, Captain Burton," said the tall but slightly hunch-backed man on the left. Like his companion, he was holding a stove pipe hat. Unlike his companion, he was extremely bald, with just a short fringe of hair around his ears. As if to compensate for this, he sported the variety of extremely long side whiskers known as "Piccadilly weepers." His face hung in a naturally maudlin expression; the mouth curved downward; the jowly cheeks drooping; the eyes woebegone. He shifted the brim of his hat through his fingers nervously.

"My name is Damien Burke."

The second man bobbed his head. He was shorter and immensely broad, with massive shoulders and long, ape-like arms. His head was crowned with an upstanding mop of pure white hair which descended before his small puffy ears in a short fringe, angling around his square jawline to a tuft beneath the heavy chin. His pale grey eyes were deeply embedded in gristly sockets; he had a splayed, many-times broken nose; and an extraordinarily wide mouth filled with large flat teeth. In his left hand, he held a big canvas bag.

"And I'm Gregory Hare," he said, in a rumbling voice. "Where do you want it?"

Burton, who'd risen from his desk, paced over to the men and held his hand out.

"Pleased to meet you," he said.

Burke looked down at the proffered hand in surprise. He licked his lips then held out his own, as if unfamiliar with such niceties.

They shook.

Hare, who had his hat in one hand and the bag in the other, moved indecisively, put on his hat, quickly shook Burton's hand, then snatched the stovepipe back off his head.

"Where do I want what?" asked Burton.

"Ah, well, there now; that's a question," replied Burke in funereal tones. "What indeed? Perhaps you have a suggestion, Captain? Messenger pipe? Canister conveyor? Communications tube? For the life of us we've not yet come up with a suitable moniker."

"Are you referring to the contrivance on Lord Palmerston's desk?"

"Why, of course, sir. But unlike the Prime Minister, you seem to be replete with desks. Is there a preferred?"

Burton indicated the desk by the windows.

"I use this one the most."

"Very good, sir. We'll have to take the floor up but it'll all be done in a jiffy and we'll leave it as we find it. Would you mind clearing the desk? We wouldn't want to disturb your work. Incidentally, sir, I read your *First Footsteps in East Africa*; most fascinating; most fascinating indeed!"

The hunchback turned to his colleague.

"Come along, Mr Hare, we don't want to inconvenience Captain Burton for longer than necessary."

"Of course not, Mr Burke," replied the ape-like Hare. "That wouldn't do at all!"

While Burton shifted books and documents, his two visitors unpacked tools from their bag and started to jemmy up the floorboards by the window.

An hour later the boards were back in place. The pipe, which entered the house below the study window, now ran under the floor until it reached Burton's desk. It then turned upward and passed through a hole in the boards and desk until it joined a steaming device identical to that which the King's agent had seen in front of Palmerston.

"The operation is simple, Captain," advised Burke. "This part here must be topped up with water every day. This dial here is how you direct your canisters. Dial one-one-one when you want to send to His Majesty, two-two-two when you want to send to the Prime Minister, and three-three-three when you need to contact us. You'll forgive me for saying so, I hope, sir, but you have a reputation for not being backward when it comes to being forward. I feel I should advise you that communicating with the king is a privilege that shouldn't be abused. In fact, I'd recommend only speaking when you're spoken to, if you get my drift."

"Understood," responded Burton. "What heats the device?"

"Don't worry about that, Captain; we take care of it at our end. The heat is conducted along a special wire in the lining of the pipe. Rather complicated. No need to go into details. Remember, dial three-three-three if you need us. You can also send a parakeet or runner—I believe you have the address?"

"Yes."

"Very good. One last thing, sir. Mr Montague Penniforth's remains were recovered by the river police in the early hours of this morning. His widow has been notified, his funeral paid for, and her pension arranged. In the future, should you encounter such unfortunate occurrences, if you can manage to have the deceased either left alone or stored somewhere, we will act the moment you notify us to ensure that disposal is civilised and respectful.

"Right then, we'll leave you to get on, Captain. We're sorry to have bothered you, aren't we Mr Hare?"

"We are, Mr Burke," rumbled Hare. "Very sorry, Captain. Goodbye."

"Goodbye, Captain," echoed Burke.

"Goodbye," said Burton.

The door closed. He heard their footsteps on the stairs. The front door opened and closed.

He crossed to the window and looked down at Montagu Place. He couldn't see them.

So that was Burke and Hare! What an extraordinary duo!

Thirty minutes later, the newly installed contraption began to shake and hiss; it rattled and whistled and a canister thunked into it. Burton opened the door on the side and caught the canister as it plopped out. He cracked off the lid and withdrew a note from inside. It read:

Gifts in the garage. A.

A for Albert. A message from the King of England!

Intrigued, he went downstairs to Mrs Angell's domain, where he unlocked and opened the back door, and ascended the exterior steps to the back yard. He crossed it and entered the garage. Inside he found two penny farthings and a rotorchair.

Later that afternoon, he used one of the velocipedes for the first time, perched high on the saddle, steaming back down to Battersea.

When he returned some hours later, he had a large basket propped on the handlebars.

§

Three days passed without progress.

There were no reported sightings of Spring Heeled Jack.

Algernon Swinburne was somewhere in the depths of the Cauldron.

Sir Richard Francis Burton fretted and worried. He tried to occupy himself with his books but couldn't concentrate; researched Moko Jumbi but found little besides the superficial resemblance to connect the African god to the stilt-walker.

Early on the morning of the fourth day there came a knock at the front door. It was young Oscar Wilde, the paper boy.

"Top o' the morning to you, Captain," he said. "I'm of the opinion that no good deed goes unpunished, but there are some people who I'm prepared to risk all for. Therefore, please take these, and I'll be bidding you good day."

He held out his hand and released something into Burton's palm, then span on his heel and walked away, turning once to wave and grin.

Burton was left holding three pebbles. A summons from The Beetle.

He acted immediately, bounding up the stairs, through his study and into the dressing room, where he donned a roughly-woven suit, chopped his beard down to stubble—though keeping his moustaches long and drooping to either side of his chin—ruffled his hair, dirtied his face, neck and hands, and slipped into a pair of scuffed and cracked boots.

When he left the house, he was not alone.

Burton was tempted to use one of his new vehicles, but where he was going, modern technology was liable to be stolen on sight or vandalised, so he waved down the first cab he saw—a horse-drawn growler—and cried: "Get me to Limehouse Cut as quickly as possible! Hurry, man!"

"Have you the fare?" asked the driver, looking at him suspiciously.

Burton impatiently flashed a handful of coins at the man.

"I'll pay you double if I'm there within thirty minutes!" he cried, pushing his companion into the four-wheeler before clambering in himself.

"Easy money!" muttered the driver, cracking his whip over the two horses' heads.

The growler jerked into motion and went flying down the street. Burton was thrown about, and banged his head as the vehicle careened around a corner, but he didn't care—speed was essential now!

The carriage skidded and swerved wildly on the wet cobbles but the driver steered it with an expert hand and delivered his passengers to St Paul's Road, close to the factory, well within the allotted time.

"Good man!" exclaimed the King's agent, passing coins up to the cabbie. "Money well earned!"

The rain was beating down hard, rinsing the city's muck into the filthy artery that ran through its middle; washing Sir Richard Francis Burton's hopes away. It could ruin his and Swinburne's plan. It could mean the poet's death.

He hurried to the factory and, leaving his companion at the bottom of the ladder, climbed it to the roof, then continued on up to the lip of the chimney.

The rain lashed his face as he dropped the three pebbles into the flue.

Minutes later, The Beetle said: "You look different."

"What's the news?" snapped Burton.

"Your friend has been taken. He was dragged out of the Squirrel Hill graveyard in Wapping by seven cloaked men. It was witnessed by one of my sweeps; a boy named Willy Cornish. He didn't see the men's faces—they wore hoods—but he says they moved in an odd fashion."

"The loup-garous," said Burton.

"Yes, I believe so. You think you can follow their trail?"

"In this rain, I fear not, but I have to try. I must go."

"Good luck, Captain Burton."

The King's agent descended to the roof, then down the side of the building to his friend waiting below.

"I hope old Ted Toppletree wasn't exaggerating about that nose of yours, Fidget!" he said. "Because if he was, we might never see Algernon Swinburne again!"

The Basset hound looked up at him mutely.

§

Swinburne's mind was a kaleidoscope of confused memories. The werewolves had carried him at great speed through the labyrinthine alleys of the city, gripping him so tightly that he could barely breathe; carrying him sometimes upright, sometimes upside down. Talons had dug into his arms and shoulders, thighs and calves; and there'd been a long dark tunnel which seemed to descend into the spongy, dripping flesh of the Earth itself.

He recalled that, at one point, he'd recovered his wits enough to start screaming at the top of his voice until his cries were smothered by a musky-smelling paw.

Then, oblivion.

He opened his eyes.

He was in a huge chamber, on an upright but slightly inclined metal rack, his limbs splayed wide; straps tight around his wrists and ankles.

Artificial light flooded the cathedral-sized space; not gas light, but the white incandescence of lightning which had somehow been locked into globes hanging from the high ceiling. Beneath them, bathed in their brilliance, was machinery the like of which Swinburne had never seen nor even imagined before. There was no steam here; it was all electricity, which fizzed and crackled across the surfaces of megalithic devices, whipping from one bizarrely designed tower to another, filling the place with the smell of ozone and with sharp snaps, claps and buzzes.

In particular, a great many bolts of energy were shooting into a chandelier like-structure suspended from the ceiling in the centre of the room. It resembled a big cast-iron wheel, with vertical stacks of disks arranged around its circumference. To these, wires and cables were affixed.

Swinburne's eyes followed their draping lines down to where they joined a crown-like construction below; a metal frame in which a number of long needles were secured, projecting a few inches outward. To these, the wires were attached. The other ends of the needles were embedded in the skull upon which the crown sat.

It was a hairless and grotesquely swollen dome, which bulged out over the ears of its owner; a head twice normal size; a phenomenal and hideous cranium! It projecting forward over the wide face below, pushing bushy brows down low over eyes which glittered coldly from within their shadow. The nose was small, the mouth wide and set sternly, the jaw decorated with a big white beard which flowed down to the man's waist—for, yes, the distorted creature was unmistakably a man.

Beneath the bloated head, a grey suit hung from a skeletal frame. The body was extremely withered, every visible inch of skin scored with wrinkles, and had rubber tubing emerging from the wrists to join devices which pumped and groaned beside the metal throne on which the man sat.

He looked, thought Swinburne, like a foetus cradled in a mechanical womb.

He also looked familiar.

"Charles Darwin!" cried the poet.

The eyes glistened, looking the poet up and down.

"You know us, boy?" Darwin's voice was deep and possessed a weirdly harmonic quality, as if two people were speaking at once.

"Of course! What's going on here? What are you up to? Who's 'us?'"

"We do not explain ourselves to children. Be quiet."

A figure silently stepped into view from behind Swinburne. It was a tall smartly-suited man with long sideburns and a handsome but entirely expressionless face. Just above his eyebrows, his head ended; the top of the skull was missing entirely, and where the brain should have been, there was a baffling device of metal and glass in which a great many tiny lights blinked on and off in a seemingly random manner. From the back of this, a cable descended to the floor and snaked across to Darwin's throne, disappearing into its base.

The machine-brained man stepped over to a trolley and lifted from it a syringe with a fearsomely long needle.

"What are you doing?" squealed Swinburne.

"This one is inquisitive, isn't he?" muttered Darwin to himself. "Yes, he is. Tall, too, which is unfortunate. Shall we test or discard immediately? Test, I think. Child, tell us: you are an orphan? Do you remember your parents? Were they also tall?"

Machine-brain levelled the syringe, its point touching Swinburne just below the centre of his forehead.

"For pity's sake, Darwin! I'm not an orphan, my parents are none of your damned business, and I'm no child! I'm twenty-four years old! I'm Algernon Charles Swinburne, the poet!"

There came a pause, then the syringe was lowered.

Machine-brain stepped away.

"You are a chimney sweep," declared Darwin. "Your skin and clothes are covered in soot. It is under your fingernails. Our collectors smelt it on you. They do not make mistakes."

Swinburne wrenched at the straps holding his wrists. They held firm.

"If by 'collectors' you mean those wolf things, I'm afraid they've been fooled this time. I'm a poet, I tell you! Let me go!"

"Fooled?"

"I was posing as a sweep."

"Why would a poet do such a thing?"

"To find out where the cursed wolves come from and why boys are being abducted!"

Darwin was silent for a moment, then:

"We are intrigued. Observe, we seem to have before us a man of a profoundly non-scientific bent. An evolutionary oddity, think you not? Of what use is a poet? Is he not merely an instance of self-indulgence; a decoration, if you will? That might be so, but pray consider the decorative qualities of certain species, say, for example, tropical birds. Do their colours and patterns not serve a purpose; to attract a mate or to confuse a predator? This creature, though his hair is of a remarkable hue, is notably puny in his development. Might we propose that his vocation has developed to compensate for his lack of physical prowess? Could it not be that, in the absence of an ability to attract a mate at a physical level, he has developed a 'song' in much the same manner as a lark, which is a small dull-coloured bird with an extravagant call?"

"What the bleeding heck are you jabbering about!" shrilled Swinburne. "Let me off this damned rack! Unbuckle these straps at once!"

Darwin's huge head leaned to one side slightly and the beady eyes blinked.

"We must ask, though; why would a poet concern himself with our research?"

"What research?" demanded Swinburne. "Tell me what's going on here. Why are you abducting chimney sweeps? And what in the name of all that's holy has happened to your head, Darwin? It's damned disgusting! Why are you attached to those contraptions? Who is this automaton?"

A strange rattling emerged from the seated figure. Was it laughter?

"My, how inquisitive it is! So many questions! We have a proposal; a minor experiment; would it not be of interest to answer the young man? We have never explained ourselves to a non-rational mind. Will he show any capacity for thought that transcends moral outrage or will the fiction of God guide his response?"

"I don't believe in God!" screeched Swinburne.

"Ah! Listen! He claims disbelief! A faithless poet! We understand they classify themselves as 'Bohemians.' On what basis does a mind that has neither scientific rationality nor superstitious faith operate? This is truly fascinating, do we not think? We do. We do. Proceed! Explain to him, and when we have analysed his response, he will be disposed of."

"What?" screamed Swinburne. "Disposed of? What does that mean?"

"Observe; the survival instinct in action," declared Darwin. "Algernon Charles Swinburne, we will explain our programme. We will then ask you to respond. Please do so clearly and in detail.

To begin with, on the subject of our head. Your reaction to it is based on aesthetic values which serve no purpose. It is this size in order to incorporate the two brains which lie within. This body is that of Charles Darwin. The individual you call an automaton was once Francis Galton. The brains of those two men have been grafted together to create a four-lobed organ with co-mingled psychic fields which allow for the instantaneous transfer of thoughts. In effect, we have become one in order to overcome the limitations of language. We are no longer forced to resort to the symbolic in order to communicate our theories to one another; communication is direct and unsullied. There can be no misunderstanding or lack of comprehension.

"The body of Francis Galton we employ as a limb, for we are confined to this machinery which Isambard Kingdom Brunel designed to support us. Unfortunately, the human body is unable to maintain two brains without mechanical assistance."

"Wait!" protested Swinburne.

"It interrupts," harmonised Darwin. "We should not feel this sensation of impatience, for have we not already established that the poetical mind operates outside the logic of the scientific mind? We cannot expect it to restrain its impulses until it has heard all the information we wish to present. Yes, we agree. We must indulge the creature. What is it, Algernon Charles Swinburne?"

The little flame-headed poet, stretched out and strapped down, with machines sizzling, spitting and shooting bolts of lightning all around him, felt as if he were trapped in a nightmare. With the squashed, gargoyle-like face of Darwin peering down at him and the figure of Dalton standing nearby, motionless but for the winking lights atop his head, the scene could have been a painting by Hieronymus Bosch come to life.

Fighting his rising hysteria, Swinburne shook his head and tried to order his thoughts.

"*The Origin of Species* made you famous—or should I say notorious—two years ago," he said. "When the church issued death threats against you, you went into hiding, but by then your face was familiar to the general public and it certainly didn't have that horrible big bonce towering over it. In other words, the machinery encasing you wasn't required until a later date. Yet '59 is also the year Brunel died, therefore he cannot possibly have designed it."

Again, the horrid rattle sounded.

"The poet makes a logical argument, though the solution to the apparent paradox is simple."

"Oh, really," said Swinburne, sarcastically. "Please enlighten me!"

"Brunel," came the response. "Step forward."

To the left of the throne, one of the huge pieces of machinery suddenly rose from the floor with a loud hiss of steam and clanged forward.

The most famous and successful engineer in the world, if this was truly Brunel, was no longer the short, dark-haired, cigar-chomping man of memory.

He stood on three triple-jointed metal legs. These were attached to a horizontal disk-shaped chassis affixed to the bottom of the main body, which, shaped like a barrel laying on its side, appeared to be constructed from wood and banded with strips of studded brass. There were domed protrusions at either end of it, each bearing nine multi-jointed arms, each arm ending in a different tool, ranging from delicate fingers to slashing blades, drills to hammers, spanners to welders.

A further dome rose from the top of Brunel's body. From this, too, arms extended—six in all—though these were more like tentacles, so long and flexible were they. Each ended in a clamp-like hand.

At various places around the body, revolving cog-wheels poked through slots in the wood, and on one shoulder—it was impossible to say whether it was the left or right because Brunel had no discernible front or back—a piston-like device slowly rose and fell. On the other, something resembling a bellows pumped up and down, making a ghastly wheezing noise. Small exhaust pipes expelled puffs of white vapour from either end of the barrel.

Amid all the electrical machinery, this great steaming hulk seemed strangely primitive.

It thumped across the floor and squatted at Swinburne's side.

A hot cloud blew from one of its vents and rolled over the poet's face.

Bells chimed from the bulky mechanism.

"Our dear friend Isambard's voice takes some getting used to," said Darwin. "He just confirmed that he is very much alive."

Swinburne laughed. "I'm dreaming!" he cried. "I'm dreaming!"

"Most interesting," said Darwin. "Observe how the poet denies the input of his senses. This is a fascinating reaction. We suggest a rupture between the corporeal sense of existence and the acquired sense of intellectual identity. Indeed. Algernon Charles Swinburne quite literally cannot believe his eyes. See how they have lost focus. We propose that this is a symptom of the medical condition termed 'shock,' caused, in this instance, by the unfamiliarity of his environment. Were he of the lower order of beasts, this would ensure his destruction. Let us continue with this diverting experiment. Perhaps a brief explanation of Brunel's continued existence will bridge the rupture? Yes, but wait; we have opened a further path of investigation. We are intrigued by the possibility that a being, when placed in an environment that is alien to it, might react in this manner. If evolution is a matter of adapt or die, then is not shock entirely counterproductive to the process? Why, then, does the condition of shock exist? What is its function? We must experiment further. Agreed. However, let us first continue with our faux chimney sweep.

"Algernon Charles Swinburne, what you are looking at might be termed a life-support machine. It is steam-powered, to allow full mobility, for the Engineers have not yet created a technique whereby sufficient electrical power might be stored in a portable container. Our colleague Isambard had himself placed inside the machine in 1859. It has kept him alive since, enabling his continued rule of the Technologists."

"Well this is all very nice," mumbled Swinburne, as far as possible cowering away from the gigantic form of Brunel. "But to get back to the bloody point, why are you abducting chimney sweeps?"

Darwin's bony fingers flexed.

"Ah. He regains focus. Excellent! Shall we tell him? Yes, proceed. We need fear nothing, for he will be destroyed shortly. Algernon Charles Swinburne;

at some future period, not very distant as measured by centuries, the civilized races of man will almost certainly exterminate and replace the savage races throughout the world."

"Is that so?"

"It is the evolutionary path. The questions which form the basis for our experimental programme are these: can the British Empire, as the dominant civilised race, hasten the process? What form shall the future Empire take? And which physical attributes will prove most beneficial to the people of the Empire?

"To this end, our experiment is comprised of three elements.

"The first is designed to remove the burden of survival from the Empire's citizens in order that they may concentrate exclusively upon the development of their scientific and inventive skills. Thus, Mr Brunel is overseeing the rapid introduction of machines which will, ultimately, fulfil all the material functions required to sustain life, from the provision and distribution of food to the creation and maintenance of dwellings."

"And what of those of us who don't want to be scientists?" interrupted Swinburne.

"The second branch of our experiment has been designed to deal with such as you. It concerns selective breeding—eugenics in its purest form. The greater mass of humanity, which has not yet evolved the ability to think rationally, is disordered and unpredictable. It is driven by animal desires which, even after the machines eliminate hunger and want, will continue to slow the evolutionary process. We therefore intend a biological intervention to bring order to the masses; a programme through which each individual will gain a specialism that contributes to the whole.

"Using chimney sweeps as our test subject, we are manipulating their biology in order that they and their descendants remain small in stature, a form which is ideal for the function they perform. Indeed, we are enhancing the boys by breeding into them additional characteristics which will serve them well in their specialism. We aim to follow their progress through successive generations, and, once the technique is perfected, we will create other specialisms, such as miners with perfect night-vision, labourers with immense physical strength, and so forth. The greater mass of humanity will become as a machine, its separate parts functioning smoothly, the whole mechanism serving the scientists.

"The third aspect of the experiment, which is being conducted by our colleague Nurse Nightingale—"

Swinburne let loose a gasp, for he knew of Florence Nightingale; it was rumoured that Richard Monckton Milnes had proposed to her ten years previously, and, though she refused him, his continued attentions had driven her to a nervous breakdown.

"—involves the raising of the lower beasts to a level where they might serve humanity more effectively."

Swinburne interrupted again: "Your wolf-men are an example of this?"

"Observe his impulsive inquisitiveness," harmonised Darwin and Galton from the single, grotesque body. "He has not the patience to gather all the facts before formulating his enquiries but must express each question the moment it occurs to him. This is not the behaviour of an evolved mind. Nevertheless, we must address him on his own terms, else how will he understand?

"Algernon Charles Swinburne; you are correct; the creatures are not men made wolves, but wolves made men. We must confess, our methodology in this area requires a great deal more testing and analysis before we can perfect it. The wolf-men have an unfortunate biological imbalance which causes a propensity for spontaneous combustion. Nurse Nightingale is looking into the problem."

"I hope she burns her fingers!" muttered Swinburne.

"We will continue. There exists a secondary experiment which combines aspects of the first and third programmes. It involves the mechanical enhancement of the human form. Behold."

Darwin gestured to Swinburne's right. The poet looked but saw only bulky contrivances, sparking electrodes, cables, pipes, flashing lights and objects his eyes could barely interpret.

Something moved.

It was the front of a large lozenge-shaped contraption; a slab of metal into which dials and gauges were set, standing upright but inclined slightly backward. It occurred to the poet that it somewhat resembled a sarcophagus, whose lid was now lifting of its own accord.

White vapour burst from its sides and fell as snowflakes to the floor.

The lid slid forward then silently glided to one side, revealing the contents within.

Swinburne saw a naked man whose pale skin glistened with frost. Tubes entered his flesh from the inside edges of the metal coffin, piercing the skin of his scarred thighs, of his arms and his neck. The upper left side of his head was missing. The left eye had been replaced with some sort of lens set in rings of brass. Above this, where there should have been forehead and scalp, there was a studded brass dome with a glass panel—like a small porthole—in its front. Just above the ear, a winding key projected.

The human part of the man's face was settled in repose and, though the bushy beard had been removed, Swinburne at once recognised the features.

"Good lord!" he gasped. "John Hanning Speke!"

"Yes," affirmed Darwin. "Soon he will be recovered sufficiently to serve us. As you see, the left lobe of his brain has been replaced with a babbage."

"A what?"

"A probability calculator crafted by our colleague, Charles Babbage. It will, among a great many other things, magnify Mr Speke's ability to analyse situations and formulate strategic responses to them. The device is powered by clockwork, for portability."

"He agreed to this?" mumbled Swinburne.

"He was in no position to agree or disagree. He was unconscious and dying. We saved his life."

The sarcophagus slid shut, hiding Speke from view.

"Algernon Charles Swinburne," said Darwin, levelling his gimlet eyes at the poet, "We would now analyse your response. Speak."

Swinburne stared bleakly at his captor.

He coughed and licked his lips.

"To summarize," the poet said, hoarsely, "you are flooding the Empire with new machines that will destabilise the current social order; you intend to create a *new* social order comprised of specialist humans who will serve as drones in what amounts to a scientific hive; and you are interfering with animal biology in order to manufacture a sub-level of mindless slaves. All this to expand the British Empire, under the rule of scientists, until it dominates the entire world. Am I right?"

Darwin nodded his huge head, and said: "We are impressed at his ability to reduce the complex to a simplistic statement which is, nevertheless, essentially correct."

"And you want my response?" asked Swinburne.

"Yes, we do."

"Very well then; here it is. You are completely, profoundly, and irreversibly *fucking mad!*"

With a blast of steam, Isambard Kingdom Brunel slowly lifted his great frame until it towered over the little poet.

"It's quite all right, Isambard," said Darwin. "Calm yourself."

The great machine froze, but for the piston on one shoulder, which rose and fell slowly, and the bellows on the other, which creaked and gasped like the respiration of a dying man.

"It's absurd!" shrilled Swinburne. "Quite apart from the moral and ethical issues, how in blue blazes can you expect to accurately monitor the three branches of the experiment when you are conducting them simultaneously in the same arena? And what about the time factor? The chimney sweeps, for example! Information from such an experiment will take generations to gather! Generations! Do you expect to live forever?"

For a third time, Darwin's rattling laugh sounded between the fizzle and claps of electrical charges.

"He has surprised us!" he declared. "He has pierced to the heart of the matter! Time, indeed, is the key, Algernon Charles Swinburne. However, we have—"

"*Stop!*"

The cry rang out from somewhere behind the poet, so loud that it echoed above the chamber's general cacophony.

"What is this interruption?" demanded Darwin, and Francis Galton's body jerked two paces forward, dragging the long cable behind it, raising its arm and brandishing the syringe like a weapon.

With a whirring noise, one of Brunel's arms shot out and a metal clamp closed on the automaton's wrist.

Bells clanged.

"Forgive us, Isambard; we were taken by surprise, that is all. Come here, Mr Oliphant; explain yourself."

As Brunel's arm retracted and Galton's lowered, Laurence Oliphant stepped into view.

"My hat!" exclaimed Swinburne. "What a merry freak show this is!"

Oliphant threw him a malicious glance.

"I don't see a mark on his forehead," said the albino. His smooth tones made the poet shudder. "Have you extracted any cells?"

"There was no need," answered Darwin. "For, despite appearances to the contrary, he is not a boy but a man."

"I know. He's Swinburne, the poet. The little idiot has been much in the company of Burton these past days."

"Is that so? We were not aware of this."

Oliphant banged the end of his cane on the floor impatiently.

"Of course not!" he snapped. "You've been too busy revealing your plans to question him about his own!"

"It was an experiment."

"Blast it! You are a machine for observing facts and grinding out conclusions but did it not cross your minds that in telling him about the programme you are giving information to the enemy?"

"We were not aware that he is an enemy."

"You fool! You should consider every man a potential enemy until he is proven otherwise."

"You are correct. It was an interesting exercise but the experiment is finished and we are satisfied. Algernon Charles Swinburne is of no further use to us. You may dispose of him outside."

"I'll do it here," said Oliphant, drawing the rapier from his cane.

"No," said Darwin. "This is a laboratory. It is a delicate environment. There must be no blood spilt here. Do it in the courtyard. Question him first. Find out how much Burton knows. Then dispose of the corpse in the furnace."

"Very well. Release him. Mr Brunel, bring him outside, please."

The blank-eyed Francis Galton placed the syringe back onto the trolley, approached Swinburne, and began to unbuckle the straps. One of Brunel's limbs unfolded and the digits at its end clamped shut around the poet's forearm.

"Get off!" screamed Swinburne. "Help! Help!"

"Enough of your histrionics," snarled Oliphant. "There's no one to hear them and I find them irritating."

"Sod off!" spat Swinburne.

Galton pulled open the last of the straps and Brunel swung the little poet up into the air.

"Ow! Ow! I can walk, curse you!"

"Follow," commanded Oliphant.

With Isambard Kingdom Brunel clanking and thudding along behind, holding the kicking and squealing Swinburne high, Laurence Oliphant crossed the vast laboratory and passed through huge double doors into a large rectangular courtyard. Swinburne was surprised to see a noonday sky above—he had no idea how long he'd been unconscious.

He instantly recognised the location; he was in Battersea Power Station, which towered around this central enclosure, a colossal copper rod rising up in each of the four corners.

"Drop him."

Brunel released the poet, who landed in a heap on the wet ground.

Oliphant held the point of his blade at Swinburne's throat.

"You may go, Brunel."

A bell chimed and the hulking machine stamped back through the doors, which closed behind it.

Oliphant stepped away and sheathed his rapier. He turned and loped across the courtyard to the entrance; a big double gate into which a normal-sized door was set. This latter he unbolted and opened.

"Your escape route," he smiled, his pink eyes glinting, the vertical pupils narrowing.

He moved away from the exit.

"Go! Run!"

Algernon Swinburne looked at the albino curiously. What was he playing at?

He scrambled to his feet and began to walk toward the door. Oliphant continued to move away, giving the poet more and more space.

"Why?" asked Swinburne.

Oliphant remained silent, the smile playing about his face, the eyes following Swinburne's every step.

The poet shrugged and increased his pace.

He was less than four feet from the portal when Oliphant suddenly sprang at him.

Swinburne shrieked and ran but the albino was phenomenally fast and swept down on the little man in a blur of movement, grabbing Swinburne by the back of the collar just as he was stepping across the threshold and yanking him backward.

Swinburne flew through the air, hit the ground, rolled in a spray of rainwater, and found himself laying exactly where Brunel had dropped him.

Oliphant cackled; a cruel, vile noise.

Swinburne staggered to his feet.

"Cat and mouse," he said under his breath. "And I'm the bloody mouse!"

§

Chapter 14

The Trail

⁊

"WHEN WE ADJUST SOME ELEMENT OF AN ANIMAL'S NATURE,
A QUITE DIFFERENT ELEMENT ALTERS OF ITS OWN ACCORD,
AS IF THERE IS SOME SYSTEM OF CHECKS AND BALANCES AT WORK.
WHAT WE CANNOT FATHOM IS WHY THE UNPLANNED CHANGES
SEEM ENTIRELY POINTLESS FROM A FUNCTIONAL PERSPECTIVE.
I AM BAFFLED. GALTON IS BAFFLED. DARWIN IS BAFFLED.
ALL WE CAN DO IS EXPERIMENT, EXPERIMENT, EXPERIMENT!"
—*FLORENCE NIGHTINGALE*

⁊

Sir Richard Francis Burton arrived at the Squirrel Hill cemetery and quickly found the area where the loup-garous had been feeding. Graves had been torn open, coffins ripped apart, and putrefying corpses shredded and gnawed at; left scattered across the wet mud.

Even though, while in Africa, he'd become fascinated by the notion of cannibalism, Burton actually possessed a deep-seated fear of the ghoulish. Anything connected with graveyards and corpses unnerved him. The many cadavers he'd seen, and even accidentally trodden on, in the East End had filled him with horror; Montague Penniforth's ravaged carcass had sickened him to the core; and now this! His mouth felt dry and his heart hammered in his chest.

At his feet, Fidget growled and whined and pulled at his lead.

Burton squatted and took the dog's head in his hands, looked into the big brown eyes.

"Listen, Fidget," he said quietly. "This damned rain has probably washed away the scent but somehow you have to find it. Do you understand? My friend's life depends on it!"

He took from his pocket a pair of Swinburne's white gloves and pressed them against the Basset hound's nose.

"Seek, Fidget! Seek!"

The dog yelped and, as Burton stood, started to snuffle about enthusiastically, moving in an ever-widening circle. Repeatedly, as he came close to the scattered bones and lumps of worm-ridden flesh, he let loose a coughing bark—*wuff!*—which Burton guessed indicated not the odour of the corpses but the scent of the werewolves. This could be useful, for if their musk was that strong, it would be easier for the dog to follow them than Swinburne.

Ultimately, this proved to be the case. Fidget led him to an area of the cemetery where, even after the rainfall, it was obvious that a struggle had taken place. Deep grooves showed where boot heels had been dragged through the mud and around them were the many footprints of loup-garous. Then all indications of Swinburne's presence vanished and the paw marks trailed away toward a collapsed section of the graveyard's wall.

"They picked him up and carried him," muttered Burton.

Fidget was gazing at him with an apologetic expression. Swinburne's trail had vanished.

"Don't worry, old fellow, the game's not over yet!"

Burton pulled Fidget over to the gap in the wall, stepped through, crouched, and pushed the dog's nose into one of the werewolf paw prints.

A deep rumble sounded in the Basset hound's chest and his snout wrinkled in disgust.

"Follow!" ordered Burton.

Fidget whined, gave a yelp, and pulled his master back toward the cemetery.

"No! Wrong direction! That way! Go!"

The hound stopped, blinked at him, looked back along the trail, turned, and started away from the wall.

"Good dog!" encouraged his new master.

Dragged along behind the excited hound, the King's agent descended the hill, skirted a long fence, and passed into a rubbish-strewn alleyway which ran between the back yards of terraced houses until it emerged onto Devonport Street. Fidget turned to the right and raced along, down the inclining road and across the main thoroughfare of Cable Street toward the River Thames. Burton was astonished at the dog's assured manner. The rain had been falling for hours, yet enough of the werewolves' scent remained for the remarkable hound to follow.

People milled about, many turning to stare at the man and the small Basset hound; there were yells and catcalls but Burton barely noticed, so intent was he on his quest.

Reaching the bank of the river, they turned right again, following the course of the Wapping Wall. The terrible reek of the city's artery assailed Burton's nostrils and turned his stomach, yet Fidget kept on, his nose able to separate one stink from another, pushing aside the distractions, focusing only on that which he'd been ordered to follow.

With the horrors of the Cauldron seething around them, they pressed on in a westerly direction for nearly two miles until London Bridge hove into view in the distance. Across the road, Burton spotted the end of Mews Street and the boarded up pawn shop where he'd met with Paul Gustave Doré.

Past the docks and the Tower of London went the man and his hound, and down a set of stone steps to a narrow walkway which ran alongside the contaminated waters of the Thames. The stone surface was slick with slime and, though the rain had abated somewhat, the muck squelched beneath Burton's tread and footing was precarious. One slip and he could end up in the river!

They passed into the gloom beneath London Bridge and there Fidget stopped and snuffled at the base of a narrow wooden door upon which a notice warned "Strictly No Entry". Burton put his shoulder to the portal and pushed. With a deep grinding noise, it scraped open, revealing a square chamber.

The King's agent reached into his coat pocket, withdrew a clockwork lantern and gave it a twist. The flame flared into life inside it and the sides of the device spilled light into the room. It was completely empty but for muddy paw prints on the floor which led through a dark archway in the opposite wall. Urged onward by the dog, Burton pushed the door shut and crossed the chamber. Beyond the archway, stone steps descended into darkness. He followed them.

The deeper he went, the damper it became, until the stone walls were literally running with water. After many minutes had passed, he finally came to the base of the stairs and here found a corridor cut through solid rock, its floor hidden beneath filthy water, with three thick pipes running along the left-hand wall. Gas mains, he supposed.

"You'll not sniff out their trail here," he muttered to Fidget, "but this is the way they must have come, so we'll press on. Here; up with you!"

He bent and hoisted the Basset hound up into his arms, then moved down into the cold water. Two steps he descended until he reached the flat floor. The liquid swirled around his knees, filling his boots and clogging his nostrils with the putrid stench of rotting fish.

Droplets fell from above, hitting the water with echoing and strangely musical plops.

He waded along the narrow tunnel, his lantern ticking in his hand, casting its fitful glow on the streaming walls and metal pipes, which shimmered and glistened in the light. Soon there was total darkness ahead, total darkness behind, and Burton experienced the same sensation he'd had when rising through the fog in the rotorchair; that he was moving but going nowhere; that this journey had no end.

He pressed on.

He was under the Thames, that was obvious, and the thought of that great weight above terrified him. He'd never been good with enclosed spaces. Bismillah! What he'd give now for the endless plains of Africa or the ever-shifting desert sands of Arabia!

"Why did I agree to this?" he whispered into Fidget's ear. "Serving an Empire whose actions I deplore, in a country I can't call home?"

Fidget whimpered and rested his chin on his master's shoulder.

Eventually, and quite unexpectedly, the tunnel ended at a flight of stairs.

Breathing a heartfelt sigh of relief, Burton stepped out of the water and ascended. He came to a room in every way identical to the one at the other end of the subterranean passage, and, setting Fidget onto the floor, he pushed the hound's nose into a paw print.

"Follow! There's a good boy!"

The dog crossed to the door opposite the entrance to the stairs and looked meaningfully at Burton, as if to say "Open it!"

The famous adventurer did so and stepped out onto another slime-covered walkway. He was still beneath London Bridge but now on the Southwark side.

He snapped off his lantern and shoved it into a pocket.

Fidget led him up onto Tooley Street where he was met with a scene of utter devastation. This part of London, the Hay's Wharf area, had been completely destroyed by a disastrous fire back in June. Its warehouses had burned for two weeks, and even now, three months later and with the rain falling upon it, the wreckage was still visibly smouldering. To the east, almost as far as the eye could see, lay a ravaged landscape; a black wasteland sprawling beneath a dirty haze which even the rain couldn't wash away.

Burton winced. This was a painful sight, for among the warehouses had been Grindlays, the place where he'd stored the bulk of the Oriental manuscripts he'd spent so much of his Army pay on while in India, plus trunks filled with Oriental and African costumes and mementoes, and a great many of his personal notebooks.

It had all been consumed by the blaze.

He remembered with grim amusement how the clerk at Grindlays head office, upon seeing his distress, had asked: "Did you lose any plate or jewellery, sir?"

"No, nothing of that nature," had replied Burton.

"Ah, well!" exclaimed the clerk, looking much happier, "That's not so bad then!"

Fidget tugged at his leash.

They turned westward and followed the river as far as Southwark Bridge before then turning inland. With his nose close to the ground, Fidget pulled the King's agent into a by-street and from there into the depths of The Borough.

Burton could see that the route the Basset hound was following would probably be quiet at night but now it was past mid-day and the streets were thronged with citizens going about their business. Pushing their way through the crowds, the man and the dog passed through alley after alley, out of The Borough and into Lambeth, through Lambeth and onto Vauxhall, until they finally emerged on Nine Elms Road. Here, the scent trail veered off the highway and through a hole in a wooden fence. It continued ahead, running parallel to the thoroughfare, and already Burton had an idea of the destination, for the sky in front of him was broken by four tall chimney-like structures.

§

Swinburne couldn't stop laughing.

His entire body hurt. He was bruised and lacerated and every injury was sending a thrill of pleasure coursing through his nerves.

Laurence Oliphant was being driven to a blind fury. He'd thrown down his sword cane, removed and dropped his jacket, rolled up his shirt sleeves, and was now setting about the poet with unrestrained viciousness.

Oh yes, he was going to kill the little man, but he'd be damned if he'd make it easy for the red-headed pipsqueak! No, a long, slow, terrifying death, that's what Swinburne was going to get.

So again and again he allowed his prey to reach that temptingly open door, and again and again he pounced on him at the last second and hurled him back into the courtyard.

And Swinburne laughed.

Oliphant circled the poet, grinned diabolically, swooped in and struck. Swinburne span into the air and thudded onto the ground, his clothes shredded, the skin beneath ripped.

He dragged himself along, a ragged bloodied mess, his eyes wild, his giggle becoming a gurgle as blood streamed from his nose and split lips.

In four long strides, Oliphant was at his side.

"What are you?" gasped Swinburne. "One of Nurse Nightingale's foul experiments?"

"Shut your mouth!"

"What did she do to you, Oliphant?"

"She saved me."

"From what?"

"Death, Swinburne, death. I overindulged in opium, became an addict, and slipped into a coma in a Limehouse drug den. Miss Nightingale rescued the functioning parts of my brain and fused them with a humanised animal."

"What animal?"

"My white panther."

"Ah, that explains it!"

"Explains what?"

"The lingering odour of cat piss I smell every time you come close."

Oliphant emitted a ferocious hiss, grabbed the poet—one hand clutching the back of his neck, the other his right thigh—lifted him, whirled around, and flung him high into the air. Swinburne smashed into the base of a high wall, dropped, rolled loosely, and lay still, his green eyes level with the ground, watching the albino's feet approaching.

Through bubbling blood, he croaked:

"Thou hast conquered, O pale Galilean;
The world has grown grey from thy breath;
We have drunken from things Lethean,
And fed on the fullness of death."

Oliphant bent over him.

"Run, little man," he whispered. "Run for the door."

Swinburne rolled onto his back and looked up into the wicked pink eyes.

"Thank you," he mumbled. "But I have it in mind to lay here and compose a poem or two, if you don't mind."

"I mind," answered Oliphant. He grabbed the poet's throat and yanked him up. Then he lifted him off his feet, fingers tight around the skinny neck, and watched with interest as his victim's face began to darken.

Swinburne kicked and struggled, clutched at his assailant's wrists, but couldn't break free.

He caught sight of something over Oliphant's shoulder and suddenly relaxed, hanging limply.

Somehow, he managed to smile.

Oliphant looked at him in wonder.

A deep commanding voice rang out: "Drop him!"

The albino whirled.

Sir Richard Francis Burton stood just inside the gate. He had picked Oliphant's swordstick up, and held it, unsheathed, in his hand. At the adventurer's feet, a small dog backed toward the door, stepped through, and hid behind it, peeking out at Oliphant.

"Burton," breathed the albino.

He let go of Swinburne, who slumped to the ground and lay still, quietly chuckling.

"Come here, you bastard," snapped the King's agent.

"I'm unarmed," revealed Oliphant, walking forward with his arms spread wide.

"I don't care."

"That's not very gentlemanly."

"There are many who claim I am not a gentleman," noted Burton. "They call me Ruffian Dick. At this particular moment in time, it's a title I intend to live down to."

He suddenly sprang at Oliphant and thrust at his heart. The feline man twisted and jumped back, the point of the rapier catching and slicing his shirt sleeve.

"I'm too quick for you, Burton!" he panted, then, lightning fast, ducked down, pounced in, and swiped at the adventurer's thigh with his sharp talons.

Burton predicted the move and caught the albino's hand in his own.

"My reactions aren't bad either," he said.

His grip tightened and bones crunched.

Oliphant screamed.

Burton dropped the rapier and sent his fist crashing into the albino's jaw.

"And I think you'll find that I'm stronger."

With his left hand mercilessly breaking the bones in Oliphant's right,

Burton set about pounding his opponent's face to a pulp. Blood spurted as the panther-man's nose snapped and flattened. Canine teeth broke. Skin tore.

Burton was thoroughly scientific about it. He revived the boxing skills of his youth, choosing where to strike with a cold detachment, timing his blows to perfection, measuring the damage to ensure that the albino suffered every crunching blow without slipping into unconsciousness.

It was more than punishment; it was torture; and Burton had no qualms about it.

As the beating continued, Fidget cautiously stepped back in through the door and began to skirt the wall toward Swinburne. Glancing repeatedly at his master, he padded around the edge of the big rectangular space then crept in until he reached Swinburne's feet. He sniffed at the blood-spattered boots, pushed his nose into the too-short trouser leg, then bit the skinny ankle.

"Yaargh!" screeched the poet.

Burton turned, and in that unguarded second, Laurence Oliphant ripped his mangled hand from the explorer's grasp and, with a sudden thrust of his legs, propelled himself away. He rolled, leaped to his feet and sprinted to the huge doors of the power station. Perfectly balanced, they swung open at his touch and slammed shut behind him.

The King's agent, who'd instantly thrown himself after the albino, crashed into the doors, pushed them, pulled them, and realised that his enemy had escaped.

He hurried over to Swinburne and shoved Fidget away.

"Are you alright, Algy?"

"Bloody ecstatic, Richard."

"Can you walk?"

"I thought I could; then that blasted dog bit me!"

"Idiot. It was just a nip. Come on, up with you."

He slipped his arm beneath the poet's shoulders and heaved him upright. There was barely an inch of his friend that wasn't smeared with blood.

"I have to get you seen to as quickly as possible," he said. "We need to get this bleeding stopped."

"It was marvellous," gasped Swinburne. "I took everything he dished out! Was that courage, Richard?"

"Yes, Algy; that was courage."

"Splendid! Absolutely splendid! Oh, by the way, John Speke is in there."

Before Burton could reply, a howl echoed from the other end of the courtyard.

"Werewolves!" breathed the King's agent. "We've got to get out of here!"

He dragged his friend toward the door in the main gate, scooping up Oliphant's swordstick on the way, but before he got there half a dozen red-cloaked wolf-men loped from an arched opening and came racing across the courtyard.

The head of the pack glared out from the shadow of its hood, displayed its sharp teeth in a terrible grin, reached out a claw toward the retreating Englishmen, then exploded into flames.

The remaining creatures scattered, diving away from the sudden inferno. In the midst of this confusion, Swinburne thrust himself away from Burton, plunged at something on the ground, snatched it up, then launched himself through the door in the gate, knocking Burton backward. They landed in a heap outside the power station with Fidget tangled in their legs.

The King's agent pushed himself up, grabbed the door and pulled it shut. There was no way to secure it from the outside, so, while the werewolves were distracted, there was only one thing to do: run!

He grabbed Swinburne, threw him over his shoulder, and took to his heels.

With the Basset hound scampering along beside him, he sprinted westwards over a patch of wasteland toward railway lines and, beyond them, the busy Kingstown Road and Chelsea Bridge.

"Hurry! They're coming!" cried Swinburne.

A quick backward glance proved the poet right; the loup-garous were pouring through the gate.

Despite his short legs, Fidget put on an astonishing show of speed and sprang ahead across the railway track. Burton tried to keep up but Swinburne's weight slowed him and now he spotted, to his right, a locomotive pelting down the line. There was no way, it seemed, to make it to the other side before the engine passed; his escape route was blocked and the wolf-men were gaining fast.

He set his mind to the task, sucked in a deep breath, and focused every ounce of his being into his pumping legs. Run! *Run!*

The events of the next seconds happened so quickly that his consciousness couldn't register them; yet he dreamed about them for many months afterward.

The locomotive was upon him.

He put everything he had into a jump across its path.

His feet left the ground.

Claws ripped through the back of his jacket and ploughed through his skin.

A deafening whistle.

A wall of metal to his right.

Scalding vapour.

Gravel slamming into him.

Rolling.

A thunderous roar.

The blur of passing wheels and, under them, flames.

A receding rumble.

Slowly dissipating steam.

The grey sky.

A spot of rain on his face.

A groan at his side.

A moment of silence.

Then:

"Ow! For Pete's sake! The blessed beast bit me again!"

Sir Richard Francis Burton started to laugh. It began in his stomach and rose through his chest and shook his whole body and he didn't want it to stop. He laughed at India. He laughed at Arabia. He laughed at Africa. He laughed at the Nile and the Royal Geographical Society and John Hanning bloody Speke. He laughed at Spring Heeled Jack and the wolf-men and the albino and that silly damned dog that kept biting Swinburne's ankle.

He laughed away his petulant anger, his resentments, his confusion and his reluctance, and when he finally stopped laughing, he was Sir Richard Francis Burton, the King's agent, in the service of the country of his birth, and it no longer mattered that he was an outsider or that he stood in opposition to the Empire's foreign policies. He had a job to do.

His laughter abated. He lay silently and looked at the grey sky.

London muttered and grumbled.

He sat up and examined Swinburne. The poet had lapsed into unconsciousness. Fidget the Basset hound was sitting at the little man's feet, happily chewing at a trouser leg.

The railway track was empty; the locomotive had disappeared from view behind a group of warehouses, though the tracks were still vibrating from its passing.

The loup-garous were nowhere to be seen; all swept away by the train.

He stood, hoisted his friend back onto his shoulder, and, using Oliphant's cane to help him balance, walked down a gravel slope toward a wooden fence beyond which lay Kingstown Road.

He was halfway down when a loud throbbing filled the air.

Burton turned and looked back at the power station. An incredible machine was rising from it; seemingly pushed upward by the boiling cone of steam that belched from its underside. It was a rotorship; an immense oval platform of grey metal with portholes set along its edge. Its front was pointed and curved upward like the prow of a galleon and from the sides, like banks of oars, pylons projected outward. At their ends, atop vertical shafts, huge wings rotated faster than the eye could follow.

Was Speke aboard that ship? And who else?

He had to get Swinburne treated; had to find out what the poet knew.

As the rotorship ascended and moved northward, Burton continued on down to the thoroughfare and made his way along to Chelsea Bridge. Here he found himself back among London's seething population. There were cries and screams as people caught side of the little man slumped over his shoulder, and in no time at all a policeman came running over.

"What's all this, sir? Has there been an accident?"

"Yes, Constable," answered Burton. "Would you flag down a carriage, for me? I have to get this fellow to a doctor!"

"I should ride along with you. I'll need to report this!"

"Fine; but hurry, man!"

The policeman ran out into the road and stopped a horse-drawn four-wheeler, ejecting its indignant passengers.

"I say! What the devil do you think you're playing at?" objected the portly old gentleman who suddenly found himself without a ride. "My wife is sixty-two, don't you know!"

"Harold!" gasped his heavily made-up spouse.

"Oh, er, sorry my dear," stammered the erstwhile passenger; then, upon spying Swinburne as Burton heaved him onto the seat, he cried: "Great Scott! The poor fellow! By all means take the carriage! By all means!"

"Much obliged," said Burton, picking up Fidget and climbing in.

The constable followed.

"Where to?" he asked.

"Bayham Street, Mornington Crescent! As fast as possible!"

The policeman repeated the address to the driver then shut the door and sat back as the vehicle jerked into motion.

"Constable Yates," he said by way of an introduction. "So what's the story? You both look proper beat up!"

"King's business, Yates! Take a look at this."

Burton took his credentials from his wallet and showed them.

"Bless me! The King's signature! You're the boss, then, sir. What can I do to help?"

Fishing his notebook out of his pocket, Burton started writing.

"We'll drop you at Scotland Yard," he said. "I want you to deliver this note to Detective-Inspector Trounce. I'm recommending an immediate police raid on Battersea Power Station!"

"The Technologist headquarters? That's rather a tall order, if you don't mind me saying so!"

Burton didn't reply, but continued to fill the page with his tiny, cramped handwriting.

The carriage swung eastward onto Grosvenor Road and from there followed the river up via Millbank, past the Houses of Parliament, and on to the Yard. Barely stopping to allow Constable Yates to hop out, it raced on along the Strand, weaving in and out of the traffic, the two horses flecked with sweat, rounded into Kingsway and continued on up Southampton Row and Eversholt Street. It shot past Mornington Crescent before careening into Bayham Street.

"Here!" shouted Burton as they reached number 3, and he leaped out as the carriage came to halt.

"Wait!"

Striding swiftly to the front door, he gave the bell-pull a violent tug and waited impatiently for a response. He was just reaching for it again when the door opened.

"Why, Captain Burton!" exclaimed Widow Wheeltapper. "How nice of you to call!"

"My apologies, ma'am, but there's been an accident. I require Sister Raghavendra's assistance. Is she at home?"

"Oh my! I shall send Polly for her at once!"

Burton stepped into the house and sprang up the stairs, calling back: "Pray don't trouble yourself, my good woman! I'll go!"

"But propriety, Captain! Propriety!" cried the old woman. Her visitor, though, was already halfway to the upper flat. He was met at the top of the stairs by Sister Raghavendra, who'd come to investigate the commotion.

"Sadhvi!" cried Burton. "I need your help! My friend has been injured! Can you come?"

"At once, Captain!" she said decisively. "A moment!"

She ducked back into her room and emerged a minute later wearing her nurse's bonnet, her jacket, and carrying a carpet bag.

They ran down the stairs and out of the front door, leaving the flustered old widow calling after them: "A chaperone! My goodness, young lady! You haven't a chaperone!"

"Montagu Place; at the double!" commanded Burton as they reached the carriage and clambered in.

The driver cracked his whip and the panting horses set off at a gallop.

Inside the rocking and bumping cabin, Sister Raghavendra examined Swinburne.

"What on earth happened to him?"

"Your albino friend happened," said Burton.

She paled, her fingers running over the poet's skin, examining the wounds, gauging their severity.

"The albino?" she gasped. "But this looks like the work of a wild animal!"

"How is he, Sister? He's been unconscious for some time."

"He's not unconscious, Captain Burton. He's asleep. He must be utterly exhausted."

Turning from Hampstead Road into Euston Road, the carriage stampeded on past velocipedes and steam-horses, between carts and hansoms, with pedestrians scattering as it thundered past, until, on Marylebone Road, the traffic became so thick that progress was slowed to a crawl.

Burton poked his head out of the window and shouted up to the driver: "Take to the back streets, man!"

The driver obeyed, and as Burton had hoped, the less direct route proved easier to navigate. Minutes later, the carriage drew up outside his home.

"Will you bring the dog?" he asked the nurse, as he stepped out and lifted Swinburne. She nodded and scooped up Fidget.

After passing a handful of coins up the the driver, Burton carried his friend to the front door, opened it, and ascended the stairs to the second floor, where he deposited Swinburne in the spare bedroom. For the first time, he noticed that the poet was clutching something. It was a coat, which Burton pulled from his hands and flung into a wardrobe.

Sister Raghavendra, who'd followed him into the room, lay Fidget down and opened her carpet bag. She started to pull out vials, rolls of bandages, and other tools of her trade.

"I'll need a basin of hot water, Captain," she advised. "This is going to take some time. I've never seen so many cuts and bruises! The poor boy must have suffered terribly."

Algernon Swinburne opened his eyes.

"I did," he muttered. "And it was glorious!"

§

It was nine o'clock in the evening and Swinburne was sitting up in bed sipping at a cup of revitalising beef broth. Sir Richard Francis Burton had carried extra chairs into the room and in them, along with himself, sat Detective-Inspector Trounce, who'd just arrived, and Sister Raghavendra. Mrs Iris Angell had permitted the young woman's unchaperoned attendance on account of her being a professional nurse and member of the Sisterhood of Noble Benevolence.

"Absolutely no show, I'm afraid," reported the Yard man, settling into his seat. "We simply couldn't get into the place; it was locked up like a fortress. The lights were blazing and we could see all manner of machinery sparking away inside but of a single man there was no sign. Lord knows what kind of glass they've used in the place; we battered at it with crowbars to absolutely no effect. As for the doors, I doubt even dynamite could shift them. I've posted men around the building, of course, but aside from that what can I do? But see here, Captain Burton; I took it on faith that you had a good reason for the raid. Perhaps you might enlighten me now?"

"For that, Detective-Inspector, we shall turn to my bed-ridden friend here. May I present Mr Algernon Swinburne, the esteemed poet," said Burton, graciously.

"And follower of de Sade!" blurted Trounce.

Mrs Angell, who was at the back of the room pouring cups of tea, cleared her throat.

"Oh, I say—I'm—er—" mumbled the detective.

Swinburne giggled and said, "Pleased to meet you, Detective-Inspector; and I assure you that despite my proclivity for the vices of the aforementioned gentleman—if gentleman is the appropriate word, which it almost certainly isn't—these wounds you see were neither self-inflicted nor delivered by request."

"Um—by Jove, that's a relief," responded Trounce, uncertainly.

"I think—" began Mrs Angell, with a glance at the Sister, but Burton held up his hand to stop her and interjected: "There are ladies present, gentlemen;

let's not forget that. Now then, Algy, perhaps you can give us an account of your experiences?"

The little poet leaned back on his pillow—his hair luminescent against its whiteness—and closed his eyes. He commenced his tale with a description of his apprenticeship with Vincent Sneed then moved on to the events in the cemetery and his subsequent confrontation with Charles Darwin.

As he spoke, he enthralled them with his choice of words and intonation, and, for the first time, Burton realised that his friend truly did possess an astonishing talent, and had the potential to be counted a literary giant if only he could remain sober for long enough to achieve it.

After Swinburne finished, there was a long silence, which was finally broken by Trounce.

"Phew!" he gasped. "They must be maniacs!"

"Triply so," noted Burton. "In the first place, they're meddling with the natural order of things; in the second, the results of their experiments will be a hopelessly tangled mix of interrelated consequences, which surely defeats the point; and in the third, even if they could separate the fruits of their endeavours, they wouldn't have anything to measure until many generations from now, by which time the experimenters themselves will be long dead. It makes no sense."

"I told Darwin as much," Swinburne informed them. "Yet he seemed confident enough. He said time was the key and was just about to tell me more when Oliphant arrived and stopped him."

"Time," pondered Burton. "Interesting. It occurred to me that, in the case of Spring Heeled Jack, time also seems to be a key—if not *the* key—element."

"And you told me Oliphant repeated almost word for word something that Jack had earlier said to you," put in Trounce.

"Yes. It's puzzling. Very puzzling indeed."

"I can have a warrant put out for Charles Darwin's arrest on grounds of abduction, illegal medical experiments, and probably murder," said Trounce. "Which will no doubt delight what remains of the church. Nurse Nightingale needs to be rounded up and questioned, too, for she certainly seems to be in the thick of it. Laurence Oliphant can be charged with the murder of little Billy Tupper. He'll dangle by the neck, I don't doubt. But as far as Isambard Kingdom Brunel is concerned, I can't arrest a man—if he is a man—for inventing machines and remaining alive after everyone thinks him dead!"

"I say," piped Swinburne. "Where's the coat? I picked up Oliphant's coat. Where is it?"

"Here," said Burton, rising and stepping to the wardrobe. He withdrew the item of clothing, which was still damp from the rain.

"I thought he might have a pocket book or something."

"Good lad!" exclaimed Trounce.

"Auguste Dupin!" smiled Swinburne, though the reference was lost on the Yard man.

Burton went through the garment. He found a silver pocket watch, a silk handkerchief, a packet of cigarettes which smelled faintly of opium, a set of peculiar items which Trounce identified as lock-picks, a key chain with four keys upon it, a pencil and, to Swinburne's delight, a small notebook.

Leafing through the pages, they found recorded all twenty-eight abductions plus the names and ages of each of the chimney sweeps. Disappointingly, this was information that The Beetle had already provided.

Various appointments that had already occurred were noted, though only the dates were given; nothing about the venue or attendees. Indecipherable markings accompanied these entries but Burton, the expert linguist, could see at a glance that they'd be impossible to decode.

There were no future assignations marked.

He sighed.

"It was an excellent try, Algy, but no luck, I'm afraid."

"Blast it!" muttered the poet.

"Excuse me, sir," interrupted Mrs Angell. "There's the hat, too."

"The hat? What hat?"

"The one that horrible albino creature left behind him after jumping through your window. I put it on the stand downstairs. Shall I fetch it?"

"Well done, Mrs Angell! But you stay put; I'll get it."

He left the room and they heard his footsteps descending.

Mrs Angell distributed cups of hot sweet tea.

Sister Raghavendra plumped Swinburne's pillow.

He sighed with delight.

Detective-Inspector Trounce reached into his pocket and pulled out a cigar, glanced at the ladies, and pushed it back in again.

Burton returned.

"I could kiss you, Mrs Angell. I found this in the hat's inner lining."

He held a small square of paper upon which a few words were written in pencil. He read it to them:

"URGENT! O confirm: DTs 2909 2300. D y? B y? N y? B."

"More code!" grunted Trounce.

"No, this isn't code, old man. This is simple abbreviation," stated Burton.

"For what?"

"Look at these letter Y's with a question mark. The simplest possible answer to a question is either 'yes' or 'no.' If these Y's represent 'yes,' then the question mark, it seems to me, is a request for confirmation."

"Ah, I follow you!" exclaimed Trounce.

"And, having just listened to Algy's story, how can we doubt that D, B and N stand for Darwin, Brunel and Nightingale?"

"By George! Now it seems obvious! And the O is Oliphant, who's being asked to confirm something about them! But who is the second B?"

"I don't know. We'll come back to that. As for what it is this mysterious B wants confirmed, the two sets of numbers give it away: it's a date and a time using the twenty-four hour clock. The 29th of September at eleven o'clock in the evening. That's this coming Sunday night. A meeting, I'll wager."

"By Jove! You're as sharp as a tack. I'd have been mulling over this note for hours! How about the DTs?"

"Delirium tremens!" suggested Swinburne enthusiastically.

"Silly ass!" smiled Burton. "I'd say it represents the location."

"If there really is a connection between Spring Heeled Jack and Oliphant, as you suspect," said Trounce softly, "mightn't DTs represent Darkening Towers? It was, after all, the home of Beresford, who was suspected of being Jack, and who was also the leader of the Rake movement before he died."

"And Oliphant is his successor!" cried Swinburne.

Burton looked at the Scotland Yard detective with an expression of admiration.

"I'd bet my right arm that you've hit the proverbial nail slap bang on its head!"

"I'm not so sure," grumbled the inspector. "It may be just a coincidence."

"Possibly; but it's a big one. Which just leaves us with the letter B. Who was Beresford's successor to the marquessate? Did he have a son?"

"No, he died without issue and the marquessate became defunct. Darkening Towers passed to his cousin, the Reverend John de la Poer Beresford, who runs a famine relief organisation in Ireland and who hasn't ever set foot on English soil. He rents the property, through an agent named Flagg, to one Henry Belljar, a recluse of whom no record seems to exist. Flagg himself has never seen Belljar; their business has always been conducted entirely by post. So there's your mysterious Mr B, Captain Burton!"

"It would seem so," responded Burton thoughtfully. "I would very much like to see this Henry Belljar. In fact, on Sunday night, if O, D, B and N are going to have a confab with him at Darkening Towers, then I think a third B should be present, too; B for Burton!"

"If you mean to say that you're going to spy on them, then you can jolly well count me in!" cried Trounce.

"And me!" chorused Swinburne.

"No," said Burton sharply. "I'm afraid I have to pull rank on you, Inspector; while you, Algy, are in no fit state. One person can move more quietly than three and I have experience in this sort of business—I was a spy for Sir Charles Napier during my time in India and undertook more than one mission where stealth was required."

"You'll at least allow me to loiter nearby?" grumbled Trounce petulantly. "Just in case you require reinforcements. Surely, though, we could forego the spying and simply raid the place with a squadron of constables?"

"If we do that," responded Burton, "We might never learn the full extent of their plans or lay our hands on Spring Heeled Jack."

"I insist on coming along too!" squealed Swinburne slapping his hands against the bedsheets. "I'll not be left out!"

"Mr Swinburne!" exclaimed Sister Raghavendra. "You'll stay in bed, sir! You are in no condition to go gallivanting around on dangerous missions!"

"I have two whole days to recover, dear lady! I shall be perfectly fine! Richard, say you'll take me!"

Burton shook his head. "You've contributed more than your fair share to this business, my friend. You nearly got yourself killed."

Swinburne flung back the sheets and scrambled upright, standing on the bed in over-sized pyjamas, bouncing slightly, twitching and jerking with excitement.

"Yes!" he cried. "Yes! I was nearly killed by that fiend! And do you know what I learned from the experience? I learned—"

He threw his arms out and nearly overbalanced. Everyone stood and moved to catch him but he recovered himself and proclaimed:

"How he that loves life overmuch shall die
The dog's death, utterly:

And he that much less loves it than he hates
All wrongdoing that is done
Anywhere always underneath the sun
Shall live a mightier life than time's or fate's."

His knees buckled and he fell back against the wall, slowly sliding back down onto the bed.

"Goodness," he exclaimed weakly. "I think I stood up rather too quickly!"

Sister Raghavendra grabbed him by the shoulders, manoeuvred him back into the bed, and tucked the sheets around him.

"Foolish man!" she snapped. "You're too exhausted to go jumping around on a mattress, let alone chasing after mysterious Mr Belljars. You'll stay put, sir, and you'll drink beef broth three times a day; isn't that right Mrs Angell?"

"Even if I have to sit on him and pour it down his throat," answered the old housekeeper.

"Richard! I am to be a prisoner?" pleaded the young poet.

"For two days at least," confirmed his host. "We'll see how you are on Sunday. Sister, will you visit?"

"Certainly, Captain Burton. Mr Swinburne is my patient; I will attend him daily until he is well."

"Bliss!" whispered Swinburne.

"And Captain," added the young nurse, "if there's any other way I can help, please don't hesitate to ask!"

Detective-Inspector Trounce picked up his bowler and dusted a flake of soot from its brim. Mrs Angell watched it float to the floor. She pursed her lips disapprovingly.

"I'll call again tomorrow, Captain," announced the Yard man pacing to the door. "We'll go over our plans for Sunday night. But, I say, do you think this Mr Belljar chappie is our jumping Jack?"

"I have no idea, Inspector," muttered Burton. "But I intend to find out!"

§

Chapter 15

Darkening Towers

❧

"I AM OPPOSED TO THE LAYING DOWN OF RULES OR CONDITIONS TO BE OBSERVED
IN THE CONSTRUCTION OF MECHANICAL DEVICES LEST THE PROGRESS OF
IMPROVEMENT TOMORROW MIGHT BE EMBARRASSED OR SHACKLED BY RECORDING
OR REGISTERING AS LAW THE PREJUDICES AND ERRORS OF THOSE SENTIMENTAL
INDIVIDUALS WHO CONSIDER THAT THERE IS A MORAL OR ETHICAL QUESTION
INHERENT IN OUR TECHNOLOGICAL ADVANCEMENT."
—ISAMBARD KINGDOM BRUNEL

❧

Darkening Towers well-suited its name.

Laying a little beyond the village of Waterford, near Hertford, the estate was some forty or fifty acres in extent, and was entirely surrounded by a high wall of rotten grey stone. Within this crumbling barrier, the ground stretched unevenly, with large areas slumped into damp, pestilent hollows, as if being eaten away from beneath. These depressions were filled with a sluggishly writhing vapour which possessed a green-tinged luminescence, and over them decayed and contorted trees squatted blackly in the moonlight, casting weird shadows and making surreptitious movements. Upon the contaminated soil grass grew in fitful clumps and weeds, brambles and tendrils twisted hither and thither as if their existence was an unavoidable agony.

In the middle of all this, crouched the half-ruined mansion.

Built on the foundations of a Norman manor-house, the glowering edifice was terribly dilapidated; its entire west wing had been ravaged by fire at some point, and was nothing but a mildewed shell, while the habitable part of the mansion had sagged, opening fissures in its vine-clad, mouldering face.

The windows were pointed arches, and the big double door of the entrance was also set in an arch of the Gothic style. At the bottom of the steps leading up to this, were two plinths upon which stone griffins sat, their once proud faces now dark with dirt and fungi, and in the shadow of one of these stood the poet, Algernon Swinburne.

Two days of rest had been all he required. Though his scratches weren't yet fully healed and his bruises had turned black, yellow and blue, Swinburne's nervous energy had hastened his recovery and his shrill insistence had finally won Sir Richard Francis Burton over.

"You can act as look-out," had said the explorer. "Nothing more; is that understood?"

So now Swinburne was watching the mansion while Burton circled around it looking for any sign of activity and a means of ingress. Meanwhile, beyond the wall, Detective-Inspector Trounce was hiding in a thicket, guarding three penny farthings and wondering why he'd been given this duty while a poet—a *poet!*—was accompanying the King's agent into danger.

Trounce would never understand Burton's motivation, for he didn't know Swinburne like the explorer did; hadn't the insight that the little man needed to face Death head on, else it would rob him of self-worth and kill him slowly via a bottle.

A slight rustle alerted Swinburne to Burton's return.

"Anything?" he hissed.

"There are two rotorships on the other side of the house," reported the

King's agent. "I'm certain the largest is the one that left the power station. People are moving around on board. Lengths of cable are running out of the main ship and into the mansion through veranda doors. We cannot get in that way without being spotted. On this side of the building everything is locked up tight. The place is a wreck but the windows and doors seem new. I'm kicking myself; I should have asked Trounce to teach me how to use Oliphant's lock-picks!"

Swinburne took out his pocket watch and angled it until the moonlight shone on its face.

"Almost eleven," he whispered. "We have to get in there!"

"I, not we," murmured Burton. "I told you, you're here to keep your eyes open, nothing else! No risk-taking!"

"If you can't find a way in, Richard, I'm going to have to take a risk."

"What are you talking about?"

"The chimney."

"Eh?"

"I can scale the vines to the roof, climb down the chimney, and open a window from the inside. I'm trained, remember?"

"No, I'll find another way."

However, though he scouted around the mansion again, Burton could find no means of entry, and reluctantly agreed to his friend's proposal.

"Stay here; I'll come and get you," breathed Swinburne.

Impulsively, Burton gripped the poet's hand and shook it.

"Good luck!" he said.

Swinburne nodded and padded away.

Moments later Burton spotted a flash of red moving quickly up the side of the building; Swinburne's hair reflecting the moonlight.

Though tiny in stature and rather frail in appearance, the poet ascended with self-assurance, testing each vine before gripping it, rapidly heaving himself up to the cornice, then throwing an arm over a gargoyle and swinging up onto it. From there, he clambered over the crenellations at the edge of the roof and disappeared from view.

Burton inhaled deeply. He hadn't realised he'd been holding his breath.

§

"Here we go again," thought Swinburne as he stepped across the flat walkway behind the faux battlement and settled himself onto the sloping roof. At least this time, if he lost his footing, he'd merely slide down to the walkway—no chance of a fatal plummet through space.

He started levering himself up over the moss-covered shingles. They were loose and cracked under his weight. Pieces slipped from under him and rattled down the slope, their noise seeming magnified by the night's silence. He thought it unlikely that anyone inside the building, on the ground floor, would hear the racket, but if anyone was in the upper rooms, there'd be trouble.

What could he do, though, except keep going? So he pushed himself on until he reached the top, and there he stood and moved to one of the chimneys.

He looked up at the sky. It was clear, cold, star-filled, with a slivered moon mounted at its apex.

He looked down the flue. It was dark, filthy, seemingly bottomless, and led straight to his enemies.

Swinburne hoisted himself onto its edge and swung his legs into the shaft. He pressed his knees against the decrepit brickwork, braced himself, then lowered himself in. Using the sides of his feet, his hands, elbows and shoulders to control his descent, he edged down into pitch darkness.

Soot crumbled away around him. He'd chosen a chimney far from the part of the mansion where Burton had seen the light, but if anyone passed by the room below, they would certainly hear the susurration of the powder landing in the hearth and would enter to investigate.

Nevertheless, he kept going, and cheered himself up by thinking about the delectable floggings Vincent Sneed had treated him to not many days previously. Where pain was concerned, Algernon Swinburne was a connoisseur. Unfortunately, the hurt from his many wounds, which now started to trouble him, was of an entirely different order from a birch or belt to the buttocks. It wasn't nearly so pleasurable!

He stopped and rested, suddenly shaken by an unanticipated wave of fatigue.

How much farther to go? There was no chink of light other than the square opening above but he felt sure that the hearth wasn't far below.

"Come on!" he mouthed silently. "The meeting must have started by now!"

Down, down, down into darkness.

His feet crunched onto ossified wood; he slipped and a metal grate clanged beneath his boots.

"Damn!" he breathed.

He felt around, found an opening and climbed through, his ankle catching a rack of fireplace tools, sending them crashing to the floor. He winced as the clanging echoed in the unlit room, seeming as loud as the bells of Big Ben.

He shuffled forward, his hands held out in front of him, feeling for any obstruction. He found none until he encountered a wall. Following this, he came to a door, groped for the doorknob, and pulled. With a guttural creak, the portal opened to reveal more darkness beyond.

He knew that the lit room which Burton had seen was somewhere off to his right and toward the back of the mansion, so rather than move in the direction of danger, he turned left and, with a hand against the wall, he crept along what he presumed was a hallway.

A few moments later, his fingers ran across another door. He opened it. Pitch black beyond.

"I'll keep going," he told himself, and passing the room, he tip-toed on to the next. It was locked, but the one after that wasn't, and when he pushed open the door, he saw a vague rectangle opposite. He crossed the room, the bare boards complaining beneath his feet, and found himself standing before a curtain-shrouded window. A yank at the material caused it to collapse into a dusty heap at his feet. Moonlight momentarily blinded him. He blinked and looked down at himself; he was completely black.

As Burton had suggested, the window was solid, though its panes were caked with dust, and looked as if it had been fitted relatively recently; the hard wood was not at all worm-eaten and the catches, which were of an ingenious and intricate design, seemed very modern. For a few minutes they resisted his exploring fingers, but then came a click, and he slid the window up and climbed through it. Dropping to the ground, he ran along the side of the building until he came to the front steps. A shadow loomed from beneath one of the griffins.

"Algy?"

"This way, Richard."

He led Burton back to the window and they climbed into Darkening Towers.

Burton pulled his lantern from his pocket and twisted it into life. Its light crawled across dirty walls, illuminating peeling paper and cracked plaster and an old portrait hanging askew. Items of furniture, hidden beneath dust sheets, stood against the walls.

Dulling the lantern's glare by holding the clockwork device inside his coat, Burton crossed to the door and passed into the hallway, with Swinburne at his heels. He saw that the floor was thick with dust aside from a trail of sooty footprints which disappeared into the third door along. Past that, they proceeded into intricate passages which wound through the mansion with a seeming disrespect for logical design.

Brushing aside cobwebs and stepping carefully over the rubble of collapsed wall and ceiling plaster and pieces of broken furniture, they moved in silence, with ears straining for any sound.

"Wait!" hissed Burton.

He twisted his torch, killing the flame.

There was a soft glow of light ahead.

"Remain here, Algy. I'll be back in a moment."

"Be careful, Richard."

Burton crept long the corridor until he reached a junction. Straight ahead, the hallway widened considerably and was free of dust and debris. To his left, a short passage led to large double doors with inset glass panels out of which light streamed. They revealed a ballroom beyond, with a gallery circling it and large chandeliers hanging from the ceiling. A lumbering machine stood within view and Burton recognised it from Swinburne's description: Isambard Kingdom Brunel. He could hear the muffled sound of bells ringing; Brunel was talking to someone.

The King's agent returned to his friend.

"They're here, Algy; in the ballroom. There's a gallery overlooking it. I'm going to find my way up to it. Your help has been invaluable but your job here is done. I want you to take the lantern, retrace our steps, get out of the window, and rejoin Detective-Inspector Trounce."

"No, Richard; I'm coming with you!" replied Swinburne stubbornly.

"I forbid it, Algy. If you want to be my assistant, you have to learn to take orders!"

"Your assistant, Richard? Are you really offering me a job?"

"If you can demonstrate the self-discipline required, then yes, I think you possess qualities that can be of considerable help to me. Moreover, I believe that you'll benefit from the experience. As I say, though, obeying orders unquestioningly is a requirement of the role."

"Then obey I shall," said Swinburne, and without further word, he took the proffered lantern and walked back the way they'd come.

Burton waited until his friend had disappeared from sight, then, keeping his head low, ran across the junction to the other side of the corridor. He moved ahead until the gloom enveloped him. If this ballroom was anything like the many he'd visited in the past, there should be a staircase to the gallery nearby. Pulling a box of lucifers from his pocket, he struck one and moved ahead until its unsteady glow revealed a door. Opening this, he entered a large cloakroom. He saw a staircase rising up to his left. Light entered the room from the top of it. He blew out his match.

Placing his feet softly and applying pressure to each step with infinite care, he silently ascended. As he neared the gallery, he dropped to all fours. He could clearly hear Isambard Kingdom Brunel's ringing, and with his remarkable ear for languages, was soon able to discern words. The famous engineer was actually speaking English, but his mechanically generated voice possessed such a bell-like quality that, for most men, the sound obscured the meaning. His current audience, though, evidentially followed him, as did the man who now wriggled forward on his belly across the gallery to the balustrade and peered down through its carved uprights.

"The experimental ornithopters have proven too unstable to fly," Brunel was saying. "Human reactions are not fast enough to make the constant adjustments to yaw and pitch which are required to keep it in the air. We are seeking a mechanical means to achieve this. A babbage would be the obvious solution, but Sir Charles is currently working in seclusion and refuses to share his knowledge."

"Then force him!" came a harsh voice from below Burton. He could not see its author but the words were spoken in a grating tone which seemed wholly unnatural to the eavesdropper.

"We do not know his current location," chimed Brunel. "And, besides, he is extremely well-protected."

"Find a way! Nurse Nightingale, your report, if you please. Have you found a solution to your problem?"

There were six individuals below, gathered around a long banqueting table the end of which disappeared beneath him. Next to Brunel, sat Laurence Oliphant, his white face swollen and cut, one eye a mere slit, his right hand encased in plaster. Opposite him, upon a cylindrical metal base, stood a throne-like seat. In it, Darwin sat with his huge head supported by a brace. The long metal needles were still embedded in his cranium, held in place by a circlet, with wires running from them into cables which coiled across the floor and out of the room's veranda doors. Another cable ran from the base of the chair into the electric brain of the Galton body, which stood silently, blank-eyed and motionless.

Nurse Florence Nightingale was also present at the table. She was a thin, severe-faced woman, tightly-corseted in a dark dress, her hair pinned back and concealed by a white bonnet.

"No, sir," she said, her voice surprisingly soft. "In every case but one, where we've raised an animal up to a human level of evolution, spontaneous combustion has sooner or later destroyed the beast. Mr Oliphant, of course, is the exception. He is the only instance where parts of a human brain— the original Laurence Oliphant's—have been grafted to the animal's. We are currently raising a second white panther, which will not receive a brain graft. If it survives, we will know that combustion is a risk associated with the species used. If it doesn't, we shall experiment further with human to animal brain grafts. I should also point out that since taking a beating from Captain Burton, Mr Oliphant's temperature has been fluctuating erratically. We are monitoring the situation."

"I'm fine," mumbled Oliphant. He spoke awkwardly through split lips and broken teeth.

"Thank you, Nurse," came the horrible voice from below. "Darwin, what progress?"

"We have so far treated nineteen chimney sweeps. Nine were rejected and destroyed on the basis of their height. The rest have been liberated."

"Will they remember?" interrupted the voice.

"No. Mr Oliphant used mesmeric influence to dominate their minds and block all memory of what occurred to them while in our hands. We will continue the programme until a hundred boys have received the treatment. As you know, we have revised our theory of pangenesis and have incorporated into it the work of the German monk, Gregor Mendel. We shall see, in the children of our sweeps, and their grandchildren and subsequent generations, the new theory—which we have named Genetic Inheritance—in action. The male offspring will become smaller until an average height of just three feet is established. With each generation, the descendants will also grow thick bristly hair—spines, almost—over their entire body. Thus they will become ideally suited to their vocation; able to fit into any flue, scraping off the soot with their bristles. Living brushes!

"If the experiment succeeds with this group of workers—which we selected due to their relatively unimportance in social terms—then we will expand it to create specialists in all fields of society.

"Of course, our ability to monitor the future generations is dependent upon you."

"You need not worry about that," snapped the voice. "I will uphold my part of the deal. The time is drawing near."

"Then tell us!" demanded Darwin. "It is time we knew the truth about Spring Heeled Jack!"

A figure shuffled into view. Burton stifled a gasp. It was an orang-utan; a large red-haired ape! Like Galton, the top of its head was missing, but rather than machinery, it had been replaced by a bell jar, filled with a yellowish liquid in which the creature's brain was immersed.

"The mysterious Mr Belljar!" thought Burton.

The primate, walking with its knuckles to the floor, circled the table.

"I brought you here for that very purpose," it grated. "Though I warn you, the story is unbelievable and contains references to things you will not understand; things that I don't understand! Parts of it I shall tell from my own experience. Other parts were told to me by a man who spoke in a strange accent; who used the English language in a way I have never heard it spoken before; and who said a great deal that was incomprehensible."

Burton tensed. His two cases had become one, and had led him to this group of rogue scientists. Now, finally, he was going to learn who—or what—Spring Heeled Jack was, and how the stilt man fitted into the picture.

"Gentlemen, dear lady, for me the story began in 1837, shortly after I gained notoriety for a childish prank in Melton Mowbery; a month after I purchased and moved into this estate."

"Bismillah!" thought the King's agent. "Henry Beresford didn't die two years ago! That ape is the Mad Marquess of Waterford!"

"But the true beginning of the tale begins a great many years from now. It begins, my friends, far into the future!"

§

The Second Part

Being the True History of Spring Heeled Jack

cx

WHO YOU THINK YOU ARE IS WHO YOU ARE.
BUT WHAT IF YOU THINK YOU ARE NOBODY?
WHAT IF YOU BANISH ALL THE LIMITS THAT DEFINE YOU?
WHAT THEN? WHO ARE YOU?

—LIBERTINE PROPAGANDA

cx

Chapter 16

❧

"Every time we are faced with a choice, and we are faced with them every minute of every day, we make a decision and follow its course into the future. But what of the abandoned options? Are they like unopened doors? Do alternative futures lie beyond them? How far would we wonder from the course we have steered were we to go back and, just once, open Door A instead of Door B?"
—*Henry de La Poer Beresford, the 3rd Marquess of Waterford*

❧

His name was Edward John Oxford, and he was born in the year 2162. He was a physicist, engineer, historian and philosopher. At the age of thirty, he invented the fish scale battery, a flake of material no bigger than a fingernail, which soaked up solar energy on one side and stored it in vast amounts on the other. The battery transformed technology and technology transformed the world.

A journalist asked: "How does it feel to single-handedly change history?"

"I haven't changed history," he replied. "History is the past."

He chuckled, as if enjoying a private joke, for though he was a genius, he was also an eccentric and obsessive; and the past was his primary fixation;

specifically, the year 1840, which was when his ancestor, also named Edward Oxford, had fired two pistols at Queen Victoria.

Both shots had missed, and the original Oxford had been acquitted on grounds of insanity and committed to Bedlam. Years later, he was released and emigrated to Australia, where he met and married the granddaughter of a couple he'd known back in London, prior to his crime. History didn't record her name, just that she was far younger than he, which wasn't unusual for the period. They began a family whose descendants wound through the generations to the Edward John Oxford of 2162.

The fish scale battery couldn't change the past. It was, however, an element of a far grander project which could; for its inventor had created it to power time travel technology.

Edward John Oxford had a plan: he was going to visit 1840 to clean the stain from his family name.

There were, of course, numerous technical challenges; the relationship between time and space being the most awkward of them. He solved this by "tethering" his device to gravitational constants: the Earth's core and distant galaxies whose position remained comparatively static. This enabled him to select an exit point in the past relative to his terrestrial position in the present; and if that exit point was already occupied by something, his device was programmed to shift him to a safe place nearby.

It was an essential function, but it caused an immense drain on his batteries, so, retaining it as an emergency measure, he found another way to minimise his chances of materialising inside a solid object.

There can be no doubt that the insanity of his ancestor had resurfaced in the inventor, for his solution was bizarre to say the least. Oxford wove his miniaturised time travel technology into a suit, the boots of which he mounted on two-foot high spring-loaded stilts. With these, he could leap twenty feet into the air, vanish from his current time, and appear in the past twenty feet above the ground in nothing more solid than air molecules.

It was crazy, but it usually worked, and when it didn't, the programming took over and moved him out of danger.

There was also a psychological issue. Oxford knew that in travelling to the Victorian age he was risking severe disorientation. He therefore included in his suit a system whereby Victorian reality would be, from his perspective, overlaid with his own 22nd century. His helmet would alter the way his brain interpreted sensory data, so that when he looked at a hansom cab, he would see and hear a modern taxi; when he observed Victorian people, he would see citizens of his own time; and towering over the skyline of 1840, he would see the skyscrapers of the 2200s. Also, because the sense of smell is most intimately connected with memory, he ensured that his would be completely nullified.

He knew that moments after his arrival in the past, he'd have to remove his suit and face Victorian London without the filter. This would only be for a short period though, and, once he'd completed his mission, he'd quickly don the suit and crank up the illusion. He hoped that he could thus avoid culture shock.

On his fortieth birthday, Edward John Oxford completed his preparations.

He dressed in mock Victorian clothing, then pulled his time suit on over the top. It was a white one-piece garment of fish scale batteries, with a rubberised cloak hanging from the shoulders which he could wrap around himself to protect the suit when it wasn't charging.

He affixed the round flat control unit to his chest and lowered the heavy helmet, which was large, black and shiny, over his head. Intricate magnetic fields flooded through his skull. Information began to pass back and forth between his brain and the helmet's powerful processor.

Bouncing on the stilts, and with a top hat in his hand, he left his laboratory and tottered into the long garden beyond.

His wife came out of the kitchen—the house was at the other end of the garden—and walked over to him, wiping her hands on a towel.

"You're going now?" she asked. "Supper is almost ready!"

"Yes," he replied. "But don't worry. Even if I'm gone for years, I'll be back in five minutes!"

"You won't return an old man, I hope!" she grumbled, and ran a hand over her distended belly. "This one will need an energetic young father!"

He laughed. "Don't be silly. This won't take long."

Bending, he kissed her on the nose.

It was nine in the evening, on February the 15th, 2202.

He instructed the suit to take him to five-thirty on the afternoon of the 10th of June, 1840; location: the upper corner of Green Park, London.

He looked at the sky.

"Am I really going to do this?" he asked himself.

In answer, he took three long strides, hit the ground with knees bent, then projected himself high into the air. His wife saw a bubble form around him and he vanished.

Edward Oxford literally jumped through time.

A moment of disorientation.

A short fall.

He thudded onto grass and bounced.

Glancing around he saw a rolling park surrounded by tall glass buildings with advertising flashing upon their sides. In the near distance, there was the ancient form of the Monarchy Museum, once known as Buckingham Palace, where the relics of England's defunct royal families were displayed.

A sonic boom echoed as a shuttle headed into orbit. People zipped overhead in their personal fliers.

Oxford ran into the wooded corner of the park, ducked into the trees, and pushed through the undergrowth until he felt safe from prying eyes. Then he stripped off the time suit and draped it over a low branch.

He reached up to his helmet, switched it off, and removed it.

A foul stench assaulted his nostrils; a mix of raw sewerage, rotting fish and burning fossil fuels.

He started to cough. The air was thick and gritty. It irritated his eyes and scraped his windpipe. He fell to his knees and clutched at his throat, gasping for oxygen. Then he remembered that he'd prepared for this and fumbled in his jacket pocket, pulling out a small instrument, which he applied to the side of his neck. He pressed the switch, it hissed, he felt a slight stinging sensation, and instantly could breathe again.

Oxford put the instrument away and rested for a moment. His inability to catch his breath had been a perceptive disorder rather than a physical one. The helmet had protected him from the idea that the atmosphere was unbreathable; now a sedative was doing the job.

Unfamiliar sounds reached him from the nearby road. Horses' hooves, the rumble of wheels, the shouts of hawkers.

He stood and straightened his clothes, placed the top hat on his head, and made his way to the edge of the thicket. As he emerged from the trees, a transformed world assailed his senses, and he was immediately shaken by a profound uneasiness.

Only the grass was familiar.

Through dense, filthy air, he saw a massive expanse of empty sky; the tall glass towers of his own time were absent, and London clung to the ground. Ahead, Buckingham Palace, now partially hidden by a high wall, looked brand new.

Quaintly costumed people were walking in the park—no, not costumed, he reminded himself; they always dressed this way—and their slow pace appeared entirely unnatural to him.

Despite the background murmur, London seemed to be slumbering under a blanket of silence.

He started to walk down the slope toward the base of Constitution Hill, struggling to overcome his growing sense of dislocation.

"Steady Edward," he muttered to himself. "Hang on, hang on. Don't let it overwhelm you. This is neither a dream nor an illusion, so stay focused, get the job done, then get back to your suit!"

He reached the wide path. The Queen's carriage would pass this way soon. My God! He was going to see Queen Victoria!

He looked around. Every single person he could see was wearing a hat or bonnet. Most of the men were bearded or wore moustaches. The women held parasols.

Slow motion. It was all in slow motion.

He examined faces. Which belonged to his ancestor? He'd never seen a photograph of the original Edward Oxford—there were none—but he hoped to see some sort of family resemblance. He stepped over the low fence lining the path, crossed to the other side, and loitered near a tree.

People started to gather along the route. He heard a remarkable range of accents and they all seemed ridiculously exaggerated. Some, which he identified as working class, were incomprehensible, while the upper classes spoke with a precision and clarity that seemed wholly artificial.

Details kept catching his eye, holding his attention with hypnotic force: the prevalence of litter and dog shit on the grass; the stains and worn patches on people's clothing; rotten teeth and rickets-twisted legs; accentuated mannerisms and lace-edged handkerchiefs; pockmarks and consumptive coughs.

"Focus!" he whispered.

He noticed a man across the way standing in a relaxed but rather arrogant manner, looking straight at him and smiling. He had a lean figure, round face and a very large moustache.

"Can he see that I don't belong here?" wondered Oxford.

A cheer went up. He looked to his right. The queen's carriage had just emerged from the palace gates, its horses guided by a postilion. Two outriders trotted along ahead of the vehicle; two more behind.

Where was his ancestor? Where was the gunman?

Ahead of him, a man wearing a top hat, blue frock-coat and white breeches, straightened, reached under his coat and moved closer to the path.

Slowly, the royal carriage approached.

"Is that him?" muttered Oxford, gazing at the back of the man's head.

Moments later, the forward outriders came alongside.

The blue-coated individual stepped over the fence, and, as the queen and her husband passed, he took three strides to keep up with their vehicle, then whipped out a flintlock pistol and fired it at them. He threw down the smoking weapon and drew a second.

Oxford yelled "No, Edward!" and ran forward.

The gunman glanced at him.

"He looks just like me!" thought Oxford, surprised.

He vaulted over the fence and grabbed his ancestor's raised arm. If he could just disarm him and drag him away, tell him to flee and forget this stupid prank.

They struggled, locked together.

"Give it up!" pleaded Oxford.

"Let go of me!" grunted the would-be assassin. "My name must be remembered. I must live through history!"

A distant voice yelled "Stop, Edward!" and a flash of lightning caught the time traveller's eye.

He looked across the park toward it. The man with the pistol did the same.

The flintlock went off, the recoil jolting both men.

The back of Queen Victoria's skull exploded.

Shit! No! That wasn't meant to happen!

He gripped the gunman, shook him, and heaved him off his feet.

His ancestor fell backward and his head hit the low cast iron fence. There was a crunch and a spike suddenly emerged from the man's eye.

"You're not dead!" exclaimed Oxford, staggering back. "You're not dead! Stand up! Run for it! Don't let them catch you!"

The assassin lay on his back, his head impaled, blood pooling beneath him.

Oxford stumbled away.

There were screams and cries; people pushing past him.

He saw Victoria; she was tiny, young, like a child's doll, and her shredded brain was oozing onto the ground.

No. No. No.

This isn't happening.

This can't happen.

This *didn't* happen.

The smiling round-faced man was suddenly at his side. "Bravo, my friend!" he muttered. "Jolly good show!"

Oxford backed away from him, feeling terrified, fell, got up again, shoved his way out of the milling crowd and ran.

"Get back to the suit," he mumbled as his legs pumped. "Try something else!"

He raced up the slope and ran into the trees.

What had caused that bolt of lightning? It had come from the same direction as the shout: "Stop, Edward!" Who had that been? He hadn't seen anyone clearly; there was too much happening.

He found his suit, slipped on the helmet, and turned it on.

A sense of well-being flooded through him as the distant noise of electric cars, passenger jets, and advertising billboards assailed his ears. He pulled on the suit and set the navigation system for three months into the past. His lunatic ancestor would be working in a public house; the Hog in the Pound on Oxford Street; that was a recorded fact.

"I'll go and talk him out of it," he whispered. "It's what I should have done in the first place."

A terrifying feeling of inevitability sank into his bones.

It won't work.

Try anyway!

It won't work.

He pushed through the undergrowth, returning to the edge of the woods.

"Step out into the open, sir!" came a voice.

Oxford froze. What now?

He crept ahead, trying to see whoever it was through the trees.

"I saw what happened; there's nothing to worry about. Come on; let's be having you!"

He remained silent.

There! A policeman!

"Sir! I saw you trying to protect the queen. I just need you to—"

Oxford plunged out into the open.

The policeman gasped, stepped back, and fell onto his bottom. He threw his baton.

The club whirled through the air and crashed into the control unit on the front of the time traveller's suit. Sparks exploded and a mild electric shock jerked through his body.

"Damn!" he cried, and bounded away. He slammed his stilts into the ground, leaped high, ordered the time jump, and winked out of the 10th of June, 1840.

The suit malfunctioned.

Instead of sending him back three months, it sent him a good deal further; and rather than shifting him half a mile northward to a secluded alley behind The Hog in the Pound, it threw him twenty-one miles beyond.

He blinked into existence fifteen feet in the air with an electric charge drilling through him, and crashed into the ground, unconscious. His limbs twitched spasmodically for thirty minutes, then he became very still.

Four hours later, a horseman narrowly avoided riding over him. The man reined in his mount and looked down at the bizarrely-costumed figure.

"By James! What have we here?" he exclaimed, dismounting.

Henry de La Poer Beresford, the 3rd Marquess of Waterford, bent and ran his fingers over the strange material of the time suit. It was like nothing he'd ever felt before.

He grasped Edward Oxford by the shoulder and shook him.

"I say old fellow, are you in the land of the living?"

There was no response.

Beresford placed his hand on the man's chest, beside the lantern-like disk, and felt the heart beating.

"Still with us, anyway," he muttered. "But what the devil are you, old thing? I've never seen the like!"

He pushed an arm under Oxford's shoulders and lifted him, then, with no small amount of difficulty, shoved him onto the horse's saddle, so that the helmeted head hung on one side of the animal and the stilted boots on the other. Beresford took the reins and led his mount back homeward, to Darkening Towers.

§

Oxford regained his senses five days later.

Henry Beresford had tried and failed to remove the time suit; he could find no buttons. He'd succeeded, however, in pulling off the boots and in sliding the helmet from the comatose man's head. He'd then placed his unexpected visitor onto a bed, with his shoulders and head propped up against pillows, and had covered him with a blanket.

Unprotected by augmented reality, Oxford's first intimation of consciousness arrived through his nose. He was forced from oblivion by the stench of stale sweat, the mustiness of unlaundered clothes, and the overwrought perfume of lavender.

He opened his eyes.

"Good afternoon," said Beresford.

Oxford blinked and looked at the clean-shaven, moon-faced man sitting beside him.

"Who are you?" he croaked, his hoarse voice sounding to him as if it came from someone else.

"My name is Henry de La Poer Beresford. I am Marquess of Waterford. And who—and, indeed, *what*—are you? Here, take this water."

Oxford took the proffered glass and quenched his thirst.

"Thank you. My name is Edward Oxford. I'm—I'm a traveller."

Beresford raised his brows.

"Is that so? To which circus do you belong?"

"What?"

"Circus, my friend. You appear to be a stilt-walker."

Oxford made no reply.

Beresford considered his guest for a moment, then said: "Yet there are no carnivals or suchlike in the area; which rather beggars the question: how did you end up in a dead faint inside the walls of my estate?"

"I don't know. Perhaps you could tell me where I am, exactly?"

"You're in Darkening Towers, near Hertford, some twenty miles or so north of central London. I found you in the grounds, unconscious, five days ago."

"Five days!"

Oxford looked down at the control panel on the front of his suit. It was dead. There was a dent on its face and scorch marks around its left edge.

Beresford said: "I apologise for the indelicacy of my next statement but, the fact is, I was unable to get you out of your costume and I fear you may have fouled it whilst in your faint."

Oxford nodded, reddening.

Beresford laid a hand on his arm.

"I shall have my man bring you a basin of hot water and some soap, towels and fresh clothing; you look to be about my size; a little taller, perhaps. I shall also instruct the cook to prepare you something. Will that be satisfactory?"

"Very much so," replied Oxford, suddenly realising that he was famished.

"Good. I shall leave you to your ablutions. Please join me in the dining room when you are ready."

He stood and walked toward the door.

"Incidentally," he said, pausing. "Your accent is unfamiliar; where are you from?"

"I was born and raised in Aldershot."

The Marquess grunted.

"No, that's not a Hampshire accent."

He opened the door to leave.

"What news of the queen?" Oxford blurted.

Beresford turned, with a puzzled expression.

"Queen? Do you mean young Victoria? She's not quite the queen yet, my friend, though His Majesty is said to be on his deathbed."

Oxford frowned.

"What date is it?"

"The 15th of June."

"Still June!"

"I beg your pardon?"

"What year?"

"The year? Why, 1837, of course!" Beresford looked at his guest curiously. "Are you having problems with your memory, Mr Oxford?"

"I—yes—a little."

"Perhaps you'll remember more once you have some food inside you. I'll see you downstairs."

He left the room and moments later his valet, a thin and stiffly-mannered gentleman, sidled in carrying a large porcelain basin, two towels and a bar of soap. The valet departed then returned with a full set of clothes. For a third time, he went away and came back, this time with a bucket of steaming water, which he poured into the basin.

Finally, he spoke:

"Will you require anything else, sir?"

"No, thank you. What's your name?"

"Brock, sir. May I offer you a shave?"

"I'll do it myself, if you don't mind."

"Very good, sir. There is a bell-pull beside the bed, here. Summon me when you're ready, and I'll escort you down to the dining room. May I take your, er, *costume* to be laundered?"

"The costume, no, Brock; I'd rather take care of that myself, if you don't mind. However, I have a suit on underneath and I'd be very grateful if you'd arrange for it to be washed. I'm afraid it's in rather a state."

Brock nodded.

Oxford sat up, removed the control panel from his chest, and slid his finger down the time suit's front seal. Brock's eyebrows rose slightly but his face remained impassive as the strange material fell open and Oxford shrugged out of it.

The suit beneath followed and was handed to the valet, along with the soiled underclothes.

Wordlessly, Brock departed.

Oxford washed, shaved awkwardly with the cut-throat razor, and put on the clothes Beresford had loaned him. They felt rough and irritating against his skin.

He turned the time suit inside-out and wiped the inner surface clean. The fish scales held no charge and, he guessed, had been flat for the past few days. A few minutes beneath the open sky would revitalise them. The control panel was severely damaged. Until it was repaired, he would be unable to travel. The most pressing problem, though, was that it was no longer able to transfer power from the suit's batteries to the helmet, which meant he had to somehow survive without augmented reality. Here, inside the house, with just a few people present, that wouldn't be a major issue. However, wider exposure to this time period might result in culture shock, which, in theory, could be intense enough to threaten his sanity.

He rang the bell and Brock reappeared.

"This way, sir," said the valet.

Oxford followed him out onto a broad landing and down an ornate staircase. As he descended, he noticed that the house was in an extreme state of disrepair. Its one-time opulence had sunk into a lazy decadence; the moulded trim around the edges of the ceilings, once painted in bright colours, was now flaked and faded; the wood-panelled walls were warped and split; the rugs, hangings and curtains were threadbare; plaster had cracked; dust and cobwebs had gathered.

They reached the foot of the stairs and passed along a corridor, turned into another, and another.

"What a house to get lost in!" muttered Oxford.

"Darkening Towers is a very old mansion, sir," commented Brock. "The man who built it was somewhat eccentric and it has been added to many times over the years. The master purchased the estate less than a month ago and has not yet had the opportunity to effect repairs."

"It's a veritable maze!"

"The dining room, sir," said Brock, opening a door.

Oxford passed through into a long shadow-filled room. It was hung all around with portraits of stern-looking elders. A chandelier hung over a banqueting table. Beresford rose as he entered.

"Ah, my dear Mr Oxford, you appear much refreshed. I trust the clothes fit you?"

"Yes, thank you," replied the time traveller, though in truth they were a little tight.

Brock ushered him to the opposite end of the table and pulled out the chair for him.

He sat.

The valet bowed toward Beresford and left the room. His place was taken by a butler, who stepped to the table and poured red wine for the two men. A couple of maids hurried back and forth, bringing plates of meat and vegetables. Beresford emptied his glass in a single gulp, was served another, and said loudly:

"So how's the memory, my friend? Has anything come back to you?"

Oxford hesitated.

He made a decision.

"My Lord Marquess—"

"Henry, please."

"Henry. I have decided to tell you everything because, the truth is, I desperately require help. Do you mind if we eat first, though? I'm half starved!"

"Not at all! Not at all! Pray settle my mind, though; you are not from a circus, are you?"

"No, I'm not."

"And your costume is something more than it seems?"

"You are very perceptive, Henry."

"Eat, Mr Oxford, we shall talk afterwards."

An hour later, the time traveller accepted a brandy, refused a cigar, and told his host almost everything. He omitted the queen's assassination and, instead, claimed that he'd travelled back through time simply to meet his ancestor.

They had moved to the morning room after the meal and were sitting, with full stomachs, in big wooden armchairs beside a crackling fire.

Beresford was drunk.

He was also incredulous.

And he was laughing.

"Great heavens above!" he roared. "You're as fine a story teller as that Dickens fellow! Have you read Pickwick?"

"Of course I have. This isn't a fiction, Henry."

"Balderdash! What can be more fictive than a man from the future being propelled into the past by a suit of clothes?"

"Yet I maintain that that's what happened."

"You're a strange one, I'll admit," declared the Marquess. "Your speech is rather too direct for an Englishman; your manner too casual by half. I have you down as a foreigner, my friend!"

"I told you; I was born and raised in Aldershot."

"In the year 2162, you say. What's that? Some three hundred and twenty-five years from now?"

"Yes."

Beresford refilled their glasses and lit another cigar.

"Let's just say I'm prepared to play along with your rum little game, Edward," he said. "You say you require my help. In what manner may I be of assistance?"

"I need you to purchase for me a complete set of watchmakers' tools."

"For what purpose?"

"I have to repair my suit's control unit. I'm hoping that watchmakers' tools will be fine enough for such work."

"Control unit?"

"The circular object you saw on my chest."

"And am I to take it that when this 'control unit' is repaired you will once again be capable of flight through time?"

"Yes."

"Phew! I have never heard such a tale in all my born natural! Yet I have it in mind to humour you! You will remain here as my guest and I shall get you your tools!"

"There is something I can tell you," said Oxford, "that might lend credence to my story."

"Really, What is that?"

"Five days from now, you will have a new monarch."

§

Slowly, over the next seven days, Henry de La Poer Beresford's amused disbelief began to waver.

The death of King William IV at Windsor Castle had, of course, been expected and came as no surprise. The fact that Oxford had predicted Victoria's ascension to the throne on the 20th of June wasn't particularly amazing; more a lucky guess, in all probability.

However, after extracting a vow of silence from his host, Oxford revealed a great deal more about the world he'd come from, especially about the different technologies and power sources available to future man. The human race, it seemed, would lose none of its inventiveness as time progressed.

It was the way the man spoke and moved, though, that most convinced the Marquess. There was something indescribably foreign about him, yet, conversely, the longer he spent with him the more Beresford believed that his odd visitor was, as he claimed, an Englishman.

"You are evidentially a sophisticated individual," he said one morning, "yet—if you'll pardon my bluntness—you lack the social graces I would expect from a gentleman."

Oxford, who was seated at a table and using the watchmakers' tools to poke at the incomprehensible innards of his "control unit," responded without looking up:

"No offence taken, Henry. I don't mean to be rude; it's just that in my time social interaction is far less ritualised. We express our feelings and opinions just as we please; openly and without restraint."

"How barbaric!" drawled the Marquess, dangling a leg over the arm of his chair. "Are you not permanently at one another's throats?"

"No more so than you Victorians."

"Victorians? Is that what we are now? Why, I suppose it is! But tell me, my friend: what possible advantage can there be in the abandonment of our 'ritualised'—as you would have it—behaviour? Are not manners the mark of a civilised man?"

"The advantage is liberty, Henry. From this century forward, the concept of liberty becomes central to personal, social, political, economic and technological developments. People do not want to feel suppressed, so great efforts are made to establish, if not true freedom, then at very least a sustainable and overwhelming illusion of it. I doubt there's ever been a time when human beings were truly free, but where—or, rather, *when*—I come from, more people believe they are than in any other period of history."

"And what do they gain from it?"

"A life in which they are able to pursue opportunities without restraint in a quest for personal fulfilment."

"Fulfilment?"

"The sense that you have explored your inherent abilities to their utmost."

"Yes, I understand," replied Beresford, thoughtfully. "But surely if a person's opportunities are unbounded, then the possibilities increase? Doesn't that make it impossible to explore them all, and extremely difficult to settle upon any one area which can be explored to the point of fulfilment?"

Oxford looked up and frowned.

"You make a good point, Henry. It's true that many people in my time are frustrated not by limitations but by an inability to make choices. They feel their lives are without direction and struggle to find their place in society."

"Whereas the humble 'Victorian' labourer," mused Beresford, "knows his place almost from birth and almost certainly never gives thought to an idea so ephemeral as 'fulfilment' except, I venture to suggest, in reference to a hearty meal and a pint of ale!"

"Done!" exclaimed Oxford.

"What?"

"The control unit. Fixed! It's a makeshift repair but it'll get me home, where I can give it a proper overhaul before coming back."

"To 1837, you mean?"

"I have some business in 1840 to take care of first but, yes, I'll come back, Henry. I'll bring you a gift from the future as a token of thanks for the hospitality you've shown me these past few days."

"For how long will you be gone?"

"My Lord Marquess, the concept still eludes you, doesn't it? I'll be back mere seconds after my departure, even if I'm away for years. Would you have Brock fetch my suit from upstairs?"

"Certainly," responded Beresford. He pulled a cord which hung beside the fireplace. "You intend to leave at once, then?"

"There's no time like the present," smiled Oxford.

The valet appeared, was given his instructions, bowed and departed.

Beresford lifted a bottle of red wine from beside his chair and took a swig from it. He wiped his mouth with the back of his hand.

Oxford eyed him disapprovingly.

"It's a little early, don't you think?" he asked.

"My dear friend; it's never too early!" advised the Marquess, languidly. "Besides, it's a wonderful restorative."

"Curing a hangover with red wine is a sure way to become an alcoholic."

"Nonsense! Besides, I can assure you that if you really do disappear into the future right before my eyes, the shock is liable to kill me unless I take a spot of wine to soften the blow!"

Brock reappeared carrying the time suit with its attached cape, the boots with their stilts, and the helmet. Oxford took the items, picked up the control unit, and followed Henry Beresford out of the room, along the hallway, around a corner and into the big ballroom. They crossed this, opened the veranda doors, and exited the house.

The man from 2202 slipped into his suit and affixed the control unit to his chest. He placed the helmet on his head, pushed his feet into the boots, heaved himself up onto his stilts, then bent and shook the hand of the man from 1837.

"You really believe it, don't you?" said Beresford.

"Yes. Wait here; I'll be back in what for you will be just a moment."

He strode out onto the grass.

Oxford had managed to restore a channel between the control unit and the helmet. It transmitted his instructions, which were read straight from his brainwaves, but the connection wasn't stable enough for the augmented reality function.

He set his destination: ten o'clock on the evening of February the 15th, 2202; location: the garden of his house in Aldershot. He hoped his supper hadn't gone cold.

It was a sunny day and his batteries required less than two minutes before they were fully charged.

"Okay," he muttered to himself. "Let's go home and start again."

He waved at the Marquess then bounded forward and jumped into the air.

"Now!" he ordered.

Reality blinked.

He fell and landed on flat ground beside a tree.

It was night.

It was not his garden.

He looked around. The lights of a small town shone behind him. A tall fence lay ahead, on the other side of a road. Low buildings were just visible in the darkness beyond it. Beside a gate, he saw a sentry box and standing in it, a man in uniform.

The man lifted something to his mouth and a spark of light flared.

Bloody hell. He was smoking! No-one smoked in 2202.

Oxford, concealed by the tree, took a couple of steps until he was better able to see the sign above the gate. It read:

British Army. North Camp. Aldershot.

This was not possible.

There had been a military base here since 1854 but it had been demolished in 2079 to make way for the town's expanding suburbs.

"Right place, wrong time!" he muttered, moving out of cover.

He approached the sentry rapidly, his stilts making a metallic clacking on the road surface. It attracted the man's attention.

"Christ almighty!" the soldier exclaimed as he saw the tall gangly figure. "Stop! State your name and b—"

Oxford slapped the weapon aside and, in a sudden fit of temper, took the man by the throat.

"What's the date?" he demanded.

The sentry's face went slack. "Wha—wha—wha—?" he gibbered.

"The date!" spat Oxford, and struck the soldier's face with the flat of his palm, once, twice, thrice, until some semblance of comprehension crept into the staring eyes.

"What's the date?" he repeated. "Day, month, year?"

"Fri-Friday, M-March the ninth," stuttered the soldier.

"Year?" urged Oxford, shaking the man.

"1877."

Oxford's hand dropped and he stepped back in surprise.

The soldier fumbled for his rifle, raised it and pulled the trigger. A bullet scored the side of Oxford's helmet, jerking his head painfully. A shout came from off to the right. He heard the sound of booted feet running on the road. He turned, paced away, ordered his suit to take him back to Darkening Towers, leaped into the air and landed in sunshine.

"You were gone less than two minutes," called the Marquess. "I'm convinced, Mr Oxford! You vanished right before my eyes! It was simply astonishing! I say, what's wrong with your helmet?"

The time traveller stumbled across the grass and collapsed to his knees at Beresford's feet. He reached up to remove his headgear and yelled in pain as heat blistered his hands.

"Careful! There some sort of blue flame dancing around your head," advised the Marquess. "Wait a moment!"

He ran in to the mansion and emerged moments later holding a curtain, which he'd ripped down from inside one of the veranda doors. Wrapping it around the helmet, he lifted it from Oxford's head and dropped it onto the grass. The curtain started to burn. Beresford used the tip of his boot to pull it away. The blue fire flickered around the uncovered black dome then shrank and died.

"I didn't get home," said Oxford, yanking his boots off.

"To the future? Why not? Where did you go?"

"I went to Aldershot, to the place where my home is, but it wasn't there yet. I landed in 1877."

"Forty years from now," said Beresford, picking up the stilt boots. "Come inside. My guess is you no longer object to alcohol?"

"It's still too early for me, Henry. If you don't mind, I'd like to sit alone for a bit. I have to work out what happened."

"Very well. I have business in London today, anyway, and will probably stay overnight, so I'll leave you to your contemplations and will see you tomorrow morning. Treat the mansion as your own."

"Thank you, Henry; you continue to be very generous; I don't know how I'd manage without you. You have been a great friend."

"Not at all; think nothing of it! As a friend, may I make an observation?"

"Of course."

"You're beginning to look a little wild about the eyes, Edward. Since your arrival here you have worked on that control unit without cease. Perhaps you should rest up for a few days. Do something different. You could come to London with me. I'm going to the Athenaeum Club. Brunel will be there; the famous engineer; have you heard of him?"

"Of course! He's still famous in my time!" said Oxford. "But I can't, Henry. I can't leave Darkening Towers. This seclusion is bearable but if I step beyond these walls I'll be confronted with a world very different from my own. Too different! It's liable to cause a severe form of culture shock from which I may never recover."

"Culture shock? What is that?"

"Think of all the things that make you the man you are today, Henry. What if they were all replaced with entirely different things? Would you still be the same man?"

"I would adapt."

"Yes, up to a point adaptation is possible, but beyond that point, destruction beckons."

"Very well, if London is too much for you, then rest here. Sleep, drink but leave off working and thinking for a few hours at least."

"I'll try."

Just after midday, the Marquess of Waterford rode out of Darkening Towers, leaving Oxford to his own devices.

Brock served a light lunch which the time traveller ate without tasting. Despite his host's advice, his mind was entirely occupied with his unsuccessful jump home. Later, he prodded and probed his helmet's hardware but without the proper tools repairs were impossible. He had to get back to 2202!

He brooded through the afternoon and into the evening, slumped in an armchair, oblivious to Brock, who occasionally appeared to tend the fire, to bring tea, and to offer food.

Eventually, after the valet had cleared his throat four times without gaining Oxford's attention, Brock said: "Excuse me, sir, do you require anything? Only it's one o'clock in the morning and I should like to retire for the night."

Oxford looked at him with faraway eyes. "What? Oh, no, go to bed, Brock. Thank you."

The valet left and Oxford remained in the chair.

The fire died.

The night passed.

The sun rose.

Brock reappeared.

He found Oxford pacing up and down.

"Shall I instruct the cook to prepare you some breakfast, sir?"

"No!" snapped Oxford. "Where's your master?"

"In London, sir. I expect he'll be back later this morning."

"Call him! I need to speak with him at once!"

"Call him, sir?"

"At once, dammit!"

"I'm afraid you've misunderstood me, sir. He is in London."

"I understood perfectly well! Get him on the—? Ah! No! Of course. I'm sorry Brock. I'm sorry. Forgive me. I'll wait. Would you tell your master I need to see him the moment he arrives?"

"I will, sir."

"Thank you."

He had to wait until three o'clock.

Beresford had barely entered the mansion before he was brought up short by a wild shout: "Where the hell have you been? I've been waiting all day!"

Passing his gloves and hat to Brock, the Marquess looked at the haggard figure who'd shouted from the door of the morning room.

"By James!" he exclaimed. "What's wrong with you, Oxford?"

"Get in here, I have to tell you something! Quick!"

Beresford shrugged and walked into the chamber, unbuttoning his riding jacket and slipping out of it.

"What's on you mind?" he said, tossing the garment over the back of a chair.

Edward Oxford, his eyes blazing, his mouth twisted into a painful grin, ran his fingers through his dishevelled hair and laughed. It was a wild, horribly pitched sound.

"I can't go back!" he yelled. "I can't go back!"

Beresford dropped into an armchair.

"Back where? Home, you mean? To 2202?"

"Yes, of course that's what I mean, you bloody fool!"

"Steady man. Calm down. Remember that you're my guest here."

Oxford wrapped his arms around himself and gazed at the Marquess.

"I killed a man," he whispered.

"You did what? When?"

"Three years from now. I killed a man by accident. He was my ancestor."

"Good lord! Sit. Tell me more."

Oxford shuffled to a chair and fell into it. He stared at the floor.

"Henry, imagine that time is a cord stretching forward from now all the way to the year 2202. Now picture a point on that cord a short distance ahead of us; the year 1840. There is a man at that point whose name, like mine, is Edward Oxford. We'll call him the Original Oxford. As you move along that line, you see this man fathering a child, and that child grows and becomes parent to another, and that one does the same, and so on and so forth until you reach 2162, when a descendant of the Original Oxford gives birth to me."

"I get the picture," said Beresford. "So what?"

"Now move forward to 2202, my fortieth birthday. I jump back from that far end of the line to 1840 and I kill the Original Oxford before then jumping to the start of the line, where we are now."

"The present moment," offered the Marquess.

"Yes. Now, at 1840, the line has been cut. The stretch of it containing all the Original Oxford descendants is no longer joined to the part of the line that we are on. It still exists, perhaps, but not for us. For us, everything after the death of the Original Oxford must be written anew. There's nothing there for me to jump forward into!"

"But you went to 1877. That's beyond the cut!"

"Yes, it is, and I've been puzzling over that all night. I think I know what happened. I think I jumped to the end of my natural life span."

"I don't understand you."

"Henry, if I remain in this time, by 1877 I will be eighty years old. Friday March the 9th, 1877, I am certain, will be, barring accidents, the end of my days."

"Do you mean to suggest that you can travel within your own allotted time, as it were, but to go beyond that you need a future which, for you, has already been established?"

"Yes, exactly."

"To all intents and purposes, then, you seem to have wiped yourself out of existence. But why, Edward? Why did you kill this man?"

"I'd rather not go into that. Like I said, it was an accident."

"So go and prevent it. If you can travel as far as 1877, then 1840 remains well within reach. Go and stop the death of the Original Oxford."

"Henry, don't you see? I'm here; I killed him; no one stopped me; therefore if I try, I will surely fail!"

"The complexities of time travel are far beyond me," answered Beresford, "but in the future you were alive and invented a time suit. That cannot have been possible if someone killed your ancestor. Yet here you are. It seems to me that just because you perceive that things occurred a certain way doesn't mean you can't go back and alter them."

Edward gazed into space.

"Yes," he whispered thoughtfully. "Yes, I suppose that's true. It's worth a try!"

He sprang to his feet.

"I have to work on the suit, Henry. There's damage to the helmet and the control unit requires further attention!"

"For pity's sake, man, rest first! You look as if you've not slept all night!"

"I haven't! There's no time for sleep!" barked Oxford, crossing to the table where his gear was laid out.

Beresford shook his head.

"Of all people," he said quietly, "I would have thought you have all the time in the world."

§

Three years later, Edward Oxford hit the ground running.

He was farther away from the other two Oxfords than he'd planned and, as he raced past a policeman, he realised that he was too late, as well; the two men were already locked together; the pistol was already raised toward the queen.

"Stop, Edward!" he bellowed.

Suddenly a bolt of energy flashed out of the control unit and into the ground. He doubled over in pain as the charge ripped through him and looked up again just as the pistol went off and Queen Victoria's head sprayed blood.

The monarch fell backward out of her carriage.

The Oxfords wrestled. The Original tripped and went down, his head smacking onto the railings.

'It was me,' thought the time traveller. 'The distraction; the shout and the flash. I looked up at myself here on the hill and in doing so moved my ancestor's arm. I caused the pistol to point at her head!'

"No!" he groaned. "No!"

The control unit let loose a shower of sparks.

He turned.

The policeman had almost caught up with him.

Oxford sprang over the constable's head and landed back in 1837.

"I can't stop it!" he told Henry de La Poer Beresford as he entered through the veranda doors. "It might not have happened at all if I hadn't gone back just now!"

He dropped his face into his hands and moaned.

"Sleep," ordered Beresford. "Once you are rested, you'll think more clearly. We'll find a solution. And remember, you have forty years in which to work on it."

"Bloody hell!" cursed Oxford. "I can't stay a Victorian recluse for the rest of my life. Besides, my wife is expecting me home for supper."

He suddenly chuckled at the contrast—the extraordinary and the mundane—and lost control of himself, throwing his head back and laughing wildly; a harsh and unbalanced noise which caused the Marquess to step back a pace.

It echoed through Darkening Towers, that horrible laughter.

Maybe it echoed through time.

§

Chapter 17

Dissuasion

~

"NOTHING IS PERMANENT, LEAST OF ALL THE THING YOU THINK OF AS I."
—HENRY DE LA POER BERESFORD, THE 3RD MARQUESS OF WATERFORD

~

Edward Oxford raved all evening until Beresford summoned Brock and together they half pushed, half carried him up the stairs and into his bedroom. They pulled off his clothes—both had learned how to unfasten the time suit—and put him to bed. He eventually fell into a fitful sleep, muttering to himself, groaning, tossing and turning.

When he shuffled into the morning room the next day, he looked gaunt and fevered, with dark circles around his eyes.

"Eat," commanded Beresford, indicating the food the butler had placed on the table.

Oxford sat and ate in a desultory manner, his eyes glazed.

"I have a question," said the Marquess.

His guest grunted.

"Where is your ancestor now; at this moment; June 1837."

"He's fifteen years old. He lives with his mother and sister in lodgings at West Place, West Square, Lambeth"

"And where will he be when you kill him?"

"Green Park."

"Then you must go to Lambeth, find him, and convince him that he'll be murdered if he visits Green Park in 1840."

Oxford leaned back in his seat and looked at the Marquess.

"Yes," he mumbled. "Yes. If I can manage it; if I can bear the exposure and hold myself together; it could work."

"Do you know where West Place is?"

"Yes, it's right beside the Imperial War Museum."

"The what?"

"The Imp—no, wait, that hasn't been built. It's—It's the Bethlehem Royal Hospital!"

"Bedlam, you mean?"

"The very place where my ancestor will spend twenty-four years of his life if I prevent myself from killing him."

"He was—is, I mean—a lunatic, then?"

"At this point in time, 1837, he's beginning to show symptoms of mental disturbance. The illness reaches its peak in 1840, when he commits a criminal act. He's caught, tried, and committed to Bedlam. Over the next couple of decades or so, he recovers his wits, though he remains incarcerated. They eventually move him to Broadmoor, then he's freed and deported to Australia where he meets and marries a girl. They have a child who is my I-don't-know-how-many-times-great grandfather."

Beresford leaned forward and rested his chin upon his hand, contemplating his strange house guest.

"But now," he muttered, "none of this will happen?"

"I came back in time to prevent his crime," answered Oxford. "But instead killed him."

"So no happy ending in Australia, then."

"He didn't have a happy ending anyway, Henry. Look at this."

Oxford pulled a wallet from his pocket and took a folded sheet of paper from it. He slid it across to Beresford. The Marquess unfolded it and saw that it was a letter, though written in no type of ink that he'd ever seen before. He read it:

Brisbane 12th November, 1888

My Darling

There was never any other but you, and that I treated you badly has pained me more even than the treasonable act I committed back in '40. I desired nought but to give you and the little one a good home and that I failed and that I was a drinker and a thief instead of the good husband I intended, this I shall regret to the end of my days, which I feel is a time not far off, as I am sickly in body as well as in heart.

I do not blame you for what you do now. You are young and can make a good life for yourself and our child back in England with your parents and I would have brought more misery upon you had you stayed here, for I have been driven by the devil since he chose me as his own when I was a mere lad. I beg of you to believe that it is his evil influence that brought misery to our family and the true soul of me never wished you anything but happiness and contentment.

You remember, my wife, that I said the mark upon your breast was a sign to me of God's forgiveness for my treachery and that in you he was rewarding me for the work I had done in hospital to restore my wits and good judgment?

I pray now that he looks mercifully upon my failure and I ask him that the mark, which so resembles a rainbow in its shape, and which lays also upon our little son's breast, should adorn every of my descendants forevermore as a sign that the great wrong I committed shall call His vengeance upon no Oxford but myself, for I it was who pulled the triggers and no other. With my death, which as I say will soon be upon me, the affair shall end and the evil attached to my name shall be wiped away.

You have ever been the finest thing in my life.
Be happy and remember only our earliest days.

Your loving husband
Edward Oxford

P.S. Remember me to your grandparents who were so kind to me when I was a lad and who, being among the first friends I ever had, I recall with immense fondness.

"It's a scan of the letter he sent to his wife after she left him and returned to her parents in England. I have the original at home. It has been passed down from generation to generation," revealed Oxford.

"Fascinating! A letter from the future!" exclaimed Beresford.

"For me, from the distant past," countered the other man. "And now, a letter that will never be written."

"Yet here it is in my hand," muttered Beresford, wonderingly. "It raises some questions, my friend. For a start, who was the wife?"

"I don't know. There's no record of her name. All I know is that she was the daughter of a family he was acquainted with in the days before he committed his crime. You'll note his postscript."

"Yes. So it was a crime of treason, was it? It must have been bad, else you wouldn't have travelled through time to prevent it."

"It was. It has been an embarrassment to my family for generations."

"But you're not going to tell me what it was—or should I say, will be?"

"No, I'd rather not."

"What of this rainbow he mentions?"

"A small birthmark above the heart, bluish and yellow in colour and

351 The Strange Affair of Spring-Heeled Jack

shaped like an arc. It has appeared sporadically on Oxfords throughout the generations. I don't have it but my mother has."

"A mark of God's forgiveness, or so the poor fellow thought," murmured Beresford. "What ultimately happened to him in your history?"

"He died a pauper in 1900."

"So if you find him at the present time and dissuade him from ever contemplating the crime, you might save him from his miserable fate—but surely this presents a problem; for if he doesn't commit the crime then he won't be sent to Australia, won't meet the girl, and your ancestors won't be born."

Oxford nodded and wearily ran his fingers through his hair.

"I thought of that before I began this venture," he admitted. "But consider this: the Original was acquainted with the girl's grandparents before he was incarcerated. There is, therefore, every chance that if he remains at liberty he will meet and woo her before she emigrates, and that she will marry him."

Beresford looked astonished.

"Good gracious, Edward; do you mean to tell me that you embarked on this scheme with only that vague possibility to protect your future existence? Are you out of your mind, man?"

"Shut the hell up!" snarled the time traveller, his eyes suddenly afire. "It's a matter of probability, and probability theory is a science of the future, so you are hardly qualified to comment, are you? You damned primitive ape!"

Beresford shot to his feet and glared at his guest.

"How dare you, sir! I'll remind you that this is my home!" he snapped. "And I'll not be spoken to in that manner! I'm going to tend to the horses. I suggest you consider your position here very carefully, Mr Oxford, because I'll be damned if I'll shelter any man who addresses me so!"

He stamped out of the room and slammed the door behind him.

Edward Oxford stared after him, then stood, moved over to the fire and watched the flames consuming the logs.

§

He landed in the grounds of Bedlam by the south-eastern wall at eleven o'clock that same night; a mere two hours into the future; it was still late June, 1837. The big hospital loomed behind him, wreathed in fog.

Vaulting over the wall, he dropped into a cemetery, which he crossed rapidly, then jumped the railings on the opposite side, hitting the cobbles of the street beyond directly in the path of a businessman, who screamed, dropped a sheaf of papers, and ran off.

Oxford looked to his left, to where the road joined a busy thoroughfare.

"That must be St George's Road; this is Geraldine Street; so West Place is straight ahead."

He heard footsteps approaching and quickly walked away from them, crossing the road and entering a mist-heavy square which had a small fenced-in public garden in the middle. Beyond the railings, trees sagged over deep wells of darkness. It was the perfect hiding place.

He knew that the Original had worked as a pot boy in a number of public houses during his early and mid teenage years before settling at The Hat and Feathers in 1839, then at the Hog in the Pound for the first few months of 1840. Where he worked this year, '37, was a mystery, but Oxford figured that since the boy was just fifteen years old, he probably laboured close to home. Lambeth was a fairly respectable borough; its pubs were more likely to stick to the regulations and close at eleven-thirty; the Original should, therefore, return home within the next couple of hours.

He didn't.

Men passed; some women; a couple of youths; but no-one resembling his ancestor.

By two in the morning, Oxford, feeling damp, stiff and chilled, stepped out from under cover, leaped straight up into the air, and landed on the same spot at eleven in the evening of the next day.

He waited.

Nothing.

He tried the following day and the next and the next.

He was exhausted, his nose was running, and his temper had frayed.

Ribbons of energy were crawling over the surface of his suit's control unit. He kept his cloak wrapped around it.

"Fuck this!" he whispered to himself.

At which point fifteen-year-old Edward Oxford sauntered past.

It was half-past midnight.

The time traveller recognised the boy immediately; it was like looking at a youthful version of himself.

He bounded over the railings, grabbed the lad by the shoulders, span him around, and punched him on the point of the jaw.

The Original slumped into his arms.

Oxford hoisted him up and carried him into the gardens.

With the boy in his arms, he leaped three and a half hours ahead. Four o'clock in the morning would be quieter.

Oxford lay his burden on the grass and squatted over him. He slapped his ancestor's face. The Original opened his eyes and screamed. Oxford clamped his hand over the open mouth.

"Shut up! Do you hear me? Shut up!"

He stared into the boy's wide eyes. The Original jerked his head in a spasmodic nod. His body was trembling wildly.

Oxford removed his hand.

"Listen to me and remember what I say."

The boy nodded again. He kept nodding.

Oxford grabbed him by the hair.

"Stop that you little idiot! I have something to tell you; instructions which you must obey!"

The Original's mouth opened and closed. Foam flecked his lips.

"Three years from now you're going to get it into your head to commit a crime. Don't fucking do it, do you understand?"

The boy made a gurgling noise. His eyes were filled with stark terror.

"If you do as you intend, your name will be remembered through history. You will bring shame on every generation that bears it. You will bring shame on *me*! Do you understand? On *me*, Edward Oxford!"

The Original started to jabber senselessly

"Keep quiet!" snapped Oxford. "Pay attention you little moron! Stay away from Constitution Hill on the 20th June, 1840. Remember that date and remember my instructions! The 20th of June, 1840! Do not go to Constitution Hill!"

The boy started to giggle hysterically. He didn't stop.

The time traveller let go of his ancestor, stood up, and looked down in disgust at the pathetic creature.

One thing was obvious: the Original was already insane.

Oxford stepped away from the lad and jumped to Green Park on 20th June, 1840, but instead of materialising a few yards from the assassination site and a few minutes before the shots were fired, he found himself way up the slope behind a large tree. Screams sounded from the path below.

Far to his right, a man was running toward a thickly wooded corner of the park. He was being chased by a policeman.

Ahead, down the slope, Prince Albert was kneeling beside his dead wife while four horsemen struggled to hold back a panicking crowd.

On the other side of the royal carriage, a man lay dead, his head impaled on a railing.

"No," breathed Oxford. "God damn it, no, no, no."

He returned to Darkening Towers and the year 1837, landing in the grounds and falling to his knees.

He remembered tackling the Original next to the queen's carriage. They had struggled, and his ancestor had said: "Let go of me! My name must be remembered. I must live through history!"

"This is not possible!" cried Oxford, and raising his face to the sky, he bellowed: "I can't be causing all of it! It's not possible! It's not possible!"

§

During the course of the next ten days, Edward Oxford was bedridden, suffering a fever which, for hours on end, caused him to rant incomprehensibly.

Henry de La Poer Beresford nursed his guest assiduously, for he'd become fascinated by this strange man from the future.

"How like gods we can be," he told Brock one day.

The valet eyed their patient dubiously. There didn't seem much god-like about the hollow-faced wretch he saw laying there, with skin pale as the sheets, stretched tautly over sharp cheekbones. Oxford seemed to have aged twenty years since his first appearance at the mansion. Deep lines now scored the flesh to either side of his mouth, around the sunken eyes and upon the forehead. His nose was thin and prominent.

"Should I send for a doctor, sir?"

"No, Brock," answered Beresford. "It's a chill, nothing more."

It was, in fact, a great deal more.

Edward Oxford was disintegrating. Submerged in a world that was alien to him, and with the knowledge that his own time no longer existed, he was disengaging from reality. Psychological bonds had loosened and slipped free; he was floating without any coordinates. He was losing his mind.

The fever broke on Tuesday the 6th of July. It happened during the night, when Oxford was awoken by screams.

For a while he lay still, not knowing where he was, then, slowly, his ragged memory returned and he groaned in despair.

The screams continued.

They echoed through the manor; a woman in terrible distress; her cries punctuated by an angry male voice.

Oxford pushed himself out of bed and rose weakly to his feet. He tottered to a chair, retrieved a gown from its back, pulled it on, and shuffled to the door.

Passing through, he entered the hall beyond and stood for a moment, supporting himself against the wall.

"Please!" came a woman's cry. "Don't do it! I can't stand any more! God have mercy!"

The commotion emanated from the Marquess's room, some way along the corridor.

Oxford took a couple of steps toward it, but suddenly the door ahead of him flew open and a naked woman crashed out of it to the floor. She scrambled to her hands and knees and started to crawl in his direction. He saw that her back was criss-crossed with red welts, some of which had cut the skin and were leaking blood.

"No more, I beg you! I beg you, my lord!" she howled.

Beresford reeled into the passage, dressed only in britches, a whip in his right hand, a bottle in the left.

He laughed demoniacally, raised his arm, and sent the whip lashing down across her rump.

"Stop it!" cried Oxford.

The woman fell on her face and lay whimpering.

"By God!" exclaimed the Marquess, looking up. "You're conscious, are you?"

"What—what's happening here?" mumbled the time traveller.

"Ha!" roared Beresford. "I'm giving this trollop all she deserves, man! And it's costing me but a few shillings! The cheap whore!"

His whip cracked down again. He laughed.

Oxford tried to say something; failed; and watched the floor swing toward him. He felt his forehead impact against it.

He knew no more.

By Wednesday afternoon, he was sitting up in bed sipping tentatively at a bowl of chicken broth. The events of the night before seemed like a vague dream.

His host entered the room dressed in his riding clothes. The Marquess had just returned from a hunt and was, once again, uproariously drunk—a not infrequent occurrence. He stumbled as he crossed to a chair and hurled himself into it.

"Back from the brink, I see! How the devil do you feel?"

"Weak," replied Oxford. "Henry, I'm sorry about the way I spoke to you."

"Fetch the damned boot jack, Brock," ordered Beresford. He grinned at his guest. "I can never get the bally things off without the old codger's help."

"What I said to you was unforgivable," continued Oxford. "I shouldn't have called you an ape."

"Pah! Forget it! Water under the bridge, what! So the Original wasn't having any of it, hey? You couldn't dissuade him? You've been babbling about it in your fever."

"Rather than talk him out of it, I think I talked him into it," admitted Oxford.

"Hah! So Victoria is fated to die, it seems! Ha ha!"

Oxford slopped soup onto his bedsheets and, with a shaking hand, placed the bowl onto the bedside table.

"I seem to have said rather too much," he croaked.

"Not at all, old man. I have no love for our little prim and proper bitch queen, and I feel I have a better grip on the affair now that I know the full story. I take it, then, that Her Majesty becomes a figure of some importance in your history?"

"She oversaw the expansion of the British Empire and a period of remarkable technological advancement."

"Brock!" yelled Beresford. "Where are you, man? These blasted boots are killing me!" He shook his head at Oxford. "We're well on our way to such circumstances anyway, Edward; I don't see how the snooty tart can possible influence the country's advancement one way or the other."

"She's a figurehead."

"Figurehead, be damned! Disposable, Edward! Disposable! Bollocks to the queen, that's what I say! Ah, Brock, at last! Get these blessed things off me, would you, you doddering old goat!"

The stony-faced valet pulled over a small three-legged stool, sat on it, lifted Beresford's right leg, placed it on his knee, and began unbuttoning the long riding boot.

"No, Edward," continued the Marquess, "If you ask me, you've been placing too much emphasis on the events of that day in 1840. We should concentrate our efforts elsewhere."

Brock inserted the jack into Beresford's boot and began to lever it off.

"There's little choice," replied Oxford. "I'm at the event in triplicate now, and on each occasion I seem a little more displaced; pushed away both geographically and chronologically, as the suit prevents me from meeting myself."

"So, as I say, perhaps you should abandon that side of it," suggested Beresford. He gave a sigh as his boot came off and Brock got to work on the other one.

"What do you suggest?"

"Leave history to run its course. Perhaps what matters is not the shape and order of events, but that you, ultimately, are in them. If you can ensure that the right girl has a child with an Oxford, you'll re-establish your ancestry.

Who gives a damn that, without Victoria, history might unwind a little differently? At least there'll be a 2202 with an Edward Oxford in it! You'll be able to go home, man!"

The time traveller stared at his hands thoughtfully.

"It's true," he muttered, "the Original did—I mean, does—have brothers. Even if I can identify the girl, though, which won't be easy, I don't see how I can force them together."

The Marquess gave a roar of laughter and, as his second boot came off, waved Brock away. The valet bowed and left the room with the foot gear in his hand.

"By heavens, for a man from the future you can by mighty slow-witted!" Beresford cried drunkenly. "You bloody well do it, man!" he slapped his knee mirthfully. "You do it! Find the little trollop and have her!"

Oxford looked at his host in shock.

"You surely aren't suggesting that I rape my own ancestor!" he said, slowly.

"Of course! Exactly that! Fuck yourself into existence, Oxford! What other option have you?"

§

Chapter 18

Preparation

❧

IT'S ALL FATE AND CHANCE.

—*ARAB PROVERB*

❧

Three days later, the idea didn't seem quite so disturbing. This wasn't because it was making more sense; it was because Oxford was making less. He felt horribly detached from his environment and, whenever Beresford or Brock spoke to him, it seemed extremely well-acted, but not real. It simply wasn't real.

On Saturday evening, as they ate dinner, he raised what had now become his main problem with the scheme. It wasn't the crime of rape, it was how to find the victim.

"I know barely a thing about her," he told the Marquess.

"You know she had a birthmark on her chest."

"Yes."

"And you know that she was considerably younger than the Original."

"Yes."

"And you know that he was acquainted with her parents and grandparents before he went to Australia."

"Yes."

"And you know that he was incarcerated in Bedlam and Broadmoor from mid-1840 until he sailed, which means he must have known them before the time of the assassination."

"Attempted assassination," corrected Oxford.

"Quite so. And you know that he worked first in The Hat and Feathers, then in the Hog in the Pound."

"That's correct."

"So there you have your starting points."

"You can't expect me to go strolling into public houses, Beresford! I can barely stand even the seclusion of Darkening Towers with just you and your staff for company!"

"No offence taken, old chap," countered the Marquess, with a wry smile. "And I'm suggesting nothing of the sort."

"Then what?"

"Simply this: I will hunt down your young lady during the course of the next two-and-a-half years, and I will meet you back here every six months to report on my progress."

"Every six months?"

"Yes! Finish your dinner, drink up, leap ahead! I'll meet you here on January the 1st, 1838!"

Six months later, Henry de La Poer Beresford, the 3rd Marquess of Waterford, looked shabbier; his mansion more decrepit.

As usual, he was in his cups.

"By James, I was beginning to think you were some sort of delusion," he slurred after Oxford appeared outside the veranda doors. "Come in out of the rain, my friend."

They walked into the ballroom, through it, and on to the morning room.

Oxford took off his helmet and boots. The helmet felt too hot and he had to smother a flame which burned around the dent made by the sentry's bullet in 1877.

"What news?" he asked.

"Will you take wine with me?

"I had some at dinner. You forget, just minutes have passed for me since we last spoke. Have you found the girl?"

"No. The yammering idiot is still living with his mother and sister. Last June he was thrown out of The Red Lion after having some sort of fit. I suppose it was after you pounced on him. Anyway, he was off work for two months then started at The Ratcatcher. I've been drinking there, in a wig and beard, calling myself Mr A W Smith. It's a squalid little hole and I'm the most regular of its regulars. I can assure you that the rest are an unprepossessing lot; just a gaggle of toothless old bastards and a smattering of poxy dollymops. I doubt our girl will spring from the loins of any of 'em. As for the Original, he's a friendless, cretinous dolt. Good behind the bar, though. Efficient. I'll keep my eye on him, of course."

Oxford held out his hand and, a little surprised, Beresford took it. They shook.

"I've never really thanked you properly, Beresford," said Oxford.

"Thank you, Edward, but it works both ways—you've given me much food for thought in our time together. I view my world in a new light. Perhaps it's time someone encouraged people to break free from its bondage; to say what they want, when they want; to freely express their sexuality; to wear whatever they wish; to be whomever they desire to be. Perhaps one day I'll make a stand; who knows?"

He hiccuped.

"A fine speech, Beresford," smiled Oxford. "If a little slurred. You should lay off the alcohol; it's bad for you."

The Marquess grinned.

"Why don't you bugger off to July the 1st, 1838," he said.

"No sooner said than done," came the reply.

The time traveller departed and half a year later they were together again. Beresford had aged.

"I'm sorry, Edward, but there's absolutely nothing to report bar the fact that he lost his job, due to his odd behaviour, and now works at Minton's Tavern. Beyond that, it's the same story: he lives with his mother; no friends; no potential among the regulars."

"Thank you, Henry. I'll see you at the end of the year."

"You'll not stay? I haven't seen you for ages! Stay and talk."

"I can't. I have to get this settled as soon as possible. I want to go home, Henry."

The Marquess sighed.

"Then go, my friend, but mark you, I'll not be satisfied with such fleeting visits. Next time, you'll remain and socialise a while!"

The next time was January the 1st, 1839.

"He handed in his resignation just before Christmas. Good news, Edward, we are entering rather more familiar territory. In a fortnight he'll start work in The Hat and Feathers. He told me so himself! You'll tarry a few hours, at least?"

"Next time."

The months passed.

To Henry de la Poer Beresford, whose riotous lifestyle was gradually adopting a surprisingly philosophical motive, the world was the world. However, had he possessed Edward Oxford's knowledge, he would have recognised that it was no longer the world of the history books. Something had diverted it from its course and it was accelerating in a different direction.

That something was the Marquess himself.

He had spoken rather too carelessly to Isambard Kingdom Brunel back in 1837, and had inadvertently planted the seed of the Technologist movement in the famous engineer, just as, thanks to Edward Oxford, he himself carried the seed of the Libertines.

The man from the future was oblivious to this state of affairs when he appeared on July the 1st, 1839.

"I've missed you, my friend," said Beresford.

"Hello Henry. I haven't missed you. I was just with you! Remember New Year's day? Help me off with my helmet, would you. Is it still burning?"

"More so than ever. And that thing on your chest is spitting fire too."

"I'll have to stay here a while to make repairs, if you don't mind."

"Good! You'll be welcome. I've missed our talks. Here, wrap this dust sheet around your head; I'll pull the helmet off."

Once the suit was removed, the two men settled in the morning room, which, by the middle of '39, was one of the few comfortable chambers left in the mouldering mansion.

"Wine?"

Oxford laughed. "You've forgotten again! I'm still digesting our dinner of two years ago!"

"By James, this takes some getting used to!"

"How are things, Beresford?"

"My reputation has spread far and wide, my friend. Do you know what they call me now?"

"What?"

"The 'Mad Marquess!' And do you know why?"

"Because you're a hopeless drunkard?"

Beresford laughed. "Well, partly. But mostly because I've been breaking through those social conventions which you claim so suppress we 'Victorians.' In fact, Edward, I have it in mind to start a movement to demolish the whole edifice of mannered behaviour. You have convinced me that man is capable of far more once he's free."

"Ambitious! And what of the boy?"

"Ah, the esteemed Original! He's been at The Hat and Feathers since January. 'Mr A W Smith' from The Ratcatcher has followed and the young lad is most flattered to learn that the aforesaid gentleman considers him the best pot boy in all of London! Ha ha! I don't know, though, Edward; it's a small tavern and I haven't seen him making any particular friends there. For a while, I thought I'd found our quarry in one Lucy Scales, an eighteen-year-old. She can't be the one he marries in Australia, of course, but she's the right age to become that girl's mother."

"Why her?" asked Oxford, his eyes glinting with interest.

"Because in February she was attacked around the corner from the tavern and his reaction to it was extreme. I wasn't there at the time but apparently he flew into a fit of hysteria and had what amounted to a mental breakdown. He recovered a couple of weeks later and went back to work."

"So you think he might have a particular attachment to this girl?"

"It crossed my mind, but on closer examination I found that he'd never met her, or her parents, or anyone who had anything to do with her."

Oxford pondered this news for a few moments, then:

"Anything else?"

"Yes; some cunning preparations on my part! The Original is obsessed with making a name for himself; he wants—and I quote— 'to live on through history.'"

"What a fool I was to approach him in my time suit," interrupted Oxford. "It scared him out of his wits, what little he has of them. He picked up on my words and twisted them to suit his delusions of grandeur."

"Those delusions are working in our favour now," offered Beresford. "I have initiated him into a secret society of my—or, rather, of A W Smith's— own invention. It's named 'Young England' and has twenty-five members."

Oxford slapped his hand down on the arm of his chair. "Please tell me you're joking! You're getting twenty-five people involved?"

"Of course not! They're all entirely fictitious, just like the organisation itself!"

"So what's the point?"

"The point is this: Young England intends to overthrow the country's aristocracy—the likes of me!—and replace them with what you might call the 'pure-bred worker.' I won't go into details, Edward, because its all nonsense. I've been spinning words and sending the poor young fellow dizzy with it. But the upshot is that each member of the organisation must find for himself a wife who embodies all the best qualities of a working girl. She must be assiduous in her duties, virtuous and demure in manner, honest and loyal and—well, the usual idiotic drivel.

"The Original is now on the lookout for such an impossible maiden. He's been primed to investigate the background of every girl he encounters. He will even hand to me a written report for each!"

Edward Oxford laughed; a brittle, edgy sound.

"You're a sly dog, my Lord Marquess, that's for sure! I must admit, though, I'm impressed with your resourcefulness."

"I'm happy to help. I'll leave you to work on your repairs now; but a little later, I insist that you'll sit and take wine with me. Agreed?"

"Agreed."

Oxford spent the evening with his host, slept, then, in the morning, jumped into the air and didn't come down until the 1st of January, 1840.

"Six months to go before the queen gets it, and things are hotting up!" announced Beresford.

"Really?" rasped Oxford. His eyes seemed to be focused elsewhere. "Tell me."

"Our man is now working in the Hog in the Pound on Oxford Street. As his most faithful customer, A W Smith, I followed him there. My fellow drinkers don't realise that I'm the famed Mad Marquess!"

"You're famous now?"

"Yes, Edward; though I suppose 'infamous' would be more accurate. I have quite a following of young bloods! Anyway, that's beside the point. As I was saying, the Original is now at The Hog in the Pound. The tavern is owned by a chap named Joseph Robinson, who lives in Battersea. Every week, he ships a group of families up from his borough for a knees up. They call themselves the Battersea Brigade, and are supposedly a protest group opposed to the building of the power station."

"What power station?"

"The Battersea Power Station; one of Brunel's rather more controversial projects."

"That makes no sense at all," objected the time traveller. "Construction of the Battersea Power Station didn't begin until the 1920s—and it had nothing to do with Brunel!"

"Um. I may be to blame for that."

"What do you mean?"

"You've told me a great many things about the future, Edward, and I promised to keep my mouth shut. I'm afraid, however, that there was a night back in '37 when I was rather the worse for wear at the Athenaeum Club. The engineer, Isambard Kingon Brunel, was there—"

"I remember that night," put in Oxford.

"Well I'm sorry to say that I blabbed rather," said Beresford. "I told Brunel about the way your people extract power from the ground. I even remembered the phrase you used to describe it: 'geothermal energy.' He was absolutely besotted by the idea, and before the year was out, he'd proposed the Battersea Experimental Power Station."

"Damn you, Henry! It's bad enough that I'll return to a future without Victoria; now you've made it one where geothermal energy has existed three hundred years ahead of its time. Don't you realise the only thing that can prevent me from totally unravelling is to return to an environment which is at least in some way familiar?"

"I'm sorry. It was a slip."

"A bad one! But tell me about this protest group; why are they significant?"

"Because the moment the Original joined the staff, he and the Brigade hit it off like nobody's business! They love the little bugger!"

"You mean he finally has friends!"

"Yes! And seven of them have daughters; all the right age to qualify as the possible mother of the Original's wife. Any one of them could have the 'Oxford birthmark' on her chest!"

"Not necessarily. It doesn't appear in every generation."

"But if it's there, finding it would be a distinct advantage; instead of having to follow all seven of the daughters until one of them gives birth to your ancestor, you'll just need to follow the one."

Oxford nodded slowly, chewed his lip, then became very still and expressionless. His face went slack.

"Edward?" prompted the Marquess. "Are you still with me?"

"Yes," Oxford mumbled, blinking suddenly. "Get me times and places where I can find the girls. I want this over and done with. I'll see you in six months."

He left.

January, February, March, April, May, June, passed.

July came.

Queen Victoria was shot dead.

Her assassin died a few moments later.

Ten days after, outside the veranda doors, Beresford greeted his visitor and said: "I took my followers to The Hog in the Pound a couple of days after Victoria was killed. I've abandoned the A W Smith disguise."

"So you're not hiding that you're the Marquess of Waterford?"

"No!" laughed Beresford. "I've be doing quite the opposite!"

"Funny. I thought your new moustache was part of a disguise. When did you grow—*God!*"

"What is it?"

"I recognise you! You were there! Watching! With a smile on your face!"

"Of course I was there, old chap! Best spectator sport ever! How could I possibly resist seeing you in action; witnessing all you've told me about? Watching the snooty cow die?"

"Henry! You could have tried to stop it!"

"Don't you think it's complicated enough already without me getting involved?"

Oxford stared at the Marquess for a moment then sighed and shrugged.

"I suppose so."

Beresford grinned. "Take off your helmet. Come inside."

"I can't stay long. My suit is on its last legs."

It was true; the white scales around the unit on Oxford's chest were badly scorched, and sparks were continuing to hiss and spit from the strange device, while the aura of blue flame around the helmet now seemed a permanent fixture.

"It does look rather unhealthy, I'll admit. Straight to business, then?"

"Please."

"Very well. The first thing I should tell you is that, not unexpectedly, the police have been sniffing around the Hog in the Pound since the shooting. They're trying to find out whether the assassination was part of a wider conspiracy and my crowd is under suspicion. We're regarded, apparently, as a bunch of dangerous anarchists."

They walked through the ballroom and passed into the corridor beyond.

"This is exactly what I intended," continued the Marquess. "It's the reason why I started taking my young bloods to the tavern; for while the coppers are concentrating on my group, they're ignoring the Battersea Brigade, which, by contrast, seems little more than a gathering of yokels.

"Then, of course, there's 'Young England,' which is baffling Scotland Yard on account of the fact that, while letters from A W Smith were found in Edward Oxford's room, there seems to be no other trace of him or his organisation.

"All in all, the wool has been well and truly pulled over the authorities' eyes."

They entered the morning room.

"And what about the girls, Henry?" asked Oxford. "Did the Original tell you anything useful about them?"

"I should say! As village idiots go, he was quite a remarkable one. He managed to gather a huge amount of information; enough for you to hop back a couple of years or so and still find them. Here, take a seat; have a spot of tiffin."

Oxford sat at the table, where Brock—who was by now Beresford's last remaining servant—had laid out a platter of bread and cheeses.

There was an expression of doubt on the time traveller's face.

"Buck up, my friend!" exclaimed the Marquess. "It's simple really. You can't get to the girls in the future because, obviously, we don't know where they'll be. You can't approach them now, because the police are on the lookout for anything unusual in connection with The Hog in the Pound. So that just leaves the past.

"I have here written descriptions of each girl: Jennifer Shepherd, Mary Stevens, Deborah Goodkind, Lizzie Fraser, Tilly Adams, Jane Alsop, and Sarah Lovitt. I also have details of the times and places where you'll most likely find them."

Oxford took the proffered paper, read it through, and suddenly became more animated.

"This is very thorough!" he exclaimed. "My ancestor did a good job. He obviously fell for your Young England story hook, line and sinker. Okay, I'm going to get to work."

"Wait! You'll not stay and eat?"

"Thank you, Henry. All being well, you'll see me again in a minute. I'll eat then."

They went out into the grounds.

"Tally ho, Edward! Bon voyage!" said Beresford.

§

Chapter 19

Hunt

സ

"IF A LITTLE KNOWLEDGE IS DANGEROUS, WHERE IS THE MAN WHO HAS SO MUCH
AS TO BE OUT OF DANGER?"
—*THOMAS HENRY HUXLEY*

സ

May 5, 1838

Every Saturday afternoon at a quarter to two, sixteen-year-old Jenny Shepherd left her parents' house in Maskelyne Close, Battersea, walked across the south western corner of the park, and called at the Calvert family home on Beechmore Road. Rather than knocking on the front door, she went down the steps to the tradesman's entrance, where she was received by Mrs Twiddle, the housekeeper.

Jenny always arrived at two and worked without a break until eight in the evening.

Her parents called it training. Mrs Twiddle called it a job. Jenny Shepherd called it slavery.

She had to admit, though, that in the six months since she started, she'd learned many skills. She could polish silver until it was as clear as a mirror; she knew how to remove stains from cotton and silk; she could set a tea tray so that it was properly balanced; she could bake bread and gut a fish; she could do a whole host of things that she hadn't been able to do before.

On this particular summer evening, as Jenny left her employer's house, she was feeling particularly exhausted, for she'd spent the entire six hours on her hands and knees scrubbing the floors. She ached all over and wanted nothing more than to be home and in bed.

It was humid and the air was thick with the clawing stench of the Thames. The sun was low but it was still light enough to cut cross the park in defiance of her father's strict edict that she should always follow the road home.

She entered through a gate, and dragged herself along the path.

Her maid's uniform felt hot and uncomfortable.

"Home. Bed," she thought, and timed it to her steps: "Home. Bed. Home. Bed. Home. Bed."

What was that?

A movement in the bush off to her left.

Probably a vagrant finding a sheltered spot for the evening; a place where the bobbies wouldn't see him and move him along.

She started to give the bush a wide berth, just in case. This corner of the park was secluded.

"You can never be too careful, Jenny my lass," she whispered, quoting her father. "Keep your eyes peeled and your ears open."

Home. Bed. Home. Bed. Home. Bed.

"Jennifer Shepherd!"

The voice, a loud whisper, came from the bush.

She stopped and looked at it. There was someone lurking in there; she could see patches of white clothing.

"Jennifer Shepherd!"

Someone who knew her!

"Who's that?" she demanded. "Is that you up to your tricks again, Herbert Stubbs? A-playin' highway man, are we? Dick Turpin is it? I'll not stand and I'll not deliver, my little lad. Ho no! It's off 'ome for me, and a nice long sleep 'twixt cool sheets. So you stay in that there bush and wait for the next mug what comes along!"

She turned and made to walk away, then stopped and faced the bush again.

"Hey, Dick Turpin!" she called. "Come and escort me 'ome like a proper little gentleman. Your mam'll be wantin' you back for tea! This is no time for little boys to be out and about!"

Silence.

"Herbert! Come out o' there at once!"

The bush rustled.

"Even highway men have to eat, my boy!" she declared. "And maybe you'll—"

She stopped dead, her mouth open, her eyes wide. Her legs began to shake.

A tall gangling figure rose up from the bush and strode out on long stork-like legs. Blue flames played around its big black head. It reached her in three strides, squatted, and grabbed her by the shoulders.

"Is there a mark on your chest?" it hissed.

She tried to move, to scream, to run, but her body wouldn't move.

"Answer me, girl!" snarled the creature. "On your chest, over the heart, is there a birthmark shaped like a rainbow?"

Home. Bed. Home. Bed. Home. Bed.

Urine trickled down her leg.

A horrible whining noise suddenly surrounded her. It started quietly but built rapidly until it hurt her ears. The thing raised an arm and swung it down, the flat of its hand cracking against her cheek. The whining stopped and she realised that it had been coming from her.

"No!" she sobbed.

"You don't have it?"

"No!" she said loudly.

"No birthmark?"

"NO!" she screamed, and tearing herself out of the monster's grasp, she hurled herself along the path, running faster than she'd ever run before, the tears streaming from her eyes, her aches and pains forgotten.

§

October 9, 1837

She was aged fifteen and had been living with her employer from Mondays to Fridays since she was twelve.

It was like being sent to gaol on a weekly basis.

The first rule of the prison was that she should only ever speak when spoken to.

The second was that whenever she encountered her mistress or master or their son in a hallway, she must turn to face the wall until they'd passed. When the son was on his own, he always brushed a hand over her bottom as he walked by, which she didn't like at all.

The third was that she was obliged to pay for anything that she damaged. This was the rule she hated the most, for Mary Stevens was a clumsy girl and the way the year had gone so far, she'd be lucky to have any money left by the end of it.

The weekends! Goodness, how she loved the weekends! Every Friday night, she left her employer's house on Lavender Hill, walked along Cut Throat Lane until she reached Clapham Common, then skirted around it to Raspberry Lane, where her parents lived, for two happy days at home.

This Saturday had been her brother's fifth birthday and her mother had sewn together a little soldier's uniform for him from scraps of material which she'd scrimped and saved over the past few months, whilst her father had carved a rifle from a long piece of driftwood.

As she walked back toward her employer's house along Cut Throat Lane, Mary remembered her brother's expression of pure joy as the gifts had been presented. How proudly he'd marched back and forth! And how eagerly, at her father's barked command, had he stood to attention with his chest out and his shoulders back.

"Now then, Private Stevens," her father had said in his sternest voice. "I see your uniform is unbuttoned. Her Majesty Queen Victoria may be new to the throne but that doesn't mean she doesn't have established rules and regulations for her brave boys in the Army! Let me tell you, young man, that bright shiny buttons are a requirement for every soldier! What say you?"

Her brother had glanced uncertainly at his mother.

"I—I—I—" he'd stammered.

At which point Mary had stepped forward and said: "I think I might be able to help. Happy birthday, Private Sevens!"

Her present to him had been six gleaming brass buttons.

She laughed to herself as she strode along, holding in her mind the image of her brother's delighted expression. Far better to dwell on that than on the week to come.

"Mary Stevens!"

The hoarse voice sounded from behind the fence at her side.

She stopped.

"Yes?"

"Are you Mary Stevens?"

"I am, sir. And who are you?"

Something flew up over the fence, over her head, and into the lane.

She cried out in shock, span around, and was grabbed by the throat.

A hideous face glared into hers and Mary's legs gave way. She dropped to the cobbles. The thing holding her followed her down, its grip not loosening, bending over her.

"Your chest, girl! Is there a mark on it?"

She tried to scream but only a croak came out.

"Stop struggling, you fool! Answer me!"

"Wha—what?" she gulped.

Suddenly the fear flooding through her galvanised her into action. She started to thrash about, her arms and legs flailing, her mouth opening wide to emit a scream.

Before any sound could emerge, the thing transferred its grip to the collar of her coat and yanked her upright by it. The garment tore open.

Finally, the scream came out.

"Shut up! Shut-up!" shouted her attacker.

But she couldn't stop.

"Fuck this!" snarled the tall, uncanny figure, and snatching at her dress, it violently jerked the material, ripping it and underclothes beneath down from her neck to her waist.

She fought wildly, twisting this way and that, hitting and kicking, shrieking at the top of her voice.

The thing, struggling to hold her, lost its grip and she fell backward into the fence with such force that it bent with a splintering crack and collapsed with her on top of it.

"Oy!" came a distant shout. "What's going on? Leave her alone!"

The thing turned its black globular head to look down the lane.

Mary heard running footsteps drawing closer.

It looked back down at her, its eyes on her chest.

She grabbed the material of her dress and drew it over herself.

"It's not you, Mary Stevens," said the thing, and suddenly it bounded high into the air.

"Bloody hell!" exclaimed a man's voice.

"What is it?" came another.

She saw the thing jumping away, taking prodigious leaps, and then it was gone and gentle hands were helping her up.

"Are you hurt, love?"

"Steady now."

"Pull your coat together, lass. Cover yourself."

"Here, take my arm. Can you walk?"

"Why, it's Mary Stevens! I know her old man!"

"What was it, Mary? What was that thing?"

"Did you see the way it jumped? Blimey, it must have springs in its heels!"

"Was it a man, Mary?"

The young girl looked around at the concerned faces.

"I don't know," she whispered.

§

January to May, 1838

Edward Oxford waited in the shade of an ugly monument in the churchyard of St David's Church on Silverthorne Road. He knew that Deborah Goodkind attended the Sunday service regularly throughout this year, yet he had been here on three consecutive Sundays in January, two in February, and this was his second in March, and hadn't seen anyone fitting her description.

"If the information the Original gave to the Marquess was wrong, I'll never find the little bitch," he muttered to himself. He laughed. He didn't know why.

There was snow on the ground. He was cold. The thermal controls in his time suit had stopped working.

People started filing out of the church. He hadn't seen her go in but he may have missed her in the crowd. He was getting a clearer view of people's faces now.

He drew back a little, concerned that the sparks from his control unit might attract attention. He pulled his cloak around it.

Half an hour later, the last straggler left the church.

"Where the hell are you?" he muttered.

He crouched, jumped up, and landed one month later and ninety minutes earlier.

It was raining heavily.

He banged his fist against the side of the monument.

"Bloody hell. Bloody hell. Come on! Come on!"

The congregation started to arrive. Their faces were obscured by hats and umbrellas.

Oxford swore and leaped to May the 25th.

After waiting for just over an hour, he saw her at last, coming out of the church.

She was a small, mousy little thing; her hair colourless, her skin white, her limbs thin and knobbly.

She said a few words to the vicar, then to an elderly woman, then to a young couple, then walked down the path, out of the churchyard, and turned left.

A strangely warm mist clung to the city but it wasn't thick enough for concealment and Oxford knew that he stood a good chance of being spotted.

He'd have to risk it.

He vaulted over the graveyard wall into someone's back garden and went from there to the next one, bounding along behind the houses that lined Silverthorne Road until he reached an alleyway. Striding to the corner, he peered around it back in the direction from whence he'd come.

Moments later, the girl walked into view.

Luck was with him; the road was quiet.

Oxford leaned against the wall and listed.

Her light footsteps grew closer.

He reached out as she passed and jerked her into the mouth of the alley; twisted her around and pushed her against a wall, clapping a hand over her mouth.

He pressed his face close to hers and asked the question.

"Is there a birthmark on your chest?"

She shook her head.

"None? Nothing shaped like a rainbow?"

Again, a shake of the head.

Oxford let go of her and, with a last look at her strangely calm face, strode away and sprang to a different time and place.

Deborah Goodkind stood motionless, her shoulders against the bricks.

She shook her head once more and smiled.

She raised her right hand and banged the heel of it against her ear.

She did it again.

And again.

And again.

And she started to giggle.

And she didn't stop.

Not until the year 1849, when she died in Bedlam.

§

October 10 and November 28, 1837

Lizzie Fraser, like Deborah Goodkind, was not where—or when—she was supposed to be.

Edward Oxford was close to where he'd accosted Mary Stevens the previous day. He was crouching behind a wall on Cedars Mews, a narrow lane leading off from Cedars Road, which crossed Lavender Hill not far to the north.

This lane was part of the route that Lizzie Fraser walked to reach her home on Taybridge Road after she finished at the haberdashery shop where she worked every day.

In theory, she passed this way at around eight o'clock each evening, but it was now Tuesday and Oxford had been here seven times so far without seeing her.

His suit was sending small shocks through him at regular intervals.

From behind the wall, he could see people passing the end of the lane. Their tightly laced clothing and restrained mannerisms were not real. Their horses and carriages were illusions. The noises of the city were an incoherent mumble scratching unceasingly at his consciousness. He vaguely remembered how, when he first arrived in the past, London had seemed weirdly silent. How wrong! How wrong! The cacophony never stopped! Nightmare. Nightmare. Nightmare.

He beat his fists against his helmeted head, burning his knuckles in the blue flame but feeling nothing.

"Every day at eight o'clock, damn you!" he groaned.

No.

He couldn't do this any more.

"Find her!" he said. Then he looked up at the clouded sky and bellowed: "Find her!"

He hurdled over the wall and ran out of the mews into the main street.

Women screamed. Men uttered exclamations.

Oxford sprang onto the side of a passing brougham. It lurched and veered to the side under his impact. The coachman gave a shout of fright. The horses whinnied and bolted, nearly jerking the stilt man loose.

"Where is Lizzie?" he screamed.

"Jesus, Joseph and Mary!" cried the driver.

"Tell me you damned clown! Where is Lizzie?"

The horses pounded through the street, with people crying out and scattering before them, the carriage swinging and swaying dangerously behind, its wheels thundering over the cobbles.

"Get off! Get off!" yelled the terror-stricken coachman.

Oxford hung on desperately, with one of his stilts dragging along the road.

The horses stampeded headlong into a small street market and their flanks caught the side of a fruit stall, sending it flying, before they then ploughed through a poultry stall and a fruit stall. Food and fragments of wood went spinning into the air.

Shouts. Screams. A police whistle.

"Fuck!" said Oxford, and hurled himself from the vehicle. He hit the ground and bounced fifteen feet into the air, landed, and started running.

A scream of dismay came from the coachman but was cut off when, with a terrific crash, the horses and carriage collided with the corner of a shop. The splintering of wood and bone was immediately drowned by the smash of breaking glass and masonry as the side of the building collapsed onto the wrecked vehicle.

Oxford sprang through the panicking crowd and started laughing hysterically as men, women and children dived out of his way.

"Go away!" he ranted. "You're all history! You're all history! Ha ha ha! Where's my ancestor? Restore! Restore!"

He jumped over a nine-foot wall into a patch of wasteland, stumbled, fell, and rolled.

Laying on his back, he dug his fingers into the grass beneath him.

"Where the hell am I?" he asked.

Shouts came from beyond the wall.

He sat and pushed himself upright, issued instructions to his control panel, took two big strides and sprang upward.

He landed back behind the wall on Mews Lane on November the 28th at a quarter to eight.

Edward Oxford squatted and wept; and he waited.

She walked past half an hour later.

Lizzie Fraser was just fourteen years old.

In the year 1837, she was considered mature enough to work. In Oxford's age, she was just a child.

The tears continued to run down his cheeks as he quietly called: "Lizzie Fraser!"

§

January 12, 1839

Tilly Adams was seventeen years old. On Saturdays, whatever the weather, she spent the mornings walking in Battersea Fields, picking flowers in the summer and catching insects in the winter. She dreamed of becoming a botanist, though she knew this was an unrealistic ambition.

"You must learn to cook, to sew, and to maintain a household," her mother insisted. "No man wants a wife who knows the names for every insect but can't grill a lamb chop. Besides, you'll be that much more successful as a mother and wife. What women scientists are there, after all?"

The destiny that her mother recommended—and which society insisted on—was, she knew, her only real option, but while she still could, she was going to walk in the park on Saturday mornings to do the thing she loved best.

"Lucanus cervus!" she exclaimed, bending to look at a large black insect which she'd spotted crawling at the side of the path. A stag beetle.

A long thin shadow fell across it.

"Tilly Adams?"

She looked up.

She fainted.

Later, a young man spotted her, took out his flask, and poured brandy between her lips.

She regained her senses, coughing and spluttering, looked down at herself, and uttered a cry of shame, for the front of her dress had been unbuttoned and her underwear pushed up.

"I didn't do it," said the young man, reddening. "I found you like that."

Tilly Adams stood up, put her clothes in order, and ran all the way home.

She never spoke about the stilt man.

She never went into Battersea Fields again.

She gave up botany and began to hunt for a husband.

§

February 19, 1838

The Alsop family had recently left Battersea, moving to the little village of Old Ford, near Hertford, so that David Alsop could take over a vacant blacksmith's on the outskirts of the little community. Being new to the neighbourhood, they hadn't yet settled in and made friends, so spent most evenings in their home.

The time traveller popped into existence above Bearbinder Lane, landed on the ground and bounced on his stilts.

It was a quarter to nine.

The lane ran along a shallow valley. There were dark fields sloping up on one side, while the village high street ran uphill to the main settlement from a junction on the other. The Alsop cottage was on the corner, secluded and a considerable distance from the other dwellings.

Mark Hodder

386

In the distance, Oxford could see a man on a ladder fiddling with a dysfunctional gas lamp. He was the only person in sight.

Walking to the cottage's front gate, the time traveller yanked at the bell-pull and heard a jangle from inside the premises. He lifted the side of his cloak and draped it over his head like a hood, hiding the helmet. He bent his knees to bring his height down. He was standing in shadow.

The front door opened and a girl walked out. As she came down the path, Oxford saw that she had a mole on her right cheek, near the corner of her mouth. He'd been lucky this time. This was Jane Alsop.

She arrived at the gate.

"Can I help you, sir?"

"I'm a policeman," he said. "There have been reports of somebody loitering along this road. Have you a candle I can borrow? I can't see anything."

"Most assuredly, sir. Please wait here while I fetch one for you."

'Good,' he thought. 'When she comes back out, she'll have to step through the gate to give it to me.'

A minute later, she reappeared, came down the path, opened the gate, stepped out onto the road, and held the light out to him.

He threw back his cloak and grabbed her by the hair, pulling her into the darkness. The candle dropped from her hand.

"Don't!" she cried.

He didn't bother to ask the question but simply clutched at her dress and tore it down to her waist.

Before he could examine her chest, though, she twisted out of his grasp, leaving him holding a clump of hair, and raced back to the cottage.

He sprang after her, slipped and staggered at the gate, regained his balance, hurled himself over it, and caught her at the threshold of the front door.

"Show me!" he hissed, pulling her around, ripping her garments away.

A piercing scream came from inside the Alsop home.

He looked up and saw a young girl standing in the hallway. She screamed again.

Oxford turned his attention back to Jane Alsop, bending her backward. He stared at her naked upper torso. Her skin was white and unmarked.

Another girl suddenly rushed from a room, grabbed Jane and wrenched her out of his grip. The door slammed in his face.

"No birthmark!" he muttered.

§

August 22, 1839

There was only one girl left to examine: Sarah Lovitt, who worked on a flower stall in the Lower Marsh Street Market, Lambeth.

Her excessively long walk between home and the stall took her through the many winding by-streets which ran alongside the Thames, so she always carried with her a posy of scented blooms which she held close to her face to ward off the river's noxious fumes.

It made her easy to identify.

Edward Oxford pounced on her in Nine Elms Lane and pulled her into a secluded walled courtyard at the side of an empty carriage house.

Sarah knew that things like this happened. Girls were forced to do things they didn't want to do and men got away with it.

'Don't fight,' she told herself. 'It will be over more quickly.'

Then her assailant turned her and she saw him.

She fought.

Fingernails raked Oxford's cheek. Teeth bit into his wrist. He lost his grip on her; regained it; was overbalanced and fell, pulling her down with him. They rolled on the dusty ground, thrashing about, her cries echoing from the walls.

"Get off me! Leave me alone! Help! Police!"

Her elbow rammed into his chin and his head snapped back.

He flew into a wild rage and pressed his whole weight onto her, forcing her down, his crazed eyes inches from hers.

She spat in his face. He banged the front of his helmet into her forehead. She went limp.

Oxford lifted himself from her and stood.

She groaned and sat up, blinked and looked at him.

"Are you from a carnival," she asked.

"No. Get up."

She clambered to her feet.

"Just answer a question and you can go," he said.

"You won't hurt me?"

"No."

A bolt of energy suddenly snapped from his control unit and hit her in the chest. She flew backward into a wall and slumped to the ground.

Oxford yelled in pain and stumbled.

"Christ!" he gasped.

Another shock jolted through him. He toppled over and passed out.

He came to his senses moments later.

"Home in time for supper," he mumbled, not knowing what he was saying.

Jane Lovitt was either dead or out cold. He giggled manically at the thought that she might be a corpse with a rainbow on her chest.

A minute later he discovered that he was wrong on both counts. She had a pulse but no birthmark.

§

It was July the 1st, 1840. Ten days had passed since the brutal assassination of Her Majesty Queen Victoria.

"Tally ho, Edward! Bon Voyage!" said Henry de La Poer Beresford in the grounds of Darkening Towers. He watched Oxford blink out of existence in mid-air, then turned and walked toward the veranda doors. Before reaching them, he heard a thud behind him.

He looked back and saw the time traveller laying in a heap on the lawn.

"That was fast!" he cried, running over to his friend. "Are you alright?"

Oxford turned over and looked up at him. Beresford stepped back in shock. The man from the future seemed to have aged twenty years.

"What the devil happened, Edward? You look terrible!"

"None of them!" rasped the stilt man. "No birthmarks! I've spent God knows how many hours exposed to your stinking damned past and all for nothing!"

Beresford dropped to his haunches, unbuckled Oxford's boots and pulled them off.

"Come on," he said. "Let's get you inside."

Two hours later, despite the removal of his malfunctioning suit, a hearty meal and a glass of brandy, Oxford had fallen into a virtually catatonic state. His eyes, the whites visible all the way around the irises, stared fixedly at the wall. The muscles to either side of his jaw clenched spasmodically. He had told Beresford very little; just that none of the Battersea Brigade girls bore the crescent-shaped mark.

The Marquess was, nevertheless, as sure as he could be that one of them would, in the not too distant future, become mother to a girl with such a mark.

Now the search must switch to that descendant.

§

The Third Part

The Battle of Old Ford and its Aftermath

cx

ALL FAITH IS FALSE, ALL FAITH IS TRUE:
TRUTH IS THE SHATTERED MIRROR STROWN
IN MYRIAD BITS; WHILE EACH BELIEVES
HIS LITTLE BIT THE WHOLE TO OWN.
—*SIR RICHARD FRANCIS BURTON*

cx

Chapter 20

Beresford Continues His Story

❧

❧

"It took him nearly four months to recover his wits," said Henry de la Poer Beresford. "Though 'recover' may be too optimistic a word, for I assure you that, by this point, the time traveller was quite demented."

Supporting himself on his knuckles, he lurched around the banqueting table as he continued his tale; and every word he uttered, in that thick guttural voice of his, was heard by Sir Richard Francis Burton, who lay hidden overhead.

"We arranged to meet again on the 25th of September, 1843. He did his vanishing trick, and, over the course of the next three years, I monitored the Battersea girls, their marriages and their subsequent children. By this time, of course, my reputation was such as to make it impossible to get close to the families, and I was unable to establish which of the daughters bore the Oxford birthmark.

"I reported this to Oxford three years to the day after he'd departed, and he flew into such a fit of temper that, had he dropped dead from apoplexy,

I would not have been surprised. For an entire night, he ranted and raged. Then he demanded that I keep track of the children, and informed me that he'd not be back until eighteen years had passed; that is to say, not until the 25th of September of this year, when the Battersea children would be of age; old enough for him to sire an ancestor by!"

"Yesterday was the 25th!" exclaimed Nurse Nightingale.

"Yes," confirmed Beresford. "His decision was a blow to me, for by now I was plotting to get rid of the insane fool and claim his suit for my own. I tried to persuade him to visit sooner—damn it; I almost begged!—but he steadfastly refused, maintaining that it would be a pointless waste of his suit's dwindling resources.

"As he left this very room through those veranda doors, I ran to the morning room, took a pistol from the cabinet there, and ran back, intending to shoot him dead in the grounds. I was too late; he was gone.

"Over the ensuing years, I never lost sight of the Battersea families, but I'll admit that after the Libertines split and the newly-formed Rake faction grew in influence, and demanded more of my attention, the whole Oxford affair became more and more dreamlike. Had I really played host to a man from the future? Might it have been a drunken hallucination?

"Eighteen years is a long time; memory plays tricks; doubt casts the past in a different light. Frankly, I never expected to see Edward Oxford again, and, after a while, I didn't much care. He became nothing more than a symbol to me; an example of 'trans-natural' man, free from the shackles of law and morals and propriety. He was Spring Heeled Jack! A myth! A bogeyman! A fantasy!

"Then disaster struck. Two years ago, in March of 1859, I broke my neck in a riding accident. I wasn't expected to live. News of this reached you, Isambard, and you sent Miss Nightingale to my assistance. She removed me from the hospital where I lay and took me to her medical laboratories, where, with consummate skill, she managed to preserve my brain by grafting it into the body of one of her experimental animals. The result, you see before you. Ma'am, I have said it before and I'll say it again: I am forever in your debt."

Nurse Nightingale acknowledged his words with a nod.

"The accident," continued the ape, "revived my interest in Edward Oxford; for, obviously, I would much prefer life as a man than life as an ape; and with his time suit, I—or someone else—could travel back to prevent the fall that put me in this position.

"You all know what happened next: I made it known to Isambard that, with his help, I could secure a time travel device. In the past, I had explained to him certain future technologies—such as geothermal and electrical power, rotor-winged flight, and engine-pulled vehicles—and he had been able to build machines based on these small insights, which Edward Oxford had given me. Isambard therefore had no reason to doubt me and communicated the possibility of time travel to you; you began your experimental programmes in the knowledge that the device will allow you to see the results; and here we are today; all reliant on that bizarre suit to achieve our aims!"

"And yesterday?" asked Laurence Oliphant. "Did he show up?"

"Yes. He did not, of course, expect to find me in this condition, but I would be lying if I told you he was shocked. The man is so far gone that everything seems an illusion to him now. Discovering that his friend the Marquess had become Mr Belljar the primate was no more strange to him than the fact that men in this day and age smoke pipes and cigars and are never seen outside without a hat upon their head!

"He didn't tarry. I handed him the list of girls and he departed."

"To find the one with the birthmark and rape her," interrupted Florence Nightingale, with distaste.

"Yes," grunted Beresford. "It's a crazy scheme, I'll admit, though it was I who thought of it.

"There are six girls. Sarah Shoemaker, daughter of Jennifer Shepherd, is sixteen years old. Unfortunately, her whole family emigrated to South Africa and I've not been able to trace her. The others though are all still in or near London. They are Marian Steephill, aged thirteen, daughter of Lizzie Fraser; Angela Tew, aged fifteen, daughter of Tilly Adams; Lucy Harkness, eighteen, daughter of Sarah Lovitt; Connie Fairweather, seventeen, daughter of Mary Stevens; and Alicia Pipkiss, fifteen, daughter of Jane Alsop.

"The seventh of the original Battersea girls—by which I mean the mothers—Deborah Goodkind, went insane after Oxford examined her back in 1838. She died childless in Bedlam some years ago."

"A paradox," observed Darwin, in his weirdly harmonic voice. "For if she, in his history, had mothered his ancestor, then in approaching her he made himself doubly extinct!"

Oliphant gave a sibilant laugh: "This time travel business seems excessively complicated!"

"More so than you imagine, my friend," croaked Beresford, "for when I gave him the list yesterday, I already possessed evidence that he's been acting upon it! Marian Steephill, Lucy Harkness and Angela Tew had already been checked for the birthmark!"

"A further paradox," commented Darwin. "We are most intrigued!"

"My Lord Marquess," said Nightingale, "Why did you not simply arrange to capture him here yesterday. You had eighteen years to organise it!"

"A good point, ma'am. As I have said, my belief in him was wavering; I was not convinced that I could trust my own memories, for the whole affair seemed utterly fantastic. Furthermore, the man who left me in 1843 was sick in mind and body, and his suit was failing. I had no guarantee that he would show up at the appointed time and since considerable resources will be required in order to capture him, I felt it best to wait until his presence was assured."

"Which it is when?"

"Tomorrow evening. One of the girls, Alicia Pipkiss, lives in the family home; the very same cottage where Oxford assaulted Jane Alsop back in

1838. It's on the outskirts of the village of Old Ford, not far from here. I told Oxford that she and her family are due to return there tomorrow evening after some years spent living overseas. This is a total fiction on my part—the girl is in the cottage now and has never travelled. I also told him that, for Miss Pipkiss, this is a fleeting visit to her family, for she will be moving to London the following day; though I don't know to where. Thus he has only one opportunity to get at her: after dark on the 27th of September!"

"Excellent!" exclaimed Darwin. "Our forces are at your disposal, Beresford!"

"As are mine!" chimed Isambard Kingdom Brunel.

"Thank you, gentlemen," responded the orang-utan. "There is, however, a problem. As Oliphant can testify, for some reason that at present eludes me, the explorer and linguist Sir Richard Francis Burton has been taking an interest in the Battersea Brigade and, together with Detective-Inspector Trounce, seems to be rather close to discovering the truth.

"Trounce has posted policemen in the vicinity of the Alsop cottage, so when Oxford appears and we strike, we must expect opposition."

Oliphant clenched his fists and hissed: "If Burton turns up, leave him to me. I insist upon it!"

The ape nodded.

"One final thing. Isambard and I made a pact that, in return for the information I have given you tonight, I will be presented with a time suit if you manage to replicate the device. Failing that, if you can only repair Oxford's suit, then I will have access to it. Agreed?"

"Yes," came the answers.

The Marquess bared his teeth, then stood and stretched his long shaggy arms.

"Then let us organise our resources," he rasped. "I already have Libertines keeping watch on the cottage. Many more will arrive tomorrow. We will also need as many Technologists and wolf-men as you can muster!"

Sir Richard Francis Burton, laying flat on the gallery above the banqueting table, had heard enough. It was time to get out of Darkening Towers while he could.

Gingerly, he eased himself backward until he crossed the threshold of the door at the top of the stairs, then, crouching low and treading softly, he descended and entered the cloakroom.

He rubbed dust from the front of his jacket and turned toward the door.

"Hello, Dick," said a soft voice.

John Hanning Speke stepped out from the shadows.

§

Chapter 21

The Gathering Forces

❧

LIEUTENANT BURTON NOW SAID, "DON'T STEP BACK, OR THEY WILL THINK WE ARE RETIRING." CHAGRINED BY THIS REBUKE AT MY MANAGEMENT IN FIGHTING, AND IMAGINING BY THE REMARK I WAS EXPECTED TO DEFEND THE CAMP, I STEPPED BOLDLY TO THE FRONT, AND FIRED AT CLOSE QUARTERS INTO THE FIRST MAN BEFORE ME.
—JOHN HANNING SPEKE

❧

"By heavens! What have they done to you!" gasped Burton, for though Swinburne had told him about Speke's surgery, seeing for himself the brass mechanism that had replaced the upper left side of his former friend's head and face was quite another thing.

"Saved me," replied Speke, quietly.

"Saved you? No, John. They've manipulated you! From the very start, they've manipulated you; made you their puppet! When you sailed from Zanzibar after our expedition, you fell in with Laurence Oliphant aboard ship, didn't you? It wasn't by chance! He was there specifically to cast a spell over you! He's a master mesmerist, John! It was he who turned you against me, he who polarised our associates at the Royal Geographical Society, and he who caused you to turn a gun upon yourself. That wound was purposely inflicted! They *wanted* to replace half your damned brain!"

"Why?"

"I don't know—but one way or the other, I'm going to find out!"

"If you live."

"Will your betrayal run that deep? We were friends. We went through hell together. I nursed you through illnesses and injuries and you did the same for me. Are you really going to throw all that away? Think, man! Think about the way things were; the way things can be again. Help me to fight these people, John!"

Suddenly Speke's face, which thus far had been entirely emotionless, was filled with perplexity, sorrow and yearning.

"Dick," he gasped. "I shouldn't—I can't—I didn't—didn't—"

He reached up to the key which projected from the machinery above his left ear and started to wind it.

"I have to—to—to decide," he stuttered.

"Don't do that!" hissed Burton, but Speke continued to twist the key which, when he removed his hand, began to turn, emitting a low ticking. Through the round glass panel above his eye, a mass of tiny cogs could be glimpsed. They started to revolve.

It appeared to Burton as if reality suddenly took on a sharper edge. The spinning wheels in Speke's head seemed to reel in divergent destinies until they touched right here, now, in this room; making of it a crossroads. One route led from India, Arabia and Africa to Fernando Po, Brazil and Damascus; the other stretched from the seeds Edward Oxford had accidentally planted in the past to an unknown future in which he, Burton, as the King's agent, would have to deal with the resultant crazy, unbalanced world.

He sensed his *doppelgänger* standing ready; they would plunge down the same road together, as one.

He backed away toward the door.

Speke turned his head to follow the movement. His human right eye was unfocused, but the rings around the glass lens of the left eye moved slightly, some clockwise, some in the opposite direction.

The key stopped revolving.

Speke made a decision.

Burton made a decision.

The King's agent dived through the door and fled down the hallway.

Speke threw is head back and bellowed: "Oliphant! Burton is here!"

As Burton raced past the junction with the short corridor leading to the ballroom, the glass doors at the end opened and the albino stepped through. Burton kept running and was swallowed by the darkness. Behind him he heard the panther-man shout: "Brunel! Get to the ship and loose the wolves!"

Guided by nothing more than memory, stumbling over debris and banging into walls, Burton retraced his steps in the direction of the room with the open window.

From not far behind him came a mocking voice: "I can see in the dark, Sir Richard!"

Down one pitch black passageway and into another; Burton veered right, then left, then right again.

"I'm coming!" sang the pursuer.

Burton yanked his pistol from his jacket, stopped, twisted, raised it and fired. The flash illuminated long walls with peeling paper and, at their far end, a white figure dressed in black, its pink eyes wide. The darkness snapped back and with it came a loud feline scream.

'Got you, you bastard!' thought Burton.

He ran on.

A light glimmered ahead.

He raised the pistol again.

"This way, Richard!" screeched a high-pitched voice.

Swinburne!

"Damnation! I told you to get back to Trounce!"

"I half obeyed your order!" grinned the little poet. "Come on, in here!"

He quickly led Burton into a room and across to an open window. As they climbed out into the grounds, a shout reached them from inside the mansion: "You'll pay your debts, Burton!"

"Run as fast as you can!" snapped the famous explorer to his friend. "They're releasing loup-garous!"

"I've had enough of them!" piped Swinburne and sped away.

The King's agent followed, surprised by the smaller man's turn of speed.

A howl rose from the far side of Darkening Towers. It was joined by a second, a third, a fourth, and more.

"Faster, Algy," Burton panted.

They tore across the uneven ground, past the knotted trees and pools of squirming mist, toward the distant wall.

Burton glanced back and saw the albino standing by the window, his right arm cradled in the left. A pack of wolf-men were flooding around the right-hand corner of the building, running on all fours.

The two men raced on, their thigh muscles burning, their breath coming in short rapid gasps.

A few moments later they reached the wall and Burton thrust the poet up onto it.

"Trounce, start the blasted engines!" screamed Swinburne.

Burton turned. The loup-garous were almost upon him. He fired two shots and one went down. The others swerved and leaped upon it, their jaws crunching into its bones, ripping the flesh. They'd obviously been half-starved to increase their ferocity, and the slight pause gave Burton the opportunity to haul himself onto the wall, lower Swinburne down to the other side, and follow. They ran across the road that bordered Beresford's estate and into a clump of trees. Engines were chugging.

"Hold on!" came Detective-Inspector Trounce's voice from the shadows. "One more!"

"Hurry, man!" cried Burton.

The last of the three penny farthings spluttered into life. The men mounted them, steered out onto the road, and accelerated away in a cloud of steam.

Behind them, a snarling loup-garou hurtled over the wall, followed immediately by the rest of the pack.

"Bloody hell!" cried Trounce, looking back. "Open your valves! They're fast! What the heck are they?"

"Hungry!" shrilled Swinburne.

The penny farthings clattered over the uneven surface of the road, rattling the teeth of the three riders. Yelping and growling, with spittle trailing from their distended jaws, the ravening animal-men loped along behind, gradually gaining on the machines.

Burton, Trounce and Swinburne swept past the corner of the Darkening Towers estate and careened onto the Waterford road. Trees flashed by; stretches of fencing, hedgerows, and beyond them, rolling fields, pale in the light of the thin crescent moon.

White steam boiled from the vehicles and trailed behind them all the way back to the thicket where Trounce had waited. Beneath the slowly rolling vapour, the loup-garous sprinted after their prey. They were close now. They could smell human flesh.

"Blast these machines!" Burton muttered. "They're not fast enough!"

His jaws snapped together as the big front wheel jerked over a pothole.

"Trounce!" he yelled. "Steer in next to Algy!"

The Yard man obeyed, though controlling the contraption proved difficult as it bounced over a particularly rough patch of road.

A long drawn-out howl sounded from just behind.

"Algy!" called Burton. "Step off your velocipede onto Trounce's!"

"What?" cried his two friends.

"Just do it, man!"

Swinburne, entirely fearless, stood in his stirrups, swung a leg over the saddle so that he was balanced on one side of the main wheel, tried to keep the wildly vibrating handlebars steady with a single hand, and reached across with the other to grasp Detective-Inspector Trounce's shoulder. Then, in one quick motion, he leaned over, put his foot on one of the mounting bars of Trounce's machine, and stepped across.

His own boneshaker rattled on, kept upright by its gyroscope. However, without his fingers holding the velocity valve open, it immediately slowed and started to fall to the rear.

Burton drew his pistol. He had three shots left. He looked back.

The wolf-men were streaming around the riderless velocipede. Burton raised his gun, took aim, breathed gently, and squeezed the trigger.

The bullet hit the penny farthing's furnace. With a startlingly loud detonation, it exploded, blasting red hot metal into the loup-garous charging along beside it. As the twisted vehicle somersaulted into the air, one of the beasts burst into flames; then a second and a third. One by one, they erupted and fell writhing to the ground, burning fiercely.

The carnage fell away behind the three men. However, four loup-garous remained in pursuit, snapping at the small back wheels of the vehicles.

"Confound it! My pistol has jammed!" shouted Burton.

Trounce passed his Colt over his shoulder to Swinburne.

"Here you are, lad. I'll steer, you shoot!"

"Terrific!" grinned the poet, happily.

He took aim, started firing, and missed with his first three shots.

"By Jove!" announced Trounce. "It takes a rare talent to avoid hitting the blighters at this range!"

Swinburne's fourth bullet found its mark and, with a blinding flash, one of the werewolves spontaneously combusted, setting fire to the beasts on either side of it. They fell back, screaming in agony as they died.

Swinburne cheered. The penny farthing jolted. He dropped the pistol.

"Curse it! Sorry Trounce, old man! I hope that didn't have any sentimental value!"

"Only in so far as it could save us from being eaten alive, you blockhead!" replied the police detective.

Burton slowed his vehicle slightly and guided it into the path of the last remaining werewolf. With the creature snapping at his legs, he reached down to the vehicle's cane holder and withdrew his recently acquired stick. Its silver top was shaped like a panther's head. It was Oliphant's sword cane, which the King's agent had laid claim to after their fight at Battersea Power Station.

Holding it between his teeth, he drew the blade, leaned over, and with cool precision pushed its point through the wolf-man's right eye and into its brain. The loup-garou crumpled onto the road.

Burton shuddered. In his peripheral vision he could see the blade's sheath sticking out from each side of his mouth. It brought back uncomfortable memories of Berbera.

He slipped the sword back into it and put the cane into the holder.

"Waterford is just ahead, then Old Ford. Which is the village after that?" he asked Trounce.

"Pipers End, I think. Why?"

"I'll tell you when we get there! We have to rouse its innkeeper and get ourselves a room. It's almost dawn, Trounce; we haven't much time to plan our campaign!"

"Campaign?"

"Yes. Tomorrow night we're going to face off with our enemies and snatch Spring Heeled Jack from right under their noses!"

§

Once again, Sir Richard Francis Burton found himself in a drinking establishment: The Cat in the Custard, Pipers End. This time, though, alcohol played no part in the proceedings. Even Swinburne showed no interest in it during the day that followed.

Soon after their arrival, the three men enjoyed strong tea in silence while awaiting a breakfast of scrambled eggs and bacon. Once this was cooked, served and consumed, they retired to a private sitting room where Burton gave an account of his experience in Darkening Towers.

Having heard the tale of Spring Heeled Jack, Detective-Inspector Trounce sat back and ran his thick fingers through his short bristly hair.

"It sounds like utter madness but I'll be damned if I don't believe it!" he exclaimed. "It explains everything! And you know, now that you've told me, I can see that the 'Mystery Hero' who struggled with Victoria's assassin had the same face as Spring Heeled Jack. I simply didn't notice it because I was distracted by the bizarreness of Jack's costume! Anyway, I'll get a message to Spearing at the Yard as soon as the post office opens. We'll have Old Ford swarming with men in no time at all."

"Hold your horses!" objected Burton. "We know the Rakes and Technologists are gathering in and around the village. If we send your men in too soon, we may capture a few—but with what can we charge them? As for Beresford and Darwin and their cohorts, they won't come anywhere near until Spring Heeled Jack arrives. Surely it's best if we amass our forces here then advance on the village when the time traveller shows up and our opponents try to capture him?"

"You mean get the lot of 'em in one fell swoop? I'm not sure I'll have enough men for that, Burton."

"Don't worry. Algy here is leaving in a moment to recruit reinforcements."

"I am?" queried Swinburne.

"Yes. Listen; this is what I want you to do—"

After issuing his instructions to the poet, he turned back to Trounce.

"May I ask a favour of you, old chap?"

"Of course!" came the ready reply.

"I promised Detective-Inspector Honesty that he'd be in at the final reckoning."

"That little popinjay? I'm not a great enthusiast, Captain Burton. He's never believed in Spring Heeled Jack."

"All the more reason to let him see the time traveller with his own eyes. Prove to him that you were right all along!"

"Yes," smiled Trounce. "I must admit, I'd take a deal of satisfaction in that. Very well, I'll have him bring the men here. What about the girl, Alicia Pipkiss? Shall we remove her from danger?"

"That won't be easy with the Rakes watching the cottage," mused Burton, "but I think it might be arranged. And what of Connie Fairweather, is she still guarded?"

"No need. The family sailed for Australia yesterday."

"Did they, by heavens! Perhaps she's the one, then! Algy, you'd better be off; you have a lot to organise. As for us, Trounce; let's get across to the post office and hammer on the door. We can't waste time waiting for it to open!"

§

At eight-thirty that morning, in a house on the outskirts of Hammersmith, Detective-Inspector Thomas Honesty placed his homburg upon his head and checked himself in the hall mirror. His moustache was perfectly even; its extravagant curls symmetrical.

He brushed lint from his shoulder and reached for his cane.

"Oh Tom!" came his wife's voice from the lounge. "Tom! There's one of those awful birds at the window!"

Honesty's carefully trimmed eyebrows rose. A messenger parakeet had never called at his house before, though plenty had tapped at his office window.

He stepped to the lounge door and passed through. The small room was an astonishing clutter of knick-knacks and ornaments. His wife, a slim, pretty woman, pointed at the window.

"Look!"

"Leave the room, Vera," he advised.

"But I want to listen! I've never heard one!"

"Bad language. Not suitable. Off you go!"

"Tom, I insist on staying! A little bad language won't offend me! I'll tell you what; I'll listen with my hands over my ears!"

Honesty looked at his wife, blinked, shrugged, and grunted: "Very well. Warned you."

He slid the window up.

"Message from Detective-Inspector nobble-thwacker Trounce and Sir Richard Francis bottom-squeezer Burton," cackled the parakeet gleefully.

Mrs Vera Honesty gave a yelp and fled from the room.

"Gather as many cretinous constables as you possibly can," continued the bird, "and get them to the filthy-cesspit village of Letty Green at the soonest possible moment. They must be in civilian garb and should all be armed with pistols and flying goggles. Avoid the verminous village of Old Ford at all cost, you mucus-bubbler. From Letty Green, the men must proceed in groups of no more than three morons at a time to The Cat in the Custard at Pipers End. It is of crucial importance that all the nose-picking men have visited this public house before sundown. Honesty, you skunk-tickler, this is a matter of national sodding importance and you can't over-estimate the number of constables required. We need a bloody army. I will take full responsibility. Get to The Cat yourself, dirt-slurper, as soon as possible. Bring with you the strumpet Sister Raghavendra of 3 Bayham Street, near Mornington Crescent. Speed is of the essence. Message ends."

"Well, I'll be blowed!" exclaimed Honesty. It was one of the longest and strangest messages he'd ever heard issue from the beak of a parakeet.

"Tosspot," squawked the bird.

"Reply," snapped the Yard man. "Message begins. Doing as you say. This better be good. Message ends. Go."

With a colourful flutter the parakeet flew from the windowsill and disappeared into the sky. Faintly, its voice floated back: "Buttock-licker!"

§

Slightly over an hour and a half later, five rotorchairs landed in a field to the west of Letty Green. Detective-Inspector Honesty climbed out of the first, removed his goggles and straightened his clothing.

He retrieved his homburg and cane from beneath the seat, then paced over to one of the other chairs and helped its driver out.

"That was utterly wonderful!" laughed Sister Raghavendra. "Though a little tricky to begin with!"

"You did well! First woman to fly!" replied Honesty.

"Really? No, surely not! Me, the first woman to fly?"

"Perhaps, my dear. Perhaps."

Honesty turned to the three men who awaited his orders.

"Remain here, Constable Krishnamurthy," he said to one. "Instruct new arrivals."

"Yes, sir."

Then to the other two men: "Venables, Ashworth; come!"

He led the girl and the two policemen to a stile in the hedgerow which surrounded the field and climbed over it into the lane beyond. As they proceeded toward nearby Pipers End, three specks appeared in the sky behind them; more rotorchairs arriving from London.

They traipsed on until, forty minutes later, they arrived at The Cat in the Custard and were shown up to the private sitting room.

"Hello, old fellow!" said Burton, shaking Honesty's hand. "I want you to listen to what Trounce has to tell you. It will sound incredible but, believe me, every word is true. We must act fast and we're relying on you."

Honesty nodded curtly and sat in the chair to which Trounce gestured.

Burton guided Sister Raghavendra out of the room and down into the empty parlour.

"Sadhvi," he said, placing his hands on her upper arms. "You said you would like to help. You can. But I may be placing you in harm's way."

"No matter," she replied eagerly. "Tell me what I must do."

§

Later that morning, a flower seller, wearing a red cloak with a hood, entered Old Ford village and started calling from door to door. It was late in the season and her basket contained only magnolias, hydrangeas, geraniums, a make-up kit, and a pistol.

Business was not good. She made few sales, though all the villagers were friendly. One, a retired soldier, who introduced himself as "Old Carter the Lamp-lighter," informed her that she was the most exotic of the blooms.

Eventually, she came to a cottage at bottom of the hill on the western edge of the village. There were two bobbies standing guard outside and one blocked her path and refused her entry.

She whispered a few words to him.

He nodded, spoke softly to the second constable, then the two men strolled away and didn't come back.

Ignoring the bell-pull beside the gate, the flower seller passed through and walked along the short path to the front door.

She knocked upon it and, a few moments later, it opened.

A short conversation followed.

The flower seller entered the cottage.

The door closed.

Twenty minutes later, it opened and she stepped out. She walked down the path, out through the gate, and back through the village.

Her basket contained magnolias, hydrangeas, and geraniums.

Old Carter the Lamp-lighter was sweeping the road in front of his house.

"Sold much?" he asked as she passed.

She shook her head and hurried on.

"Funny," he mumbled. "The exotic bloom seems to have faded."

As she exited Old Ford along the south road, a man detached himself from the shadow of a tree and wandered along some distance behind her.

A little time later, the flower seller arrived at The Cat in the Custard in the neighbouring village of Pipers End and sat in the parlour, waiting. The man who'd followed her entered.

"Miss Pipkiss?" he asked.

"Yes," she answered nervously.

"I'm Detective-Inspector Trounce. I can assure you that you're quite safe now."

Alicia Pipkiss pulled back her hood. Her dark skin was much paler around the edges of her hairline and behind the ears and back of the neck.

"Can I wash this make-up off?" she asked.

A deep and mellow voice from across the room said: "I'll ask the landlord to heat some water for you."

A man had entered. He was big and had a fierce, scarred face which was bruised and cut.

"Hello Alicia," he said. "I'm Captain Richard Burton. I'm working with Scotland Yard."

She nodded.

"I have to ask you a rather personal question. I hope you don't mind."

She swallowed and shook her head.

"Alicia, do you happen to have a birthmark? Something shaped like a rainbow?"

Alicia Pipkiss cleared her throat and put down the basket of flowers.

She looked up into Burton's eyes.

"Yes," she said. "As a matter of fact, I do."

Back in the cottage in Old Ford, Mrs Jane Pipkiss nee Alsop, one time victim of Spring Heeled Jack, handed her guest a cup of tea.

Sister Sadhvi Raghavendra accepted it with a smile and placed it on the table next to her chair.

She sat and waited, the tea at her side, a pistol in her hand.

§

The hundred and eleven men of Letty Green village met on the cricket field at lunchtime to discuss the strange state of the sky. It was filled with streamers of white vapour which were coming in from the south, veering to the west over the little settlement, and dropping groundward to the east.

"It's comets, that's what is is!" claimed one.

"You mean meteors!" corrected another. "And they don't turn in the sky like what these 'uns are doing!"

"Maybe these 'uns are a new sort!"

"Maybe you ain't got no brain!"

The discussion went back and forth for half an hour until it was suggested that they head out of the village to see where the trails of vapour ended. This plan was immediately approved and, arming themselves with shovels and garden forks, broom handles and walking sticks, and the occasional blunderbuss and flintlock, the mob swarmed out of Letty Green, climbed the hill to the west, and stopped dead on its brow. The field below them was filled with rotorchairs.

"What in heaven's name is going on here?" muttered the villager who'd somehow emerged as the leader of the crowd.

He led them down the lane until they came to a stile which gave access to the field. A man, standing beside it, smiled at them.

"Good day, gentlemen," he said. "I'm Constable Krishnamurthy of the Metropolitan Police—and I have just become a recruiting officer!"

§

Old Carter the Lamp-lighter had never seen so many strangers in the village. More particularly, he'd never seen so many well-dressed strangers. And even more particularly, he'd never seen so many well-dressed strangers carrying paper bags in one hand, canes in the other, and with small rucksacks upon their backs.

It occurred to him that the road needed sweeping again.

Five minutes later he nodded his head at a smart, paper bag-carrying stranger and said: "Good day!"

The man nodded haughtily, flourished his cane, and walked on.

Fifteen minutes later another one appeared.

Old Carter the Lamp-lighter nodded at him and said: "Good day! Fine weather, hey?"

The man looked him up and down, muttered "G'day!" and pushed past.

When the next appeared, Old Carter the Lamp-lighter stood in his path, grinned broadly, raised his cap, and said breezily, "How do you do, sir! Welcome to Old Ford! You've picked a fine day for a stroll! What's in the bag?"

The man stopped and looked at him, taken aback. "I say!" he exclaimed.

"I do too!" agreed Old Carter the Lamp-lighter. "I say it's a lovely day to go for a walk with a paper bag under your arm! What's in it? A picnic, perhaps?"

"Why, yes, that's it; a picnic! What!" exclaimed the stranger, and made to move away.

"Up your arse!" said the bag.

The two men looked at it.

"Sandwiches?" suggested Old Carter the Lamp-lighter.

"Parakeet," mumbled the stranger, sheepishly.

"Ah, yes. Training it perhaps?"

"Yes, that's right. Training. Seeing how fast it can fly back to the London, what!"

"Gas belcher!" announced the bag.

"Is it a convention?" asked Old Carter the Lamp-lighter.

"A con—con—a what?"

"A convention, old bean. A gathering of the Oft-spotted Parakeet Trainers of Old London Town? I say, you're not the chaps who teach 'em how to swear, are you?"

"Blasted impertinence!" exploded the stranger. "Let me past!"

"I do apologise!" said Old Carter the Lamp-lighter, standing aside. "Incidentally, the fishing's not good in that direction. No water, you see."

"The fishing? What in blue blazes are you on about now?"

"There's a length of netting hanging out of your rucksack."

The stranger strode away, swinging his cane, his countenance flushed with anger.

"Have a splendid day!" called Old Carter the Lamp-lighter after him.

"Goat fiddler!" called the bag.

§

Sneaking along from the untended land to the north, a poacher approached the field opposite the Alsop cottage and quietly slipped into the thick border of trees that surrounded it. It was a good field for rabbits but there'd been police outside the cottage these past few days and he'd been too nervous to check his traps. Were the coppers still there? He was going to have a look.

Treading softly, as was his habit, he moved furtively from bole to bole.

Suddenly, a feeling of unease gripped him.

He froze.

He was not alone.

He could sense a presence.

Moistening his lips with his tongue, he crouched, held his breath and listened.

All he could hear was birdsong.

A lot of it.

Too much!

An absolute cacophony!

"Maggotous duffers! Cross-eyed poseurs! Scrubbers! Bounders! Dirty baggage! Dolts! Filthy blackguards! Decomposing scumbags! Poodle rubbers! Piss heads!"

The poacher looked around him in bewilderment. What the hell? The trees seemed to have more birds in them than he'd ever known—and they were screaming insults!

"Bastards! Stink-brains! Stupid fungus-lickers! Lobotomised chumps! Tangle-tongued inbreds! Curs! Fish-faced idiots! Balloon-heads! Little shits! Witless pigstickers! Crap masters! Buffoons!"

His unease turned to superstitious dread.

The poacher was just about to turn and take to his heels when an uncomfortable feeling in his neck stopped him. He looked down and his stubbled chin bumped into a wet red blade which projected from his throat. He coughed blood onto it and watched as it slid back into his neck and out of sight.

"My apologies," said a soft voice from behind.

The poacher died and slid to the loamy earth.

The man who'd killed him sheathed his swordstick. Like all his fellow Rakes, he was well-dressed, carried a bagged birdcage in one hand and had a rucksack on his back.

Little by little, the Rakes had occupied the shadows under the trees around the field and now there were hundreds of them.

§

By the time twilight was descending over the village, there were no more smart, bag carrying, cane brandishing strangers for Old Carter the Lamp-lighter to accost.

He'd swept the street until it was practically shining. Now he was settling into his armchair to enjoy a cup of tea and a hot buttered crumpet.

He placed the tea cup on the arm of his chair, raised the crumpet to his open mouth, and stopped.

The cup was rattling in its saucer.

"What in the name of all that's holy is happening now?" he muttered, lowering the crumpet and standing up. He crossed to the window and looked out. There was nothing to see, but he could hear an odd thrumming.

Moving to the front door, he opened it just in time to see a plush leather armchair descend from the sky.

It landed across the street from his cottage; the spinning wings above it slowing down; the paradiddle of its motor becoming lazier; steam rolling away.

The noise stopped. The wings became still. The man in the seat pushed his goggles up onto his forehead, lit a pipe, and began to smoke.

Old Carter the Lamp-lighter sighed and stepped out of his house. He closed the front door, walked down the path, opened the gate, crossed the spotlessly clean street, stood next to the chair, and said: "Sangappa."

The man looked up, and with his pipe stem clenched between his teeth, mumbled: "Beg pardon?"

"Sangappa," repeated Old Carter the Lamp-lighter. "It's the best leather softener money can buy. They send it over from India. Hard to find and a mite expensive but worth every penny. There's nothing to top it. Sangappa. It'd do that chair of yours a world of good, take my word for it."

"I do," said the man, raising a pair of binoculars to his eyes and directing them down the street.

Old Carter the Lamp-lighter ate his crumpet and chewed thoughtfully while he looked to where the lenses were pointing; at the high street's junction with Bearbinder Lane; the lower end of the village, beyond which fields and woods sloped up to the next hill.

"Bird-watching?" he asked, after a pause.

"Sort of."

"Parakeets?"

The man lowered his glasses and looked at the villager.

"Funny you should say that."

"It's been a funny sort of day. Police, are you?"

"What makes you think so?"

"Your boots."

"Ah. Oh dear."

"Good for boots, too, that Sangappa is. They're in the woods."

"The parakeets, you mean?"

"Yes. In cages, in bags, in the hands of men, in the woods."

"How many? Men, that is."

"An infestation, I should say. Is that one of 'em new clockwork lamps?"

He pointed to a cylindrical object resting in a coil of rope between the constable's police-issue boots.

"Yes, it is."

"Do me out of job, that would, if it weren't for the fact that I'm twice retired."

"Twice?"

"Yes. Good, is it? Bright?"

"Very bright indeed, Mr—?"

"They call me Old Carter the Lamp-lighter, sir, on account of the fact that I used to be a lamp-lighter before I retired."

"I thought that might be their reason."

"Detective, are you?"

"No. Constable. What else are you retired from?"

"Soldiering. King's Royal Rifle Corps. They have nets too."

"As well as rifles?"

"I mean the men in the woods, sir. Nets and parakeets."

"I see. Well thank you, Mr Old Carter the Lamp-lighter. I'm Constable Krishnamurthy. Your information is most useful. Would you accept a little advice?"

"Only fair, sir. I advised you about Sangappa, after all."

"You did. In return, my advice is this: stay indoors this evening!"

§

The policemen and Letty Green villagers left Pipers End as the sun was setting. They moved in a wide silent arc toward Old Ford and the south, west and northern borders of the Alsop field.

Detective-Inspector Thomas Honesty led the men to the south.

Detective-Inspector William Trounce led the men to the west.

Sir Richard Francis Burton led the men to the north.

Meanwhile, opposite the lower eastern end of the field, in the isolated cottage, the Alsop family hunched around a table in the candlelit cellar and played games of whist, while above them, on a chair in the hallway, Sister

Raghavendra sat facing the front door. She held a revolver in her lap and kept her finger on the trigger.

Farther to the east, beyond the village, near a derelict farmhouse, six rotorchairs landed. Their drivers sat and watched Old Ford. If they saw Constable Krishnamurthy's chair rise from it, they would fire up their engines and follow him.

The forces marshalled by Sir Richard Francis Burton were ready to pounce.

However, so were the forces gathered by the opposition.

Beneath the trees surrounding the Alsop field, the Rakes slouched insouciantly and endured the insults hurled at them from the caged birds.

In Darkening Towers, on the outskirts of Waterford, three miles to the west of Old Ford, the orang-utan known as Mr Belljar, who was actually Henry de La Poer Beresford, the Mad Marquess, impatiently paced up and down the huge empty ballroom, its chandelier blazing above him. The light would attract any parakeet that happened to have a message for him.

Outside, in the grounds, two rotorships sat. The largest, which dwarfed the other, had its engines idling. It contained Charles Darwin, the automaton Francis Galton, Nurse Florence Nightingale, Isambard Kingdom Brunel, John Hanning Speke, and a great many Technologists.

Along the shadow of a hedgerow between Waterford and Old Ford, an injured albino limped eastward. At his heels, following obediently, were twenty-three robed and hooded figures who walked with a peculiar lurching gait and who occasionally emitted slavering growls, like starving dogs.

Soon these forces would meet.

It was just a matter of time.

§

GROW A MOUSTACHE

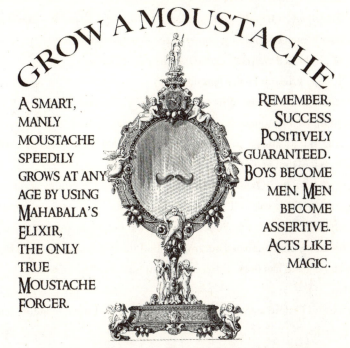

A SMART, MANLY MOUSTACHE SPEEDILY GROWS AT ANY AGE BY USING MAHABALA'S ELIXIR, THE ONLY TRUE MOUSTACHE FORCER.

REMEMBER, SUCCESS POSITIVELY GUARANTEED. BOYS BECOME MEN. MEN BECOME ASSERTIVE. ACTS LIKE MAGIC.

Box (sent in plain cover) for 6d and 1d for postage. Send 7d to:
Rameswaram Importers Co., 42 Hobbes Lane, Newbury, Berkshire.

Chapter 22

The Battle of Old Ford

On September the 25th, 1861, Spring Heeled Jack bounced onto the brown, dying lawn outside the veranda doors of Darkening Towers. They stood open and the lights were on in the ballroom. He stalked in.

"Henry! Henry, where are you?"

"Stay there, Oxford!" commanded a brash, ugly voice. It came from behind a French screen in the corner of the big, decrepit room.

"Who the hell are you?" demanded the time traveller.

"It's me, Edward; Henry Beresford."

"You sound different. Why are you hiding? Come out!"

Fire suddenly erupted from the control unit on his chest.

"The suit is almost dead!" he groaned, smothering it with his cloak. "Come out, damn you!"

"Listen to me, Oxford. This is important. I had a serious accident," gurgled the thick voice. "I broke my neck. They had to perform extreme surgery to preserve my life. Prepare yourself. I'm not the man I used to be."

An orang-utan lumbered out from behind the screen. The top of its head was missing and had been replaced by a liquid-filled bell-jar in which a brain floated.

Edward Oxford started to laugh. "You've got to be fucking kidding me!" he gasped.

"It's temporary, I hope," said the orang-utan.

Oxford doubled over, his laughter rising in pitch, echoing in the large chamber.

"This world—is—fuck—fucking—*insane*!" he screamed.

"Calm down, Edward! It's strange for me, too. I was beginning to think I'd dreamed you up. I can hardly believe you're real after all this time."

The orang-utan lurched toward the stilt-walker and reached out a hand to him.

Spring Heeled Jack staggered back.

"Don't touch me, ape!" he cried.

"Alright! Alright! Just try to control yourself, man! I have the list of girls for you!"

Oxford looked at the primate.

"Is it *really* you, Henry?"

"Yes."

"And you were successful?"

"In the main, yes."

"In the main? What do you mean 'in the main?'"

"One of the families moved to South Africa. I've lost track of them."

"Well find them, you fool! She could be the one!"

"I'm doing all I can, Edward. In the meantime, I have the descriptions and locations of Angela Tew, Marian Steephill, Connie Fairweather, Lucy Harkness, and Alicia Pipkiss."

The ape shuffled across to the banqueting table—which Oxford saw had been moved from the dining room—and took from it a sheet of paper which he then handed to the time traveller.

"I'm sorry about the writing. It's difficult. I don't have proper thumbs."

Oxford looked at the names scrawled messily on the paper.

"They are all children of the original Battersea Brigade daughters," continued the orang-utan. "One of them is your ancestor, of that I am certain. Be aware that your opportunity with the Pipkiss girl is limited. I know where she will be the night after tomorrow, but before and after that, her movements are unclear."

"Very well," replied Spring Heeled Jack. He read down the list. "Ah," he said. "She won't be far from here. The same cottage as before!"

"Yes."

"And the South African girl?"

"Sarah Shoemaker. I have sent agents to track her down," lied Beresford.

"Good. I'll not delay; I must act while the suit still functions. What is to become of you?"

"I hope to have a new body soon. Will you return?"

"Yes. If I'm successful and I restore my genealogical history, I'll come to say goodbye before returning to my time. If I'm unsuccessful, we'll know that the Shoemaker girl is the one and I'll need your help to find her. I must go now."

"Goodbye, Edward."

Oxford nodded and strode out into the grounds. He looked back over his shoulder and saw the orang-utan silhouetted in the doorway. He started to laugh again. Ridiculous world. None of it was real. He jumped.

He was still laughing when he landed on Wix's Lane, between Battersea and Clapham, at seven in the evening on the 2nd of August, 1861. He immediately vaulted over a fence into an area of waste land which local residents used as a rubbish tip. A shout from the street told him that he'd been spotted. He hopped away over piles of rubbish.

Moments later, he arrived at the back of the houses on Taybridge Road. He identified the fifth one along and approached its high back wall. He was just tall enough to look over it.

A gas lamp was on in the kitchen and through the window he could see a woman washing dishes in a basin. Last time he'd seen her, she'd been just fourteen years old. Now Lizzie Fraser was thirty-eight. She looked careworn and exhausted, with a haunted expression around her eyes.

A young girl came into view; the daughter, Marian.

The mother said something.

Marian replied.

She moved away from the window.

The back door opened.

The girl stepped into the yard and walked over to a small chicken coup. She bent over it.

Edward Oxford vaulted over the wall, landed behind her, pressed a hand over her mouth, wrapped an arm around her slim body, lifted her off her feet, and leaped back over the wall clutching her tightly.

An agonised scream came from the kitchen.

Damn! The mother had seen him!

He whirled the young girl around and grabbed her by the upper arms, shook her and growled: "You're Marian Steephill, yes? Answer me!"

She nodded, her face contorted with fear.

The screams from beyond the wall became hysterical.

Without further ado, Oxford grabbed Marian's dress and ripped it away. He clawed at the slip beneath until her skin was bared.

There was no birthmark.

He pushed her away and ran back into the rubbish tip, took three giant strides, soared into the air, and landed in Patcham Terrace at ten in the evening of the 6th of September, 1861.

It was a warm night. The street was empty but he could hear a vehicle approaching. He pressed himself into the shadows as it passed; a motorised penny farthing, leaving a cloud of steam behind it. He shook his head and chuckled. Impossible. There was no such thing!

Lucy Harkness, the daughter of Sarah Lovitt, lived at number 12 with her parents. It was Friday; her mother and father would be at The Tremors public house.

Oxford walked up to the door, which opened straight onto the pavement—there were no front gardens in this road—and knocked on it. He bent to bring his height down below the transom window.

"Who is it?" came a muffled girl's voice.

"Constable Dickson," said Oxford. "Lucy Harkness?"

"Yes."

"Has there been a break-in here?"

"No, not at all, sir."

"Would you allow me to check your back windows, miss. There's an intruder in the area."

"Wait a minute."

He heard a bolt being drawn back.

The door cracked open.

He threw his weight against it, knocking the girl backward onto the floor.

Slamming the door shut behind him and crouching so as to avoid the ceiling, he paced forward until he was next to the prone girl.

She was shaking so hard that her teeth were chattering.

He reached down and pulled apart the buttons of her blouse.

She didn't resist.

He pushed aside her underclothes.

No birthmark.

All of a sudden, her body arched upward and her eyes rolled into her head. She was having some sort of fit.

Oxford backed away nervously, fumbled with the door until it opened, stepped out and jumped.

He thudded into the ground at five o'clock in the morning on Thursday the 19th of September, 1861. He'd landed on a dark misty pathway in Hoblingwell Wood near Mickleham village.

He ducked into the cover of the trees and waited.

A few minutes later he saw the light of an oil lamp approaching.

He stepped out.

"Who's that there?" demanded a girl's voice.

Suddenly she turned and started running.

He sprang after and caught her, yanked her around and savagely rent her clothing; ripping it wildly until her naked skin was exposed. Bending her backward, he placed his face close to her chest. Blue light from his burning helmet reflected off her pale, unmarked skin.

He looked up into her face.

"Not you!"

Then he dropped her and jumped away—but landed in the same time, and in the same place.

"Shit!" he spat.

The leap from Battersea to his current location had drained the suit's power. Now he'd have to wait until dawn, when the sunlight would recharge it.

He paced along the path, out of the woods, across a road and into a field. He sat beneath a gnarled oak, the mist curling around him, and waited. A feeling of drowsiness overtook him.

"Is this what I've come to?" he thought. "A man who rips the dresses from teenage girls, like some sort of sexual pervert? God, I want to go home! I want to have supper with my wife! I want to put my hand on her belly and feel the child kick."

About thirty minutes later, he was roused by a shout.

He looked up.

A crowd of people were charging toward him, waving pitchforks and clubs.

He hauled himself upright and ran away.

His legs ached.

He was exhausted.

When was it he last slept? He couldn't remember. Probably years ago. Literally!

He stumbled on. The villagers followed.

Sometimes he out-distanced them and stopped to rest. Then they'd come back into view, yelling and brandishing their makeshift weapons like crazed animals.

If they caught him, they'd kill him, of that he was sure.

As dawn broke, Spring Heeled Jack, Edward John Oxford, the man from the distant future, sprang on his stilts from one field into the next, over hedgerows and across roads, over a golf course and into the shelter of some woods.

He pushed through the trees, leaned against one, and tried to regain his breath.

The sun was up but it was misty and the light too weak to recharge his batteries quickly.

Something irritated his ear; a distant vibration; the sound of a machine.

As it increased, he recognised it. It was the noise made by rotor blades.

Closer it came, until the tree at his back began to vibrate.

He looked up as it flew overhead and caught sight of a ludicrous flying contraption.

Edward Oxford didn't believe anything he saw any more. The world was one giant fairy story; a crazed jumble of talking apes and horse drawn carriages and accentuated manners and the stink of unprocessed sewerage and, now, flying chairs which trailed steam.

The machine approached again, at such a low altitude that the trees thrashed beneath its downdraught.

"Oh, will you please piss off and leave me alone!" he yelled.

It passed above him. He crouched, leaped, shot up through the twigs and leaves, and caught hold of the side of the machine. It rocked and careened sideways.

The man at its controls turned and looked at him through a pair of goggles.

"I said piss off!" shouted Oxford.

He reached out and grabbed the man by the wrist.

The machine spiralled out of control and crashed into the trees.

Oxford was knocked from its side and fell spinning through the foliage. He thumped into the ground and lay still, winded, his shoulder hurting.

He got to his knees. He could hear the whistle of steam off to his left. Pushing himself upright, he walked in the direction of the sound until the wrecked machine came into view.

A man was laying face down beside it. He rolled over as Oxford stepped over him with a stilt to either side.

The time traveller squatted.

"Who are you?" he asked. The man had a vaguely familiar face; dark, savage, powerful, but also scarred, battered and bruised.

"You know damned well who I am!" exclaimed the man.

"I don't. I've never seen you before, though I must admit, I feel I should know you."

"Never seen me! You gave me this damned black eye! Or maybe that was your brother?"

Edward Oxford grinned. More nonsense! More of this world's idiocy!

"I don't have a brother," he said, "I don't even have parents!"

He threw back his head and laughed.

The man beneath him shifted uncomfortably.

Oxford looked down at his face.

So familiar. It was so familiar.

"Where have I seen you before?" he muttered. "Famous, are you?"

"Comparatively," answered the man, and started to wriggle out from between the stilts. Oxford reached down and clutched the front of his coat, stopping him from moving.

"Stay still," he barked.

He searched his memory; thought about the history of this period; the biographies he'd read and the old black and white photographs he'd seen.

The name came to him.

'Fucking hell!' he thought. 'You're joking!'

But it wasn't a joke. There was no doubt about it. He knew who this man was.

"Yes, I know you now," he muttered. "Sir Richard Francis Burton! One of the great Victorians!"

"What the hell is a Victorian?" snarled Burton.

Shouts reached them from the distance. There were people approaching— and, too, the far off chopping of another flying machine.

"Listen Burton," hissed Oxford. "I have no idea why you're here but you have to leave me alone to do what I have to do. I know it's not a good thing but I don't mean the girls any harm. If you or anyone else stops me, I can't get back and I won't be able to repair the damage. Everything will stay this way—and it's wrong! It's wrong! This is not the way things are meant to be! Do you understand?"

"Not in the slightest," replied Burton. "Let me up, damn it!"

Oxford let go of the man's coat and Burton pushed himself out from between the stilts and got to his feet.

"So what exactly is it you need to do?"

"Restore, Burton!" replied the time traveller. "Restore!"

"Restore what?"

"Myself. You. Everything! Do you honestly think the world should have talking orang-utans in it? Isn't it obvious to you that something is desperately wrong?"

"Talking orang—?" began Burton.

"Captain Burton!" came a distant shout.

Oxford looked up through the trees as the second flying machine drew closer.

"The mist has cleared and the sun is high enough," he muttered to himself. "I should be able to recharge."

"Charge at what?" demanded Burton. "You're speaking in riddles, man!"

"Time to go," said Oxford. He laughed. "Time to go!"

Burton suddenly dived at him.

Oxford twisted out of the way and, as the famous Victorian crashed past him, he strode away.

"Sir Richard Francis Burton," he hissed to himself. "That's all I bloody well need!"

Ducking under branches, he moved from bole to bole until he emerged from the woods back onto the golf course. Off to the south, he saw a horde of policemen and villagers milling about. A police whistle blew and a roar went up from the crowd. They surged toward him.

Oxford bounded away and circled the course. He only had to remain in the sunlight for a couple of minutes; it would be enough.

In enormous hops, he ran around the perimeter while the mob surged back and forth trying to cut him off.

He passed the edge of the trees again and saw Burton standing there. The man ran out to intercept him. Oxford bounded over his head.

"Stay out of it, Burton!" he shouted.

He took six more strides and sprang high.

At the apex of his jump, he ordered the suit to flip him to the next destination and, at exactly the same moment, realised that the second flying machine was too close; almost touching him.

He landed in the Alsop field on the night of the 27th of September, 1861, with fragments of the machine accompanying him. He hit the ground awkwardly, floundered, and fell. Bits of twisted metal thudded into the earth around him. One piece embedded itself in his right forearm. He screamed with pain and yanked it out. Blood splashed over the scales of his suit.

Spring Heeled Jack rolled to all fours and hauled himself upright. He held his arm and winced. He looked down the sloping field and forgot the pain.

It was all so familiar.

There were the lights of Old Ford; there was Bearbinder Lane; and there was the cottage where Jane Alsop lived, and where he would now find her daughter, Alicia Pipkiss.

He had no no reason to think that she was the girl with the rainbow birthmark, but all of a sudden that's exactly what he did think.

He smiled.

Something came spinning through the air, hit his stilts, and wrapped itself around them.

He toppled sideways and fell onto his injured arm. Another scream was torn from his throat.

What the—?

He looked down and saw that he'd been enmeshed in bolas; a throwing weapon consisting of a cord with weights at either end.

Men rushed out of the trees. A lot of men. They threw nets over him.

Colourful birds exploded into the air.

§

In Old Ford, Constable Krishnamurthy saw the flock of parakeets rising upward. They wheeled around then flew westward. Firing up his rotorchair, he ascended on a column of boiling vapour and steered the craft toward the field. Some distance behind him, by the ruined farmhouse, six more rotorchairs rose.

To the north, west and south of the field, Burton, Trounce and Honesty also saw the birds. They ordered their men forward.

Not far behind Trounce's team, Laurence Oliphant turned to the twenty-three red-robed figures and snapped: "Go! Attack! Feast!"

They threw back their hoods and howled.

§

Men piled onto Spring Heeled Jack, holding his arms away from his chest. They hauled him upright. He struggled wildly and became entangled in netting. One punched him hard in the stomach. He doubled over and vomited.

"Sorry, old thing. Had to immobilise you, what!" said the aggressor.

"Blast it," said another. "We have company."

The Rakes, gathered around the time traveller, suddenly found themselves surrounded by men who were charging out from the very same trees they'd just vacated. The Libertine extremists formed a circle around their prisoner, faced outward, and drew their rapiers from their canes.

The advancing forces pulled goggles down from their foreheads to cover their eyes, reached into their jackets, and withdrew truncheons and pistols.

"I am Detective-Inspector Trounce of Scotland Yard," roared a voice. "I command you, in the name of His Majesty King Albert, to lay down your weapons and give yourselves up!"

"Not likely!" came a reply.

The Rakes chuckled and brandished their swords.

Seven rotorchairs began to circle the field. Bright lamps blazed beneath them, suspended on ropes, illuminating the scene, sending long black shadows angling across it.

"We need reinforcements," Oxford heard one of his captors mutter.

"Don't worry. They're coming," answered another.

§

A parakeet landed on the threshold of the veranda doors at Darkening Towers.

"Message for Henry bog-breath Beresford!" it squawked into the ballroom.

Another fluttered down beside it: "Message for the limp-wristed Marquess of Waterford!"

And another: "Message for the highly hideous Henry Beresford!"

And more:

"Message for Henry bastard-of-bastards Beresford!"

"Message for Henry tweak-nibbler Beresford!"

"Message for the mange-ridden Marquess!"

"Message for barmy flesh-puller Beresford!"

"Message for the Marquess of buttock-wobbling Waterford!"

"Bloody hell!" exclaimed Henry de La Poer Beresford, the 3rd Marquess of Waterford, as a colourful tidal wave of parakeets swept into the room to insult him.

"Message begins," they chorused deafeningly. "He's arrived, you bollock-groper. Message ends."

The glass-headed orang-utan blundered through them, waving its long arms, sending up a fluttering mass of colour. He lurched out into the grounds and bawled: "Get the steam up! Get the steam up! He's here! Spring Heeled Jack is here!"

The gigantic rotorship trembled as its crankshafts started turning, spinning the rotors. It vented steam from its exhausts. Men ran between it and the smaller vessel, which was landed nearby.

Beresford tumbled up the ramp, passing a man whose head was half brass; John Speke, who, with the key over his left ear slowly revolving, raced to the smaller craft.

The Mad Marquess entered the mighty Technologist ship and the ramp withdrew behind him.

The doors clanged shut.

With a powerful roar, the colossal platform lifted into the air.

§

Sir Richard Francis Burton, his eyes covered by leather-bound goggles, his cane held in his belt, plunged into the amassed Rakes and laid about him with his rapier. The blade clicked and clacked against those of his enemies, and, though he was vastly outnumbered, his skill was such that he disarmed or disabled man after man without sustaining even a scratch himself.

Beside and behind him, police constables pushed forward, swiping swordsticks aside with their truncheons, lashing out with fists and boots.

It occurred to the King's agent that last time he'd been in a position such as this, it had ended in disaster.

"Not this time!" he grunted, leaning into the *manchette* and watching with satisfaction as his opponent flinched, cried out, dropped his sword and clutched at his pierced wrist.

Soon, the crush of men became too tight for swordplay and his left fist became his primary weapon, smashing into jaws, noses and foreheads. He grinned savagely, thankful to have at last reached the final reckoning with his enemies, glorying in the battle.

He laughed when he caught sight of Detective-Inspector Honesty. The slightly built man appeared to be boxing under the Marquess of Queensbury rules, as had been demonstrated for the first time last June by the heavyweight pugilist Jem Mace, who'd won the Championship of England against Sam Hurst. Honesty's back was ramrod straight; he was dancing and dodging on his toes; his left fist was defending his chin, while his right was jabbing again and again into the face of his infuriated adversary. He appeared to be making no headway until, quite without warning, he swerved, stepped in, and whipped his left fist up in a devastating uppercut. His opponent's feet left the ground and the man flopped to the ground, out for the count.

"Bravo!" cheered Burton.

A pistol shot detonated somewhere behind him.

"No, man!" came Trounce's cry. "Take them alive!"

A terrible scream echoed across the field.

Something howled triumphantly.

"Werewolves!" yelled another voice.

More pistol shots sounded.

Something burst into flames.

A fist clouted the side of Burton's head. He reeled, recovered, and hit back, his knuckles crunching into his enemy's mouth, breaking teeth. The man went down and Burton stumbled over him, falling onto all fours.

"Burton! This is your doing!" hissed a voice.

He looked up, straight into the insane eyes of Spring Heeled Jack. With his captors distracted, the stilt-walker had managed to untangle himself from the bolas and netting and now crouched, ready to leap away.

"I told you not to interfere—but I'll stop you, Burton!" snarled the bizarre figure. "I'll stop you!"

Burton lunged at him and went sprawling as Edward Oxford launched himself high into the air. The King's agent rolled to his back just in time to see the stilt-walker vanish. His view was suddenly blocked as a loup-garou came swooping down upon him. Reflexively, he swung his rapier up, catching the beast in the throat. Its heavy weight slid down the blade and thumped onto him. Talons ripped down his upper right arm, slicing through the material and the skin beneath.

The creature went limp. Fierce heat began to emanate from it.

Burton quickly heaved it aside, stood up and stepped back.

The werewolf exploded into flames.

Men were fighting all around him, the battle now spreading across the field.

Loup-garous slunk through the crowd, pouncing and tearing with their teeth and claws.

He saw, in the near distance, Laurence Oliphant easing a sword out of a man's stomach.

The air throbbed.

A huge flying platform slid over the tops of the trees, a wall of steam bubbling out beneath it, enveloping the battleground.

Doors opened in its sides and ropes were thrown out.

Men came sliding down into the swirling vapour.

The Technologists had arrived.

'We're outnumbered!' thought Burton.

§

Edward Oxford landed in Green Park on Sunday the 8th of September, 1861. It was eleven-thirty and the night was bitterly cold and misty.

He was near the trees at the top of the slope. Next to the path below, he could see a tall monument on the spot where Queen Victoria had been assassinated.

Ducking into the gloom of the trees, he stood and considered. Where would he find Sir Richard Francis Burton?

He couldn't recall where the man lived nor the location of the Royal Geographical Society. There was, however, the Cannibal Club above Bartoloni's Italian restaurant in Leicester Square. He remembered reading about that place and the eccentrics it attracted. He knew that Burton went there regularly.

Not long ago, the prospect of visiting Leicester Square without the protection of augmented reality would have filled him with dread. Now, though, he was so numbed by the preposterous environment in which he was trapped that he felt almost immune to it. An illusion. A dream. It was nothing more than that. He wasn't even sure why he had come here, and hardly cared. He clung to the only things that made sense to him, despite their patent absurdity: he had to get to the Pipkiss girl; there was only one night on which to do it; and the famous explorer Sir Richard Francis Burton had arranged an ambush to stop him.

Oxford didn't realise that opposing forces were battling over him. His broken mind latched onto just one thing: in order to have supper with his wife on February the 15th in the year 2202, he had to stop Burton from interfering on the 27th of September in the year 1861.

Surely that wouldn't be too difficult?

He closed his eyes and swayed for a moment.

"No!" he thought. "Don't let go! Get it done! Get it done now!"

He jumped and landed five hours later in Panton Street behind Leicester Square. At that time of night it was empty but, afraid of being spotted, he immediately sprang up onto the roof of one of the buildings facing the street, and from there to a higher one. He leaping from building to building until he eventually found a chimney stack overlooking Bartoloni's, against which he could sit. Before settling, though, he jumped high and landed next to the stack the following night, just as Big Ben chimed midnight.

It was a long cold wait and he didn't see Burton.

At three in the morning he gave up and moved ahead to the next night, the 9th of September.

Again, nothing.

The next night the club members gathered, had a good time, and departed at two in the morning.

Burton wasn't among them.

Spring Heeled Jack tried the next evening, and the next, and kept going, waiting hour upon hour, until exhaustion overwhelmed him and he slept, slumped against the chimney. He awoke at dawn, swore at himself, and moved through time again.

On Wednesday the 16th, he finally caught sight of his man.

Sir Richard Francis Burton stumbled out of Bartoloni's at one o'clock in the morning.

He was quite plainly drunk.

As he staggered along, Spring Heeled Jack followed, hopping from rooftop to rooftop, his eyes fixed on the man below.

He trailed his quarry through the streets and alleys, and wondered whether the explorer had any destination in mind, for he seemed to be wandering aimlessly.

Oxford took a great leap over the canyon of Charing Cross Road, landed on a sloping roof, slid down it, got a grip, and sprang to the next building.

He kept moving across the city like a bizarre grasshopper.

Something big and white flapped overhead. It was an enormous swan, dragging a box-kite behind it. A man looked down at him from the canvas carriage and yelled: "What the dickens is that?"

Spring Heeled Jack ignored him, dismissing the swan and its passenger as an illusion, for such things didn't exist in the Victorian Age, and followed his prey into a seedy section of the city until, eventually, Burton entered a long lonely alley.

"This will do!" whispered the stilt-walker to himself.

He raced ahead, soared over warehouses, and, after waiting for another of those crazily-designed penny farthings to pass by, he dropped into the thoroughfare below.

A huge metal lobster-like thing rounded a corner and clanked toward him. Multiple arms beneath it flashed this way and that, picking litter off the street. He watched it as it lurched by, amazed by the sight, and suddenly wondered if somehow he was on another planet. As it passed the mouth of the alleyway down which Burton was approaching, the contraption sounded a siren. The eerie ululation echoed into the distance and was then drowned by a terrific hiss as steam poured from the back of the mechanism and billowed across the cobbles.

Spring Heeled Jack lurched through the cloud and entered the alley.

He emerged from the steam and faced his enemy.

Sir Richard Francis Burton stopped and looked up at him, then stumbled backward and pressed himself against the side of the passage.

"Burton!" said the time traveller, stalking toward the famous Victorian. "Richard Francis bloody Burton!"

He jumped at the man and hit him, sending him spinning across to the opposite wall.

"I told you once to stay out of it!" he spat. "You didn't listen!"

He grabbed the explorer by the hair and glared into his face.

"I'll not tell you again! Leave me alone!"

"W-what?" gasped Burton.

"Just stay out of it! The affair is none of your damned business!"

"What affair?"

Oxford snarled: "Don't play the innocent! I don't want to to kill you. But I swear to you, if you don't keep your nose out of it, I'll break your fucking neck!"

"I have no idea what you're talking about!" cried Burton.

"I'm talking about you organising forces against me! It's not what you're meant to be doing! Your destiny lays elsewhere. Do you understand?"

He slammed his forearm into Burton's face.

"I said, do you understand?"

"No!" the man gasped.

"Then I'll spell it out for you," growled Oxford. He yanked the explorer round, shoved him against the wall, and punched him three times in the mouth:

"Do what—you're *supposed*—to do!"

Burton raised a hand in weak protest.

"How can I possibly know what I'm supposed to do?" he mumbled. Blood oozed from his mouth.

Spring Heeled Jack jerked the explorer's head up and looked directly into his eyes.

"You are *supposed* to marry Isabel and be sent from one fucking miserable consulship to another. Your career is *supposed* to peak in three years when you debate the Nile question with Speke and the silly sod shoots himself dead. You are *supposed* to write books and die."

"What the hell are you babbling about?" Burton shouted. "The debate was cancelled. Speke shot himself yesterday—he's not dead!"

Edward John Oxford, the scientist and historian, froze. How could this be? He knew the facts. They couldn't be wrong. They were well-documented. Speke's death was one of the great mysteries of the period. Biographers had endlessly debated it, wondering whether it was suicide or an accident! Slowly, he absorbed the things he'd seen; the strange machines and the weird animals.

"No!" he said softly. "No! I'm a historian! I know what happened. It was 1864 not 1861. I know—"

He stopped. What had he done? How could so much have changed?

"God damn it!" he groaned. "Why does it have to be so complicated? Maybe if I kill you? But if the death of just one person has already done all this—?"

Burton suddenly slipped out of his hands and shoved him hard. Oxford lost his balance, staggered away, and fell against the opposite wall.

They stood facing each other.

"Listen to me you bastard!" said Oxford tightly. "For your own good, next time you see me, don't come near!"

"I don't know you!" answered Burton. "And, believe me, if I never see you again, I'll not regret it one iota!"

The time traveller was opening his mouth to reply when his control unit malfunctioned and sliced him through with an electric charge. He yelled in agony and almost collapsed from the pain of it.

He looked across at his adversary and suddenly saw him clearly, as if a curtain of fog had lifted. He marvelled at the brutal lines of the man's bloodied face.

"The irony is," he said, "that I'm running out of time. You're in my way, and you're making the situation much worse."

"What situation? Explain!" demanded the explorer.

A ripple of electric shocks ran through Oxford. He flinched. His muscles jerked. The suit sounded an alarm in the centre of his skull. It was dying.

"Marry the bitch, Burton," he groaned. "Settle down. Become consul in Fernando Po, Brazil, Damascus and wherever the fuck else they send you. Write your damned books. But, above all, leave me alone! Do you understand? *Leave me the fuck alone!*"

Chapter 23

In Cold Blood

❧

❧

"There he is!" yelled one of the Rakes.

Burton turned back and looked at the spot he'd just left. Spring Heeled Jack was standing over the ashes of the fallen loup-garou. Ribbons of steam curled around him.

"Shit!" screamed the stilt-walker. "Why didn't you fucking listen, Burton!"

Two Rakes dived at the tall lanky figure and knocked him sideways to the ground. Burton made to move toward them but a sixth sense warned him that danger was at his back. He dodged and something sizzled past his neck, gouging a furrow through the skin, burning the edges of the wound. Twisting, he found himself facing a Technologist who was holding a strange crossbow-like weapon. A belt of pointed bolts hung beneath it and the man was in the act of pulling back a lever which, the instant that Burton looked, caused the topmost bolt to clunk up into the snub barrel. The Technologist raised the weapon and pointed it at the King's agent. At the same moment, to his right, a Letty Green villager, who was wielding a hat-stand like a staff, swung it into the chest of a Rake. His victim, thrown off balance, floundered into the gunman; the crossbow gave a sharp puff of compressed steam, and the bolt ripped through Burton's coat, missing his thigh by inches. The edges of the hole caught fire.

Burton slapped the material and lunged at the man, caught him around the waist, and sent him crashing down. He knocked him senseless with a left hook and snatched up the weapon. There was some sort of heating element beneath the grip. Four thin pipes passed from it into a cylinder positioned over the barrel. He pulled back the lever at the side of the crossbow as he'd seen the man do. The next bolt slotted into place.

Sheathing his blade, Burton took aim at one of the slavering werewolves. With the steam from the rotorship above, and the swaying lights from the circling rotorchairs, the scene of the battle crawled with dark and distorting shadows, making it difficult to focus on the target; nevertheless, his aim was true, and the bolt tunnelled through the beast's brain. The wolf-man fell, twitched, and lay still.

Burton reloaded and looked around in time to see three Rakes hoisting Spring Heeled Jack above their heads and running with him up the slope toward the western end of the field. He lifted the crossbow and shot one of the three in the leg. The man fell with a cry of pain and lay jerking spasmodically while the other two dropped the struggling time traveller. One of them caught the next bolt in his shoulder and went down with a screech. The remaining man began to spin bolas, his eyes fixed on Burton. The King's agent shot him in the arm before he could let fly.

"Trounce! Honesty" bellowed Burton, spotting the two men fighting nearby. "Jack is here! Help me!"

Detective-Inspector Honesty was engaged in fisticuffs with a huge brute of a man; a Technologist who, by the state of his clothes and skin, was evidentially employed to stoke the boilers of the gargantuan ship hovering above. The svelte Yard man was dwarfed by him, yet, miraculously, seemed to avoid every swipe of the mammoth fists while planting his own again and again on the block-like jaw above him. Even as Burton watched, the Technologist's knees wobbled and gave way. The big man dropped to a sitting position, and—*bang!*—his head snapped to the left as Honesty's fist met the solid jawbone. *Bang!*—it was smacked to the right. The Technologist lay down and slept.

The slim detective shook his hands, flexed his fingers, and ran over to Burton with a smile on his face.

Detective-Inspector Trounce, meanwhile, was displaying a much more basic form of combat. Truncheon in hand, he was moving from Technologist to Technologist, Rake to Rake, walloping them over the head.

He, too, paced over to Burton.

"The fight is moving up the field!" he shouted. "They have more men than us! We're losing constables fast, Captain!"

"Where's your Jumping Jack character?" asked Honesty, wiping a spot of blood from his goggles.

"There!" said Burton, but as he pointed to where Edward Oxford had fallen, the stilt man suddenly bounded up and sprang away, a shower of sparks and blue flame trailing behind him.

"After him! Don't let him escape!"

Oxford took two mighty strides, plucked a shovel out of a villager's hand, whacked the man on the head with it, then started laying about himself indiscriminately.

Trounce and Honesty sprinted toward him.

Burton raised the crossbow and took aim at Spring Heeled Jack's left leg. He began to apply pressure to the trigger.

A blade slid out of his upper right arm, then withdrew.

With a cry of pain, Burton dropped the Technologist weapon, its bolt sizzling into the air.

He turned and faced Laurence Oliphant.

"From behind, Oliphant?" he asked, stepping back and drawing his blade left-handed.

"I'm not feeling gentlemanly today," answered the albino. "Fighting with my off-hand doesn't agree with me; though I have, at least, evened things up on that score."

"How is your paw? Haven't you licked it better yet? And a bullet in the arm just above it; poor little kitten."

Their swords clicked together.

Blood ran down the fingers of Burton's right hand and dripped onto the grass.

"I see you have my blade," observed Oliphant. "I want it back. I had it specially made. It's a very fine piece."

"That's true. It's wonderfully balanced," agreed Burton. "I have it in mind to keep it as a souvenir; something to remember you by after I run it through you. Don't you find it nicely ironic that the blade you commissioned is the one that'll pierce your dastardly heart?"

They circled each other.

Oliphant's sword blurred through the air. Burton countered it with ease and pricked the panther man's shoulder.

"My my!" exclaimed the King's agent. "You aren't nearly so fast today!"

Oliphant bared his canines.

Over his opponent's shoulder, Burton saw Trounce knocked to the ground by a wolf-man. Detective-Inspector Honesty crossed to his colleague, pulled out a pistol and put a bullet through the monster's skull. He looked up and saw Burton; raised his pistol and pointed it at the back of Oliphant's head. Burton shook his own slightly, as if to say "No. This one is mine."

Honesty gave a curt nod and plunged back into the battle, chasing after Spring Heeled Jack.

Oliphant lunged and almost caught Burton in the chest. The King's agent barely managed to parry, but parry he did, then turned the tables with an *une-deux* of such power that the albino's sword not only flew from his hand but also broke into two pieces.

He levelled his blade at his adversary's throat.

Oliphant laughed viciously, stepped back and drew a pistol, aiming it between Burton's eyes.

The King's agent lowered his blade.

"What a blackguard you are!" he sneered.

Oliphant's feline eyes narrowed. His finger applied pressure to the trigger.

A dark object smacked into his face and exploded in a cloud of black dust. He fell backward. His gun cracked and the bullet flew wild.

"Yaah-hooo!" came a cry from above.

Burton looked up and saw Algernon Swinburne grinning down at him from a madly tumbling box-kite which was being towed along by a huge swan. A great flock of the giant birds was flying in from the south, their feathers startlingly white against the night sky; the lamps from the rotorchairs shining off them.

In each kite—with the exception of Swinburne's—sat two boys, chimney sweeps, who were eagerly throwing bags of soot down onto the combatants below.

Now it became apparent why the all policemen were wearing goggles, for while it was true that they had to frequently wipe the black powder from their eyepieces, at least their eyes were protected. Not so the Rakes and Technologists! As the air clouded with the dust, which whirled through the steam as it was blasted by the rotorship overhead, the enemy forces stumbled around half blinded. Man after man, with watering eyes, walked into a descending truncheon and fell senseless onto the grass.

Meanwhile, the sweeps, directed by Swinburne, split into two groups. The first continued to circle under the rotorship; the kites whipped about by its downdraught; the boys throwing soot bombs. The second group peeled off and swooped out, up and over the massive ship, then began to wheel above it. The boys took out metal rods—handle sections of their chimney brushes— and dropped them onto the spinning wings beneath. Loud clangs sounded and chunks of the damaged wings streaked out sideways, spinning away over the trees that bordered the field.

It had the desired effect; very slowly, the rotorship began to retreat, sliding westward at a snail's pace.

Laurence Oliphant kicked Burton's legs out from under him. The famous explorer sprawled onto the ground and cried out as pain lanced through his injured arm. The panther-man hurled himself onto him. They rolled, punching, scratching, biting, kicking, forcing their elbows into each others' throats, head-butting and scrambling for an unbreakable hold. Burton had the skill, the strength and the training, but Oliphant possessed animal savagery; his mock manners had fallen away to reveal the beast within, and the King's agent felt as if he were back in Africa, fighting hand to hand with one of that continent's great cats.

It was impossible to get a grip on the albino, and Burton's strength drained rapidly as he weathered the storm of slashing claws and snapping teeth. Then Oliphant's brow hammered into his face with such force that for a second Burton saw nothing but stars. His vision returned as the panther man bent over his throat, with his jaw distending unnaturally, his dripping canines glinting with wicked intent.

A rope slid across Burton's outstretched hand. He snatched at it and, in one lightning fast motion, coiled it about the albino's neck. With a choking cough, the panther-man was yanked backward and dragged from him, slid across the grass, then was hauled into the air. He swung, kicking and jerking convulsively at the end of the line, which descended from one of the departing rotorship's open doors. Then he became still, his white face blackening, until he limply vanished into the cloud of steam and soot.

"Still hanging around with the wrong crowd!" observed Burton.

There came a sudden flash and Oliphant's body swung back into view, burning brightly; he had spontaneously combusted.

Burton watched as the blazing corpse vanished into the pall again, then he located the crossbow, picked it up, and went in search of Honesty and Trounce.

Visibility was severely hampered by the black dust which moved through the air and clung to his goggles but it seemed to him that the battle had thinned out, with less men fighting and a great many laying dead or unconscious on the grass.

The mist parted and a massive swan emerged from it. Flying extremely low, it shot past him, the long leather straps attached to its harness trailing behind to a box-kite in which a red-headed passenger was yelling: "The cottage!"

It was Swinburne—and his message was clear!

Burton started running down the field.

§

Up in the well-swept high street of the village, Old Carter the Lamplighter was attempting to restrain his neighbours.

"It ain't nothing to concern us!" he announced. "I happen to know that it's a police matter and they'll not brook interference from common folk!"

"Who're you calling common?" shouted a middle-aged man. "Old Ford is our village! It's bad enough we had Spring Heeled Jack back in '38—now we have to put up with giant swans, wolf-things, and all manner of flying contraptions! It ain't natural, I tell you!"

"Aye!" came a cry of agreement. "There's a bloody curse on this village!"

"There ain't no such thing as curses!" objected Old Carter the Lamp-lighter.

"Then how do you explain all that malarkey?" shouted another, pointing at the battle in the field across the small valley. "I tell you, it's the old mansion in Waterford that's the cause of it! There's been an ill wind blowing through Old Ford ever since the Mad Marquess took up residence there back in '37!"

"It's true!" called a voice from the back of the crowd. "He may be dead but he's not forgotten! His ghost haunts that place!"

"Darkening Towers was built by a mad 'un and it's had mad 'uns in it ever since!" a woman screamed. "We should have burnt it to the ground years ago!"

"And what about this Mr Belljar blighter? Has anyone actually seen him?"

"No!" they roared.

"Who is he? Why did he come here?"

"Look! Look! The flying ship is leaving! It's heading toward Waterford!"

"It's going to Darkening Towers, I'll warrant!"

"Let's follow! Let's find out who Belljar is, once and for all!"

"Aye, and if it's him what brought this madness upon us, let's string him up!"

"Bravo!"

"Aye!"

"Hang him!"

"Stop, you fools!" yelled Old Carter the Lamp-lighter, but no-one listened, and soon, brandishing makeshift weapons and burning torches, the mob was descending toward Bearbinder Lane, which, if they followed it to the right, would eventually lead to the main thoroughfare to Waterford.

"What the heck!" sighed Old Carter the Lamp-lighter. "If you can't beat 'em, join 'em!"

He hurried after his neighbours.

Down the hill they marched until, at the bottom, with the Alsop field sloping up before them, they came to the cottage.

Four constables, who'd been guarding the premises since the fight commenced, came forward.

"Folks! You should return to your homes at once!" said one. "It's not safe here!"

"Aye!" cried a villager. "And it'll never be safe until we're rid of Darkening Towers!"

"It's true!" shouted another. "We're going to burn the accursed place to the ground!"

The constable shook his head. "You'll be doing no such thing!"

Suddenly one of the women screamed and pointed at the field. They turned and saw the dirty cloud parting as a dreadful apparition came hopping toward them. The tall gangling creature was familiar to them all; it had been associated with Old Ford ever since it attacked Jane Alsop twenty-three years ago on the very spot where they were standing. It was Spring Heeled Jack!

With cries of terror, the villagers scattered as the grotesque bogeyman ploughed into them swinging a shovel left and right, while shrieking: "Get away! Get away!"

The constables were mown down by his frenzied attack. The villagers raced away. The cottage was left unprotected.

The stilt man threw the shovel aside and vaulted over the gate, stalked up the pathway, and slammed his shoulder into the front door. It swung open. He bent and peered into the hallway.

A young woman was standing in it. She held a pistol levelled at his head.

"Tell me, girl; do you have a birthmark on your chest?" he demanded.

"I'm not Alicia Pipkiss," she replied coolly. "She's been taken to a place of safety. You'll never find her."

He expelled a sulphuric hiss of fury and for a second Sister Raghavendra thought he was going to pounce upon her, but then a voice rang out:

"Edward John Oxford!"

Spring Heeled Jack whirled around.

Sir Richard Francis Burton was standing at the gate.

He held a strange weapon in his hand.

He pulled the trigger.

A bolt crackled through the air and thudded into the time suit's control unit.

Oxford screamed and convulsed as lines of energy writhed up and down his body.

He tottered, nearly fell, crouched, leaped, and vanished.

"Bismillah! Where the hell has he gone now?" muttered Burton.

He heard his name called from the battlefield. It was Detective-Inspector Trounce, who was waving his bowler above his head to attract the explorer's attention. He strained to hear what the man was shouting.

"He's here! He's here! The Technologists have him!"

§

When Spring Heeled Jack leaped out of 1861 with the energised crossbow bolt embedded in his suit's control unit, he had no clear idea of a destination. His mind had been pushed to the brink of unconsciousness by an electrical discharge. He jumped without considering a landing place and, for a split second, or possibly an eternity, he floated beyond time.

He fragmented.

All the elements that had made Edward Oxford the man he was separated from one another and drifted apart. Decisions taken were unmade and became choices; successes and failures reverted to opportunities and challenges; characteristics disengaged and withdrew to become influences.

He lost cohesion until nothing of him remained except potential.

Yet, set apart from this strange process, something observed and wailed and grieved as it watched itself disintegrate into ever smaller components.

It was that same something which clung despairingly to one final possibility; that issued a last command to the ebbing time suit; that hoped against all evidence to the contrary that another attempt to dissuade the original Edward Oxford from assassinating Queen Victoria might—just *might*—work, and wipe this crazy version of history out of existence.

Spring Heeled Jack popped into existence above Green Dragon Alley on the 27th of February, 1838, hit the ground, fell, and dragged himself into an angle in the narrow passageway.

He pulled the suit's cloak over his head, seeking darkness and a moment to remember, to gather his thoughts.

Who was he?

Where was he?

Why was he here?

What must he do?

There was a name: Edward Oxford—the Original.

And a place: The Hat and Feathers.

And an enemy: Burton.

And a voice: "Are you sick, mister? Shall I fetch help?"

He pulled the cloak aside and looked up. A young girl was standing looking at him; a child, also female, just behind her.

He had to rape her, or someone like her.

Rape?

What was he thinking? He'd never done anything like that in his life; he wasn't capable of such brutality! Why was he contemplating such a foul act? Why was his head filled with all this violence? Rape and ripping girl's dresses and assassination and fighting and—

He screamed at the horror of all he'd done and all he'd considered.

A jagged line of energy lashed out from his helmet and struck the girl in the face.

She was thrown onto the muddy cobbles. She started to convulse.

The younger girl scrambled over to her, shouting: "What have you done? Help! Help!"

Spring Heeled Jack pushed himself to its feet and yelled: "This is your fault, Burton!"

As he paced away along the alley—less a man than a disjointed bundle of possibilities—he was jolted again and again by shocks.

An emergency program in the damaged control unit suddenly activated. A voice in Spring Heeled Jack's head ordered him to jump into the air. Reflexively, he did so. With its very last resource, the suit flipped him back to where he'd come from, moving him a little to the west to prevent him from colliding with himself.

Thirty seconds after he'd leaped away from Burton, he dropped onto the Alsop field straight into the hands of the retreating Technologists.

§

"The Technologists have Oxford!" shouted Detective-Inspector Trounce as Burton approached. "They're making away with him."

Burton peered through the gloom at the battle raging at the top of the field. Policemen, led by Detective-Inspector Honesty, together with what remained of the Letty Green villagers, were engaged in hand to hand combat with a line of Rakes who were holding them at bay while, farther up the field, the Technologists swarmed up the ropes to the rotorship, whose prow was slowly passing over the western line of trees.

Swinburne and his chimney sweeps, swooping around the vast platform, were unable to do further damage to it, having run out of things to throw.

Even as he watched, Burton saw Spring Heeled Jack, who appeared to be unconscious, being hauled up into the massive flying machine.

"If you're fighting them buggers, we're with you!" came a voice. He turned and saw an elderly man leading a group of villagers. They were all squinting; their eyes watering as particles of soot drifted into them.

"Old Carter the Lamp-lighter at your service, sir!" declared the man. "We're from Old Ford, and we're sick to the back teeth of Spring Heeled Jack!"

"Good man!" said Trounce. He pointed to the struggling men. "Do what you can!"

"Aye, sir! Come on lads, let's have at 'em!"

He led the villagers away.

Burton pulled his shirt from his trousers, ripped a strip from its hem, and, with Trounce's help, bound his bleeding arm.

He glanced toward the rotorship. He knew what he had to do. There was no question. No doubt. No *doppelgänger* haunting him with alternatives.

"I need a rotorchair," he told the Yard man. "I'm going to see if I can wave one of them down."

"Use this," said Trounce, handing over his police whistle.

Burton ran back to the bottom of the field, where the soot was less dense, and began signalling to the flying machines as they passed overhead, waving his arms and blowing short blasts on the whistle. The fourth to fly by turned and descended.

"Nearly missed you!" announced Constable Krishnamurthy as he climbed out of the seat. "Bad visibility. The lamp caught you, though. You look like the devil!"

"I need your machine!" barked Burton, throwing himself into the leather chair. He pulled his panther-headed swordstick from his belt and pushed it under the seat.

"How much fuel?"

"Enough, unless you're flying to Brighton," responded the constable.

The King's agent nodded and eased the machine into the air.

As he gained altitude, the soot and steam fell away beneath him. It was crawling with light and shadows as the other rotorchairs circled through it.

Ahead, shining silver in the starlight, the Technologist's ship was slowly picking up speed.

Burton accelerated toward it.

A swan slid up beside his vehicle. He looked over and saw Swinburne waving at him from the box-kite. The poet was grinning broadly; obviously enjoying himself. He mouthed something but Burton couldn't hear above the sound of his machine, so he just gave a thumbs-up and pointed to the rotorship. Swinburne nodded.

They flew on.

By soaring high over the ship's outspread spinning wings, they were able to avoid the turbulence and descend onto the vast platform. There was a wide railed walkway around the circumference of the oval-shaped vessel and a long structure in the central area. Burton put down on the walkway. For Swinburne, landing was a riskier business. He flew his swan low over the platform and pulled the emergency release strap which cut his box-kite free from the bird. Tumbling through the air, the kite hit the deck and slid along it until it brought up hard against the railing. Swinburne shot out of the canvas and disappeared overboard.

With a sick feeling in his stomach, Burton ran over to the rail and looked down.

The poet smiled up at him. He was gripping the edge of the deck with his fingertips, dangling over the long drop.

"Culver Cliff!" he exclaimed, as his friend pulled him to safety. "What now?"

"The final reckoning, I hope," replied the King's agent, unsheathing his sword. "We can't allow Darwin and his cronies to continue with their insane experiments. People should have the right to shape their own destiny, don't you think?"

"Isn't that a contradiction, Richard?"

"We'll save the philosophical argument for later, Algy. Right now, we have to get inside this thing. Do you have a pistol?"

Swinburne drew a Colt from his jacket.

With a nod of approval, Burton began to move around the edge of the central structure. The great ship vibrated beneath their feet as the two men peered into portholes, seeing empty rooms with bunks and tables, offices with desks and cabinets, and engineering stations, some of which contained men who seemed to be monitoring gauges or making adjustments to valves.

They passed two doors which opened onto such stations, and these they ignored, for the rooms were too well occupied. The third, though, gave access to a switchboard room in which just one Technologist laboured, and into this they sprang. Burton held his rapier to the man's throat while Swinburne crossed the room and locked the door.

"If you value your life, you'll not cry out," advised the King's agent.

The Technologist swallowed and nodded, raising his hands.

"Tell me the layout of the ship," ordered Burton. "Be succinct."

"Two decks," the man responded, speaking rapidly. "This one has the crew cabins and various maintenance and monitoring rooms, all arranged around a central corridor with stairs to the main deck at either end. The main deck is much larger. There are eight engine rooms arranged around the central section which matches the dimensions of this upper deck. The rear third contains the boilers, water tanks, furnace and coal rooms. The middle third houses the main turbine. The forward section contains the flight cabin."

"Good," snapped Burton. "Is Darwin aboard?"

"Yes, in the flight cabin."

"Brunel?"

"Yes. Probably in the turbine room."

"Beresford?"

"Who?"

"The ape."

"With Darwin."

"Nightingale?"

"Yes; I don't know where."

"Speke?"

"Is he the one with the babbage in his head?"

"Yes."

"No. He disembarked before we left. He's on a second ship at Darkening Towers. It's fitted out as a medical laboratory."

"I see. How do we get to the flight cabin without attracting undue attention?"

"Two rooms forward of this there's a storage bay with an access ladder leading down to a maintenance corridor between the turbine room and the flight room. It opens onto both."

"Good. You've been helpful."

"I don't want to die."

"I'm not a killer," responded Burton. "However, I do have to render you unconscious. Which would you prefer; a crack on the jaw or mesmerism?"

"None of that mind control hocus-pocus, if you don't mind!" exclaimed the man.

He stuck out his chin.

Burton hit it.

Swinburne caught the man as he fell and laid him gently on the floor.

"If only they were all so willing!" he mused.

"Algy, I won't be able to punch them all. You may have to disable a man or two. Try not to kill anyone. Aim for the legs."

"Understood."

They unlocked the door and checked the corridor. It was clear, and they were able to get to the storage bay unmolested. The room was filled with huge rolls of soft insulating material. When they climbed down the short ladder to the maintenance passage on the deck below, they saw the same stuff lining the walls behind the pipes and tubes which ran the length of it.

Halfway along the corridor, on either side, the conduits curved up over large double doors; one leading back to the turbine room, the other to the flight cabin. Burton eased the latter open an inch and looked through at the large room beyond.

At its far end—the prow of the ship—in front of large windows, two technologists were standing at the vessel's controls. A third was nearby, next to a console, with a speaking tube in his hand.

Darwin was in his metal throne in the centre of the room. Wires and cables connected him to a horizontal wheel-like structure which was affixed to the metal ceiling; it was very similar to the one Swinburne had seen in Battersea Power Station.

A thick cable ran across the floor from Darwin to the automaton that had once been Francis Galton. It was standing next to a trolley to which Spring Heeled Jack had been strapped. The time traveller's helmet had been removed and lay on a table nearby.

Henry Beresford was lumbering up and down beside the prisoner.

"Why aren't they answering!" he barked.

"I don't know, sir," answered the man at the speaking tube. "But we're undermanned at the moment and damage to the wings is causing severe instability. I imagine they have their hands full back there."

"They might, but she doesn't!" yelled the orang-utan. "She's a nurse not a bloody mechanic!"

"We have observed that she is infatuated with Brunel," put in Darwin.

"Pah!" grunted the orang-utan. "Go and find her and drag her here by her bloody hair. We can't allow Oxford to die. We need his knowledge."

"Yes, sir!" replied the crewman, sliding the speaking tube into its slot. He hurried to the door.

Burton and Swinburne stood back, one to either side of it.

The man stepped through, closed the portal, saw Swinburne, opened his mouth, then emitted a strangled squeak as Burton's thick left forearm slid around his neck and squeezed. The King's agent used the fingers of his right hand to apply pressure to points on the man's neck and, seconds later, the Technologist slipped into unconsciousness.

They dragged him into a corner and returned to the door.

The Galton automaton was pulling off Edward Oxford's spring-loaded stilts.

"An ingenious design," noted Darwin. "Though Brunel will appreciate it more than we can."

"Never mind the damned boots!" exclaimed Beresford. "How long until we reach the mansion?"

"About ten minutes, sir," answered one of the men at the controls.

"Go faster!"

"That's impossible, sir. The wings will fly apart if we try!"

"I'm not interested in your confounded excuses!"

"We must keep his body alive until we transfer him to the medical ship," said Darwin. "After that, it won't matter; Nurse Nightingale can extract his brain and place it in a life support container. There will be—"

He stopped. His huge double-brained cranium turned. His beady eyes settled on the two men who'd silently entered the room.

"We take it you're Sir Richard Francis Burton?" he harmonised. "And the little poet Swinburne we are acquainted with, of course."

Henry Beresford span to face the door. He bared his great teeth and made to leap at the intruders.

"The legs, Algy," said Burton quietly.

Swinburne raised his pistol and fired.

A hole appeared in the bell jar, just above the orang-utan's right eye.

"Oops!" said Swinburne.

Liquid started to stream from the hole.

Beresford stuck a finger into it, halting the flow.

Liquid continued to leak from a second opening at the back of the jar.

Miraculously, the bullet had missed the floating brain.

One of the technologists at the ship's controls slumped to the floor. The bullet hadn't missed him.

"Double oops," muttered the poet. "My apologies, Richard. I didn't mean to do that."

"Get the nurse! Get the nurse!" screeched Beresford.

"Or a couple of corks," suggested Swinburne.

"Move your walking corpse away from Oxford, Darwin," ordered Burton, striding to the trolley.

The double-brained scientist obeyed the command; Galton stepped back.

Burton looked down at the time traveller. His eyes were wild but recognition flickered at the back of them, and he said to the famous explorer: "You died in 1890. Heart failure."

A shiver ran down Burton's spine.

"Sir!" cried the man at the controls. "I can't do this on my own! She's losing altitude fast!"

"Where in God's name is Nightingale!" wailed Beresford.

"Algy," said Burton. "Step outside and guard the door. Don't let anyone in. Do whatever's necessary."

"But—" began the poet.

"Swinburne!" barked the King's agent. "You half obeyed my last order. This time I need more. Is that understood?"

"Yes, sir," answered the poet quietly. He walked out of the room and closed the door behind him.

"Damn you to hell, Burton," said Beresford weakly. He collapsed down onto his haunches and sat with a finger in each of the holes in the bell jar. Liquid continued to dribble out. The top third of his brain was already uncovered.

Burton looked down at Oxford.

"I know who you are," he said. "I know what you've been trying to do."

"You died in 1890," repeated the stilt man.

"So you say. It doesn't matter. Everyone dies. What I'm interested in is what makes everyone live."

"Intriguing," said Darwin.

"I've made extreme decisions in my life," continued Burton. "I decided to do things that most men would never do. I've been driven by I don't know what to—to—"

"To find your place," offered Edward Oxford. The madness died from his eyes. "To find yourself. You were displaced by a childhood spent being dragged from one country to another. Ever since, you've been looking for points of stability. Things you could associate yourself with. Permanent coordinates."

"Coordinates. Yes, I see what you mean."

"They make us who we are, Burton. They give us identity. I made a mistake. I chose as one of my coordinates an event from ancient history which, in my opinion, brought shame to my name. I tried to erase it, and ended up erasing something that made me."

A tear trickled from Oxford's cheek.

Darwin chuckled and said: "This is most gratifying. How simple it is to construct a new future. Yes. We are most fascinated. The possibilities are endless. However, we must establish whether one future replaces the other or if they run concurrently. Once we have the time suit, we must construct a method through which this can be ascertained."

"Don't let him have the suit," whispered Oxford. "Free me. I don't care about myself any more, I'm a discontinued man, but let me restore history!"

Beresford toppled onto his side.

"Help me, Darwin," he gurgled. "I feel so drained."

"I altered one thing," said Oxford. "Just one thing! But the consequences have changed everything. You're not meant to be doing what you're doing now!"

"The problem, Oxford," replied Burton, "is that, though the future isn't what it used to be, I like it the way it is."

"Most gratifying. Most gratifying!" uttered Darwin. "Here we see the human organism selecting its own path of evolution!"

Henry de la Poer Beresford whispered "Free!" and a horrible rattle issued from his throat.

A gunshot came from beyond the door.

"She going down!" yelled the man at the controls.

"And if the Technologists get their hands on your suit," continued Burton, "the very idea of history will become a thing of the past."

"We're going to crash!" screamed the ship's operator, and he made to run for the door, but the Francis Galton automaton was standing behind him and, clamping its hands around the man's neck, it held him in front of the controls.

"We command you to fly the ship!" ordered Darwin.

"I can't! I can't!"

"You must!"

Burton reached down and took hold of Oxford's head.

"In cold blood?" asked the time traveller.

"Whatever is necessary," replied Burton.

"What will it achieve?"

Sir Richard Francis Burton looked the man in the eyes.

"Stable coordinates," he said.

"Enjoy your reboot," whispered Spring Heeled Jack.

Burton yanked Edward John Oxford's head around, breaking his neck.

"That was a serious mistake," said Darwin. "However, what's done is done. Now get us out of here before the vessel is destroyed. Bring the corpse, the helmet and the boots."

The King's agent glanced at the windows and saw Darkening Towers looming large in them.

"No, Darwin," he said. "The time suit must be destroyed. Your experiments must end."

"We disagree. Allow us at least to debate the point with you before you act. We propose to you, Burton, that access to time travel will allow us to finally put to rest the great delusion of a God who intercedes in human affairs. We will eliminate the absurd notions of fate and destiny. We will choose our own paths through time. We will place reins on the process of evolution to steer it where we will!"

"So nothing will happen by chance?" suggested Burton.

"Precisely! Save the time suit!"

"And you?"

"And us! Yes, save us!"

Burton glanced at the window.

"We would have your response," came Darwin's double-toned voice. "What do you say?"

The King's agent paced over to the door. He looked back at the malformed scientist.

"I'm sorry," he said. "There will be no debate today."

"The evolved must survive!" cried the scientist.

Burton opened the door and passed through. Swinburne was holding Nurse Nightingale at bay with his pistol. A man lay on the floor clutching his bleeding side.

"I was aiming at his leg, I swear!" claimed the poet.

Burton gripped Nightingale by the arm and dragged her to the access ladder.

"Up!" he ordered.

"No," she replied.

He punched her forehead and she collapsed into his arms.

"No time for niceties," he said. "Up you go, Algy!"

Swinburne ascended and Burton followed, with the woman over his shoulder.

Less than a minute later, the front of the titanic rotorship collided with Darkening Towers. The ancient mansion exploded into a cloud of flying bricks, masonry and glass. Crumpling metal screamed as it tore through the building and hit the earth.

The inhabitants of nearby Waterford were jerked out of their sleep by the terrifying sound of destruction. The floor shook beneath their beds and their house windows shattered as the ship ploughed a wide furrow through the grounds of the Beresford estate before finally coming to rest almost a quarter of a mile beyond; a mass of torn and twisted metal.

For a moment a strange sort of calm descended and it seemed that the devastation was complete. Then, one after the other, the ship's boilers exploded; a series of terrific detonations which blew the back half of the ship to pieces, throwing debris hundreds of feet into the air and sending a thick pall of steam rolling outward.

Finally, the scene of the crash became quiet but for occasional clangs and squeals as the wreckage settled.

Of Darkening Towers, nothing remained except a smear across the landscape.

§

Burton had no idea how long he'd been unconscious. Wrapped in a roll of the thick insulating material, he'd been thrown violently around the small storage bay until his senses were shaken from him. Now, as they returned, he gingerly tested each limb, and though his right arm pained him where Oliphant's sword had pierced it, he found that all his bones were intact.

With much difficulty, he wriggled out of the material onto the slanting and twisted deck, pulled his clockwork lantern from his pocket, and surveyed the ruins around him by its light. The bay was almost ripped in half; the floor was buckled and stars glinted through a wide and jagged gash in the ceiling.

The swathes of insulation were in disarray; the roll he'd bundled Florence Nightingale into had come undone and she lay awkwardly amid the tangle. He crawled over to her and found that she was alive, though out cold.

The folds that contained Swinburne were underneath a tangle of girders from the ruined roof. One long thin fragment of metal had been driven right into the bundle, and when Burton peered into the end of the roll, he could see a red stain within. For a second, fear gripped him, as he imagined his friend dead, but he then realised that the patch of crimson was actually the poet's hair.

"Algernon?" he called. "Can you hear me?"

"Yes," came the muffled response.

"It may take a while to get you out of there. You're underneath a pile of debris. Are you hurt?"

"There's something sharp sticking into my left buttock. It's not as thrilling as it sounds!"

"I'll get help as quickly as I can."

"And you, Richard? Are you in one piece?"

"Apart from having my brains scrambled, yes. Hold on! I can hear movement. My light may have attracted someone."

The sound of metal being shifted had reached him, and he wondered whether Detective-Inspector Trounce had arrived in a rotorchair while he was unconscious. However, as the noise increased, he realised that something of far greater weight than the burly Scotland Yard man was approaching.

He looked up as mechanical grippers closed over the edges of the torn roof and peeled the metal back with a horrible squeal.

Isambard Kingdom Brunel thudded into view, towering overhead. The arms on one side of him were twisted and bent out of shape.

There was a moment of silent, broken only by the wheezing of his bellows, then he chimed: "She is alive?"

"Yes," replied Burton. "Merely unconscious. I wrapped her in this material to protect her from the worst of it."

A pause, then arms stretched down into the room, slid beneath the prone nurse, and lifted her out.

"I thank you, Sir Richard. I am in your debt," rang the huge machine.

It retreated from view and they heard it stamping over the wreckage, onto the earth, and away into the distance.

Burton began to clear the fallen beams away from Swinburne.

Some time later he heard a rotorship rising into the air and departing.

"That must be the medical laboratory," he said to the trapped poet. "Speke is aboard. I wonder where he and Brunel will go?"

Ten minutes or so passed before he heard the approaching paradiddle of rotorchairs, climbed out onto the roof of the wrecked ship, and waved down Detective-Inspector Trounce.

Exhaustion hit him.

"By God!" he muttered. "Africa was child's play compared to this!"

§

Chapter 24

Conclusion

༜

"FROM TOO MUCH LOVE OF LIVING,
FROM HOPE AND FEAR SET FREE,
WE THANK WITH BRIEF THANKSGIVING
WHATEVER GODS MAY BE
THAT NO LIFE LIVES FOR EVER;
THAT DEAD MEN RISE UP NEVER;
THAT EVEN THE WEARIEST RIVER
WINDS SOMEWHERE SAFE TO SEA"
—*ALGERNON CHARLES SWINBURNE*

༜

"It's incredible!" exclaimed Mrs Iris Angell for the umpteenth time. "Poor Mr Speke. I don't say he was ever a bad man, but perhaps a little lacking in rectitude. He certainly didn't deserve to fall into the hands of that immoral crowd. What will become of him, I wonder?"

"I don't know; but I feel I haven't seen the last of him. Have you finished?"

Mrs Angell was sitting at one of Sir Richard Francis Burton's desks, where she'd been writing out two copies of his report.

"Yes. I must say, Sir Richard, your handwriting leaves a lot to be desired.

I suggest you have a poke around in the attic. If I remember rightly one of my late husband's fancies was some sort of mechanical writing device. An 'autoscribe,' I think he called it. You play it like a piano and it prints onto paper, like a press."

"Thank you, Mother Angell; that sounds like it might be useful."

The old dame stood and rubbed a crick from her back. She passed the two copies to Burton then crossed to the study door.

"I must get back to the kitchen. Your guests will be here in half an hour or so. I expect they'll appreciate some cold cuts and so forth?"

"That would be excellent. Thank you."

She departed.

Burton rolled one of the copies and placed it into a canister. This he put into the messenger pipe. With a blast of steam, it went on its way to Buckingham Palace. A few moments later, he sent the second copy to 10 Downing Street.

He prepared the study for his guests; stoking the fire, arranging armchairs around it, refilling the brandy decanter.

He sat and read for half an hour.

Algernon Swinburne was the first to arrive. Like Burton, he was covered in yellowing bruises and healing injuries. He was limping slightly.

"Your little paper boy, Oscar, just accosted me on the street," he announced. "He asked me to pass on his congratulations and he hopes you're recovering from your injuries."

"How the dickens did he get wind of it?" exclaimed Burton. "There's been nothing said to the press!"

"You know what these newsboys are like," replied Swinburne, easing himself carefully into a chair. "They know a great deal about far too much. He also asked me to advise you that 'one can survive everything, nowadays, except death, and live down everything except a good reputation.'"

Burton laughed.

"Quips is being exceptionally optimistic. I hardly think our little victory is enough to mend my reputation. Richard Burton might be battered and bruised but 'Ruffian Dick' is alive and well, I'm sure!"

"That might be true in certain quarters, but, for certain, your stock has risen with King Albert and Lord Palmerston, and that's what matters. I'll have a brandy, please; but purely for medicinal reasons."

"How are you, Algy? Recovering?"

"Yes, though the hole in my arse cheek hurts like blazes. I fear I shall have to skip my birchings for a few weeks."

"Bad news for London's houses of ill repute," noted Burton, pouring his friend's drink. "They'll have to tighten their belts, if you'll pardon the pun."

"Thank you," said Swinburne, accepting the glass. "By the sound of those thundering footsteps, old Trounce is coming up the stairs."

The door opened and the thick-set Yard man stomped in.

"Greetings both!" he announced, slapping his bowler onto a desk. "The confounded fog is closing in again. Every pea-souper is a bonanza for the criminal classes! I tell you, I'm going to have my work cut out for me over the next few days. I say, Burton, what the heck did Spring Heeled Jack mean?"

"When?" asked the King's agent.

Trounce threw himself into an armchair and stretched out his legs to warm his feet by the fire. He took a proffered cigar from his host.

"You said he told you to—what was it?—'enjoy your boots?'"

"No. He said 'enjoy your reboot.' A curious turn of phrase. Language is a malleable thing, old chap; it follows a process much like Darwin's evolution; parts of it become defunct and fade from usage, while new forms develop to fit particular needs. I have little doubt that 'reboot' has a very specific significance in the future. His future, at least."

"The meaning seems clear enough," mused Swinburne. "Replacing your old boots with new ones is like preparing yourself for a new and potentially long journey. Your old boots may not last for the duration, so you re-boot, as it were, before you set off. Like re-shoeing a horse."

"It seems as good an explanation as any," agreed Burton. "And it fits the context."

He handed Trounce a brandy and, with his own, sat down and lit a cigar.

"Detective-Inspector Honesty should be along soon. Have you two made your peace?"

"I'll say!" enthused the police detective. "The man saved me from a werewolf! He may look like a whippet but he fights like a tiger. I saw him taking on men twice his size with his bare hands—and he downed the blighters! Besides, when the dust had settled he came over, shook my hand and apologised for ever doubting me. I'm not one to hold a grudge, especially against a man like that!"

"Ow!" yelled Swinburne. "Bloody dog!"

"Come here, Fidget!" ordered Burton. "Sorry, Algy. I forgot he was in the room!"

The Basset hound hung his head and ambled over to its master, settling at his feet, from where it gazed fixedly at Swinburne's ankles.

"Blessed pest!" grumbled the poet.

"You owe this blessed pest your life," observed Burton. "Excuse me a moment."

He'd heard a rattle from the messenger tube. A canister thunked into it as he reached the desk. It was a message from Palmerston: *Burke and Hare dismantled wreckage. Remains of Darwin, Galton, Beresford and Oxford identified. Time suit recovered and destroyed. Good work.*

"Palmerston says the time suit has been destroyed," he told his guests.

"Do you believe him?" asked Trounce.

"Not at all. It will at least have been put out of harm's way, though."

"We can but hope," muttered Swinburne.

Mrs Angell entered with a tray of cold meats, pickles, sliced bread and a pot of coffee. Detective-Inspector Honesty stepped in behind her.

"Sorry, late!" he said. "Came on velocipede. Broke down. Accursed things."

"Have a seat, Honesty! Thank you, Mrs Angell," said Burton.

His housekeeper glanced dolefully at Honesty's well-greased hair and thought about her antimacassars as she left the study.

The newly-arrived policeman sat, refused a brandy, and lit a pipe.

"A hundred and twenty-six men in custody," he declared. "Seventy-two Rakes. Fifty-four Technologists. All charged with assault."

"And Brunel?" asked Burton, returning to his chair.

"Location unknown. Nothing to charge him with."

"And to be frank," added Trounce, "the Chief Commissioner is reluctant to press charges, anyway. As far as most people are concerned, Isambard Kingdom Brunel died a national hero a couple of years ago. The powers that be are reluctant to expose his continued existence, the thing that he's become, or the fact that he appears to have crossed ethical boundaries."

"And Florence Nightingale?" asked Swinburne.

"Same," said Honesty. "No charges."

"She's a strange one," mused Swinburne.

"Not as strange as the Edward Oxfords," grunted Trounce. "I still can't get to grips with the fact that the man I saw trying to stop the assassination of Queen Victoria was struggling with his own ancestor, and was the same man as the stilt-walker who ran past me, the same man as the stilt-walker who jumped out of the trees, and the same man we fought over in the Battle of Old Ford twenty years later! Good lord! Time travel! It's more than I can cope with!"

Burton blew out a plume of cigar smoke.

"That's the least of it. We removed the cause but we didn't repair the damage. The fact of the matter is that we live in a world that shouldn't exist.

Oxford changed the course of history. His presence sent out ripples which altered everything. If I understand it correctly, this period of time should be called the Victorian Age, and if you care to get up and look out of the window, what you'll see bears only a superficial resemblance to what you'd be looking at had he never travelled back through time."

"And we are changed, too," added Swinburne. "Our time has presented us with different opportunities and challenges; we are not the same as the people recorded in Oxford's history!"

"If we made it into his history at all!" muttered Trounce.

Sir Richard Francis Burton shifted uneasily in his chair.

Marry the bitch. Settle down. Become consul in Fernando Po, Brazil, Damascus and wherever the fuck else they send you.

§

For the remainder of that evening, the four men relaxed together, discussed the case, and cemented their friendship. By the time the guests took their leave, another London particular had settled over the city and ash was falling from the dark sky. They waited until they heard a brougham creeping along, called for it, and said their goodbyes.

Burton retired back to his study and sat with a book on his lap. His eyes slid over the words without taking them in. He hung his arm over the edge of the chair, his fingers idly fondling Fidget's ears.

He looked down at the Basset hound.

"I killed a man, Fidget; cold-bloodedly broke his neck with my bare hands. Palmerston would say it was my duty—that I had to do it to preserve the Empire—but the truth is that I did it to preserve my own existence, as it is now!"

He rested his head on the back of the chair and cleared his mind; used his

Sufi training to focus inward, searching for any awareness of a newly incurred karmic debt.

He found none, and was jolted from his meditation by a tapping at the window. Fidget barked. It was a parakeet.

"Message from scum-hugger Henry Arundell. Please meet me at the stinking Venetia at noon tomorrow. Message ends."

"Reply," said Burton. "Message begins. I'll be there. Message ends."

"Underwear-nabber!"

§

The next morning he donned his Sikh costume and delivered a bag of books to The Beetle, then returned home, washed and changed, and made his way through the fog to the Venetia Hotel. He arrived a little early and, after one of the doormen had brushed the ash from his hat and shoulders, made his way to the lounge and sat contemplating the silver panther head of his cane until Isabel's father arrived.

He stood and shook the older man's hand. They had a difficult relationship, these two; a grudging respect.

Isabel's mother had always disapproved of Burton. To start with, she clung to the dwindling Catholic faith, whereas Burton was rumoured to be a Muslim, though he actually held no religious allegiances at all. Then, of course, there was his reputation; the dark rumours and general consensus that he was "not one of us."

Henry Arundell had none of his wife's prejudices. He did, however, love his daughter, and wanted only the best for her. He'd never been convinced that Burton was the best.

They sat.

"She's gone," Arundell said, without any preliminaries.

"What?" exclaimed Burton.

"Isabel packed her things and left the family home some few days ago—on the 21st. We suspected that the two of you had fallen out over some matter and she was taking a holiday to think things over. Yesterday we received this."

He handed Burton a letter.

Trieste, 25th September, 1861

My Dearest Mama and Papa,

Richard has broken off our engagement and I feel my life as it was, and as I expected it to be, has ended. I had considered that I was fated to be with him from the very first instant I laid eyes on him in Boulogne ten years ago. It had been my intention that we should travel to the East together and settle there. I find it almost inconceivable that it should be him who denies me this destiny.

How can it be that a future which had seemed to me set in stone can be so altered by another? Is Life so fickle a thing that we are helplessly cast about by whims that are not even our own?

I cannot bear it.

Mama, Papa, I will be mistress of my own fate! I will be answerable for my own mistakes and I will claim credit for my own triumphs! Though the world may change around me, it will be I who chooses how to meet its challenges and disappointments, and nobody else.

The world! I now understand that we inhabit two worlds. There is the wider one that we live upon yet see but a fraction of, and there is the one which consists of the immediate influences from which we take our form. The first expands us; the latter contracts us. Richard was of the second world; from him I gained a sense of my own being, its limits and its character. Now he is gone and I find that I am uncontained.

What do I do? Do I retreat from this breech and hide from the infringing outer world? Or do I flow out into it to discover new possibilities and perhaps to take on a new shape for myself?

You know your daughter, dear parents! I will not flinch!

Richard has made my long-held vision of the future impossible. Should I therefore abandon it all? NO, I say! NO!

I am in Trieste en route to Damascus. I know not what awaits me there. I hardly care. Whatever; I will at least be creating an Isabel Burton who is defined by her own choices.

I do not know when I will be back.

I will write.

You are more dear to me than anything.

With deepest love
Your Isabel

"By heaven, but she's headstrong!" exclaimed Burton, handing the letter back to Henry Arundell.

"Always was!" agreed the older man. "Like her grandmother. By George, man! What made you do it? Leave her, I mean. I thought you loved her!"

"I do, sir. Make no mistake about it; I do. I was given a choice by Lord Palmerston; I could either accept a pitiful consulship on a disease-ridden island or I could serve the country in a capacity which, though hazardous, would offer far more by way of personal fulfilment. In either case, Isabel, had she become my wife, would've been placed in a perilous position. I broke off our engagement to protect her."

Arundell grunted, and said: "And in consequence, she's gone gallivanting off to Arabia on her own where, surely, she'll be at equal risk!"

"No, sir; don't let the popular image deceive you. The Arabs are an honourable race and she'll be in no more danger there than she would if she were in, say, Brighton. London is a hundred times more dangerous than Damascus."

"Are you sure?"

"I promise you. It's in the British Empire's interest to portray other cultures as barbarous and uncivilised; that way there's less of an outcry when we conquer them and steal their resources. Lies have to be propagated if we are to retain the moral high ground."

Arundell shifted in his seat uncomfortably. To him, such statements seemed traitorous.

"Be that as it may," he grumbled, "I'm not at all happy. I'm concerned for my little girl's welfare and I hold you responsible."

"I cannot help that. The decisions I make are based on what I think is best. The decisions she makes are based on what *she* feels is best. The decisions you make, likewise. We all act on what we know, what we see, what we are told and how we feel. The simple fact of the matter is that not a single one of us operates under identical influences. That, sir, is why the future is always uncertain."

Henry Arundell stood and placed his hat upon his head.

"I am not mollified, sir," he said, somewhat resentfully.

Burton got to his feet.

"Neither am I."

Isabel's father nodded and left.

Sir Richard Francis Burton wandered over to the bar and took a shot of whisky. A few minutes later, he put on his topper and his coat and, swinging his cane, walked out of the hotel and along the pavement toward Montagu Place.

The thick fog embraced him.

It was silent.

It was mysterious.

It was timeless.

"It makes it seem as if," he thought, "my world doesn't really exist."

THE END

Appendix

Meanwhile, in the Victorian Age …

Sir Richard Francis Burton

After they completed their expedition to Africa's central lake region in 1859, John Hanning Speke returned to London ahead of Richard Francis Burton and claimed credit for the discovery of the source of the Nile. Some weeks later, Burton arrived and their feud commenced. The following year, while Burton toured America, Speke returned to the lakes but failed to collect convincing evidence that his assertion was correct.

In 1861, Burton married Isabel and accepted the consulship of Fernando Po. He did not allow his new wife to accompany him there and they didn't see each other again until December the following year.

Burton's duties on the disease-ridden island ended in 1864. That same year, in September, he was due to debate the Nile question with Speke at a meeting of the Royal Geographical Society in Bath. The day before the scheduled encounter, Speke died from a gunshot wound to his side while out hunting.

His death marked a turning point in Burton's career.

Burton became consul in Brazil, then Damascus, and finally in Trieste, and spent the rest of his life focusing on his writing rather than on exploration.

Queen Victoria did not award him a knighthood until 1886.

He died from heart failure in 1890. Controversy followed, when it became known that Isabel had burned many of his papers, notebooks and unpublished manuscripts.

Algernon Charles Swinburne

In 1866, Swinburne caused a sensation with the publication of Poems and Ballads I and quickly became the enfant terrible of the Victorian literary scene. Though he was quickly hailed as one of England's premier poets, his alcoholism took a heavy toll on both his health and career. He also diverted much of his energy into his fascination with birchings and sexual deviancy—he had a condition known to modern medicine as algolagnia, which causes pain to be interpreted as pleasure—and critics generally agree that he never lived up to his potential.

In 1879, when he was forty-two years old, Swinburne suffered a mental and physical breakdown and was removed from the temptations of the London social scene by his friend Theodore Watts. For the remainder of his life, Swinburne lived in relative seclusion with Watts, losing his rebellious streak and settling into comfortable respectability until his death in 1909.

Swinburne's words "—of shame: what is it? Of virtue: we can miss it. Of sin: we can kiss it. And it's no longer sin." form part of his poem *Before Dawn* which appeared in *Poems and Ballads, First Series. The Poems of Algernon Charles Swinburne*. 6 vols. London: Chatto, 1904.

"Not with dreams, but with blood and with iron, shall a nation be moulded to last," is from his poem, *A Word for the Country*, (undated).

"Thou hast conquered, O pale Galilean;
The world has grown grey from thy breath;
We have drunken from things Lethean,
And fed on the fullness of death,"
is from *Hymn to Prosperpine*, which appeared in *The Poems of Algernon Charles Swinburne*, 6 vols. London: Chatto, 1904.

"How he that loves life overmuch shall die
The dog's death, utterly:
And he that much less loves it than he hates
All wrongdoing that is done
Anywhere always underneath the sun
Shall live a mightier life than time's or fate's."
is from Thalassius, Songs of the Springtides which appeared in The Poems of Algernon Charles Swinburne. 6 vols. London: Chatto, 1904.

John Hanning Speke

Much might be said about Speke's attitude toward Burton after their expedition to the lakes; his actions definitely raise questions about his character. However, it is quite wrong to accuse him of cowardice. Certainly, this is what he thought Burton had done when the explorer published his account of the attack at Berbera. Speke felt that Burton's command "Don't step back! They'll think that we're retiring!" was a personal slight. There is no evidence to suggest, though, that Burton ever meant it as such.

Without the advantage of flight, Speke's second expedition to Africa's central lake region took as long as the first. The subsequent debate with Burton, therefore, was not scheduled for September 1861, but September 1864.

Oscar Wilde

The Great Irish Famine lasted from 1845 to 1852. Oscar Wilde was not a refugee from it, nor was he an orphan or paper boy.

As an adult he became a playwright, poet, author and controversial celebrity. His epigrams are still celebrated today. They include:

"By giving us the opinions of the uneducated, journalism keeps us in touch with the ignorance of the community."

"There is luxury in self-reproach. When we blame ourselves, we feel no one else has a right to blame us."

"I am so clever that sometimes I don't understand a single word of what I'm saying."

"I have the simplest tastes. I am always satisfied with the best."

"When I was young, I thought money was the most important thing in life. Now that I'm old—I know it is."

"One can survive everything, nowadays, except death, and live down everything except a good reputation."

Wilde died in 1900.

Laurence Oliphant

Laurence Oliphant never kept a white panther as a pet. He did, however, nurture John Hanning Speke's resentment of Burton.

In 1861, he became first secretary of the British legation in Japan but soon after accepting the post there was an attack on the legation during which he was severely wounded, losing the full use of his hand.

After a failed stint in parliament, he showed more promise as a novelist but then fell under the influence of the spiritualist prophet, Thomas Lake Harris. From 1868, he lived as a farm labourer in Harris's cult, not breaking free until 1881.

He spent the rest of his life as an author until his death in 1888.

Richard Monckton Milnes

Richard Monckton Milnes, one of Burton's best friends, was a poet and politician. He was a patron of literature and possessed a massive collection of erotic books.

Milnes never said: "The Eugenicists are beginning to call their filthy experimentations '*Genetics*,' after the Ancient Greek '*Genesis*,' meaning '*Origin*.' This is in response to the work of Gregor Mendel, an Augustinian priest. A priest! Can there be any greater hypocrite than a priest who meddles with Creation?"

The significance of Gregor Johann Mendel's work was not recognised until the turn of the 20th century, long after his death. He eventually became known as the father of modern genetics.

Milnes died in 1885.

Isambard Kingdom Brunel

Isambard Kingdom Brunel actually said: "I am opposed to the laying down of rules or conditions to be observed in the construction of bridges lest the progress of improvement tomorrow might be embarrassed or shackled by recording or registering as law the prejudices or errors of today."

Brunel planned his "atmospheric railway" as an extension of the GWR line, intending that it should stretch from Exeter toward Plymouth. A section of the route operated from 1847 to 1848 but, after the leather flap-valves were eaten by rats, Brunel abandoned the project.

He was not involved in the building of the London Underground, the first line of which opened in 1863. He did, however, complete the Thames Tunnel, which had been designed by his father, Marc Brunel. This was later purchased by a consortium of six railway companies and, in 1884, the District and the Metropolitan line began to operate a service through it.

Brunel designed and built the Great Western Railway, a number of bridges—most famously the Clifton Suspension Bridge in Bristol—and ocean liners, including the massive 700ft *Great Eastern*.

In 2002, the BBC conducted a public poll to determine the "100 Greatest Britons." Isambard Kingdom Brunel came in second place, after Winston Churchill.

He died in 1859.

Henry John Temple, 3rd Viscount Palmerston

Lord Palmerston was British Prime Minister from 1855 to 1858 and again from 1859 to 1865, when he died in office. He did not have any plastic surgery.

Paul Gustave Doré

The French artist's association with London didn't begin until the mid-1860s. His book of engravings, *London: A Pilgrimage,* was published in 1872. He died in 1883.

Constable William Trounce

There is no record of Constable William Trounce having been present at the scene when Edward Oxford tried, and failed, to assassinate Queen Victoria in 1840. However, on 29 May 1842, another assassination attempt was made, this time by a young man named John Francis. After firing a pistol at the monarch, Francis was seized by Constable William Trounce. History does not record what happened to the brave policeman after this brief moment of fame.

The Battersea Power Station

The station was not proposed by Isambard Kingdom Brunel and didn't exist during Queen Victoria's reign. Its construction commenced in March 1929. It still stands, though abandoned and derelict.

29 Hanbury Street, Spitalfields

This premises is where the body of Annie Chapman, one of Jack the Ripper's victims, was discovered on the morning of 8th September 1888. Her mutilated body was found in the back yard.

Florence Nightingale

The "Lady of the Lamp" did not say "When we adjust some element of an animal's nature, a quite different element alters of its own accord, as if there is some system of checks and balances at work. What we cannot fathom is why the unplanned changes seem entirely pointless from a functional perspective. I am baffled. Galton is baffled. Darwin is baffled. All we can do is experiment, experiment, experiment!"

Florence Nightingale revolutionised nursing and is rightfully regarded as one of British history's greatest women. She died at the age of 90 in 1910.

Henry de La Poer Beresford, the 3rd Marquess of Waterford

The Mad Marquess never said: "Every time we are faced with a choice, and we are faced with them every minute of every day, we make a decision and follow its course into the future. But what of the abandoned options? Are they like unopened doors? Do alternative futures lie beyond them? How far would we wonder from the course we have steered were we to go back and, just once, open Door A instead of Door B?"

In 1842, he married and put his wild youth behind him.

He died in a horse riding accident in 1859.

Spring Heeled Jack

Spring Heeled Jack is one of the great mysteries of the Victorian age (and beyond). Somewhat akin to the Mothman of West Virginia, this ghost, or apparition, or creature, or trickster, leaped out at unsuspecting victims over a period covering 1837 to 1888 and even on into the 20th century (though the main sightings were from 1837 to 1877—the subsequent ones may have been hoaxes, copycats, or something else entirely).

There is no recorded incident of a time traveller visiting the Victorian Age ...